THE
SECRET OF
ALPINE
VALLEY

THE SECRET OF ALPINE VALLEY

PAUL CREHAN

2014

BODA BOOKS

Published by

Boda Books
2355 Westwood Blvd. #907
Los Angeles, CA 90064

www.paulcrehan.com

ISBN 978-0-615-98107-9
Library of Congress Control Number: 2014905261

Cover artwork: Jeff Bennett
2013 © Jeff Bennett / lindgrensmith.com

Cover layout: Jeff Bennett & Joe Larios

Printed book production: Grace Peirce
Great Life Press (greatlifepress.com)

Publisher's Cataloging-in-Publication Data
Crehan, Paul.
The Secret of Alpine Valley / Paul Crehan.
        pages cm
     ISBN: 978-0-615-98107-9 (pbk.)
     ISBN: 978-0-615-92057-3 (e-book)
   1. Sasquatch—Fiction.   2. Teenage girls—Family relationships—Fiction. 3. Northwest, Pacific—Fiction. 4. Hoaxes—Fiction.   I. Title.
   PZ7.C8634 Se 2014
   [Fic]—dc23

                                                              2014905261

For Mom

Note to Reader

THIS STORY HAS A HAPPY ENDING. WELL, AS HAPPY AN ending as real life will allow. In other words, this story is not a fairy tale—and I want to warn you about that right at the top. So please, only turn the page if you've got stomach enough for truth. If you don't, it's better that you put this story down. Maybe go clean your room instead, or go get some fro-yo. Or Skype Grandma—you haven't spoken to her in a while, and don't you feel the tiniest bit guilty about that?

Prologue

HERE'S WHAT WAS GOING ON IN ANNIE'S MIND: WE need a plan or this town will die.

Here's what was going on in Preston's mind: Without a good plan, this town is toast.

Here's what was going on in Millard's mind: What can we do to save this town?

Here's what was going on in Edna's mind: I'd like ham for lunch.

In sum, three out of four people in Alpine Valley were worried about its future, and *four* out of four people knew that every plan they'd come up with hadn't worked. Raise taxes, lower taxes, sell this, sell that. Didn't matter. Nothing worked.

But truthfully, I'm not interested in starting this story with what Annie, Preston, and Millard were thinking—and I'm *really* not interested in what Edna was thinking, especially since I'm not fond of ham. Or her. (Sorry, but it's the truth.)

No, what I'm interested in is starting this story with *action*, and the action currently going on is Melissa getting ready for school, although you'll have to take my word for it, since we're here and Melissa is up the trail of words, rushing around in Chapter One. But don't worry—she'll still be rushing around by the time we get there: I know her well enough to say that with confidence.

And why should I want to start this story with Melissa in the first place, especially since you might argue that it should start with her brother, Peter? Because without her, there'd be no story at all.

So it's with Melissa that we shall start.

Chapter One

*I*F SHE HAD HER TEETH BRUSHED AND OUTFIT SELECTED before she saw Miss Dorothy crossing the street, she could walk to the bus stop. If she didn't, she'd have to run, and Melissa hated running for the school bus, because she'd have her top tucked into her pants just so; and her hair looking just so; and if she ran, the breezes made flyaway wisps of her hair, and her top rode up and bulged at her beltline, and she could *never* get it tucked back in as perfectly as she had had it, and she could *never* get her hair back the way it had been.

These weren't the biggest problems in life—Melissa got that—after all, people were starving in India, but still, these were annoyances, and she could do without them; and she *could*—if only her teeth were brushed and outfit selected before she saw Miss Dorothy crossing the street.

So she looked everywhere except through the window, because in fact, her teeth *weren't* brushed and she *hadn't* decided on what to wear.

She could, of course, look at the clock on her nightstand to see how close to eight it might be, but the clock was not as accurate as Miss Dorothy. No clock was as accurate as Miss Dorothy. People knew that. The whole town knew that. No one set a timepiece by the towering *bong-bong* clock at City Hall; they set it by her, and if you saw Miss Dorothy crossing Main Street on her way to Merle's

1

for coffee, it was without a doubt eight o'clock; and if you weren't at that point swinging your backpack up onto your shoulder and walking out of your bedroom, you could be sure that you'd be running the last three blocks to the bus stop.

You might think, and I hope you do (while Melissa considers between the white and aqua socks in her hands), that every once in awhile a person would get lucky, and the bus itself would run late. But unfortunately, the town's only other scarily punctual person was the school bus driver, Terry Troy, and even before the doors of the old weathered bus yawned open, you heard Terry from behind the glass shouting, "Let's go! Let's go!" And as the kids raced up the steps, he studied his watch, while drumming his fingers on the dashboard, so that it sounded like a horse galloping away as fast as it could.

The school was only a mile away; as for traffic—in *this* tiny town?; and even if part of Terry's job were, I don't know, to do a hula dance for each and every kid who stepped onto the bus, he'd *still* get them to school well before the bell rang. But each and every morning, Terry pleaded, "Let's go, children, hurry! Please!"

And now (and I find this surprisingly coincidental, because I've just been telling you about Mr. Troy), his pleading voice came to Melissa's mind as she pulled on the first aqua sock, and, as she straightened out the heel, she thought, *How come Mr. Troy is always afraid of being late? It'd be impossible. So it's not really about getting us to school on time. It's about something else…right? But what? Where does he have to be?*

And in the nine or ten seconds it took Melissa to ask herself these questions, something magnificent happened—and before this story hurries on (although we'll let Melissa do so), I must pause to tell you what that magnificent thing was.

Let me say first that it's not that Melissa was a self-centered kid, it's just that she was twelve, and wondering why another person might fear what he feared, or do as he did, was not something she had done before. So now, in asking herself why Mr. Troy was afraid of being late, she was doing nothing less than stepping off the path of childhood and up onto the path of adulthood, where one sees the world as a place filled with others, who have their own fears. And places to be.

Not that she herself understood that she'd just ascended to this trail: it had happened without her paying any attention to it; so I'm thrilled that I was able to capture for you that magnificent transition that, without these words, Melissa herself would never have been aware of.

Unfortunately, Melissa never got around to actually *asking* anyone what the answer to her questions might be, because now, in the next moment, she got distracted by a dozen other thoughts flying around in her head—like whether there might be a quiz today, and how much homework she might have tonight, because her favorite show was on at eight, and how come Kenny Piersall never passed notes to her but only to Janet McPhee—and then, the hours of the day passing—eight a.m., nine a.m., ten a.m.— she got further distracted by everything that happened at school, and then, the days passing, even *more* distracted —and changed forever—by the events of this story; and so, though she had wondered what Terry Troy might be afraid of, she never did find out, because not long after this story takes place, he died while sitting at a picnic table by himself in Ranger Park, during the town's annual Fall Festival Fireworks Show.

And quite sadly, no one else in the park knew he was dead— they never looked his way; and no one *would* know, until the grounds crew came the next evening and found him, still sitting upright at the picnic table, his one hand placed over the other, as if he were waiting for something. Or someone. Patiently.

Everything about him, the crew noted (well, *I* noted), was perfectly still, except for the sweep of the second hand on his wristwatch, still going around, like a man with a torch turning in a circle to keep back a dozen gathered wolves.

"What happened?" everyone asked.

"I suspect his heart got him."

That's how Doc Cabot answered the people of this town; and everyone knew there was more freight in his train of thought than those few linked-together words might indicate.

Curious, the crew had opened the picnic basket Terry had with him, and inside they found a picnic dinner—for two.

No one questioned claimed to have made a date with Terry—that is, no one *questioned*. Maybe there was someone out there who *should* have been questioned, but wasn't. And why did that person fail to show up?—unless that person *had* shown up, found Terry dead, and had run away. But most people thought that Terry had no date at all, and was hoping that someone, *anyone*, might find a way to that distant table and join him.

But all that—this quiet little mystery—would be later, and though part of town history, it would remain on the margin of it, like Terry at his picnic table at the margin of the park. Because by the time of his death, the town had become preoccupied and transformed by the events I am about to relate.

But in the here and *now*, Melissa was racing to her closet (having finished staring at her rumpled bedspread and scratching her arm, though why she should have zoned out like that when she knew she had to hurry, I couldn't say), and it was in yanking open the closet door that she threw a furtive glance out her window—and there was Miss Dorothy, crossing the street!

Melissa said a word she was *not* supposed to say and was very glad she hadn't yelled it—but wait, her mother was already at her council meeting—they met extra early on Mondays—so she wouldn't have heard it anyway—and she raced into the bathroom, got out her toothbrush—fumbled it—it went into the toilet bowl—oh, for heaven's *sake!*—so forget brushing her teeth (but at least that would save her time) and she ran back to her closet—and almost blindly yanked out a pair of jeans, a top, and a pair of sneaks, and now, finished tying them, she grabbed her backpack, slung it onto her shoulder and raced out the door—already annoyed and yet trying to remind herself that she was lucky to be living here, and not in India—until she realized that she hadn't done anything with her hair, and then she said *again* what she wasn't supposed to say—and this time *very* loudly—because her mom wasn't home, but up the street, there at City Hall.

And Melissa ran down the porch, across the lawn, and down the sidewalk, and there in the distance, the bus pulled up to the stop.

Chapter Two

IF YOU'D NEVER MET EDNA BEFORE, YOU'D FIND YOUR-self looking twice to make sure that wasn't a real beehive on top of her head.

Whenever Melissa saw her in town, she liked thinking about the things Edna could hide in that hair of hers. For instance:

—If she wanted to sneak a dog into a fancy restaurant, she could easily get a teacup Chihuahua past the maître d', maybe two, though if the dogs started barking at one another up there in her hair, that'd call attention to Edna, so best to hide only one dog; and certainly she'd want to walk it before she hid it—because what if the dog had to go? Edna would have a whole new definition of the word 'hairdo.' (This made Melissa laugh out loud when she thought of it, and that made her wonder if anybody else would find it funny. 'Hairdo.' Maybe not. Maybe people would even think she was gross or weird, so maybe she'd just keep this one to herself.) But what else? This:

—If Edna didn't have any money and wanted candy from a store, she could probably make off with a dozen bags of M&M's.

—If she were a secret agent, she could steal the enemy's weapons plans, fold them up into a little square, put them into an Altoids tin and push it into her hair, and walk across the border, whistling a tune—and she'd *still* have room for goggles, fins, and snorkel for swimming back to her ship, anchored in secret off the coast. Okay, that was going too far: the hairdo couldn't hold *that* much. The fins would have to go. Edna would have to swim back to her ship without the fins.

But that was what *Melissa* thought, and we're not talking about Melissa at this exact moment.

No, we're talking about Edna, here at City Hall, which, by the way, the bus has just passed—in fact, if you looked out the window you'd see the exhaust disappearing into the morning air, and she's just said, "We could do pies."

She looked around the table to see what her fellow council members thought of her idea. Her look was smug, however, and she was thinking, Let's see anyone top *that*. Interestingly, by the way, if you were to look over Edna's shoulder and out through the window, you'd now see Melissa running by, waving and hollering.

Annie LaPeer, the town's mayor (and Melissa's mother—and no, she didn't see her daughter running past, and it's a good thing, because Melissa would have gotten another scolding tonight), gave Edna a flicker of a smile. Her idea was moronic, even maddening. The town needed *far* more money to fix the streets than any bake sale would supply; but what really bugged Annie was how out of touch Edna was—to think that enough people in town had any kind of disposable income: Most people were jobless, many losing their homes, and a few—and a few more every day—were going hungry. How many wet-eyed mothers with quivering lips had Annie seen at Merle's checkout stand, poor Merle going broke because he kept extending credit? And here Edna thought anybody had the seven or eight dollars to plunk down for a *pie*?

Millard Barnes, the town's pharmacist, rolled his eyes. Millard was a very nice man—always extending credit to people when they couldn't afford their medicines, but still, that was his favorite thing to do whenever anyone said the least little thing he thought stupid: He'd roll his eyes.

Sitting next to him, Skeet Hillsborough, the editor of the town's paper, *The Alpine Voice*, pressed his lips together hard to make a dam against his building emotion—which nevertheless burst through. "For the love of *god*, Edna!"

Seven people sat around this oval oak table. They listened to the old-fashioned fan blades creak as they turned 'round overhead. When was the last time anybody had gotten up there and oiled them?

Annie tugged nervously at the hem of her realtor's blazer. Mayor though she was, she, like everyone else around this table, had a full-time job, and she wanted to wrap things up and get to it. For the first time in months, she had prospective buyers—a young couple all the way from Phoenix, Arizona, who had read how depressed the economy was up here and thought they might get a home in these parts for very little. And they were right; and Annie didn't want to be late.

"Well, Edna," Annie found herself saying, and then really wasn't sure what to say after that.

"*Rhubarb* pies," added Edna. "We could do a whole *bunch* of rhubarb pies. People *love* rhubarb."

"Rhubarb," Annie said, "I'll take that under advisement."

"I hate rhubarb!" Bulie Olsen announced—or was it more accurate to say 'yelled'? Bulie was a retired mill foreman, and the scream of the saws over five decades had impaired his hearing so badly that he announced—or yelled—a lot, just so he could hear himself. But at the moment, it was hard to tell whether Bulie was *announcing*, so that he could hear himself, or *yelling*, because he was mad at Edna.

"Duly noted," Annie said to Bulie. "We'll let the minutes reflect that you hate rhubarb. Now, anyone else?"

"I'm not fond of it, either," Preston Mayhugh said.

"I *meant*," Annie said, shooting Preston a look, "does anyone else have a *proffer* on raising funds for *street* repair?"

"Why do you hate rhubarb?" asked Edna, folding her arms tightly across her chest and glaring at Bulie.

"Edna!" said Annie, trying not to lose her cool and not doing such a good job of it. "Can we stay focused here?"

"I *am* focused," Edna said, "and as far as I can see, I'm the only one at this table who has offered—*proffered*—any idea on how to raise money to get our potholes and sidewalks fixed!"

Well, this was true; and everyone around the table had to admit it. Millard tugged at the collar of his white pharmacist's tunic. Preston, the high school football, basketball, and baseball coach, suddenly got interested in the state of his cuticles. Shirley Considine shrugged, staring into her coffee cup.

In the silence, they all couldn't help but listen to the ceiling fans squeaking as they went 'round and 'round.

Annie was so glum that she forgot for a moment that she had somewhere to be. "Well," she said after several long seconds, "if we don't have any alternative means for raising the money we need— *realistic means*," she added, looking squarely at Edna, "then we see that we've got *no* choice but to— ."

"Annie—Madame Mayor," Shirley broke in, "we *can't*. People have only got lint in their pockets!"

Annie set her jaw. She knew as well as anyone that that was the truth, but still what choice did she have?

Preston studied Annie's face. Though pretty, it could look formidable—almost fierce—when its owner set her mind on something—which she had just done.

He had come to know her various looks well since he'd moved here a decade ago, when the town was thriving and could afford to hire someone to develop a sports program at the high school.

Whether it was the football, basketball, or baseball team— and usually the same dozen guys played all three sports—The Alpine Valley Bears seldom won. No one in town minded, because everyone knew that with only thirty boys enrolled in school—many of whom had to hustle off at three o'clock to the jobs they'd managed to find—there wasn't a big pool of talent to draw from, nor time to practice beyond the one-hour of P.E. during the school day.

And anyway, when the town had decided to fund a sports

program, it was never with any expectation of winning. Everyone knew tiny Alpine Valley couldn't compete with the big high schools on the other side of the mountain. No, all that the town wanted was to give their boys something to do; channel their energy some.

Of course, now that the town was this close to broke, Preston had to wonder how soon it would be before everyone started wondering how important it was, really, to give a few high school boys something to do—which was the same thing as wondering how important it was to pay his salary.

But that was a concern for another day. Today, Preston had to worry about mowing the football field and re-painting the bleacher seats—though at the moment, he was more worried about Annie, standing there trying to look steeled to her decision, which would prove unpopular with her fellow Alpine-ites; and would probably cost her many a sleepless night; and *certainly* her job as mayor. But did all that have to happen *today*? Did Annie—Madame Mayor— really have to bang her gavel down *today* and order that a new tax be imposed on everyone?

Well, yes, she had to—and everyone knew it, even though they weren't going to like it one bit, especially since raising taxes— *again*—was going to be the last straw for a lot more people. They would have to pack up and leave. Because Shirley was right and barely exaggerating: people only had lint in their pockets.

Still, Preston just didn't want to hear the news now, today; and anyway, he liked Annie (more than he liked to admit), and he liked her as mayor, too, so, before she could un-set that jaw of hers and make new taxes the harsh new law and reality, he said:

"*Wait*. I mean, excuse me, Madame Mayor," and here Preston showed everyone his watch, and even tapped it, "but we're past time, and I move to adjourn. We can pick up tomorrow."

Her jaw still set, and a little surprised that Preston would interrupt like that, but not entirely ungrateful, either (Preston could see that in her eyes), Annie said, "Well. Does anyone second that?"

"I do!" Bulie yelled/announced, his chair already scraping back across the floor. "I can't spend all day in here yammering about rhubarb!"

"Then the motion carries to adjourn," Annie said, and she quickly picked up her gavel and banged it on the table.

At that, everyone else pushed back, got up, and filtered off to their days.

But wait.

Before we move to Chapter Three, let's rewind, as Peter LaPeer might say, all the way back to Chapter One. Let's turn our attention to Miss Dorothy as she's crossing the street to Merle's, sky-blue pillbox hat crowning her head, the pink of her scalp showing through the curls of her white hair, purse in the crook of her arm, gloves in hand.

Besides being distinguished for her punctuality, she was distinguished for her age. At ninety-one, she was the town's oldest citizen, and if anybody could claim title to being the most beloved, it was she. Probably because of her invariably sunny attitude, which always made people smile.

It's not that Miss Dorothy was a simpleton that she could always be so happy, it's that after living so long, and having lost so much, she had developed quite an eye for seeing kindness and goodness in people and places most overlooked. So she found much to make her happy.

She was a widow and had been for decades. She'd only been married eleven years when her husband Maxwell, a sawyer, died. He had been walking up a trail into the woods when the entire face of the mountain gave way in a slide. He and four other men were killed, their bodies never found. Over time, the misery of that fact eroded; eroded the more she thought about how she could always look up at the mountain, deadly but beautiful, and know that her beloved husband was and would always be a part of it. Over time, too, she felt less and less sorry for herself and mad at God, and more and more grateful that she had had eleven years with such a man as Maxwell Dodd. There was no one like him when she married him, and never his equal thereafter. He was as rare as the kind of landslide that took him; and though Miss Dorothy was never quite sure what that might mean, she liked the thought of it.

But Maxwell wasn't her only loss. She and he had had two children, and they too had died—and long ago. Their son, also Maxwell, died in a war on a foreign shore—his body, too, never found. What she had of him were his loving letters home, which she still took out and read and laughed and cried over at least once a month.

Her daughter, Eleanor, had died in childbirth along with the baby. Her husband, who just plain disappeared after the tragedy, had tried to get her to Taylorville and the local hospital there, but the road is long and terribly twisty, and she and the baby died on the way.

And after that, Miss Dorothy was alone; and remained alone; and over time got used to the fact; and over time knew gratitude for the happiness of the children she had been given. She had had them in her life, and still and every day had memories of them, which were as clear, and as moving, and as satisfying, as anything that she experienced, or saw, or felt, in any one day of her life.

Which was simple.

And peaceful.

Mostly pain-free.

And punctual.

Miss Dorothy had things to do.

At ninety-one, she knew she couldn't possibly have too many years left, and if she had one last wish, it was that she be allowed to die in Alpine Valley, her beloved home. That thought, that she die gazing at the mountain of which her husband was a part, was her one deep hope, and that she might be denied it, her one deep fear. Because the town was in trouble. And what if it were to die before she did? What if she then had to go to Cascade City, to that *facility*, and she died in a place she did not love, looking out at a parking lot? And with that thought, Miss Dorothy signaled Merle that she was through with her coffee (and apple danish—"Particularly good, Merle!"), and that she'd like the check, please.

Chapter Three

WITH HER REAL ESTATE BLAZER OVER HER ARM AND her shoes in her hand, Annie went barefoot up the lush green and windblown hill, sun in her hair like joy in a body.

From the front porch of his hilltop cabin, Dr. Samuel Cabot watched her approach. Maybe it was his big round glasses, or something about his face, or both things together, but Dr. Cabot looked like an owl. Annie wondered if Dr. Cabot knew he looked like an owl and didn't much care one way or the other, or outright cultivated the look, wanting people to think of him as an owl, because it was an animal thought wise. Either way, Annie thought, he *was* wise, and her best and oldest friend, though forty years separated them.

"I'm going to guess," Dr. Cabot said, as Annie crested the hill and headed toward his porch, "that Edna suggested a bake sale."

Annie merely nodded—she was catching her breath. Dr. Cabot sat down on the top step of his porch and patted the space next to him.

"But even she," Annie now said, as she approached, "is beginning to understand the gravity of our times." She plopped herself down next to Dr. Cabot. "Because she brought out her biggest gun yet: Her great aunt whatever-her-name was's rhubarb pie."

"Ah, yes. Beulah-Mae," Dr. Cabot said. "Sure-fire sales. Fetched three dollars a slice, even back in the day."

"Couldn't get that now," Annie said.

Dr. Cabot shrugged. "No mill, no money."

Annie squinted into a spot in the valley below. "And John Chamberlain just *sits* there."

Dr. Cabot directed his gaze to where Annie was looking and surveyed the sprawling, rusting, fenced-in mill-works. Boards where windows used to be. Weeds.

"Three more families are moving next week. Did you know that, Sam?"

Dr. Cabot nodded and now shifted his gaze from the mill-works to the whole of the valley spread out below them. "Perhaps we were only meant to be here for a little while, Annie."

She grimaced and looked at him. "Sam, no...*preparing* me, all right? I do *not* want to lose this place."

Sam Cabot chuffed a laugh. "You don't? *I'm* the one grew up with the trees."

"*Man*, Sam," Annie said, "I came up here for a little, 'Go get 'em, tiger,' you know? Not 'Prepare to meet thy doom.'"

"Is it that?" Sam asked, "or embracing reality?"

"It's embracing hopelessness. Sam, we're not dead." Annie flung a finger toward the mountain range off to their left. "That tourist dollar we need is just beyond the Twin Mountains there. If we could just cut a road *between* them— ."

"Annie..."

"No! Really! If we could just cut a road between them, we could link up with Taylorville—and the highway!"

Annie turned abruptly and looked at Sam. He was looking at her, searchingly, but in a kindly way, too. Annie had to look away. "I know," she said, looking at the ground, and back at reality. "Where would we ever get the money to build a road?"

"It's more than that," Sam said. "Why would tourists come *here*? Even with a more direct road, we're seven miles this way of Taylorville, and we don't have any more rustic charm than they do. Less, actually. If I pull off the Coast Highway to see charming little Taylorville, am I really going to travel another seven miles—of mountain road—to see a tiny little *mill* town?"

"Well, we're very nice here," said Annie. They laughed. But it was glum. "Most of us, anyway," she continued, her face going dark.

Sam reached out and took Annie's hand. He placed it between both of his and squeezed it gently. "Gotta let it go, Annie," he said. "Let *him* go."

"Oh, I've let him go, all right," she said.

Sam gave her a smile, but it was sad. "Along with peace of mind...and trust..."

"*Sam,*" Annie said, "it is what it is. Divorce is...Who is it easy for? No one. We're getting through, all right? The way people do."

Sam raised one shoulder in the world's slowest shrug. "Well," he said, "Melissa's all right, I'll grant you. But Peter? He's getting fat, Annie."

"He's a little stressy, sure. But Sam, *really*. You're worrying, and...you shouldn't! And anyway, blah, blah, *blah*." Annie got up quickly. "And you know where the new road begins? Main Street! So I'm going to fix it! Those potholes? History!"

Sam gazed at her. With big owl eyes. "You're changing the subject. And your road is a dream. You know it."

Annie deflated, shoulders sagging. "Gee, Sam, didn't you used to be, I don't know, *cheerier*?"

"You used to be younger. And all you had were scrapes on your knees."

The two of them regarded each other for a long moment, and then Annie rushed up to Sam and bending over, embraced him. "Don't *worry*, Sam! Please! Everything's going to be okay. It *is* okay! This town will come alive again! We all will! I know it!"

Chapter Four

ELISSA DIDN'T MIND SETTING THE TABLE. DOING so appealed to her practical side: It was better to have everything laid out than to have everyone scrambling around when dinner was ready, trying to get their plates, silverware, and glasses. That made for confusion; everyone in everyone else's way.

Besides, a set table was beautiful. The plates gleamed; the silverware shined; and the glasses reflected and sometimes refracted the light, making small rainbows on the table. So yes, it was good to set the table, and Melissa didn't mind the chore one bit.

The only thing she minded was setting the table in the same way every night. Why were there rules about where the salad plate should be, and the fork, and the knife and spoon, and how the napkin should be folded? Weren't there other ways to place these things so that they were still convenient to the person sitting down to eat, and still pretty to look at?

Melissa certainly thought so. So for a while now, she'd been challenging herself to come up with inventive ways to set the table. Her brother, Peter, didn't mind how she did it—he just cared about the food, and scooping as much as possible onto his plate; and her mom not only didn't mind how she set the table, it always made her laugh to see what she'd come up with—not that *funny* was what Melissa was going for with her various designs. She would have preferred a 'How beautiful!' or at the least, a

17

'How creative,' but laughter wasn't bad. It wasn't disapproval—her dad's specialty.

She particularly liked what she was coming up with tonight. She'd gotten a wineglass out of the cabinet for her mom and made it a pedestal for her plate—a blue plate, from the fine china stack; and she made an origami swan out of a paper napkin (well, it was *almost* a swan; Melissa wasn't great at origami—not yet), placing it in the middle of the plate, hoping her mother would get it that the swan was swimming in a pretty blue pond. She laid her mother's fork, knife, and spoon in one column to the right of the plate, placing them one inch apart from one another. She didn't know why she did that, or why they had to be one inch apart from one another, but it looked good that way.

"What do you think of *that*?" Melissa asked Muffin, giving the spoon the last perfect little adjustment. Muffin responded the way she always did (she was apparently a big fan of Melissa's work) by thumping her tail on the linoleum of the kitchen floor. "I appreciate your approval," Melissa said to her. Muffin licked her nose in response—her own nose; not Melissa's.

And then Muffin barked—her happy bark—when she heard the screen door to the pantry creak open, and, barking still, she padded into the pantry, which adjoined the kitchen. Melissa heard her mom greeting Muffin and telling her what a good girl she was, and then heard the click-click-click of her mom's high heels as she came through the pantry toward the kitchen. Her *heels*, Melissa thought, Mom must have shown a house today. Good—she'd be happy.

"Hi, honey," Annie said as she entered the kitchen, Muffin leading the way. Annie had her briefcase under her arm while she sorted through the mail in her hands.

"Hi. I started dinner," Melissa said.

"Uh-huh," said Annie, showing concern over the letter she was opening—a bill—and as she scanned it, her mouth got that pursed look it got, but then she quickly looked up from the bill at

Melissa and said, "I mean, thank you, honey. Sorry. Long day."

Passing her daughter, Annie kissed her on top of the head and now put her briefcase, mail, and keys on the kitchen counter. "Your brother home?"

"Library. He said he'd be home soon."

Annie went to the refrigerator and was about to open it when she saw what was front and center on the freezer door, stuck to it with a magnet.

"Well, *hel*-lo!" Annie said, removing Melissa's story. "'The Monster in the Woods,'" Annie intoned, reading the title.

"I got an A+."

"So I see. What's it about?"

"A monster in the woods."

"Har-har. And *specifically*?"

Annie put the story back up on the freezer door, opened the fridge, and began taking out things for a salad.

"It's about this monster," Melissa said. "He has two mouths. One can breathe fire, and one can chew up trees and then spit them out. Like a wood chipper."

"My," said Annie, "that's an impressive skill-set. Can I borrow him for council meetings—help me keep order?"

Now, at about the same time that Annie and Melissa were getting things ready for dinner, Peter LaPeer, Annie's son and Melissa's brother, was exiting the library. He had so many books in his backpack that he hadn't been able to zip it up all the way. He was polishing off a bag of chips, which he had only opened two or three seconds before. Peter was fourteen. You wouldn't call him a loner, exactly, because he would have liked to have had friends, but he wasn't good at making them. Deep in his heart, this fact bothered him. But deep in his heart was a place Peter didn't like going— not that he could put that fact into words; but since Dad had left, he felt afraid, and like there were frightening things out there—I mean *in* there, in his heart.

Pushing the last of the chips into his mouth, Peter caught sight of Preston, off in the distance, mowing the grass of the football field. Peter would have to pass by him since the man stood—mowed—between him and his home. But that was okay with Peter. He liked Coach Mayhugh.

Peter was no athlete and never attended any of the games, as most of the kids did, but Coach never seemed to hold that against him, and in fact was always friendly toward him. Which kind of surprised Peter, because he couldn't say the same about his dad. His dad was great—just great!—but Peter had to admit that his dad had, well, *moods,* and there were times when he didn't know Peter was talking to him. But that was understandable, because his dad was super-busy. The only veterinarian in the whole *county,* so he had a lot on his mind.

"Hey, Coach," Peter said as he approached Preston from behind, and Preston turned around to see him.

"Ah, young Scorsese," Preston said. He always called Peter that—the name of one of Hollywood's greatest directors. *"Gone With the Wind?"* he asked him.

Ever since—somehow, some way—Preston had learned that Peter was a film buff, he'd quiz him, whenever he saw him, about when particular films had been released and who had directed them.

"1939. Victor Fleming," Peter answered, now walking beside Preston as he pushed the mower up the field.

"Lawrence of Arabia?"

"1962. David Lean," Peter replied.

"Animal House?"

"My mother won't let me rent it."

"I should talk to the woman," said Preston. "Your education is not complete. In the meantime, look out for that— ." Preston was not able to complete his warning before Peter fell over a field bench. "—bench," Preston concluded.

He let go of the mower handle and went over to Peter to help him up. But, super-embarrassed, Peter was getting up quickly and was all the way up by the time Preston got to him. Peter's books had popped out of his backpack and lay in a loose heap on the ground.

Preston helped him gather them up. "*Seven Wonders of Cryptozoology,*" he said, reading the title of the book he'd just picked up from the grass. He opened the book and turned to the table of contents. "The New Jersey Devil," he read, "West Virginia's Mothman...For what class is this?"

"Mrs. Barbour's," said Peter.

"Champy?" Preston said, looking up from the table of contents. "What's that?"

"Lives in Lake Champlain? In New York? The Adirondacks? North America's version of the Loch Ness Monster?"

"Bigfoot," said Preston, eyes back on the table of contents. "Pages 101 to 152. Big chapter." He began leafing through the pages. "Why is Mrs. Barbour having you read this stuff?"

"We have to do a report?" Peter said. "We have to determine if there's any evidence these creatures exist, and if there *isn't*, why do people all over the world insist they do?"

"Okay," said Preston. "I get it." He now turned the book around to show Peter a picture he'd come across. "Where's this?"

Peter looked at the picture Preston was showing him and as quickly as possible read the caption to himself. He didn't want Coach to think he couldn't answer his question. Peter wasn't athletic, but he wasn't *about* to let Coach think he wasn't smart. "That's Willow Creek, California," he said. "That statue is of Bigfoot. The people there call their town the Bigfoot Capital of the World. Obvious example of mass psychosis." Peter had no idea where he'd come up with words like 'mass psychosis,' but they sounded smart, and anyway it occurred to him that he might Google 'mass psychosis,' and see if he couldn't use it to answer the question of why people might insist that fairy tale creatures actually existed.

"Obvious," Preston said, and he handed Peter the book. "Well, good luck with writing up your diagnosis." He headed back for his mower.

"Thanks," Peter said, cramming this last book into his backpack with the others. "And good luck with your mowing." Well, *that* was stupid, Peter thought. Good luck with your *mowing*?

"*Jaws*?" Preston said, taking hold of the mower handle.

"What?" Peter asked.

"*Jaws*?" Preston repeated.

"Oh. 1975. Steven Spielberg. And like that one? Mrs. Barbour said it was a classic example of the power of fiction. It was a book first."

"I read it. Peter Benchley."

"Yeah. Because, like, there have always been great white sharks attacking people? But they still went to the beach? But when they put one in a novel, people stayed away for the longest time. I'm going to put in my paper that that shows that fiction can have more *bite* than reality. Get it? *Bite*?"

"I do, young squire. And I like it. Well done."

Peter shrugged casually, but, though he tried, couldn't keep out of his face the joy he felt at Preston's approval; and when he realized that he was probably failing miserably in looking casual, looking cool, and embarrassed by that, he quickly turned with a, "Well, anyway. Gotta go. See you around, Coach."

"Have a good evening, young Scorsese," Preston said, pushing the mower up the field.

Chapter Five

$\mathcal{I}$ HAVEN'T YET TALKED ABOUT THE BARNETT BROTHERS, Boyd and Floyd, and perhaps now's a good time to do so, since they seldom drove into town, but had decided to do so tonight, and here they came.

As they drove down Main Street, BAM! Their truck went into a pothole and out, Floyd banging his head on the ceiling of the cab. But he didn't say ouch, or even react. All he said was, "That one's new."

A full second went by; then Boyd and Floyd said at the exact same moment, "I remember when they built this road."

Boyd had a smile on his face; and Floyd, looking at his brother, said, "I say that that much?"

"Every time we come in," Boyd said.

"Okay," said Floyd, thinking things through. "Well, here's something I *don't* say every time: Rah-gun-schnobbin-flagon-schnabbers."

"You're right," said Boyd, "that's not something one hears every day."

Reaching Eddie's Bar and Grill, they pulled up to the curb, parked, and got out. Eddie's was a big treat for them. Whenever they had managed to scrape together a little extra money, they treated themselves to a ride down the mountain for some cheeseburgers and beers.

They opened the door to Eddie's and went in.

Now, it just so happened that that's also where Preston was going tonight. He had changed after work into a nice pair of slacks and a nice shirt, and was walking down Main, here and there stepping into the street to avoid a particularly broken-up, mountainous, or sinkhole-y patch of the sidewalk. That was another thing the town would have to attend to—the sidewalks. They were falling apart. He passed Alpine Valley's town square.

It wasn't much of a square, to tell you the truth. It comprised a chest-high war memorial to honor the sons who had fallen in foreign wars, a flagpole, several iron benches painted green, and—what else?—that was about it. Except that Preston saw Reverend Flambeau sitting on one of the benches and tossing pieces of bread to the pigeons who were out past their bedtimes. Flambeau wasn't really the good reverend's name. It was Lambeau, but some time back Dr. Cabot had started calling him Flambeau—'torch,' in French. He said it was an appropriate name for a man dedicated to leading people down right paths. Lambeau knew what the town called him and didn't mind.

Preston raised a hand in greeting. Flambeau smiled broadly, and after Preston passed him, went back to feeding his flock. Preston knew that the good reverend was kind of a lonely guy, but for some reason, he just couldn't bring himself to say anything more to him than, "Good morning," or afternoon or evening, whatever it was, and maybe make a comment to him about the weather.

Maybe, Preston told himself, if Flambeau were a regular fixture in town, he'd have more opportunity to get to know him; but Flambeau traveled a circuit throughout three counties, tending to the spiritual needs of the far-flung towns in these parts of the Pacific Northwest.

If Flambeau were here this time of night, on a weekday, it was a good bet that somebody in town was sick, though Preston hoped not dying, or...had anybody had a baby recently?...he couldn't remember...but maybe he was here to baptize a baby? He knew that Flambeau had a little apartment attached to the church in Cascade City, but otherwise, and mostly, it seemed, he lived in his camper, going from town to town.

Alpine Valley was the northernmost town on Flambeau's route, and was separated from the nearest town, Taylorville, by seven miles. Maybe that doesn't sound like a lot, but that was seven miles of twisting, and here and there *treacherous*, mountain road. So any trip from here to Taylorville was an hour and a half. Longer, of course—a *lot* longer—during winter months, when snow and ice became big issues for drivers.

But, Preston thought, winter weather never kept Flambeau from coming here. You saw him just as much in the winter as you did in the summer.

He was a good man, thought Preston, so maybe one day he'd actually sit and talk with him. But then Preston's stomach did a somersault. So no, he'd just keep things to a wave, a comment, a smile; and he was sorry if Flambeau might be lonely, but he believed in God, right? So he had God to keep him company; and God's company had to be a lot better than Preston Mayhugh's, right? And anyway, Preston was busy. Really, very busy. Reaching Eddie's, he pushed open the door and entered.

When his eyes adjusted to the light in the place, Preston caught sight of his cousin, Larry Salisbury, seated at the bar. He headed toward him.

It was Larry, in fact, who had told Preston ten years ago that there might be a job opening in Alpine Valley, and why didn't he drive down from Taylorville and see if he couldn't interview for it?

Preston was a big man—six-two and solid, built like the point guard he had been in college, but Larry dwarfed him. Preston had never asked his cousin how tall he was or how much he weighed, but he guessed that the man had to be at least six-six and no less than three-hundred pounds. But gentle?—he was gentle as a *fawn*, and so it always surprised everybody when they learned that Larry was a cop.

"Hey, cuz," Preston said, coming up to Larry. They greeted each other, Preston ordered a beer, and they settled in for a chat. Then at some point for some reason that wasn't entirely clear to Preston at the time, he said to Larry, "Do you remember when we were kids and used to visit Grandpa Earl in Cascade City?"

"Of course."

"Do you remember we'd be making s'mores in the fire-pit, and he used to try to scare us with his stories about the Alpine Ape?"

Larry laughed. "'You don't get out of them woods before dark, the Ape's gonna *git* you boys.'" He laughed again, and Preston laughed with him.

"But," Preston said, "it was like...he kind of believed it."

"Nah," said Larry, "and Grandma said that myth was moldy when *they* were kids."

"Gentlemen!"

Preston and Larry turned to find that Boyd and Floyd had come up to greet them.

"Hey," Preston said, "long time no. You just getting in?"

"We've been dining," Boyd said, "like civilized adults." He jerked a thumb over his shoulder. "We were at that table in the corner."

"Pull up a seat and have a beer," Larry said.

As they sat, Floyd ordered beers for himself and his brother, and Boyd said, "So what's the talk o' the town, gents?"

"Preston has been feeling nostalgia for his youth," Larry said.

Preston chuffed a laugh. "I was talking about the Alpine Ape. You guys ever heard of the Alpine Ape?"

Floyd laughed. "Our grandpap used to tell stories about him."

"Exactly," said Preston.

"Well, I've *seen* him," Boyd said. "Of course, I was liquored up at the time. I tend to think that might work against my credibility."

"But you think you saw him?" asked Preston.

"He was as real to me as the time I saw Miss America in a bikini, beckoning for me to join her for a swim in the river."

"Wow," Floyd said. "What part of the river?"

Boyd shook his head. "Floyd, for god's sake," he said. "Madame Barkeep!" he called to the bartender, "I'm going to need one more of these beers if I'm going to withstand my brother for too much longer."

Chapter Six

*B*ACK AT THE LAPEER HOME, ANNIE SAT AT THE kitchen table, her open briefcase in front of her. It didn't remind her (because she was too busy to think about it, but at the moment, it does remind me) of a large mouth of a beast waiting for her to reach into it, so it could bite off her arm.

She was flipping through some documents, and here and there underlining important sentences with a yellow-highlighter. Her dinner—a hot-dog casserole and salad—sat uneaten, pushed to her right.

At the other end of the table, Melissa made gloriously strange whipped cream stalagmites on top of scoops of ice cream. Dessert for the three of them. But in Melissa's mind, she was serving art more than ice cream—not that she might put it in words like that, but that was her thinking.

Peter stood at the sink, washing the dishes, excitedly talking to Annie as he did so.

"And Coach Mayhugh was mowing the field? And he called me young Scorsese?"

"Honey," Annie said to him, without looking up from the document she was reading, "you don't always have to go up with your *sentences*? Like *this*? You're not asking me a question. You're *telling* me something. Making a *statement*."

"Coach Mayhugh was mowing the field."

"Excellent," Annie said.

"And he said, '*Animal House*?'"

"Ah-ah," said Annie.

"No, Mom, that's what *he* said? I mean, that's what he *said*."

"Okay," said Annie, but something in the document had arrested her attention—something she didn't like.

Peter looked at his mother as she frowned at the document. "Never mind," he said.

"Come on," said Annie, her eyes still on the document, "don't be a spoilsport. Keep going."

"No," Peter said, "it's all right. It's okay." He dried his hands on a dishtowel and headed out of the kitchen.

"Peter," Annie called, but he didn't stop or turn back; just disappeared down the hall.

"He must be having his period," Melissa said.

"Melissa!" said Annie.

"Well, that's what he's acting like."

Peter's room was dominated by movie posters on every wall, posters of the old great classics. *Citizen Kane. King Kong. Stagecoach. City Lights.*

He plopped himself into his chair at his desk and took out a couple of the books from his backpack. But his attention was drawn to the screen saver on his laptop. A family photo. Annie, Peter, Melissa, and their dad, Dave. All of them close to the camera and making goofy faces. Better days...

Peter took out a bag of M&M's from his drawer and opened them just as Annie knocked.

"Come in," he said, putting the M&M's back in the drawer, and closing it.

"Okay, so what's the deal?" Annie asked as she entered, closing the door behind her.

"Nothing," said Peter. "It's cool."

Annie sat on Peter's bed. She watched him pull out a couple

of more books from his backpack. She glanced at the screen saver; now away, now into her palms. "Look. Peter," she said. "Your dad and I..."

"Mom," Peter said, "it's cool. *Really.*"

Annie opened her mouth. But what to say? She really didn't know. She closed her mouth. That damned screen saver. It really dominated the room.

Chapter Seven

$\mathcal{L}$IKE PETER, PRESTON WAS ALSO SITTING IN FRONT OF his laptop. Of course, truth to tell, it was much later in the night now, and Peter was in bed by this point. So it would have been more accurate, and probably more grammatical, to have written, *As Peter had been doing, Preston was sitting in front of his laptop.* But I'm not sure I like the sound of that. But anyway, Preston was gazing at his laptop screen, absorbed in research.

He clicked on a picture of the Willow Creek statue of Bigfoot—the same picture he'd seen in Peter's book.

He clicked on a picture of the town of Willow Creek—crowded, touristy, a busy main street.

He clicked on a picture of two tourists pointing at a sign that read 'Burlington, Vermont, Home of the Lake Champlain Monster.'

He clicked on a picture—a very grainy, black and white picture—of what looked like a dinosaur-like creature, swimming. You saw his slender neck and dinosaur-looking head. This was supposed to be 'Champy.'

Preston moved his mouse to 'File,' clicked on it, then dragged the arrow down to 'Print.'

He raised his index finger up from his mouse, thinking—and thinking again—whether he should do what he was about to do—and then let that finger come down like a hammer.

Chapter Eight

*B*ANG! ANNIE'S GAVEL CAME DOWN HARD.

"Okay, ladies and gentlemen," she said, "council is now in session."

"No rhubarb!" announced Bulie, even before Annie had laid down her gavel. "And I don't want to talk about pies!"

"Rest assured, Bulie," she said, "there'll be no discussion of either rhubarb or pies."

"Well, *wait* a minute," Edna said. "That's awfully high-handed."

"All right," said Annie, "the motion put forward is, 'No rhubarb or pies shall be discussed.' All in favor..."

"Aye!" said everyone at the table but Edna.

"The motion carries," said Annie.

"Well, I *never*," said Edna, looking off and looking both hurt and mad.

Annie would have liked to have said something nice to her, placate her a bit, but she wanted to get to her ugly task and be done with it as quickly as possible. "Ladies and gentlemen of the council," she said, "I've looked and looked, and there's no way out. By Charter Title Six-One, I'm exercising my emergency executive privilege and raising the municipal road tax..." and here she paused, not for dramatic effect, but because she *really* didn't want to say what she had to say, "...by seven percent."

"Seven percent?!" cried Skeet.

"We just can't!" Millard said.

"Annie—Madame Mayor!" said Shirley.

"Ladies and *gentlemen!*" Annie said, banging her gavel and trying to bring everyone back to order.

Only Preston, sitting quietly, seemed to understand that by invoking executive privilege, Annie was taking the burden of the unpopular decision entirely on to herself. Council members would be spared having to defend their votes to their friends and neighbors; and anyway, he guessed that she'd *never* have gotten a majority vote for a seven percent hike; and seven percent—as Annie had discovered last night while reading her documents—was the gulp-inducing number it would take to get Alpine Valley's roads even *half*-repaired.

The hue and cry continued, and Annie kept banging her gavel—but to no avail. So Preston did what he'd never done before—not to adults, anyway, only to his athletes. He blew his whistle at them.

It shocked them all into silence.

"Look, ladies and gentlemen," he said, "and I'm sorry about that, but...Madame Mayor, may I have the floor?"

Shocked by the whistle-blowing, and upset by the hue and cry, Annie merely nodded—and anyway, it would be nice to have the attention off of her, if only for a minute.

"Thank you, Madame Mayor," Preston said, and then, sitting up straight, and clearing his throat, he said, "I have a question, and it may sound like a strange question. But I assure you it's important. Who here remembers their grandparents, the old folk, talking about the Alpine Valley Ape?"

Everyone blinked at Preston, for awhile.

"The Alpine Valley *Ape?*" Shirley asked, frowning, confused.

Bulie chuckled. "He was like the Boogey Man," he said.

"Did anybody ever see him?" asked Preston.

"Oh, well, you know how it is," said Bulie. "Campfire stuff."

"Okay," Preston said, "okay," and he opened the file that lay in front of him. He started handing around copies of the pictures he'd printed out last night. "Now this first picture," he said.

"Bigfoot," said Millard, looking as his copy.

"No, he wasn't like that," said Bulie. "He wasn't tall like this. He was shorter. Shaggy. Like one of them dwarves. Hairy."

"There *was* no Hairy," Millard said. "It was Doc, Sleepy— ."

"Happy was one," offered Skeet.

"Wasn't there a Sneezy?" Shirley asked.

"I don't mean his *name* was Hairy!" announced—yelled— Bulie. "*He* was hairy! The ape!"

"Fine," Preston said, hoping to put a quick end to this digression. "Never mind the dwarves for a moment. Let's consider this picture of Bigfoot. Look carefully. What do you see?"

"No visible genitalia," said Edna.

Preston, thrown off track, looked at her. Annie looked at her. It was their turn to blink.

"Um, yes," Preston resumed, "but I mean, *behind* him. The town. Look at the town."

"People on the street," Shirley said. "So?"

"Look at your second picture," Preston said. "Different angle. Same town. What do you see?"

"Well, cars," Skeet said.

"Look at the license plates," said Preston.

"Idaho," Millard said.

"New York. Florida," Skeet said. "Colorado."

"I don't like where this is going, Mr. Mayhugh," said Annie, glancing at him over the picture in her hands.

"Annie—Madame Mayor," Shirley said, sitting up, the light beginning to dawn in her face, "the streets are *full*."

"I *see* that the streets are full, Shirley," Annie said, "but— ."

"Now look, folks," said Preston, cutting her off—and hoping she wouldn't cut *him* off—but he *had* to press his advantage—"I'm no kind of artist, but..." He got up from his chair and hurried to an easel he'd set up. Nobody had paid any attention to it before now. "Look here." He turned over a blank, covering sheet of paper to reveal a badly done, but still comprehensible illustration of the town of Alpine Valley: You could make out City Hall and its clock tower...The town square...Merle's Grocery Café...the grammar school...the high school beyond that...and Main Street—*filled with people*. In the foreground, nearest the viewer, and dominating Preston's illustration, was a huge statue of a bizarre-looking creature holding up a sign that said, 'Welcome to Alpine Valley.'

"Well, I'll be dad-gummed," Millard said.

"But he's not real," Annie said.

"So we *make* him real!" said Preston.

"How?" asked Shirley.

Preston smiled broadly—glad she asked that—and raced back to his folder and extracted more pictures, which he passed around. "A few strange, unexplainable footprints here or there—like these in the pictures, see? They're supposed to be of Bigfoot. It's nonsense, of course, but it makes a lot of people go, 'Whoa,' and makes them believe—right? And look at this photo—this is supposed to be Champy. New York's version of a Loch Ness monster. Well, we could do something like this. Fake a few photos, even fake a video and post it online—even send it to the news stations!"

Preston paused. He suddenly sensed a change in the atmosphere. The group had been with him, but he felt them retreating. Ah. The word 'fake.' They weren't sure about this *faking* business. He saw Shirley shift uncomfortably in her seat. Bulie furrowed his brow as he stroked his chin.

"Well, I don't know," Skeet said.

Preston nodded, nodded and swallowed. He still hadn't played his ace. He hadn't wanted to play it so soon in his presentation, but he was losing them. "Do you know," he asked the council, "how much money the city of Willow Creek, California made last summer? Two point seven million tourist dollars."

There was a beat as everyone around the table considered this information; then Shirley said, "We could modify some snowshoes for making the creature's tracks." She demonstrated with her hands, pretending they were snowshoes, and walking them up the table.

"Shirley!" Annie said, shocked at her.

Everyone looked at Annie.

Preston licked his lips.

"Ladies and *gentlemen*," Annie said. "I mean, essentially you're talking about lying!"

"But it's a fun lie!" said Skeet. "It's fun!"

"It may be fun, but it's fraud," said Annie. "What will we be teaching our kids?"

"But it's all wink-wink, nudge-nudge," Preston said. "Everyone will know it's horse manure, but it's fun for their kids—and maybe for themselves, they'll be tapping into, or satisfying, a need."

"*Mis*ter Mayhugh," said Annie.

"These people," said Preston, quickly grabbing and holding up a picture of the tourists in Vermont, "are locked in by freeways and mini-malls. There are no deep, dark woods that contain a 'what if.' We're giving them that. If they come, it's because they're lying to themselves, which is really saying they're *fantasizing*. They get to be kids again. Around Bulie's campfire."

"How very pretty," said Annie. "But is that truly your *motive*, Mr. Mayhugh? Is your motive to give people a good time? Your motive is to take their money, while *faking* it that this creature is actually *here*. 'Come on, everybody, give us your money for a chance to see...absolutely nothing.' That's deception. And fraud. You want our kids to watch us lie and fake things? You want us to impart to our kids that it's okay to lie to get out of a problem? How about this?: Do you want to say to your kid, 'Honey, when a tourist asks you, *Is there really a monster here*? that you should lie and say, 'Yes, sir.'"

"I don't have any kids," Skeet said.

"Annie, we don't have any options," said Millard.

"It's Madam Mayor," said Annie, "and yes we *do*. We raise

taxes. We tighten our belt a little more. We work harder."

"No one in this town could work harder than they do, Madam Mayor," said Preston. "Look, our creature, our ape, is just a variation on a theme. The same people who chase after Bigfoot and fly off after the Loch Ness Monster—they'll come *here*."

"But at least these people—your people in this town here," and Annie grabbed up a copy of the picture of Willow Creek, "for them there may be a modicum of real belief. You know, somebody saw *something* strange. But us—we'd just be making it up *wholesale*."

There was a silence in the room, but for the creaking of the fans above.

"Madam Mayor," said Preston, "members of the council. Two point seven million dollars. *In one summer*. Not only enough to fix the streets, and sidewalks, but enough to at least *start* a road that'll get us more quickly to Taylorville. And Shirley?" added Preston, "does anybody on this council—does anybody in *town*—know better than *you* how great it would be to get to Taylorville quickly?"

"Well," Shirley said, "I guess not."

There was another silence as everyone thought about this. Because it was true, a straight road to Taylorville would mean a world of good to Shirley—and especially to her son, who was wheelchair-bound thanks to handicaps and seizures, and in need of weekly visits to the doctors in Taylorville.

"I ask for a vote," Preston said. "Do we create an ape? All in favor..."

"Aye!" everyone said, except for Annie, who was openly glaring at Preston. How dare he commandeer this meeting? How dare he ask for a vote? Only the mayor could ask for a vote!

"Wait a minute!" Annie said. "Wait! This is— ."

"Motion carries!" announced Bulie, grabbing Annie's gavel, and now banging it on the desk.

"Bulie!" Annie cried, shocked by what he'd done, and about to cry at everyone's, well, *betrayal* of her, and their good sense, and their *morals!* "Well, then," she said, swallowing hard, trying to recover her poise, I see that I have been..."—and she searched for a word she could say aloud—"*out-maneuvered*. Yes. Out-maneuvered. But I'm still Mayor and I still have executive administrative privileges, and I'll invoke them and say that you will *not* be allowed to use city chambers, or assemble in city hall, for any of...*this*."

She stormed away from the table and to and through the door. It slammed behind her.

There was yet another silence, the members of the council either looking in pain or shock at the closed door, or at one another—to gauge how others might be feeling about all this that had transpired—or just down at the table, as Shirley was.

Preston looked miserable. He believed in his idea. He thought it would help. But he had *never* wanted to hurt Annie. And boy had he done *that*.

The ceiling fans creaked. Then Edna cleared her throat. "Dopey," she said.

As one, everyone turned to look at her.

"And Grumpy and Bashful," she added; and as they all continued staring at her, she got angry and said, "Well, I know I'm right! Go look it up!"

Chapter Nine

*T*HEY WERE STAPLED TO EVERY TELEPHONE POLE IN town—one was taped to the flagpole in the square—and another was stuck on the bayonet of the Civil War soldier in the war memorial—which was a little rude, but got the job done, because everyone passing the square wanted to see what the sign stuck on the bayonet said.

'Want to Save This Town?'

That's what it said in big bold letters. Underneath them, one read,

'Saturday. 8p.m. High School Auditorium.'

And that's why at eight o'clock on Saturday night, Main Street was deserted. Even Eddie's Bar and Grill was closed—and Eddie *never* closed his bar and grill—not even on Christmas Day.

But there he was, about the middle of the overflow crowd in the auditorium. Not a single seat was empty, and the people making a collar around the seats stood three deep.

And everyone was in the dark—physical dark, not dark in the sense of not understanding something, because, at this very moment, Preston was giving them a slide-show presentation, and explaining point by point how, in fact, they could all help save this town.

"Point number three," Preston was saying. "The creature we

come up with can't be too much like a bear, or people will say, 'Ah, they're just seeing bears.'" Preston, up on the auditorium stage, now clicked the next slide into place, and everyone saw—and laughed at—a picture of a cartoon bear holding a beehive and, unwilling to surrender it, swatting at the bees angrily circling him.

(It had crossed Preston's mind to add a little joke here about Edna's hairdo, but then he thought better of it: It might hurt her feelings. It might *not,* because she was a pretty good sport about the ribbing she took because of it, but since he'd screwed things up with Annie, he didn't feel like taking any chances with Edna.)

"On the other hand," Preston continued, "he can't be too out-landish—advice I got from Chrissy Covington."

The audience roared with laughter, and Chrissy shouted a mock-annoyed, "Hey!" She loved the attention, as Preston abso-lutely knew she would. Chrissy was the town's young thespian, with dreams in her head of going to Broadway—and the *other* things she had in her head were multiple piercings and studs; and *on* her head, there was a pink and black rooster tail hairdo. Glittery silver eye-shadow completed the picture.

And perhaps it's not so surprising to hear that Melissa (who was not here tonight: her mother wouldn't allow her to come) looked up to Chrissy and admired her unique sense of style—though it was hard for Melissa to imagine *ever* getting studs in her nose and at the corners of her eyes. How brave Chrissy was!

When the laughter died down, Preston continued. "But the biggest thing to remember is that we can't make our creature a Bigfoot. Just about every state in the Union claims to have one; and as our town is hard to get to, why would anybody come here to try and see ours?"

While the crowd thought this through, Peter slipped into the back of the auditorium. He had wanted to come late, and to slip into the back like this, so people wouldn't look at him—for the usual reason that he just didn't want people to *look* at him, but also, tonight, for the added reason that since he had sneaked out of the house to be here, he didn't want anybody saying to his mom tomorrow, 'Oh, I saw Peter at the meeting last night.'

He had told his mother that, because he was exhausted from staying up late last night working on his essay for Mrs. Barbour (which was true), he thought he'd turn in early. But instead, he only snapped off his light—and crawled out the window. His mother would check on him, of course, but he'd seen *Ferris Beuller's Day Off*, and though he didn't have a dummy to rig up the way Ferris did, he *did* have a bunch of foam rubber he'd found in a dumpster, and which he'd cut up into shapes and glued together so that it looked (more or less) like a body. And he put his pajamas on it and pulled the covers up high.

But anyway, here he was, and the door was closing behind him as, up on the stage, Preston was saying, "No, we need something special. Something different."

And just at that moment, the door slammed shut behind Peter, startling him, and worse, quite a few people in the auditorium, too. They turned around and *looked* at him. Peter wanted to pull the ground up over his head.

"And we need special and different *people*," Preston said. "People who can make this *happen*, make this *convincing*. Well, guess what? There's a lot of talent in this town. A *lot*. So I don't think it will be hard at all to come up with an amazing creature—and a plan for springing him on the world. Ladies and gentlemen, we can *do* this!"

There was a lot more applause than Preston had anticipated, perhaps because Annie's disgust at his idea—and consequently, her disgust with him—loomed large in his mind, and he thought there'd be a lot more people like her in the crowd. Maybe those people had stayed away—except, well, it looked as if everyone in town was here. But then, Preston *did* notice that there *were* people out there in the crowd whose faces showed either doubt about this big idea or outright hostility toward it. They had frowns on their faces, and in many cases, their arms folded tightly across their chests. Some of these people were outright glaring at Preston, the way Annie had.

He licked his lips fast and continued, "Now, I propose we break up into committees. For instance, we'll need a committee to *conceive* of the creature. What does he *look* like? How does he *behave*? I think Mr. Pierce, our science teacher, should team up with Miss Ames, our creative writing teacher, and come up with an idea."

As it just so happened, Miss Ames, shy as a mouse, always keeping as close as possible to the walls when walking down halls, happened to be sitting in front of Mr. Pierce, who now tapped her on the back of the shoulder, once, and almost imperceptibly, with the tip of his finger. She jumped and turned quickly. He gave her a little wave, and though he had planned on smiling, the fear in her face scared him, so what *she* saw was an overly wide-eyed man doing something peculiar with his fingers.

He, too, was shy; in fact—though it hardly seems possible—shyer than Miss Ames. But in that moment just prior to tapping her on the shoulder—maybe because he felt emboldened by the attention Preston had given him—he thought, *What could a tap hurt?* But after she'd turned on him in fear, he, like Peter earlier, wanted to pull the earth up over his head. This was *not* a promising start to their collaboration.

But what Mr. Pierce didn't notice, quickly dropping his gaze to the floor, his face on fire with embarrassment, was that Miss Ames' face had changed from fearful to something resembling gladness. She was blushing, too, but she looked, well, something close to happy.

"Then," Preston was saying, "we're going to need a committee to actually *make* the creature. I mean, we'll need a costume or something, right? And I'm hoping Miss Dorothy Dodd and the Alpine Valley Sewing Circle can take care of that."

Miss Dorothy, sitting in the front row and blushing, put an 'Oh, my' hand to her chest. Her two oldest friends, Millicent and

Gertrude (and I'm sorry to say I've forgotten their last names), sat on either side of her, and Gertrude seized Miss Dorothy's free hand and inhaled sharply, happily; and Millicent plucked Miss Dorothy's sleeve.

Preston smiled at all three of them, and there was not only happiness for them in that smile, but gratitude, too, that three of the town's oldest and most respected citizens should apparently be on board with all this. "Okay," said Preston, now looking at the crowd, "we're also going to need a committee to get the word out on the creature. *Witnesses*—who can get other people to believe what they say is true. And I'm hoping that Miss DuMonde, our drama teacher, can head that committee."

At that, Ramona DuMonde, a large woman with an unruly cloud of red hair, big ruby rings (not real rubies, of course—not on a teacher's salary), gold hoop earrings, and a necklace of blocky multi-colored stones, stood up from her seat—also in the front row—and blew Preston a kiss, then turned around and, putting her palms together as if in prayer, bowed to the audience, though there was only a smattering of applause. Turning back to Preston, and with a flourish of her hand, she said, "I shall accept the position!"

Preston replied thank you, waited for her to take her seat again—and he had to wait several moments—and then said, "Finally, we're going to need someone to *be* the creature!"

"I nominate my husband!" a woman yelled from the audience. "He's some kind of creature, all right!"

Pretty much everyone laughed, and Miss Dorothy did, too, after Millicent leaned in to repeat what the woman had said.

"All right, all right," Preston said, trying to get everyone quiet again, "what we're going to do is hold auditions. Male, female, young, old—doesn't matter: The person who's most convincing as something, well, I don't know, *beast*-like, *ape*-like, is going to win."

"And I'm telling you—that's going to be my *husband*," the same woman shouted, and again she got laughs, though not nearly as many as the first time.

You can't tell the same joke twice, Peter thought—something he'd read in a biography of Charlie Chaplin. But mostly Peter was thinking about how much he wanted to be a part of all this. This was the greatest thing that had ever happened in Alpine Valley, as far as he knew, and certainly the most exciting thing in *his* life.

"Well, I guess that's it, ladies and gentlemen," Preston said, "There are sign-up sheets for the various committees at the foot of the stage here. So what do you say? Shall we get started and *save this town*?"

While most everyone else applauded, whistled, and cheered, Peter looked anxious. The sign-up sheets were at the *foot of the stage*? He'd have to walk all the way down the aisle to the front if he wanted to sign up, everyone *looking* at him, and a few of these people—you could be *sure*—would see his mother tomorrow and tell her he'd been here. But oh how he wanted to sign up! And Peter took a step forward—then turned around and hurried out of the auditorium.

Now, that Peter had hurried away is understandable, given his character and legitimate fear that his mother might discover what he'd done. But what's surprising is that Preston, watching the crowd surge forward to sign up for this or that, suddenly turned pale and hurried off stage.

There was a door on the side of the auditorium, and Preston, sweat beads forming on his brow, pushed through it, and walking quickly, he now broke into a run; and going faster and faster, he didn't look like a man running *to* something, but a man running *from* something—like from a monster.

And in a way this was true, because the monster was a memory, a memory that rose up and came after him every now and again, especially when Preston was feeling particularly good; and he was feeling particularly good just now—well not *now*, because he was frightened to death *now,* but a few seconds ago, when he was up on that stage and seeing that the town had embraced his idea and that, holy moly, this town might be saved, after all!

But if you could read Preston's horrified eyes as he ran, they would tell this story:

It's twenty-four years ago, and Preston is eleven years old. He's standing on the bank of the Alpine River. He's standing next to his ten-year-old brother Nickie. They have boogie-boards under their arms, and they're watching the river. It's fast, full, roily, and it plunges over a cataract a hundred yards downstream.

"It's still up," says Nickie. "We shouldn't try it."

"C'mon," says Preston. "We can do it. Really—we can do it! We just ride to that group of boulders there, about the middle—see?—how they make the river fork? And we just go to the right. See how much gentler it is on that side? And we paddle to the islet."

"I'm not gonna do it," Nickie says.

"Ah, don't be yellow," says Preston.

"I'm not yellow!" says Nickie.

"I think you're yellow," Preston says, and suddenly, as if something invisible, like a thought, has yanked him into the water, he's belly-whumped on his board, and is heading for the fast slick middle of the river. "See ya later, ya sissy-mary!"

"I'm not a sissy-mary!" Nickie calls, and though he stands there for a moment, a second, a third, biting his lip, he now runs into the water and belly-whumps onto his board and paddles after his brother.

Preston meantime doesn't find himself so much reaching the fast middle of the river as getting yanked into it, and while only moments before he was yelling "Whoo-hoo!" he isn't now. He's trying to get his board aimed at the boulders ahead, and he's paddling and kicking for them—but the current is strong and pulls him left, away from them. He's on the verge of being swept past them, and toward the cataract.

He jerks his head around to look at Nickie; Nickie, because he's still starting out, showing more conviction on his face than fear—and "Nickie!" Preston yells, "Go back!"

Preston turns his head around; and while with his right arm he tries to keep the board pressed to his torso, he frantically paddles with the left, and frantically kicks with his legs, and tries to resist the torque his body and motions are making—which torque will roll him under into certain death.

His left arm on fire and cramping up, his legs on fire, he's within two seconds of being swept to the cataract, but animal fear makes him take a faster half-dozen furious strokes—and he's snatched into the current that whisks him around the boulders into swift, but less swift, and more easily managed water. He'll make it to the islet ahead to the right.

Nickie, now yanked into the middle of the river, strokes furiously—and with rising panic. He saw how Preston succeeded, and is trying to do so, too. But he's not nearly as strong as his brother. He can't outfight this current. He is swept past the boulders.

"Preston!" he yells.

"Nickie!" yells Preston, and Nickie looks at Preston with horror as he goes past—and now he's separated from his board and goes under.

"Nickie!" Preston screams, and the last he sees of his brother is his tumbling body as it goes over the cataract and disappears forever, except as it lives in this memory yanking Preston after him.

His clothes soaked in sweat, Preston has left the lights of the town far behind, and he's raced into the dark woods, wanting to be lost, lost forever.

Chapter Ten

ANNIE WATCHED ALL THESE VERY IMPORTANT Government Types in their power suits and power ties, shiny shoes and shiny briefcases, hurrying up and down the marble-floored and colonnaded hallway of the State Capitol building. If she shouted—and believe me, she was thinking about doing so—the shout would echo off these walls for a good long time.

She herself sat forlornly on a bench—a cold marble bench—in that same hallway. She clutched rolled-up charts to her chest. Her briefcase sat on the floor at her feet. It was not shiny. It was scuffed, and about as beat-up as Annie felt.

She caught sight of Trevor Westley coming through the door a few yards off from where she sat. He was followed by three Very Important Types who looked surprisingly like Trevor—just older versions of him. One of these guys was wearing cologne. Annie wanted to put a hand to her nose—kind of shield her nostrils: the scent was that strong and unpleasant. But she didn't. Trevor and the three men shook hands all around, and while the older Trevors went off down the hall, young Trevor turned and came toward Annie.

"I didn't do well in there, did I, Trev?" she asked as he approached.

He sat next to her on the bench. He sighed. "It wasn't you, Annie. You had nothing to do well with."

"Trevor," she said, "*please*. The state *has* to float us a loan." She motioned with her chin toward the three Important Types retreating down the hall "Try something *else* with them. I mean, *talk* to them. *Something.* Twist their arms—*something.*"

Trevor sighed again. "And if Alpine Valley defaults on the loan—which it will?" He sat back and rested his head against the cold wall. "Look. Annie. I love that little town, too. Me, you, the McGuire Brothers. Your mom's caramel apples..."

Annie sat up and toward him. "And wasn't that the best time in your *life,* Trev?"

He smiled, sadly. "Of course. But Annie, what can I do?" He motioned with his head toward the Important Types. "The Dudes have spoken."

A worried frown on her face, Annie searched Trevor's eyes— first the left one, then the right—certainly the answer she wanted to hear was in one of them; was in Trevor *somewhere.*

He looked away. "I'm sorry, Annie."

With her free hand—she was still clutching her charts to her chest (and though I don't know what her charts depicted, it's a pretty good bet that they showed how one might build a road to Taylorville)—she grabbed Trevor's wrist. "Trevor, don't give up!"

"Annie," he said.

She let go of his wrist and looked away.

Trevor gave a small laugh. "You're doing that thing you do," he said. "You've got your jaw all set—that *I-mean-business* look." Normally, Annie would have laughed—at herself. But these weren't normal times—not for Annie.

She looked at him—pretty hard, too—like a glare. "Well, I *do* mean business. And *I'm* not giving up. I'm going to write your *dudes* a letter. And then write them again. And then write them *again.* We need that money. We need that road!"

"Annie."

"Trevor, they have to listen!"

"Annie."

She abruptly got up, grabbing her briefcase. "Your cologne stinks, Trevor." She walked briskly away.

Chapter Eleven

$\mathcal{A}$T ABOUT THE SAME TIME THAT ANNIE WAS WALKING away from Trevor (and by the way, it wasn't *he* who had been wearing the foul-smelling cologne, but one of his colleagues—it's just that the scent got on him), Melissa was standing at the front of Room 5B at Alpine Valley Elementary and reading her latest story to the class.

And her teacher, Miss Sarah Watkins was looking on—horror-stricken.

"And then," Melissa read, "the wax figure of Zoltan the Madman sprang through the glass. The tourists ran. But one little girl fell, and Zoltan grabbed her and bit off the top of her head. The brain inside was quivering like Jell-O, as if it were frightened of the fate that awaited it."

As Melissa continued, the horrified Miss Watkins stopped listening and starting writing something down on a pad of paper—and I'll tell you now that what she was writing was a note home to Melissa's mother.

Meantime, just up the street at the high school, in Room 7H, Peter was putting the finishing touches on the second of two side by side panels, like panels in a comic strip, or better, like two frames in a film strip, which, in fact, is what the panels were supposed to represent.

While he worked, his teacher droned on about... well, Peter had no idea; and if called upon to answer a question, he'd be in big trouble, because not only would he have to ask his teacher to please repeat the question—making the man more than a little angry with him—all of the other kids would turn around and stare at him. But he couldn't stop sketching.

The first panel showed an apelike creature in the background, mid-stride as he emerges from behind a huge rock in the forest. In the foreground, one saw a female hiker, turned toward the viewer, and screaming.

The content of the second panel—the screaming woman, the huge rock, the sky, the very ground—it's all tilted at a severe angle; and in the foreground, at the far right corner of the picture, one saw the back of the creature's head and his elbow, the creature apparently having jostled the camera badly as it runs away, disappearing from the frame.

Now finished with the sketch, Peter— .

But here his teacher interrupted both him and this story—so we'll never know what Peter was about to do, but it couldn't have been *too* important—the important stuff in this scene is already told, and the sketches done—and the teacher barked, "Peter! I asked you a question!"

Peter's heart began to thump hard, then harder, as everyone turned around to stare at him. Not only did he not know the answer, he had been so absorbed in his sketching that he even forgot he was in math class, as all the numbers on the blackboard now told him he was. He'd thought he was in history or something.

Interestingly, while Peter asked his teacher to please repeat the question, it was right next door, in 7G, that Miss Ames and Mr. Pierce, the heads of the committee tasked with conceiving of the town's creature, were having their first meeting.

Neither had a class to teach this period, so they had an hour free.

When Miss Ames adjusted the blinds against a too-bright

sun, the room became prettily atmospheric, as softened light pen-
etrated the shadows, as happens in the forest when sunlight filters
through the canopy of trees and makes beautiful and magical certain turns in the path.

"Well, that might be a *little* dark," Mr. Pierce said, and Miss
Ames said, "Oh, it's fine, it's lovely," and then gulped because it
shocked her that she should not only have contradicted Mr. Pierce,
but should have said anything at all. She thought about going back
to the blinds and re-adjusting them, but she did, in fact, find the
light lovely the way it was now, and Mr. Pierce looked so nice in it,
his glasses and tie-tack glinting so nicely, so she just returned to
the student desk she had been sitting in, and, before re-taking her
seat, she pushed it right up to Mr. Pierce's desk, so that they just
kissed. "You were saying, Mr. Pierce?" she asked.

"Um, well," Mr. Pierce said, not at all sure why they needed
to be sitting so closely together—unless perhaps Miss Ames had
difficulty hearing, in which case, why hadn't he been informed of
this? It would have been helpful, in fact, *advisable* for the principal
to have informed him of his colleague's impairment. He'd have to
have a word with the man. "I was *saying*," Mr. Pierce continued,
raising the volume of his voice, "that I don't think our creature
should be *too* frightening. Families won't *come*."

"Yes, of course," Miss Ames said, either not aware that Mr.
Pierce had increased the volume of his voice, or paying it no mind
that he did, "but we don't want him completely docile. We want
him a little wild."

Both of them had thermos cups of tea on their desks, which
sent steam into the almost golden atmosphere in which they found
themselves.

"Well, all right," said Mr. Pierce, and he jotted down 'a little
wild' on his notepad. "Perhaps he *brachiates*," he added, looking up
at Miss Ames.

"Oh, I like the sound of that," she said. "What is that?"

"He swings from trees," answered Mr. Pierce, now jotting

down 'brachiates,' and, inspiration striking, he wrote, even as he said it, "so that means his arms are long—and strong," and then looking up—and for Miss Ames's benefit, because he knew his volume had dropped as he had concentrated on his writing—"He has *muscular arms.*"

"Hmmm," said Miss Ames, as if she'd just tasted something delicious, and smiling at Mr. Pierce through the steam of her tea, she said, "Muscular arms, you say?"

"Indeed," said Mr. Pierce, now convinced that, since she had just asked for confirmation about what he'd said, the poor woman was most definitely hard of hearing.

Chapter Twelve

$\mathcal{A}$NNIE SAT AT A TABLE AT A FAST-FOOD PLACE ON THE highway. All kinds of trucks hurtling past shook the window before her. She had only taken two bites of her hamburger and two sips of her Diet Coke before she'd pushed aside her tray. Her briefcase was once again open before her, looking like it wanted to have her for lunch. She had her cell phone to her ear and was listening to her own voice on the answering machine at home telling her to leave a message after the beep, which she now did.

"Hi, sweeties," she said, "it's me. I left the capitol a couple of hours ago and should be home around seven. I'll stop at Merle's to pick up something for dinner. Call me if you need anything. Okay, love you. Bye." She snapped closed the phone and gazed at the contents of her briefcase. Surely the town's salvation was in there somewhere; somewhere in all these papers, these printouts—and there was her mail—yesterday's; she hadn't opened it yet. She took out the stack and began going through it. Bill. Bill. Bill. Certified letter. *Certified letter*? She hadn't signed for anything. Had Melissa signed for it, or Peter, and had forgotten to tell her that it had come?

She tore it open, began to read, and her eyes widened—and she gasped so loudly that every single person waiting in line to order turned around and looked at her.

While a now alarmed Annie was neglecting her lunch, Miss Dorothy and the ladies of the Alpine Valley Sewing Circle were happily digesting theirs, and, the dishes all washed and dried, they had turned their attention to their job: creating the look for the creature Mr. Pierce and Miss Ames had conceived of.

Mr. Pierce had come to Miss Dorothy's house with the notes he and Miss Ames had made, and had found the ladies preparing their luncheon, as only people their age called 'lunch.'

They had, of course, invited him to join them, but he had papers to grade, he said—though he really didn't. The ladies had passed around and discussed the notes all through luncheon, and unfortunately, there were now big drops and splotches of Waldorf Salad dressing, coffee, mayonnaise, and something they called 'piccalilli' all over the notes, obscuring certain important words and phrases. No matter. The ladies were *quite* confident that they'd come up with just the right look for the creature, and anyway, several of them, in their haste to get to this important meeting, had left their homes without their glasses, so they wouldn't have been able to read the notes anyway; and Alice Tobin—their best sewer— didn't have her hearing aid turned on, so she wasn't going to hear any instructions anybody might give her—although, even if she *could* hear them, she wouldn't follow them. Alice liked things her way, which everybody knew, so why argue with her? You can't win with a half-deaf woman who doesn't want to listen to you in the first place.

Still and all, while dining, their discussion of the notes had been focused and serious-minded. But Miss Dorothy, ever the gracious hostess, had made the mistake of serving sherry with luncheon, and the ladies, so buoyant with the fact that they had great purpose now and had been entrusted with a job so vital to the town's interest, had taken quite a few joyous nips—well not nips (I was trying to be polite), but entire joyous *glassfuls* of sherry, and they were no longer too terribly focused or serious-minded. In fact, Peggy Piersall was out wandering around in front of Miss

Dorothy's house, petting her marigolds, and Teresa Considine (Shirley's grandmother) was lolled in Miss Dorothy's love seat, asleep and snoring.

But the rest were wide-awake and, if not terribly focused, terribly busy and enthusiastic. There were little groups of ladies here, and little groups of ladies there, sewing—their practiced fingers so deft and still nimble—and calling for more sherry—loudly—so Miss Dorothy could hear—and though it was hard to see what they were actually creating, since things were being created in pieces, or sections—little group by little group—and who could concentrate anyway with all the *nattering* going on?—and unfortunately the noise and commotion have caused me to lose my way with this sentence, so I'm just going to have to stop it, and start a new one.

At the top of the stairs, to which he'd gone in hasty retreat, Miss Dorothy's little dog (whose name I don't remember) watched all the ladies and their goings-on with great uncertainty. Every time one of them laughed raucously, or several at the same time did, the poor thing whined; and it's possible he thought about running out his doggy door to go outside and get away from all this. But as Miss Dorothy could tell you—and would—the little dear *never* went outside unless Miss Dorothy was right by his side. So what a waste that doggy door had been!

The little group of ladies nearest him (*Winston* was his name—I just remembered it!) had a big box in their midst. It was marked 'Halloween,' and Mary-Ellen Pennybaker had had her grandson, Roger, tote it over to Miss Dorothy's for her. Mary-Ellen was a saver, and she had years' and *years'* worth of Halloween costumes and decorations saved up in this box. She had been confident that most everything they would need to create the look for the creature would be in here. And it appeared she was right.

Millicent (whose last name I *still* can't come up with) had pulled a Wolfman costume out of the box and taken it to her little group; and Gertrude (ditto the parenthetical foregoing) had pulled out a gorilla costume. Peggy Piersall, who had wandered in from outside at some point I missed (since I've been busy telling you all this) was now busy with a pair of pliers, yanking out the fangs from a hard plastic Count Dracula mask.

Somehow, at some point, a decision about the look of the creature's head had been made—or Miss Dorothy had made the decision herself (accounts differ)—but anyway, there it was now, in Miss Dorothy's lap, as Miss Dorothy tied off the last stitch. The head looked...great. Convincing. It might have been more Ape-like (as far as some were concerned) than Mr. Pierce's and Miss Ames's notes had specified, but somehow, as particularly the older folk later said, it just plain *looked right*, like what they visualized out of their parents' stories.

Quite happy herself with the head she'd created, Miss Dorothy slipped it over her head.

"What do you think, girls?" she called, and though her voice was muffled, those nearest her heard her; and as they began to laugh with glee, the others took note and began looking over, at which point, Miss Dorothy got up from her chair, and, because she could see through the eyeholes, began walking up and down the area in front of her chair, doing her version of an ape walk, and scrabbling at the air in front of her with her fingers—as if they were claws. "Grrr! Grrr!" she said.

The ladies erupted in laughter, Millicent actually falling from the ottoman on which she sat, Teresa Considine waking up, and Winston running down the hall and under Miss Dorothy's bed.

Chapter Thirteen

SUCH A BUSY DAY IT HAD BEEN SO FAR IN ALPINE VALLEY —and it remained busy.

If you had driven from Miss Dorothy's at about four p.m.—which was about the time the ladies had come together to form a close circle, to stitch together the various parts of the ape into a single whole (except for the feet—that'd be the Barnett Brothers' responsibility)—and had gone to the high school and had entered Ramona DuMonde's classroom, you would have been surprised (I am) to see giant Larry Salisbury, in his cop uniform, standing in front of the class and reading from a script in his hand.

"'Whoa,'" Larry read, his eyes glued to the page, "'Whoa, Where's the fire?'"

Sitting in a school seat in the front row, directly in front of Larry, Ramona winced. She may or may not have wanted Larry to see her do that, but she was dramatic, and would probably have winced like that even if she were alone in the room and listening to Larry on tape.

"No, no, Officer Salisbury," she said, "there's not *really* a fire. You're just a friendly cop trying to get these people to slow down.—And anyway, you weren't the least bit believable."

"Okay," said Larry, "but I'll remind you I'm no actor."

"Oh, no need to remind me, Officer," Ramona said, and everyone in class, except for Larry, laughed.

She pushed herself up out of the seat and walked up to Larry. She stood at his side, a copy of the script in her hand. Ramona was a big gal, but she looked downright small next to Larry, and she liked that.

It was a full class. There'd be need for a lot of witnesses—townspeople who could convince others that they were telling the truth about what they'd seen. Preston hadn't tasked Ramona to come up with any kind of scenarios for fooling people—he hadn't thought of it, and of course he wouldn't have—*he* wasn't in theater, so Ramona had taken it upon herself to create said scenarios while training her many student-witnesses to deliver credible lines.

"Now, class," she said, "listen." Everyone sat up straight and gave her their undivided attention. "And Officer Salisbury," she said to him, "watch me carefully."

Ramona tossed her curls and closed her eyes, in order to get into character, and said, not read—she already had everyone's parts memorized—"'Whoa! Whoa! Where's the fire?'"

When she was finished, there was silence in the room. She'd been *real*. That was *perfect*. *Exactly* how someone might say it! The class couldn't help but break into applause.

Miss DuMonde couldn't suppress the satisfaction growing in her eyes. It was in her smile, too. "Do you *see*, Officer Salisbury?" she said, turning and looking up at him.

"Well, I *see*," he said, "but I don't know that I can *do*."

"Oh, I'm sure you can, Officer Salisbury, or I'm sure you *will*," she said. "But you've been enough on the hot seat, brave soul. Have a seat." And as Larry got all of himself moving toward his seat in the back, Miss DuMonde said, "Well, now, Mrs. Carnody, why don't you come up here and take a whack at your lines?"

The high school gym was just a pine cone's throw away from Miss DuMonde's classroom, and there, inside, Bulie was going ape.

"I reckon that's enough," he said when he was through and standing quietly in the center of the basketball court.

Preston sat slack-jawed. Mr. Pierce sat slack-jawed. Miss Ames sat slack-jawed.

The three were sitting side by side at a long table. They were the judges for the 'Ape Auditions,' as the hastily scrawled poster hanging on the open gym door indicated.

The three of them couldn't tell you whether Bulie was actually good, that is, right for the role or not. It was just the sight of Bulie Peppersmith behaving so...so...like *that* that left them speechless. There'd been roaring. There'd been yipping. There'd even been something that sounded like German. And then he'd topped it all off with a somersault. *Why?*

"Um," said Preston, trying to regain his bearings, "thank you. Bulie. We'll let you know."

"Suits me," said Bulie, and he turned and went back to the bleachers where the other people auditioning sat, along with quite a few town folk simply out for a good show. And boy, had he given them one.

Consulting his clipboard, Preston now called, "Millard?"

Millard, dressed in his pharmacist's tunic, hurried out of the bleachers and to the center of the basketball floor. He smiled at the judges. They smiled back. He kept smiling.

"Um, Millard," said Preston, "you can go ahead."

"Oh," said Millard. "Yes, of course." He cleared his throat.

He went ape.

It was...it was...I can't *begin* to describe it to you, except to say that at one point he began making leaps like they make in ballet, jetés, I think they're called; and he had so much change in his pockets that he jingled all over the place, so he sounded more funny than scary; and then when the change began flying out whenever he made a particularly energetic move, it was hard to concentrate on him, because one's attention went to the coins bouncing everywhere, or rolling all the way across the gym floor.

Edna came next, and she lost her dentures, and that surprised people because no one knew Edna wore dentures. When they hit the floor they broke, which was too bad, because now she'd have to go all the way to Cascade City to get them fixed. On the plus side, she was remarkably good. Very convincing as a wild animal. Mr. Pierce had made five inked stars by her name—five stars being his top grade, and Miss Ames had made four. Preston had only written 'WTF!' by Edna's name.

Skeet auditioned after Edna. Walking around, and rather slowly, while clawing at the air, he said, "I'm a big scary monster, and I'm coming to get you. Roar!" (Yes, he actually *said* roar. He didn't *make* a roar.) "So you'd better run! Here I come! Roar *again!*"

Since it didn't appear that Skeet was joking, or trying to be ironic, and actually thought that this is what their ape should be *doing*, Preston had his second occasion to go slack-jawed. He wondered if Skeet had missed the proverbial memo. Did he not *get* it that they were trying for a *realistic* creature—not a pretend creature; that this was not about your favorite uncle running around in the backyard at a BBQ scaring the delightedly screeching four-year-olds?

"Roar *super* loud!" said Skeet; and Preston, seeing people in the bleachers exchanging worried looks, wondered if Skeet had had a little stroke while he'd sat waiting his turn. Maybe he'd bumped his head pretty badly on the way here? Preston looked to see if Doc Cabot was in the bleachers. He wasn't. But maybe someone should call him?

"Well, what do you think?" asked Skeet when he was through—and Preston was not about to tell him what he thought, not in public.

"I think," said Preston, "that, um, may I have a word with you outside, Skeet?"

Well, there's really no need to take you outside and make you privy to the conversation between a worried Preston and a nonplussed Skeet. But the upshot of it was that Preston was assured that Skeet was all right. He'd just *really* misinterpreted what 'fun' meant when the council had been talking about how 'fun' this whole thing might be—'convincing' tourists that there was a 'monster' here. Skeet had, in fact, conceived of all of this as if it *were* something like a backyard goof, somebody's uncle running around and scaring kids. As he told Preston the following day, he'd had an idea of Disneyland in his head; an idea of some big costumed character going up and down Main Street the way Disney characters, like Goofy, and Mickey, and Captain Hook, went up Disneyland's Main Street. "Gee," he said to Preston, "I guess I really missed the boat, didn't I?"

And Preston told him not to worry about it—and he laughed it off—though he was thinking that from now on he'd have to question what he read in Skeet's newspaper, *The Alpine Voice*. Holy moly, he thought, if Skeet hadn't understood a concept so simple that even the *kids* here got it, how could anybody be sure that Skeet was understanding and interpreting correctly the events he was reporting on?

Shirley went ape after Skeet, and it was hard to tell if Shirley was pretty good because she was pretty good, or because *anybody* would look good after Skeet. She had to cut her audition short, however, because Shirley had (and I hope you don't get offended by this—but it's the truth—and what I'm about to say really happened) enormous breasts, and she hadn't put on the right kind of bra for something as strenuous as the routine she was now doing, and those breasts were swinging wildly every which way and, really, might have smacked a short man in the face and knocked him down, if he'd stood too close to her side; and of course the teenaged boys in the stands started to snicker, and Shirley either heard them or became aware herself that she must look a sight, and so she just stopped abruptly, and blushing said, "Okay, well, thanks." And though she thought about walking right out the door, she bravely turned and went back to the bleachers.

Preston was glad she had stopped when she did because he himself was only seconds away from bursting out laughing: already he'd been digging his fingernails into his palms to keep himself from doing that.

Mr. Pierce had given her four stars, though, and Miss Ames, looking over, noted that. She only gave Shirley one.

Several more people got up to audition after Shirley, including Boyd and Floyd, who had driven in to do so, and while Boyd was okay (two stars from Mr. Pierce; two from Miss Ames; and an OMG from Preston), his brother simply stood center court and recited the 'To be or not to be' monologue from *Hamlet*. Preston considered questioning Floyd about it as in, *Why*?, but then nixed the idea. He liked Floyd, and Floyd inhabited a slightly different world from the rest of humanity, and if Floyd wanted to audition for the Alpine Valley Ape by doing a Shakespearean monologue, who was hurt by the experience? No one. So he simply thanked him, and a smiling Floyd went back to the stands.

When Preston looked down at his clipboard, he was surprised to see Miss Ames's name there, but in pencil so light, he looked again to make sure he'd really seen it. "Miss Ames?" he said, turning to her. "You're auditioning?"

She nodded, her neck and face turning pink. "I won't vote for myself," she said, although it was almost inaudible.

"Sure," said Preston, shrugging.

Beginning to visibly shake, Miss Ames toed off her shoes, and then, her blush going from pink to red, padded barefoot to center court. Still shaking, she undid the bun in her hair and shook it out, and then gazing at the floor, as if reading a message there, quickly started gathering up her hair to work it back into a bun, and headed back toward her seat. "I'm sorry," she said in a near-whisper, to no one, to everyone.

"Are you sure?" Preston said, knowing that she was, but trying to be encouraging; and then surprising him, but not as much as it surprised the man himself, Mr. Pierce piped up, and in a voice that didn't sound to him like his own, said, "But surely, Miss Ames, you should try. You have the best sense of the ape, I should think." These words stopped Miss Ames in her tracks, and she glanced at Mr. Pierce, who normally would have looked away, but found himself holding her eyes. Then suddenly, madly, impulsively, her eyes locked on Mr. Pierce, Miss Ames undid her bun again and began to make slow, curvy S-shapes with her body, like a plant many feet below the surface of the sea, and while she was doing this, her eyes still locked on Mr. Pierce's—but now as if to look away were to die—she began to make what sounded like—but you had to listen closely because it was faint—a growl.

Preston couldn't have been more amazed and, in truth, he was a little afraid. What was wrong with Miss Ames? Mr. Pierce, in the meantime, looked a *lot* afraid.

The teenaged boys in the stands sat shocked, sat mesmerized. But then, so did everybody. And then very suddenly, as if the real Miss Ames had returned to her body, Miss Ames twirled her hair up into its bun and beet-red padded back to her seat. She sat. She worked her toes into her shoes.

When Preston saw that Miss Ames wasn't looking their way, or asking anything like, *Well, how did I do*, or even *expecting* any comment from them, it occurred to him that Miss Ames's aim had not been to audition. What had he missed? Preston wondered. What the heck had just gone *on*? Clearly this had something to do with Mr. Pierce—*everything* to do with Mr. Pierce—but just as clearly, it couldn't have been to please him. The man sat mortified, alarm in his eyes, which were locked on his notepad. He wasn't about to look Miss Ames's way. He wasn't about to look anybody's way. And he wasn't making any stars. Instead, whether he himself noted it or not, he was making a furious circular motion with his hand, inscribing into the paper a tight cyclone of blue ink, a cyclone that got darker and denser and was about to tear through the paper and maybe take Mr. Pierce with it—which I don't think he would have minded.

Preston glanced into the bleachers, his unconscious way of saying that he'd rather be anywhere else but at this table, between these two people, and he noted how the teenaged boys were either still gaping at Miss Ames or gazing at her. The men, he noted, were, too. The women were the most shocked of all. It was not only because of the inappropriateness of the display, but because it had come from *Miss Ames*, the squeaky little mouse who was so frightened to say anything at all at parent-teacher conferences beyond formula phrases like, *He works well with others.*

"Well, okay," Preston said, "thank you, Miss Ames, for that...," but he couldn't think of the words, so concluded with, "for *that*."

He consulted his clipboard. How many more names? Four. "Derrick?" he said, "You're up."

Derrick Merrick (and yes, that's his name, I'm not making it up) bounded down the steps to center court. He was the school's best athlete—a standout in everything. He was on the small side, though, and that was going to keep him from playing college ball. It broke Preston's heart a little that he couldn't develop a gymnastics program here—principally because gymnastics was not something Preston knew anything about—because there were several boys here who would have made first-rate gymnasts, and Derrick the best of them all.

"Should I just go, Coach?" Derrick asked.

"Whenever you're ready, yes."

And boy how Derrick went. I'll tell you now, since you've already guessed it, that Derrick became the Alpine Valley Ape. He was the one to don the costume Miss Dorothy and the ladies had created.

He ran to the end of the gym and climbed the rope, using only his hands, and then in a wink, got himself turned upside-down and came down the rope using only his feet and legs, while beating on his chest with his hands. He ran to the other end of the gym where there was an old pommel horse that hadn't been used in decades and had just sat in the corner because, well, no one actually *saw* it anymore, and he quickly dragged it out and made all kinds of moves on it, then vaulted over it. Well, why do I need to go on? You know Derrick wins the audition, and he was magnificent— agile, ape-like—without being *too* much like an ape, and more like something that might be a cousin to it—and his smallish size was actually an advantage here. Nobody could really say why that was so, but they just felt that it was, and later, the old folk would recall that their parents might have mentioned in their yarns that the Alpine Valley Ape was about the size of a year-old black bear.

When Derrick was through, everyone in the stands stood as one and applauded and cheered. So did all three judges. There were actually tears in Preston's eyes, and Mr. Pierce, forgetting his terror of her, turned to Miss Ames and impulsively grabbing her elbow, said, "He *got* it, didn't he? He understood exactly what we wanted!" And Miss Ames had stars in her eyes—and a lot more than five.

The three other people on the list after Derrick decided not to try out; and as one of those people was Chrissy Covington, that may better than anything else convey to you how perfect everyone thought Derrick Merrick was to play the part of the Alpine Valley Ape.

Chapter Fourteen

𝒯HE DARK BEGINNING TO GATHER, ANNIE FLIPPED ON her lights, and did so just as she approached, and now lit up, the sign that said, 'Welcome to Alpine Valley. Population 581. Elevation 8,467 feet.' We should change the sign, Annie thought. We've got less than half that number of people now, and no one feels very elevated. The sign was leaning over, like a chopped down tree heading for the earth, bang.

Annie pulled over, parked, got out of her Jeep and ran back toward the sign. In the red light of her taillights she pulled and *pulled* to get that sign back *up*.

Succeeding in doing so, and more happy about that than a normally happy person might be—a sign that Annie had too few opportunities for success lately (and in case you've been won-dering, that couple from Phoenix had decided against buying a house in Alpine Valley—they found the town 'depressing')—Annie wiped her hands clean and headed back to her Jeep.

As she took the last bend in the road, she saw the few lights of her hometown twinkling in the distance, so faint, and so fragile looking, against all this thick, encroaching darkness. God, how she loved her little town. Tears welled up in her eyes. But no, she couldn't cry. What she had discovered at lunch... no, there was no time for tears; she didn't have the luxury of tears.

She pulled up in front of Merle's. She was surprised to see

on the clock in her Jeep that it was only 7:30pm. It felt like it was closing in on midnight. She took a slow, deep, calming—perhaps suppressing—breath.

Inside the grocery/café, Merle was ringing up Millard's potato, pork chop, and can of spinach. Shirley stood next to Millard, next in line, her son Walter, in his wheelchair, next to her. She had Walter covered up in a blanket. He was smiling, though I guess it had been something of a challenging evening for him, breathing-wise, since he had his oxygen tank with him tonight, strapped to the back of the wheelchair. Slender plastic tubes went into his nostrils.

"Nah," Merle said to Millard, "you weren't the worst, and anyway, you gave everyone a pretty good laugh—scrambling around for your change under the bleachers, your butt in the air."

Walter laughed and clapped his hands, in that sort-of clapping thing he was able to do, and his laugh was more a rasp than anything else, but it made Shirley happy to hear it.

The little bells over Merle's door jingled as Annie pushed through.

"Annie," said Merle, "you really missed it today. Biggest laughs we've had around here in a long time."

"Yeah, well," Annie said, grabbing a hand basket from the small stack by the entrance. "Hey, Millard. Shirley. Walter."

"It was *fun*, Annie," Shirley said.

"I'm sure it was. Yes," said Annie, trying to mean it (especially since she saw how happy Walter looked—and when was the last time anybody in town saw a smile on that kid's face?). "Any pies left, Merle?"

"Back there somewhere," he said.

Annie thanked him and headed for the back of the store. Merle shared a look with Millard and Shirley. Merle shrugged.

In passing the junk food rack, Annie stopped; started to go on; stopped—and quickly grabbed some cookies—of *course* she shouldn't be buying these for Peter—and she thrust them into the basket.

She hurried to the shelf where Merle stocked his breads and pies. One little pie was left. Apple. She put it into her basket, and, as she turned, she banged her basket into Preston's.

"Madame Mayor," Preston said.

"Coach Mayhugh."

"State turned us down?" he asked.

"You knew I was going?"

"Small town," said Preston.

"My dears!" cried Gertrude. Annie and Preston turned to see Gertrude and Millicent coming down the aisle. They all exchanged happy hellos and Gertrude gave Preston a warm hug. "Oh, *Preston*," she said, "this is all such fun! We had so much fun today!"

"Are there any pies left?" Millicent asked, squinting at the shelves, giving them an up and down. "The girls have the munchies."

"Sure," said Annie, "here," and she handed her apple pie to Millicent.

"Oh, but we're not going to take your pie, dear," she said.

"Yes, we are," said Gertrude. "Thank you, Annie, dear. Come along, Millicent, before she changes her mind." And the two ladies turned and left the aisle, Gertrude tottering once.

"Is it me?" asked Preston, "or did they both seem a little... blitzed?"

Annie turned back to Preston, and ignoring the question, if she heard it at all, said, "This...*thing* you're doing. It's so... amateurish. We'll look stupid. The rubes, the desperate rubes of Alpine Valley."

"I think we can do this," Preston said. "And it's already paying off." He made a motion with his head, indicating Gertrude and Millicent, whose progress toward the cash register you could follow by the sound of their giggling. "You saw their faces. There's hope here."

"That's the worst part of it," Annie said. "You've got everyone floating around on bubbles. Don't you know life hates that? It wants to go pop, pop, pop—and then *wham*. And we'll all have you to thank, Mr. Mayhugh."

The two looked at each other for a second, but then that second became an uncomfortable two. Annie's face burned as she looked away, because this was *terrible*; an *impossible* situation.

Because she saw in Mayhugh's eyes that he was thinking, *What a sad woman*, and she just *knew* that he was thinking about her divorce, and how bitter she must be because of it; and okay, a *little* of her personal situation had crossed her mind when she'd said those hurtful words just now. But what was *chiefly* on her mind—what *really* pushed through her lips that *pop, pop, pop*—was what she couldn't share with this guy; not yet, anyway. Not here and now; so she'd have to *endure* this incorrect thinking of his— this *totally* wrong—well, mostly wrong—*thinking*; and it made her want to scream at him that he had *no* idea what he was talking about, but she couldn't do that, of course, because he hadn't said a thing; though he was *oh* so eloquent with those eyes, and suddenly she turned and walked quickly away up the aisle. She needed air. She needed it fast. She had to get away from this man.

Of course—well, maybe not of course, so let's say, in fact— what Annie just *knew* Preston was thinking wasn't what he was thinking at all.

What Preston had been thinking was how much pressure he was under. Annie LaPeer had just made that *oh-so-clear*. He *did* have them all floating around on bubbles. On a dream. And they *were* just amateurs. They were going to be exposed as frauds, silly frauds. Because he didn't know how to fake things! No one here did! Even if they got as far as attracting a few curious tourists, they'd end up laughing at these amateur-night hicks.

Preston was still thinking these same thoughts as he headed for bed that night. About to pull back his covers, he turned instead and headed to his desk. He got out his legal pads, well-worn, well-thumbed-through, and looked at all the copious notes he'd been making; the list of things to do; the questions to ask. But was he asking himself the *right* questions, or *enough* questions? He had worried about the costume shedding its non-natural fibers, and people getting ahold of them and putting them under a micro-scope—and *laughing*; and that would be the end of them...He had worried about the tracks Boyd and Floyd had volunteered to make. *Boyd and Floyd*? He liked them, and they were good craftsmen, but...*really*? What did they know about biology and animal phys-iology? Nothing! How were they going to make tracks that, say, a first-year veterinarian student wouldn't know were complete fakes? And all these people 'acting'?

What *had* he been thinking?

And as *she* was getting ready for bed, Annie went into the bathroom and opened the medicine cabinet. Out came the tooth-brush and toothpaste. As she closed the cabinet door, Annie saw tears streaming down the face of the woman who looked out at her. That woman knew something no one else did.

The numbers had been wrong.

The letter she'd read was from the town's bank in Taylorville. They were sorry, but they had made a banking error in the town's favor; and had only now corrected it. The new balance had only four figures in it. Not five. And Annie and the council had paid bills based on five; not four figures. All those checks Edna, as comp-troller, had signed and put in the mail last week—several, many, would come back any day now.

With shaking hands, Annie had gotten out her calculator there in the fast-food place. She'd crunched the numbers. What the town could expect in income this month was not going to be enough to cover their debts or meet their obligations.

She wanted to throw up, but she did not. How many days did they have before they couldn't meet payroll for city services? Or keep the lights on, the gas piped in? In other words, how many days left did they have as a town?

And she had been worried about *potholes* and *sidewalks*, and a *tax* increase? Wow, weren't *those* the good old days, when they could survive by putting band-aids on things. But the patient had cancer; stage-four cancer. And she hadn't known it.

Annie started to shake, and she put down her toothbrush and sobbed when she thought about Miss Dorothy. Who would take care of her when she, like everyone else, would have no choice but to leave town? She'd have no money, because she wouldn't be able to sell her house. Who would buy a house in a town that was no longer a town? And there was no assisted living in Tayloville, and she'd seen the facility in Cascade City. It was huge. Impersonal. She'd seen roaches.

Days. They had days. And then they were done.

Only a miracle was going to save them; and—anger rose in Annie now—Preston Mayhugh and his merry little band did *not* have what it would take to pull this off.

She just *knew* it.

Chapter Fifteen

A ROOSTER CROWED—WHICH WORKS OUT GREAT FOR me because I was searching for a way to indicate right at the beginning of this chapter that it was early the next day—and what indicates that better than a rooster crowing? So if I ever meet that rooster, I'm going to have to thank him for helping me out.

Of course, I wonder if he'll understand that he's being thanked, and how does one thank a rooster? Give him a little chicken feed? I can't think what else a rooster might like. You can't pat a rooster on the head—not much to pat, really, and maybe he wouldn't like that, so he'd hardly feel thanked, assuming roosters can sense someone's gratitude at all.

But I'm off track. But you know who's been making tracks, while I've been nattering, and the rooster crowing? Boyd and Floyd.

That's Floyd you see, halfway up that small bald hill, and it looks as if he's wearing snow shoes, doesn't it?, and now back to the past tense...

"Boyd!" he called to his brother, "come out and see! What do you think?"

"Okay!" Boyd called. He wiped his hands on a rag and put the rag down on the worktable. Spread out over it were books from the library in Cascade City, the books open to photos of animal tracks, as preserved in hardened mud, or in the whisper of dust covering a desert floor—coyote, mountain lion, wolf, bear, deer—ape, monkey. There were even a few photos of what were supposed to be Bigfoot tracks.

Boyd and Floyd, you should know, had been up all night studying these pictures. They, too, had a copy of Mr. Pierce's and Miss Ames's notes, and had been asking themselves good questions about what kind of tracks an animal as those two had envisioned might leave behind.

It was toward midnight that they thought they might try working up something that borrowed a little from the ape, and a little from the bear.

On a separate table lay their tools—awls, shears, pliers, saws, drills, along with a dozen pairs of old snow shoes that they now felt glad they had never thrown out.

Throughout the small hours of the morning, those snow shoes had been taken apart and made into something new, or modified—made narrower or broader, shorter or longer, the webbings torn out and replaced with wood plates carved up with ridges and whorls and crests and knobs, or the webbings re-webbed to create a pattern that, impressed into the earth, might suggest the kind of track an Alpine Valley Ape might leave.

And this latest pair of 'track-makers,' as Floyd had decided to call them, were now strapped to Floyd's feet. Ready to experiment, he had walked out of their work shed all the way to the top of the small bald hill. He'd only been halfway up when this chapter began, but as I've been telling what I've been telling you, he's been walking on and up to the top.

Boyd, in the meantime, walked out of the work shed into the new morning sun. He fished his glasses out of the top pocket of his overalls and put them on. Seeing the path Floyd had made, he headed over to it, and now bending over, his hands on his knees, he studied each set of footprints as he paralleled Floyd's path and followed it all the way to where it ended at Floyd, at the top of the hill.

"Well," Boyd said, and he stood erect. His brother was gazing from the top of the hill to the choppy sea of the tops of all the trees spread out below them. He put his arm over his brother's shoulder. "No one can say we didn't do the best we could."

Chapter Sixteen

*C*HAPTER SIXTEEN DOES NOT HAVE A ROOSTER TO TELL us the time of day it is. It has something— *someone*—better for the job, because she was always oh so accurate. And now since you've guessed who it is, I won't waste any more time, but will get right into the story.

Miss Dorothy, heading for Merle's, was still a dozen steps away from her favorite spot for crossing the street. Per usual, she warily eyed the concrete slabs of the sidewalk that rose up between her and the crossing spot. They looked like they'd been pushed up by the same forces that pushed mountains up out of the sea—and they had, only to a far lesser degree.

What the poet Robert Frost called 'the frozen groundswell' of the earth (not to mention the tree roots pushing up under the sidewalk from so many trees all around, and, like bucking broncs, unseating man's little concrete slabs, tossing them up and to the side) had made a treacherous zone for someone like Miss Dorothy, who survived on spindly, fragile legs, making the people here worry about her, especially Merle, every morning, who had made it a habit to hasten out and escort Miss Dorothy down the sidewalk and across the street—though there were usually enough people around to gladly do that for her (and him). She was thinking 'blueberry muffin,' this morning, as she raised an orthopedic shoe over a ridge in the walk that didn't seem to be this high only yesterday, and that's when Merle caught sight of her through his window.

"She's preoccupied," he said to Claude, who sipped his coffee as he leaned on Merle's counter. "Take care of your change," he added, "if you have to go," and Merle hurried out of the store and into the street. Claude reached into the cash register and took out two pennies and a nickel. He put a lid on his coffee, preparing to follow Merle out the door.

Claude was a miller, that is, he was a miller until Mr. Chamberlain closed the mill. He loved the work, and the only reason he, like most others, didn't pack up and leave for greener pastures is that Claude was an optimist, every day *certain* that Mr. Chamberlain would come to his senses and re-open the mill, and he was a bachelor and didn't have a family to support.

It was hard to say what Claude did to support himself, since he never had anywhere he particularly had to be. But Merle, his oldest friend, would tell you that Claude still had his first nickel, meaning that Claude was very thrifty and was probably living on savings.

Every now and again Claude went hiking with Terry Troy, and he did chores for several of the ladies of the sewing circle—often driving them to Taylorville for whatever they needed there, or all the way to Cascade City. He enjoyed driving the ladies. They had great stories about the early days of the valley, and Claude was always half-entertaining the idea of writing a history of the valley one day: He found it *so* rich and interesting and thought that others might, too. In turn, the ladies never lost interest in asking Claude about the day John Chamberlain's son died. Because Claude had been there when it happened.

It's not that Claude relished telling the story—he didn't—it's just that talking about the day helped him express it—literally—that is, helped him get it *out,* as if it were toxic fluid building up inside of him.

But today Claude had to get going because Ramona had agreed to see him in her classroom this morning. He *knew* he wasn't delivering his lines well; not playing his part well. As Ramona had impressed upon everyone, they'd be playing their parts *full-time*. In any moment of any day, since a tourist might engage you in conversation, or a reporter might, you had to be convincing as the person who saw what he saw. So now, his coffee in hand, he went out the door only these few seconds after Merle, who had reached Miss Dorothy—and only in the nick of time.

She had just put one orthopedic shoe down, over the ridge, and was lifting the other over it, but not high enough, and her toe caught on it, and she pitched forward, and a bit sideways, heading for the street, and would have landed there, like a felled tree, except that Merle had grabbed her and held her up.

"Whoa, there, Miss Dorothy," he said. "You all right?"

Steadied, Miss Dorothy pushed her hat aright and readjusted her purse in the crook of her arm. She plucked at her clothing here and there to set things right. "I'm fine, Merle. Thank you."

"That sidewalk's a *menace*. And this street!" Watch your step now," he said to her, as, taking her arm, he led her across the street in a sometimes lateral path to avoid the larger potholes. "Damned minefield," he muttered.

"It's a beautiful day, isn't it, Merle?" Miss Dorothy asked him—and it was the kind of thing she'd often ask him to divert his attention from the mutterings he was apt to engage in whenever something displeased him.

"Yes, yes, beautiful day."

Reaching safety, they stepped into Merle's Grocery Café.

You should know, by the way, that Melissa was *not*, in the meantime, running to the bus stop. It was a Saturday. She was in her backyard, and we'll get to her in a minute.

Our interest now—well, *mine*—and I hope it'll be yours, too—is in Annie, who, at this moment, was walking out the front door of her home.

She had on her realtor's blazer, but more as cover than any-thing else. People knew she often worked on Saturdays—they'd see her in her little glass-fronted office—and so to the office she would go. But not to do any realty work. She'd be doing the obsessive work she'd been doing of late, that is, looking for a way out; a way to save the town—and already she knew she was wasting her time, so she couldn't really tell you, rationally, *why* she was heading off to her office. She felt like a fraud. But going off to the office was a normal thing to do; and right now, because things were panic-inducing, she needed as much normal as possible.

She had her briefcase in hand, too, the poor thing getting more and more beat-up, and heavier. (The briefcase, not Annie. If anything, Annie was getting skinnier, because she wasn't eating.)

She heard the ring of a bicycle bell and looked up to see Sarah Watkins, Melissa's teacher, coming up the sidewalk—*bump*-buh-buh-buh-buh-*bump*—the poor dear's head rattling on top of her neck like...like...well, Annie couldn't say, she wasn't a writer.

Sarah came to a stop in front of Annie's gate, which Annie now came through, greeting her, a fraudulently happy smile on her face.

"Morning, Sarah! Where you riding?"

"Slauson's Ridge." Sarah was decked out in helmet, bicycle shorts, bicycle shoes and tank-top. She had a daypack on her back. "I wanted to swing by—catch you before you left for work." Sarah straddled her bike and took off her daypack. She unzipped it. "I wanted to talk to you about Melissa's latest story."

"The A+ thrilled her. Thanks."

"No, I mean— I'm glad, but I mean, the *latest* story. *This* one. You can flip to the end."

Sarah handed the story to Annie, who took it as she put down her briefcase. She began to read, not flipping to the end.

Sarah looked off, to give Annie privacy, but then, a little anxious, looked back at her and, even as Annie read, said, "I guess my concern is—how is Melissa adjusting? I mean, post-divorce and all."

"She's adjusting," Annie said, maybe a little more tersely than she should have—Sarah was a good friend, and very sweet. She only had Melissa's best interest at heart.

"Good. Good," said Sarah. "It's just that her stories have become..."

"Vivid?"

"Violent," answered Sarah. "I mean, *way* out there. It's like... she wants attention. The wrong kind."

"The brain quivering like Jell-O," Annie said, looking at the end of Melissa's story. "I like that. What do you call that? The simile. I don't know where she gets the talent." She handed the story back to Sarah and gave her a big smile.

"Okay..." said Sarah, looking at Annie, and not sure what to say, since she seemed so...*sanguine* about this, like nothing was wrong.

"Sarah," Annie said, looking at her carefully. "She's *o-kay*. We might be only muddling through, but we're *muddling through*—and even a little better than that."

"Well, okay," answered Sarah, though she really wasn't sure this was okay. She took back the story Annie extended to her (and only much later in the day, while riding the trail along Slauson's Ridge, did she realize that she had wanted Annie to *keep* the story, not hand it back), and she put it into her daypack.

"But—you know—I appreciate your concern for her." Annie put a hand on her friend's arm. "For *us*."

For the first time in this meeting, Sarah smiled. It was a tentative smile, but sweet all the same. "Of course," she said. "Well, look, I'll let you get off to work."

"Enjoy your ride."

Sarah peddled off. Annie watched her go, and when Sarah had turned a corner and ridden out of sight, Annie pushed back through her gate and went back to the house.

In the backyard, and still in her pajamas, Melissa was painting Muffin's nails. Muffin sat on the picnic table, her paw in Melissa's hand. Muffin's collar today was the black one adorned with aqua sequins (aqua currently being Melissa's favorite color), as well as silver beads—with a pink bead, here and there, to give what Melissa called 'a little bit of accent.'

"Honey, what are you doing to Muffin?" Annie asked as she came into the backyard, walking across the lawn carefully. She'd put her briefcase down in the house, but she still had on her heels and blazer.

"She needs a pedicure," Melissa said.

"She's going to lick it off," said Annie.

"It's only food coloring."

Annie sat down on the picnic table bench. She rubbed one of Muffin's ears. Muffin loved that.

"Are we about to have some kind of talk?" Melissa asked, her eyes on her work.

Annie didn't respond, her eyes on her own nails, though a manicure was the farthest thing from her mind, and anyway *way* beyond her budget. "You know. Honey. Before your dad and I..." But what to say?

"Split up," Melissa said encouragingly, but also in an effort to move things along. If they were going to have to have a talk, might as well get to it.

"Split up. Yes. Before that, you liked, you've *always* liked horror stories—right?"

"Yeah."

"Okay. Okay. How come?" Annie now asked.

"I don't know. I like 'em. Are you going to let me buy *Friday the 13th*?"

"No."

"You let Peter buy that French film, and it has boobies in it."

"Well, that's— . It *does*? He said it was an art film."

"My ass."

"Melissa!"

"Well, it's true!"

Annie didn't know what to say. She worried one hand with

the other. Her train of thought had been smacked off track by this whole new train. Weren't her kids teething and learning to walk only yesterday? "Where *is* your brother, by the way?" she asked.

"Big Rock," Melissa answered.

"Big Rock? All the way up there?"

"You know," said Melissa, "the ape thing. Coach Mayhugh, Derrick Merrick, all them."

"*Mayhugh*?" Annie said it so explosively that it scared both Melissa and Muffin, Muffin jerking her paw out of Melissa's hand.

Chapter Seventeen

SWEAT STREAMED INTO PRESTON'S EYES, MAKING THEM sting and making them blurry, but he didn't *dare* wipe them—not at this moment. For the first time today, he'd been able to follow Derrick's actions with his camcorder—keeping the kid in frame.

The actions they had decided on were simple enough. Derrick was to swing from a branch, land on the ground, look toward Preston—exhibit alarm at being seen, make a brief charge at him, but then exhibit fear and run away into the woods.

Derrick was doing his job well—and so well that even Chrissy Covington, who was here to help out, was impressed. She had noticed that over the last couple of days, she had developed a little thing for Derrick, to whom she'd never before paid any attention. But she noted, too, that she was even a little jealous of him. What if *he* were the one who ended up the big actor—the one with all the talent? So she was a little confused. She liked this guy, but everyone kept saying he was an amazing actor. Maybe she *should* have gone ahead and auditioned the other day. *Then* they'd have seen—have been *reminded*—who the great actor was around here. But this was *wrong* to be thinking this, she thought, and *look* at him—he's just so sweet—and look how *cute* he is—running around like that.

"Ah...*heck*!" said Preston, wanting to say something else, but he was supposed to be a good example. "Sorry, Derrick. I lost you again—dang." He wiped his eyes, his brow.

Worn out, Derrick put his hands to his knees and pulled all the oxygen he could into his lungs. He was dressed in the lower half of the ape costume, Boyd and Floyd's track-makers on his feet. The track-makers were now covered in the fur they had picked up from Miss Dorothy's the night before. As Derrick and Preston were so far only rehearsing their actions and camera moves, Derrick didn't need to bear the weight of the full costume yet.

"It's okay, Coach," Derrick said, having caught enough breath. "But do you mind if I take a breather? I'm getting tired."

"Yeah, take a break," Preston said. "*I'm* the one who has to keep going. I'm not getting the hang of this camera." Preston made a quick look around at some of the other boys who had come up with him—several scouts from the local troop. They were under or up in trees, and either sawing limbs or elongating them. He saw one boy at a workbench (two sawhorses and a pine board) sawing a branch in two. "Hey, Benny," he said.

"Yes, Coach?"

"Run around like an ape for a minute. You're pretty good at that sort of thing."

"Sure!"

As Benny ran around like an ape, Preston practiced following him with the camera. But he just wasn't getting it.

It surprised Preston that he should be so inept at this. It had never crossed his mind that he wouldn't be able to take convincing pictures of the Alpine Valley Ape. But all he was doing was producing shots that looked as amateurish as Annie LaPeer had predicted they'd be. When Preston played back his video on the camcorder, all he saw was the truth: Some yo-yo with a camera was filming some kid in an ape suit who was pretending to be some wild beast.

Sure, it would be a lot easier if he could shoot Derrick's actions in little sections, and then edit them together. But then that would make it look like a movie, like someone had staged all this, and then pieced together the best parts. And that wouldn't look natural; wouldn't look like someone had *just happened* to catch something on camera as they were passing by.

Only now did Preston realize how much thinking should have gone into this *ahead* of time. He should have mapped out *ahead* of time all the actions that had to take place. He should have thought through where the camera had to be to capture the actions, but so that they looked natural. And *certainly*, as he was thinking right this instant, he should have taken the position of the sun into consideration. There was so much *glare* everywhere, making Derrick difficult to see, and so many things were *reflecting* the light, too—making so much shine that that *also* tended to obscure your view of Derrick. Most vexing of all to Preston, you really had to think like an *actor* in moving this camera around. What was the *character* of this person holding the camera? He'd only be of a certain level of skill with it—right?—if he were just some regular joe out on a hike. And how would he react when he saw the ape? How scared would he be? Scared, but not so scared that he wouldn't *also* be amazed and *know* you had to keep the camera on this thing you were seeing...and the camera movements would have to convey, to show in themselves, the tenseness and shakiness in the guy's body. The movements couldn't be *too* dramatically shaky, nor could they be too steady...and there were certain things the character would *say*, that the audio would pick up, certain half-scared, half intrigued things...oh, *man*, thought Preston, there were a *hundred* things he should have thought about, and on top of all *this*, as good as Derrick was, he looked too human, and Preston didn't know what to say to him to get him to look more like an ape...and he hadn't even *begun* to work with the Carnodys, who were to play the hikers, although (and this was of some comfort) he knew that Ramona DuMonde had been working with them on their acting. Still, he had to direct them for the *camera*—when to move, where exactly, how...

Preston had to stop thinking. He was feeling overwhelmed. But one thing was clear: He didn't have what it took to pull this off. He was in trouble. This whole enterprise was in trouble, and it was going to collapse because *he*, Preston Mayhugh, fearless leader— .

"Excuse me, Coach?"

Preston turned. "Peter!" he said. He was quite surprised to see him. "What are you doing here?"

Peter ignored the question. "You're taking the video of Derrick today?"

"Well, not so far."

Behind Preston, Peter noticed two scouts pointing at him. Then one, looking directly at Peter, mimed gobbling up food, while the other laughed.

Preston, noticing that Peter was looking at something behind him, and obviously upset by it—*hurt* by it?, Preston wondered—turned and saw the two scouts, the one still gobbling, the other laughing. He glared at them, and the scouts quickly got busy elsewhere.

Turning around to Peter and studying him for a moment, he said, "What's on your mind, young Scorsese?"

"Can I do it?"

"Do what?"

"Do the filming? I have some ideas?"

"Peter, your mother doesn't approve of all this."

"I know. She thinks it's going to fail. But I'm good at it? I mean, filming? I mean, I'm *good* at it. And, I mean, I think I know what's needed."

Preston studied Peter's face. He saw imploring doing battle with confidence; determination battling the desire to run away.

The two of them felt the presence and eyes of the scouts around them. This would really be good for this kid to shine here today, thought Preston, and he knew in his heart that the kid would be a lot better at this than he would.

On the other hand, Preston knew the world of hurt he'd be in with Annie LaPeer—and the world of hurt he'd give *her*—if he handed Peter this camera. On the other hand, everything was going to fall apart if it were left to Preston to take this video—and then, yeah, pop, pop, pop and *wham*—he'd be leaving the town in worse shape than before. And really, c'mon, it was just a few seconds of video, right? Not even half a minute.

He handed Peter the camera.

I think it was about an hour after Preston had handed Peter the camera that Annie roared into the clearing at the trailhead for Big Rock. She stormed out of her Jeep, glaring at Preston's truck. She slammed the door, grabbed her daypack from the back of the Jeep, and headed up the trail.

But back to Peter. He had taken charge. That camera in his hand— it was like Excalibur. The boy was transformed.

"Okay, let's try it again. Mrs. Carnody, you ready?"

"Rarin' to go."

Judy Carnody stood at her mark, walking stick in hand, good solid hiking boots on her feet.

Her husband, Al, stood directly behind Peter and close—the idea being that Al was the one taking this video.

Preston himself had come to the very reasonable conclusion that a couple the Carnodys' ages (mid-sixties) probably wouldn't be taking video with their cell phone, but, a bit behind the times, would tote a camcorder along on a simple day-hike. Preston thought that that might add just one more realistic touch to everything. Peter wasn't sure he agreed—he'd seen Old Lady Piersall use her cell phone to take video of her acanthus—and thought Preston might have been over-thinking things, but he kept this thought to himself, and his cell phone in his pocket; and anyway, the camcorder was a good one and would do the trick.

"Derrick?" Peter now called. "You ready?"

Derrick squatted on a low branch in the tree off to Mrs. Carnody's right. He was dressed in full ape costume now. "Ready!" he called, his voice muffled by the mask, but audible nonetheless. He was really hot inside that costume, and sweating like crazy. He was trying to stay positive, but he thought that if Coach Mayhugh couldn't get the shots, then certainly Peter LaPeer wasn't going to. But he was going to be a trouper. That's what Chrissy Covington said he was, and he didn't know what that meant, but he was going to be one.

"All right, then, quiet please, everyone!" announced Peter. "And...Action!"

Mrs. Carnody started walking up the trail, and turning directly toward the camera, she said, "Oh, Al, for heaven's sake, are you going to film me all day?"

With his head just over Peter's head (so that Peter could feel his breath in his hair), Al said, "You don't want the grandkids to see their grandma?"

"You're gonna bore them stiff," Mrs. Carnody said, and the line was so believably delivered that Preston, standing off to the side, made a mental note to thank Ramona: *man*, was she training these people well!

Then, "What's that?" asked Mrs. Carnody, hearing something, (that is, 'hearing something'), and turning from the camera to look off to her right.

"What's *what*?" asked Al, from behind the camera—Peter still keeping the camera on Mrs. Carnody; and now Derrick, outside of the viewfinder's frame, jumped from his branch—his shadow covering and passing over Mrs. Carnody, who ducked with a cry of alarm, and as she did, Peter jerked the camera as a person startled by the startlement of another might, the jerky move causing the camera to catch only a glimpse of Derrick's side as Derrick landed on the ground and leapt behind a tree—all of which was exactly what Peter wanted.

Mrs. Carnody dashed toward the camera, exhaling, "What *was* that?!" as Al with a laugh of relief more than amusement said, "Some kind of raccoon, that's— . Whoa!" And as Mrs. Carnody ran past the camera, disappearing from the viewfinder's frame, Peter again jerked the camera, this time severely, like a startled, shaky Al might—scared, but still wanting to follow the action of this 'thing' now running along behind the trees.

As Al, per prior instruction, now quickly stepped aside to get out of Peter's way—though staying at Peter's side to parallel him—Peter backed up fast, the camcorder still more or less pointed in Derrick's direction; and, masterfully, Peter got Derrick glancing toward him for a split second before disappearing, sunlight between trees spotlighting *some* of Derrick's head and *some* of his torso.

"Oh, my god," said a panting, frightened, mesmerized Al (and really, that Ramona—she'd worked *wonders*); and now Peter turned and ran—Al peeling off, his line delivered, job done—as if following after Mrs. Carnody (which of course he was actually doing), the camcorder still on, but pointing at the ground, everything a blur now, though the sound was still on, and catching Al's (well, Peter's) panting as he ran away, Derrick in the background noisily running away through the snapping branches one could hear.

"Okay," Peter now said, stopping; and breathing hard, he turned and walked back to his original place. "Let's see what we've got." Mrs. Carnody followed him back.

Derrick came snapping back through the branches, and Al, Preston, and three or four of the scouts, along with Chrissy, all converged on Peter, crowding up behind him and right close to the sides of the camera.

Peter had taken a lot into consideration when planning out this sequence—like whether shadows—his and Al's, would be an issue, and whether Al's voice from behind him would sound natural, as if Al were the one holding the camera—and did his own panting sound like it might plausibly be coming from Al? As for capturing Derrick's actions in a realistic way, well, that was the biggest issue of all. Suddenly, feeling the press of all these people around him—all these hopeful, vitally curious people—Peter did not want to hit 'Play.'

As for Preston, his heart pounded hard. It flashed through his mind that the last time it pounded this badly was many years ago, during a basketball game in college. The crowd was chanting his name. There was one second left on the clock. If he made the shot, the team would go to the finals. If he missed, they'd lose the game and have to go home. He missed.

Peter took a slow deep breath...and hit 'Play.'

They all watched. And listened. And when this brief thirteen seconds of video was over, Preston half-screamed, half-shouted, thrusting his arms into the air.

"It looks real!" one of the scouts shouted. "Like how it would be!"

"Oh, my god, Peter!" Chrissy said, "oh, my god!" That from Chrissy Covington? High praise indeed.

Preston jumped around, pumping both fists in the air, still half-screaming, half-shouting, and Chrissy wondered if Coach Mayhugh shouldn't have auditioned for the Ape.

"Nice work, everybody," said Peter, as matter-of-factly, as professionally as possible, though of course he was bursting with joy inside. This was, without a doubt, the best moment in Peter LaPeer's life. "Let's do a second pass at this angle, then think of something different."

"Did I do okay, Peter?" Derrick asked him, turning to him and rubbing his hands—well, his big paws—together; and as he still had the ape head on, he really did look like an ape quite concerned about pleasing this human.

But before Peter could tell him that he'd been great, he heard: "Peter LaPeer!"

Peter turned, and so did everyone else, and they saw Annie hurrying off the trail and into this small clearing—their staging area. "What are you doing?!" Annie cried, and approaching Peter, she said, "You know how I feel about this!" Then catching sight of Preston, she turned to him and said, "And *you* know how I feel about this!"

"Madam Mayor—Mrs. LaPeer," Preston began, "please. Can we just talk over there?"

Annie ignored him and whipped back around to Peter. "I thought you *got* things! That you were *bright*! Unlike some *flim-flam*, some *liar*, some— ." She abruptly stopped, but the point was made—her feelings about Preston crystal clear—and he was stung; and though she was probably glad that he was, her focus had already shifted: She was, she saw, embarrassing her son, hugely. Yes, she was mad, but she was embarrassing her child in front of all these people, and she felt terrible for him and ashamed of herself. Not sure what next to say, if anything, though wanting to yell at Peter, and wanting to get him *away* from these people, and from all *this*, still, she couldn't embarrass him any further by demanding he come along with her now, like some small child. So though she was about to say, "Come on! We're leaving!" she didn't. She just turned and hurried back the way she came, hoping that Peter would follow; and Peter would have—but he was rooted to the spot from shock and embarrassment.

"Whoa," said Benny, "what a bitch."

Peter whirled on him. "Shut up!"

Preston whirled on Benny, too. "Shut your trap, Benny! And that goes for all of you!" he shouted. He hurried after Annie.

Peter, his camera still in his hand, wanted to die; felt he *was* dying.

Derrick, that head still on, came up to him. "Sorry, dude," he said. "But anyway, you did great, all right?" He clapped him on the back with his big paw.

In the meantime, Annie was close to running up the trail, and now she heard behind her, "Madam Mayor! Mrs. LaPeer! Annie!"

Not stopping, not turning around, she yelled, "How dare you!"

Preston, catching up to her, said, "How dare *you*! You do *not* do that in front of my students!"

Annie stopped and so abruptly that Preston would have bumped into her had it not been for his athlete's reflexes and grace—but it was close. "What are you doing to me?!" she said, and it was almost a wail.

Preston was struck to the core by that, by her pain, but he said, "I beg your pardon, but this is not all about you! This town's going to die without a road!"

"This is all a lie!" Annie shouted.

"Why don't you just get over yourself!" he shouted back.

Annie slapped him hard across the face.

"Great," said Preston, the blood charging to the right side of his face and turning it almost purple. "This is…"

Tears sprang to Annie's eyes.

"Look," said Preston, "I'm sorry."

"Bastard," said Annie, and she turned and ran up the trail.

Preston watched her go and, deciding that he had nothing to gain from trying to follow her, turned to head back to the clearing. He stopped abruptly when he saw several scouts, gathered, watching him. He could see that they hadn't just now arrived. They'd witnessed pretty much everything. "And more good news," he said to himself.

It was fully night by the time Preston's truck pulled up to the curb on Main Street. Scouts piled in the back started hopping out. Peter piled out, too. He took the camcorder from his daypack.

"Everyone straight home now," Preston said. "Tomorrow is another busy day."

Peter stepped up to Preston. "Here," he said, handing him the camera. "The best sequence is the very first. I'd go with that."

"Ah, yes," said Preston, taking it. "Peter, listen. I disrespected your mother's wishes."

"It's all right."

"It isn't. And I'm sorry." Preston meant for his 'I'm sorry' to convey apologies to Peter for having disrespected his mom. But Peter heard it as 'I'm sorry'—you won't be participating in any more shooting.

"Okay, Coach. Good luck." Peter stepped back from the truck and now turned and headed home.

Preston watched him, then turning, couldn't help but see the camcorder: he'd put it on the dash after Peter had handed it to him. He sat back, regarding it. So much trouble…

He put the truck in gear, made a U-turn, and headed home.

As Peter was about to turn a corner, wondering how much and what kind of trouble he was going to be in with his mom, he heard the *ding-ding*, *ding-ding* of someone's open car door. He also heard someone laughing—snickering, actually.

Turning the corner, Peter saw just ahead an older man slumped in the street, his back against the side of his SUV, the door open. An empty bottle stood between the man's legs. Three scouts squatted next to the man. One of them was lifting the man's wallet from his breast pocket; another was tying his shoelaces together, as the third looked on. His job, apparently, was to do the snickering.

Peter stopped in his tracks. What to do? "Hey, guys," he said.

"It's Old Man Chamberlain!" the scout with the wallet said, and he took out the cash he found.

"Come on, guys," Peter said, afraid now.

"Shut up, chubs," said the snickering scout, and he rose, and before Peter could figure out what to say or do next, the old man woke up with a roar and flailed his arms, frightening the three thieves, so that the one with the wallet and cash dropped both and, not at all considering the fate of his buddies, ran away for all he was worth—only to be passed by the scout who had tied the shoelaces together. The scout who had called Peter a name ran off in the opposite direction.

Many seconds too late, Mr. Chamberlain thought to grab his empty bottle and hurl it after the thieves. It arced in the night and landed a good five yards away, but surprisingly didn't break. It skittered to the curb, where it came to rest.

Peter stood frozen in place, watching Chamberlain as the man struggled up to a standing position. He weaved where he stood, arms out for balance, and when he thought he'd gained some, he took a step forward—or tried to—and down he went into the street. He landed hard on his side, also smacking the side of his face. For a second Peter thought the man had been knocked out: he was that still.

But then Chamberlain roused himself with a groan and got himself into sitting position. He began taking off his shoes.

"You all right, Mr. Chamberlain?" Peter asked. "You just have to untie them," he added, trying to be helpful.

"Get away," Chamberlain said, succeeding in removing his shoes from his feet. "Help me."

Peter didn't know what to do. These were two contradictory orders. He remained standing where he was, and once again Chamberlain struggled up to a standing position; and once again he weaved in place, arms out, and, still weaving, turned toward his car. He took a very uncertain, round-ish step toward it, whereupon Peter found himself hurrying up to him and getting him by the arm the way he'd seen Merle do on many occasions with Miss Dorothy. Chamberlain leaned into him heavily, so that Peter had to take quick little side steps so that he wouldn't fall, with Chamberlain landing on top of him. Regaining his balance, Peter got himself and Chamberlain moving forward, toward the SUV, that door still *ding-ding, ding-ding-ing*.

Chamberlain extended an arm toward the open door—to grab it, use it for balance—but Peter said, "You shouldn't drive. Here. Back seat."

"I'm driving!" roared Chamberlain, scaring Peter.

"Please," said Peter, and with Chamberlain leaning on him so heavily that Peter was sure he was going to fall this time, he reached out for the passenger door handle like reaching out for a lifeline, and grabbing it, opened the door. "Here, Mr. Chamberlain, here," he said, managing, by fits and starts, and awkwardly—but managing nonetheless—to set Mr. Chamberlain down on the back seat, perpendicular to the car.

"You can't drive," Chamberlain said.

"My dad showed me."

"Who's your dad?"

"Dave LaPeer."

Chamberlain baked a laugh. "*That* jackass!"

"He is not!" Peter said.

"Okay, son, fine."

"He isn't! You want me to leave you?!"

"Yes," said Chamberlain—and he really meant it. But Peter couldn't just leave him.

"Look. Just. Look, get in the car. I'll take you home." Peter grabbed Chamberlain's legs between knees and ankles, and lifting them up, tried to turn Chamberlain in toward the car. It was hard, almost impossible work, because Chamberlain wasn't helping at all. Those legs were dead weight. But then, helpfully, Chamberlain passed out and fell to the side—most of him falling between the back of the front seat and the bench of the backseat.

Though all of Chamberlain was now dead weight, at least it wasn't resistant dead weight. It took Peter a good five minutes to push, pull, and maneuver the man's body enough so that Peter could close the back seat door.

He then got up into the driver's seat of the SUV and closed the door, *whumph*, the *ding-ding* noise stopping. The keys were in the ignition. Chamberlain wasn't extra-tall, but still a lot taller than Peter. He had to move the seat up. He adjusted the mirrors— took a long time doing it. He started the car and slowly depressed the gas pedal and the car went forward, more quickly than Peter would have liked. He hit the brake—hard.

And pretty much in that fashion—stop-start; stop-start; stop-start, Peter got Mr. Chamberlain home.

Chamberlain's one remaining servant got him out of the car and up to bed.

Peter never noted that the servant didn't thank him.

Chapter Eighteen

*M*ISS AMES BRACED A LADDER AGAINST A TREE, looking upward. Though her hair was still in its bun, she was wearing shorts and a tee, and hiking boots.

Mr. Pierce stood very near to the top of the ladder she was bracing, and though he was still wearing a long-sleeved shirt, the kind he wore to school, he wasn't wearing a tie, and shockingly (as far as his students on hand were concerned), *the sleeves were rolled up—and to the elbow!* He was still wearing his eternal tan Dockers, but *had* he been wearing shorts, it were possible that several of his students might have succumbed to shock. The rolled-up sleeves were enough radical change for *anyone's* system, and they'd be talked about for days to come—much as Miss Ames in her cute little shorts would be.

Mr. Pierce had one of Derrick's ape feet in his hands, and was very vigorously scraping the claws along the bark. These claw marks would be one of several realistic signs or bits of evidence of the ape's presence.

Mr. Pierce knew who Boyd and Floyd were, of course, but he doubted that he had ever exchanged even a word with them. But now, in this moment, he thought he might. He was *most* impressed with the strength and integrity of the foot's design, and how strong yet flexible these claws were—so life-like! It might do to offer a word of congratulations—and certainly he would like to learn the thinking and process they followed to achieve this excellent result.

Mr. Pierce was also thinking about Miss Ames, below. He was still somewhat frightened of her, but, he noted, there was that adverb—*somewhat*. The fright had lessened; and he noted the presence of, well, *curiosity*, if he thought about her—well, *when* he thought about her, as he had been doing (but *only* off and on, he said to himself) since that evening in the gymnasium; and he was shocked at her legs—two of them, and bare, there below him. Yes, of course, it was stupid of him to be shocked that this woman had legs, but heretofore, he'd never seen them. She always wore long skirts—tweeds and wools—and really, her legs, heretofore, were nothing other than the limbs the woman would have had to possess if she were to perambulate; and yet now here they *were*—exposed, distinct—sunlight on them, and, well, they were quite...beautiful, and it made him feel faint to look at them—even to think of them.

"Are you all right, Mr. Pierce?" Miss Ames called up to him.

"Yes. Fine. Thank you."

"It looked like you almost fell there."

"No, no! I'm all right." He suddenly wanted to turn and look at those legs, but he was feeling...he didn't know how he was feeling...but strange, and he both liked it and didn't. He scraped at the bark even harder.

Not too far from the two of them, in full costume—minus the one foot Mr. Pierce held—Derrick laid himself down into a barely mudded patch of forest earth. Several townspeople surrounded him, a couple with brooms made of bound together tree branches, and one man with a bucket, half-filled with water: the mudded patch had been created. Several long seconds passed, and it looked like Derrick was sleeping—and indeed that was the key to this idea.

"Think that's enough time?" he asked.

The man with the bucket shrugged. "Let's see. We can always do it again. Lots of trees."

Derrick got up. Everyone bent and peered at the impression

of his side captured in the earth.

"I think that's all right," the man said, whereupon everyone but Derrick took out a magnifying glass and got to his or her knees: It wouldn't do for any scientist who might come around to find even a *single* hair from any fake fur trapped in this impression left by a real sleeping Alpine Valley Ape. Of course, the opposite problem had been discussed earlier in the morning, the discussion led by Mr. Pierce: Was it realistic that a creature lying on the ground wouldn't leave *something* of himself behind—at least a hair or two or more, if not a tuft? The answer was no, but what were they going to do? The best they could do was at least not leave evidence of *themselves* behind.

After a very long while, the townspeople decided the impression was pristine. With aching backs and crackling joints, they pushed themselves up and walked away from the impression under the tree, the townspeople with the branch-brooms, making brisk sweeps of the area all around, eradicating hand prints, knee prints, footprints—and hoping to bury, obscure, or chase away, whatever particulate matter from all their bodies they themselves might have left behind.

Looking over at this group, finished with its job and dispersing, Preston now crossed 'Impression of the Ape—Sleeping. Under a tree?' off the list of things that had to be accomplished today. He went over to the rock he'd been sitting on to study his list and the timeline he'd created. Were they on schedule, or falling behind? They'd only have the sun for so many hours, and he still had to get everyone down the trail before it got dark.

And there on the rock next to his sat Melissa. She had her mountain bike leaned against a third rock. Her bike helmet was still on her head.

"Melissa," he said.

"Don't worry, Coach. Just came to look. I have no intention of helping."

"Thank you. You're very kind. Look, about your...You know what happened with your mom and me."

Melissa shrugged. "Mom is...She's been kinda funny since my dad left."

"Yes, I'm sorry about your dad. And all."

"That's all right. He sucked."

Preston sat bolt upright, shocked at both her language and that this little girl should—*would*—characterize her father like that.

Melissa, noting his shock, merely shrugged again. "As a dad. As a husband."

"Okay, Melissa," said Preston, trying to put a stop to this, "this might not be stuff your mom would want you saying—or discussing with— ."

"The county vet," Melissa went on, "always had to spend the night with some filly." She looked up at Preston. "That was a pun."

"Some filly. Roger that."

"He fooled around."

"I *got* it. Melissa— ."

"She doesn't think I know any of this, but my bedroom was next to theirs. Peter misses him. But that's because they played catch together once or twice. Maybe only *once*. But for Peter, that was the greatest day ever. And he doesn't even *like* sports."

"Okay, well— ."

"He used to call her stupid. And other things." Melissa looked off.

"Melissa," Preston said, "I'm... really sorry."

"Anyway," she said, "Mom's cool, just... Anyway, when does all this start?"

Preston glanced at Melissa—her face—wondering if he had any kind of role here. What to say to this girl? He wanted to say something...helpful...or encouraging. But all he could find in his head were clichés. Maybe just listening had been enough. "Well," he said, exhaling, and regarding the folk busy at work all around them, "I'd say we're ready enough after today. We just need some hikers. Real hikers, to come through the area."

"And then you set everything in motion?"

"And then we set everything in motion."

"You must be nervous," Melissa said. "Everyone counting on you and all."

Preston exhaled so hard that he went lightheaded and felt on the verge of passing out.

"Are you all right?" Melissa asked.

No, he wasn't. Not at all. "Oh, sure," he said.

Chapter Nineteen

THE REAL HIKERS WERE NAMED DANE AND GLORIA, AND they showed up in town the very next day, pushing through the door of Merle's Grocery/Café, the little bells jingling.

But before I tell you about what happened next, I think it's important that you understand *why* the town had decided that the presence of hikers was necessary.

Originally, the plan for setting everything in motion had been to send Peter's tape to KWCS, the biggest news station in Cascade City. This was the plan that had carried after vigorous discussion amongst the Ape Steering Committee members, democratically made up of young and old, male and female (and held in Mr. Pierce's classroom, Preston, Ramona, and Mr. Pierce chairing).

Most of the younger members had pushed for sending Peter's tape to Liveleak, or YouTube, or whatever; or having the Carnodys open a Facebook account or whatever, and posting the video there. But after further discussion, it was decided that web-sters might think the video had been faked—sent out for a goof. Plus, there were a *lot* of faked videos out there in cyberspace—none, they had to admit, that looked nearly as good as Peter's, but still, people might say, 'Well, this one's especially good, but of course it's a fake,' and before you knew it, their tape would be yesterday's news and forgotten. And anyway, Chrissy had chimed in, there was still something about seeing something on the *news* that gave it a credibility

101

it couldn't have on YouTube, or Facebook, or whatever. She very much liked it that Mr. Pierce, who had never given her anything other than a 'C,' said, "I agree with Chrissy." Miss DuMonde said she agreed, too, (but that didn't mean as much to Chrissy, since she only got 'A's' from Miss DuMonde). And then everyone was agreeing: Yes, send the tape to the news.

And with a *note*—which Miss Ames would compose along with the Carnodys. Miss Ames would lean on her skill-set to come up with a succinct, credible little story providing the background and context for the tape, and the Carnodys would put everything into their own words, which was *vital*, since the voice of the note would have to be consistent with the Carnodys' voice. Reason: When and if the Carnodys were interviewed on TV, you didn't want someone to grow suspicious if they didn't think the Carnodys sounded like people who did write, or *could* have written, the story behind the tape.

Ironically, when Miss Ames—an English teacher—saw that Mr. Carnody's punctuation had been perfect, it was *she* who said they had to re-write the whole thing and misplace a comma here and there, and maybe include a misplaced modifier, a split infinitive, and a dangling participle.

Mrs. Carnody, in turn, thought it might be a good idea to drop one of Miss Ames's details—about Mr. Carnody noting the snapping of branches—because it didn't seem like something her husband was likely to note—though *he* argued that he *would* have noted it (and believe me, that little back-and-forth between husband and wife cost them a good twenty minutes), and anyway, Mrs. Carnody asked, didn't the addition of that detail sound a *wee* bit like a writer at work? And though Miss Ames was quite proud of that detail, she immediately saw the wisdom in what Mrs. Carnody was saying. The line was dropped.

But, as I said, sending the tape along with the note to the news station had been the *original* plan, Preston volunteering to drop the tape in the mailbox, since his house was nearest to it. (*It.*

There was only *one* mailbox these days. The local post office had been decommissioned last summer—not enough mail coming to or going out of Alpine Valley to justify the operations costs; and the three other mailboxes in the area—two in town and one out at the mill—had been unbolted and carted off.)

But on the night after everything had been settled, Miss Ames couldn't sleep, but tossed and turned, and called Mr. Pierce early the next morning to ask if the steering committee could meet again in emergency session. She had concerns.

This is a summary of what she said before the committee:

Consider you're someone at the news station in receipt of this video. You're a *news* station, not an entertainment station, and how *newsworthy* might a video be that a *viewer*—not a scientist, not a forest ranger, no one with *credentials*—claims is of some heretofore unknown creature? Wouldn't airing such a video undercut the station's credibility as a news source; as people who know what news is and *isn't*. Further, you can't have your station *gee-whiz* the footage, and then expect your station to be taken seriously as a place that does investigative reporting—and the Cascade City news station prided itself on its investigative reporting.

(And by the way, speaking of newsworthiness, I think it's valuable to report that 'heretofore,' was, well, *heretofore*, a word that Miss Ames had only infrequently used in her life, but was now dropping into her conversations all the time. This would indicate, don't you think, that Mr. Pierce's presence in her life was looming larger and larger? He was invading her lexicon; he was in her locutions. Of further note, the only one who seemed fully aware of this was Preston. Miss Ames herself was only partially aware of this. Mr. Pierce not at all.)

But Miss Ames was going on:

If the person in receipt of the video doesn't *immediately dismiss* it as hokum and toss it in the trashcan, it may be that he or she will only give the tape a fast, I'm-really-busy look and conclude that a couple of gullible hikers had simply caught sight of a *bear*, and, owing to the sun, the camera angle, whatever, had only *thought* they'd caught a glimpse of something unknown—when they hadn't—and there it goes in the trashcan.

But, said Miss Ames, if we have people, like a couple of hikers—and this is important—*not associated with this town,* be the first to see something, something amazing, then they'll do a lot of work for us. *They'll* be the ones trying to get people to believe *them*, and no one will think this town has been up to something. And then, as the hikers are being doubted, and questioned, and busily trying to convince people of what they saw, then we actually *hand-deliver the tape*—that is, the Carnodys do, looking chagrined and worried, their story being, look, just the other day, we caught on tape what you're about to see, and we didn't do anything with it because we *ourselves* thought it was only a bear; and, well, we didn't want to embarrass ourselves; and we're actually not real sure we want *you* to see it, because maybe people will think we're trying to fake something, but anyway, now that those *hikers* saw something, it makes us think that, well, shoot, maybe we *did* see something.

And, Miss Ames continued, because the time and date stamp will appear on the Carnodys' video, and because that date will be prior to the date the hikers come forward, then the news people will see that the Carnodys weren't people just now trying to capitalize on something, or piggyback their ruse on to someone else's: it will appear—it will *be*— that they had shot this video before the hikers told their tale—and that will reinforce their statement that they *hadn't* wanted anyone to see the tape.

Context, Miss Ames, concluded. With the hikers—a *disinterested party*, meaning people with nothing to gain from their claims—leading the way; and the Carnodys playing at being reluctant and embarrassed, then *certainly* a news station will think twice before refusing to consider airing the video—especially as the station has competitors. Sure, KWSC is the biggest station in Cascade City, but there are two others—and KWSC would have to mull over the possibility of being scooped—and they'd want to avoid that.

If the creature captured on tape *is* something no one can explain away, they'd *certainly* want to be the first to show it to the world.

So, Miss Ames concluded, let's wait for some hikers to play our herald. Hikers first; tape delivery to the news station second.

It was quite an impassioned little speech and carried a lot more weight than it might have coming from anybody else, because Miss Ames seldom said anything at all, and then, seldom above a whisper—and here she was speaking *up* and with confidence. Everything she said sounded reasonable—debatable, to be sure— but reasonable; and she spoke with such confidence that everyone on the committee felt persuaded that she had to be right.

So wait for hikers they would.

Which brings us back to Dane and Gloria, who are now bringing their groceries up to Merle's cash register, Claude standing nearby, sipping a coffee—while I bring us back to past tense and the story as it unfolded:

"You folks find everything you need?" Merle asked them.

"Yes, sir. Thanks," said Dane, pushing the drinks and snacks and whatnot toward Merle so he could ring them up, and as he began doing so, Claude asked, "Where you young folks from?"

"Los Angeles, California," Dane answered. "You guys heard of it?"

Merle and Claude couldn't help exchanging a look. The look was fast, but contained a lot, in fact this whole dialogue (which wasn't said in words, but only through their eyes):

"Did that kid just ask us if we've ever heard of Los Angeles, California?"

"How stupid does he think we are?"

"Probably pretty stupid—real backwoods rubes. But this is great, right?"

"Yes! He's exactly who we want! Anybody stupid enough to think we might not have heard of Los Angeles, California is exactly the kind of pinhead we need to buy into our ruse."

"Sure," Merle answered Dane, "I might have heard of it."

"We're on semester break," Gloria now volunteered, "and decided to hike the entire Forestal Range. But don't worry, we're practicing safe sex."

In trying not to let his coffee go spraying out of his mouth— as in, *What wall did* that *come off of?*—Claude only succeeded in getting coffee all over his shirt. He beat the heat out of it with his hand.

"Uh-huh," Merle said to her, having no idea what to say. "Well, good for you. I mean, about the…" But he didn't finish, because he wasn't sure he meant *good for you* for hiking the whole range, or *good for you* for…the other thing. So he just got busy checking the price on the water purification tablets these two were buying.

But Claude quickly came to his aid. "Wow! Good for you, all right. Hiking the whole Forestal? That's impressive. But, you know, around here—just stick to the trails, okay?"

"Why? What do you mean?" Dane asked.

"Ah, now, Claude," Merle said. "Just stop that. And that'll be thirteen-forty, my young friend," he said to Dane.

"I'm just saying…" Claude said, and gave a half-shrug.

"What?" asked Gloria "What are you saying?"

"Nothing," Merle said, taking the twenty Dane handed him. "Claude's just local color. Likes to pull everyone's leg."

"I am *not*," said Claude, looking heated. "And you shouldn't be nonchalant about people's lives."

Merle winked at the young people. "He's good, isn't he? And six-sixty is your change," he said to Dane, handing it to him.

"What are you *talking* about?" Dane asked.

"Nothing," Merle said. "Claude, *really*…"

"He's been seen again," Claude said, ignoring Merle. "The Ape. The Alpine Valley Ape."

Gloria went wide-eyed. "You mean…*Bigfoot*? You guys have a Bigfoot?!"

"He's not a Bigfoot!" Merle and Claude said at the exact same moment.

Dane and Gloria looked from Merle to Claude, trying to figure this all out.

"I *mean*," said Merle, "he'd be nothing like a Bigfoot, if he existed, which he doesn't. Except in some people's very active imaginations."

"Look," said Claude to Dane and Gloria. "Just stick to the trails. You'll be fine. But just stick to the trails."

As Dane looked at Claude, trying to determine how serious this guy might be, a smile began to grow on his face—and then it bloomed. "I've got an *uncle* like you!" he said. "Full of jokes and *amazing* at keeping a straight face."

"Well," said Merle, hurrying from behind the counter to get the door for the young people, "he's got your number there, Claude."

"I tried," said Claude. "My conscience is clear."

Gloria smiled at him uncertainly, as she and Dane headed for the door.

"Well, thank you kindly," Merle said, holding the door open and giving off a vibe that he wanted them out of there as quickly as possible. "Now you young folks have a good time. Hiking and... whatever else."

And as soon as Dane and Gloria cleared the door, Merle closed it.

"Well," he said to Claude, as the two of them watched a perplexed Dane and Gloria make their way up the street, "what do you think?"

"Maybe. Let's call the boys. But I gotta say, for a first time? I think we were great!"

Chapter Twenty

'THE BOYS' TO WHOM CLAUDE WAS REFERRING WERE Boyd and Floyd, and they were once again in their work shed. But this time they had all kinds of old record albums on their work-table, albums they'd also gotten from the library in Cascade City.

The album covers had titles like, *Sounds of the Wild*, and *Jungle Calls*, and *Know Your Primates*. Also on the table was an old-fashioned record player (and who had one of *those* any more?), and an assemblage of inventively connected recording machinery that had big black, red, and ivory-colored knobs on it, and little orange lights lit up under tiny glass domes, and dials with needles that could arc from a green zone to a red zone.

To this strange assemblage, Boyd and Floyd had hooked up an old, thigh-high, black-fronted, wood-framed stereo speaker (and when was the last time you saw one of *those*—if ever?), and a tiny, shiny, flimsy, silver-faced speaker from a cheap car stereo system. And wired to all of this was an old-fashioned nickel-plated microphone.

The product of all this was the tape cassette (!) that Boyd held in his hand. "Shall we give it a whirl?" he asked his brother, and he put the tape into a small, chipped, paint-spattered cassette player. He hit 'Play.'

And if you had been in that work shed with them, you would have heard the eerie, strange, but oddly beautiful voice of the

Alpine Valley Ape filling the air. But since you *hadn't* been in the work shed with them, I've had to tell you that that's what filled the air—not that I was there, either, but I'm in the unique position of knowing things.

Blending together the squeak of a dolphin, the roar of a lion, the angry screech of a macaque, the growl of a bear, the squawk of a parrot, the honk of a goose, and interestingly, nothing at all from an ape, the brothers came up with one marvel of a beastly sound. Imagine plopping all those animal sounds into a blender, hitting 'Puree,' and pouring it out—that's what was pouring out of the speakers right now—one pure, unique voice.

Boyd hit 'Off,' and the voice of the ape disappeared, replaced by silence in the work shed. Then:

"That's his very *voice!*" said Floyd, and Boyd nodded happily.

The ape was becoming more and more real to them.

It was as the brothers were cleaning up the shed—putting all the records into their jackets, and disassembling all their recording machinery, that Boyd's cell phone rang—Merle and Claude on the other end. Boyd listened.

"Well, this is timing," he said to Floyd, as he hung up.

"What?" Floyd asked.

"My brother," said Boyd, "the town's more beneficent future approaches on four legs." "It's time for us to go meet it."

"That was a mouthful. What does it mean?"

"Hikers," Boyd said. "They're headed this way." Grabbing a screwdriver, Boyd added, "I'll disassemble what we'll need. Would you be so kind as to get the backpacks?"

"Sure. But, Boyd, hikers have *two* legs," Floyd said.

"Think it through, my brother."

As Floyd headed out of the shed to go get the backpacks, he suddenly paused. "*Oh*," he said, the light having dawned. "*Two* hikers. *Four* legs!"

Chapter Twenty-One

I THOUGHT ABOUT MAKING CHAPTER TWENTY-ONE A part of Chapter Twenty—which is now above you, well, *behind* you, since it's in your past, though it isn't really, since it's a part of you as something absorbed into your brain, and which will be present within you forever, even if, years from now, you can't recall it—so that it only remains with you as something *having been*. But as you absorbed Chapter Twenty, it had to go somewhere in you; room had to be made for it; and therefore it altered something in you, like a prior arrangement, or mood; and in entering, it had to touch, effect, *affect*, or alter, perhaps even spark, something else already present in you, and so it *changed* you, if only a tiny bit. In sum, you were one way, one kind of person, at Chapter Nineteen, and now you're a *different* person because you've absorbed Chapter Twenty—and you'll be *yet a different* person—if only in a very tiny way—after you've absorbed *this* chapter, Twenty-One, which I decided should be a separate chapter because the material you're about to read—to absorb—is, I think, important enough that it warrants the attention its own chapter would give it.

Because it's about the tiny moments, the small changes, that on the surface don't look like much, but—once you start thinking about them—reveal themselves to be important, as they will just a paragraph below you, where your future lies, and where LaPeer family relationships—or *dynamics*—change, and in an easy-to-miss, but still, important way.

And so we come upon what happened in Annie LaPeer's kitchen, as Boyd and Floyd are making a swift way into the woods...

Annie and Peter sat at the table. Peter has polished off his breakfast. Annie has barely touched hers.

She'd been up since four a.m., trying to put words together for the council, words that would also be published in *The Alpine Voice* about how they all might help one another face the grim reality of the death of their town; how to do it with dignity and grace. But no matter how many drafts of her speech she tried, nothing came out right; and so she had decided to try again tomorrow, maybe the next day; and of course she'd also been online looking into apartments she and the kids might get in Cascade City—where there was far more opportunity for employment than in Taylorville. At least her ex kept up with child support, and Annie had savings enough that they could survive for three months if she couldn't find a job in that time...ninety days...

Through the kitchen window, just over the sink, Annie and Peter could, if they stood up from their chairs—see Mel streaking this way past the window, and disappearing, and now streaking that way, and disappearing, making big soap bubbles fly from a string-less tennis racket she has in one hand (a plastic bucket of soap solution in the other).

Muffin chased the bubbles, which Annie and Peter would only have seen if they had stepped up to the window: Muffin was too small to be seen from where they were, even if they had stood. Some of the bubbles knocked against the window and went pop. But Annie and Peter couldn't hear that, of course, and they didn't see it. They weren't aware that that was happening. They'd been sitting in silence for a while, at the same table, occupying different worlds.

As she gave her plate a quarter turn, looking at Peter from the corner of her eye, Annie said, "Hey, I've got an idea. Let's grab the inner tubes, go to the river. We haven't done anything as a family in a while." She got up and rapped on the window to get Melissa's attention. She motioned her in.

"No, that's okay," Peter said, getting up from the table. "I've got homework." He grabbed his plate, to take it to the sink.

"Look, Peter," Annie said, "I'm sorry. The other day...in front of Mayhugh...and everybody."

"It was embarrassing!" Peter said, loudly. "It was scary!"

"I'm sorry, honey. I was...No excuse. *But*. You *did* disobey me. You knew how I felt about what's happening here."

"Everybody knows it's just *fun*."

"Peter, lots of things are fun that aren't right. People will be spending money to try to see something that doesn't exist, and we're telling them it does. That's called fraud, and people go to prison for it."

The screen door creaked open and banged shut, and Melissa came into the kitchen.

"What is it?" she asked her mother. "What's up?"

But Annie's attention was wholly on her son. "Peter," she said, eyes steady on him.

But he wouldn't look at her. He kept his eyes on the plate in his hand.

Melissa looked from one to the other, then said, "'And suddenly, there was a distinct chill in the air.'"

Peter put his dish in the sink, and without another word, walked out of the kitchen.

"Mom," said Melissa.

"Yes—what?" Annie said.

Melissa pointed at her plate. "Your breakfast. Please eat it. Do you want to just waste away? Do you want to just disappear?"

"No," said Annie. "Look, I'll take one bite." And she did; took a bite of her scrambled eggs, then wiped her mouth, got up, put her plate in the sink, and walked out of the kitchen, in the opposite direction from Peter.

Melissa watched her go. She put her hands on her hips.

"What am I going to do with these two?" She turned and set about washing the dishes.

Chapter Twenty-Two

$\mathcal{B}$OYD AND FLOYD SAT BEHIND A HUNTER'S BLIND halfway up a long gentle slope that bordered the hiking trail below them.

Boyd kept watchful eyes up the trail, from which direction Dane and Gloria would come.

Floyd, meantime, made last-minute, fine-tuning adjustments to their public address system, which included the cassette player—microphone pointed at it—the two speakers, and a home-made and complicated battery pack—to generate the electricity needed to make everything work.

Lying in the grass next to Floyd was a pair of track-makers—a duplicate of Derrick's they had thought would come in handy— exactly for occasions such as this.

"I could run down and make more tracks," Floyd offered.

"We've got enough," Boyd said.

"What if this doesn't work?" Floyd worried.

"Floyd," Boyd said, his eyes still on the trail, "put something in your mouth and chew on *that*."

Floyd shrugged. "I could eat."

"Capital thinking," said Boyd, and Floyd rummaged around in his backpack. "Ah," he said, "can of franks and beans." He withdrew it from the backpack. "This'll hit the spot."

Now, while Boyd and Floyd waited for them, Dane and Gloria, a quarter of a mile up the trail, played a guessing game as they hiked along—or trudged along. It was getting fairly steep here.

"Okay," Dane said, "what's *this* one?" He whistled the first four notes of a tune.

"*Hawaii 5-0*," said Gloria.

"Right. Your turn."

Gloria whistled the first four notes of the musical theme for *The Dick Van Dyke Show*, which she'd discovered in re-runs on cable, and she just *knew* Dane wouldn't get it—but he *did*. So now the score was tied, seven-seven.

And on the game went for another thirty minutes and through a ten-minute rest stop, wherein they each had a banana and drank half a liter of water, both looking around, squinting from the sun, and trying to figure out what TV themes they knew that hadn't been used already. Then each, almost simultaneously, though they didn't know it, got a really good one.

"You ready?" Dane asked, swinging his backpack up onto his back.

"Yup," said Gloria, doing the same. "Whose turn is it?"

"Mine," Dane said. "Okay, how about this?" he asked, as they headed off, and he whistled the first four notes of *Bewitched*.

Boyd heard these notes and sat bolt upright. "They're here!" he said to his brother, keeping his voice low. He couldn't see the hikers yet, but who else would be whistling?

"*Bewitched*," Gloria said, and now she and Dane rounded a rock face and came into Boyd's view. Impulsively, excitedly, he reached out and seized his brother's arm.

But Floyd merely nodded. He couldn't share his brother's enthusiasm. He didn't look too good. He held his stomach with both hands.

"My turn," Gloria said.

The game was tied again, at nineteen-nineteen (the winner being the first to twenty-one), and Gloria thought for *sure* she'd win with the theme that had come to her (from *Mister Ed*—she hadn't seen those re-runs since she was a kid!), and in fact, she was just forming her lips into a whistle, when she stopped suddenly. "Dane," she said. But as he only responded, "Hm?" and kept on walking up the trail, she said loudly, "Dane!"

Even though he didn't feel good, Floyd took interest in Gloria's sharp cry. He joined his brother in gazing down on them, their eyes just over the top of the blind. They watched Dane walk back toward Gloria. They saw Gloria pointing at the ground.

"Look!" she said.

Dane squatted down to take a closer look at one of Floyd's ape tracks. "*Whoa*," he breathed. He looked up the trail, and so did she, to see and follow more ape tracks that went up the trail about ten more yards, then disappeared into trailside foliage.

"Let's go back," Gloria, said, "I'm scared."

But Dane chuckled. "It's just that dude!" he said. "At that store!"

"Why is he laughing?" Boyd whispered, more to himself than to his brother. "That's not good...*not* good...He *suspects*..."

"Brother, I'm not feeling good," Floyd said. "I think I ate those franks and beans too fast."

"Shh!" Boyd hissed and slapped at his brother's arm. He then reached over and gave a small adjustment to the larger speaker, to point it more toward where the hikers now stood.

Gloria squatted down and studied the track in front of her. "But they don't look, I don't know, fake. And they look, like, *new*. Like not real old."

"Well, then not that dude, but some crony, you know?"

Gloria stood up and looked all around, nervously. Dane stood, too. "The thing is," she said, "that other guy—the grocer guy? He kept trying to shush the other guy, the one warning us."

"Because it was malarkey, and the dude was just trying to scare us!" Dane said.

"No," said Gloria, glancing at Dane as her eyes passed his, as she continued looking around. "I think grocer guy knows it's true, too. But he doesn't like people talking about it—because it's bad for business. Who would come here, right? That's really why he was telling him to hush up. Didn't you notice that he couldn't get us out of his store fast enough?"

"Yeah," said Dane, frowning now, because she was making sense. "He did look nervous."

Floyd groaned, very softly, holding his stomach. "Oh, brother, this is...this is not good," he whispered, and he turned away from his brother and, to take pressure off his stomach, got to his hands and knees, and he groaned softly again.

"Quiet, my brother," Boyd whispered. "Hold on...," and he extended his arm toward the cassette player. He put his finger on the 'Play' button. "Three...two...*one*."

And as if the countdown had been for him, Floyd blasted a huge fart, directly into the microphone, toward which his butt was facing, and the speaker—maybe it was old, but it was of *excellent* quality—broadcast that fart wonderfully far. Birds from every-where flew out of trees.

Gloria cried, "What was that?!"

Boyd angrily slapped Floyd all over. "Floyd! *Floyd!*" he said, trying to keep his voice to a whisper, but Floyd only farted again, even more loudly.

"It sounds angry!" said Dane.

"Baby..." said Gloria.

"Yeah, let's go! Let's go!" Dane said, and the two took off run-ning, back the way they had come.

They both screamed when Floyd farted a third time.

Boyd watched the two young hikers round the rock face and disappear. He was mad, but he was chewing the inner side of his lower lip the way he did when he was thinking some startling new information through.

Floyd lay on his back, holding his stomach and moaning.

"All our hard work," Boyd said, meaning all the hard work

they had put into creating the voice of the ape; but even by the time he had uttered these words, the complaint behind them was already fading as something that he was really angry about, or even thinking about. After all, Boyd thought, chewing his lip, their objective had been to frighten the hikers, making them think they'd come upon the Alpine Valley Ape—and hadn't they accomplished that?

Though still looking in the direction Dane and Gloria had gone, and half-expecting them to return at any moment (once they calmed down and got it through their heads that what they'd heard couldn't have been from any beast, in a manner of speaking), Boyd said, "I don't know, my brother, but it may be that you're an unexpected genius."

Boyd turned, unzipped a pouch on his backpack, and got out his cell phone.

Three minutes later, in town, Preston snapped closed his phone. He turned to face those gathered here in Merle's store—Ramona, Larry, Skeet, Millard, Merle, Claude, Shirley, and her son, Walter.

(How did all these people come to assemble here so quickly, since they all had jobs or busy schedules?, you ask—or you might have—though I know for a fact that three readers in Pocatello, six in Miami, four in Albuquerque, seven in Pittsburgh, six in New York, nine in Boston, another nine in Chicago, and two in Honolulu, *did* ask, and *didn't* find it believable that a cop, like Larry, and a pharmacist, like Millard, and a teacher, a reporter, and a woman with a special needs kid, could all just *drop everything* and hurry to Merle's store. All I can say—as I told these readers—is that even though it might not *sound* believable—it was actually the truth that they all managed to get there. As the saying goes, even though I just made it up, *Sometimes it's the truth that's the most unbelievable thing of all.*)

"*What?*" asked Ramona, anxious that the next thing to happen should happen.

"That was Boyd," replied Preston. "We have success! The hikers are running this way—and scared out of their wits!"

Everyone beamed, a few exhaling great relief, because until such time as you see the fruit of your labor, you'll find yourself wondering if you were merely wasting your time, or even crazy, to have put such effort into it, and Ramona made very fast *pitti-pat* applause with her hands while she jumped up and down, which was an interesting sight, given how large she was.

"All right," said Preston, "Larry? Skeet? You guys ready?"

The two men nodded gravely, the seriousness of their upcoming responsibility coming to mind and replacing their joy.

Of course, everyone would have to wait: it would be at least an hour and a half before Dane and Gloria would make it back to town, even if they ran all the way, which they were unlikely to do. Fear's a great motivator, but there were a lot of uphill moments in the trail back to town, and those moments would definitely force the two to walk, and slowly.

It was the longest ninety minutes of these people's lives, and they did nothing in those minutes but anxiously sit, or stand, or both, peering compulsively out of Merle's windows—and then suddenly, but were they dreaming?, here came Dane and Gloria running into town, down Main Street. Shirley saw them first. "Here they are!" she almost screamed.

Preston leapt up from the stacked cases of canned goods he'd been sitting on. "All right, everybody, look sharp! Larry, you're up!"

Realizing they had reached town, and feeling somewhat safe for the first time in one hour and forty-six minutes, Dane and Gloria slowed down. They walked, breathing hard.

They looked terrible. Sweat had shrink-wrapped their clothing to their bodies, and dust had caked them head to toe, making them look like strange ochre-colored people from another planet. They looked around, almost wildly, for someone to tell their tale to, then reacted swiftly—re-frightened—when they heard a door open. "Officer! Officer!" they yelled, and they ran toward Larry, coming out of Merle's store.

"Whoa. Whoa," Larry said. "Where is the fire?"

Inside Merle's, peering out at Larry through the window, Ramona now covered her eyes. "Oh, my god," she said, "he's *awful*." (He was. Even though he had practiced hard, Larry had just delivered his lines the way he had the very first day he'd read them in class.)

Preston winced. "C'*mon*, Larry," he said, watching his cousin through the window, "get it together, pal."

"We saw it! We heard it! We saw the footprints! They were huge!" Dane and Gloria were speaking at the same time, overlapping each other.

"Now, now," said Larry. "Slow down. There. What are you talking about? There."

"Oh, my *god*," Ramona said again. "Preston," she said, turning to him, "can you go out and shoot him?"

"He's the one with the gun," Preston replied.

"The ape!" Gloria said. "The Alpine Valley Ape! We heard him! We saw his prints!"

"Ha. Ha. Ha," said Larry. "Those boys there at the grocery..." And here Larry stopped and jerked a thumb over his shoulder to indicate Merle's, remembering what the script said to do at this point, "...they've got you all..." And here Larry stopped again, but this time because he'd forgotten his lines. "They've got you all..." He frowned, trying to remember what he was supposed to say here.

"Oh, *no*," breathed Ramona and Preston at the same time, as they watched all their efforts go up in flames.

"Excited?" Gloria said to Larry. "They've got us all *excited*?"

"No," said Larry, thinking hard—that wasn't it.

"Frightened?" Gloria offered.

"No..."

Dane and Gloria looked at each other, then Dane turned to Larry and said, "Riled up?"

"That's it!" said Larry. "Very good! They've got you all riled up!"

"If I distract him," Ramona said to Preston, "you can grab

his gun, shoot him, and put us all out of our misery."

"No! No!" Gloria said. "It's true! We heard it!"

"We saw the tracks!" said Dane. "Those guys in the store know what they're talking about!"

Exaggeratedly, Larry crossed his arms over his chest and gave them an exaggerated skeptical look. He even stroked his jaw—exaggeratedly.

(I don't need to bring you into the store for you to see Ramona's and Preston's reactions, except I will note that Ramona had passed out, on her back, and Preston was trying to revive her.)

But now here came Skeet, up the street. (Per prior arrangement, he had slipped out the back of Merle's and gone down the street a bit. Perhaps he'll save the day.) Skeet had a camera around his neck and a reporter's notepad sticking out of his jacket pocket. He headed toward Larry—casually—as if just happening upon him.

"Well, what's going on here, officer? Is there any trouble the town should know about?"

Though you might not believe it could be possible, Skeet's acting was worse than Larry's.

Inside Merle's, a revived Ramona was sobbing in Preston's arms.

"Shh...shh...," he said, trying to comfort her. Then, "Millard, Shirley, Walter—go! Your turn!"

Millard, and Shirley pushing Walter, came out of the store, Millard with a small bag of groceries as a prop.

Preston watched them join the knot of people in the middle of Main Street. Millard had been tasked with looking sheepish—even a little reluctant—while he said to Larry that, well, officer, he hadn't told anybody this, but in March, he saw some tracks he thought looked funny, like nothing he'd seen.

Shirley's job was to be bold about what she'd heard and seen: She told Larry in no uncertain terms that she had seen the ape last June, up at Big Rock—and no one had believed *her*, either—and that had made her mad. So I do not think these young people are just trying to prank us, she said. We're not! We're not! Dane and Gloria pleaded. We're not making this up! We swear!

And now Preston watched Merle and Claude join the scene. Claude had the easy job: All he had to do was say things like, 'I told you so!' And, looking very concerned, inquire as to whether Dane and Gloria were all right. Merle had the hard job. Because when Larry, looking concerned, and even a little persuaded that Dane and Gloria were a) not just riled up; and b) telling the truth, he was supposed to turn to Merle and say, 'Merle, you got anything to add here?' Whereupon, Merle was to try to look all guilty, and shifty, and—if he could pull it off—get his lower lip to quiver, as he finally blurted out, 'All right! All right! *Maybe* I saw him up by the mill. But it *could* have been a bear!"

And now Preston watched as Dane and Gloria pressed in on him a little and said, 'It wasn't a bear! You *saw* him, mister! You *know* it! You *know* you did! You saw the Alpine Valley Ape!'

While all this was going, Skeet was going around taking photographs—real photographs—while merely making a show of taking down notes, getting quotes from Dane and Gloria, and asking for the correct spellings of their names—playing up his character of local reporter, which of course he actually was. But though Skeet certainly needed the pictures for publication, he had pretty much already written up the story—with the help of Miss Ames.

(By the way, he had resented her help. But after Preston had had his conversation with Skeet after Skeet's ape audition, in which conversation Skeet had revealed how badly he'd misinterpreted the concept of the ruse, Preston couldn't really trust him to write up the story correctly. Actually, he *could* have, now that Skeet understood what the deal was, but Preston couldn't be persuaded otherwise, which left a bad taste in Skeet's mouth. But when Miss Ames read Skeet's first draft and said that she thought it 'sounds just like all your other stories,' and that he shouldn't 'change a single word,' Skeet felt highly gratified and decided to get over being miffed.

It never occurred to Skeet that Miss Ames was very cleverly and politely not complimenting him. But still, she *had* thought Skeet's story would do the trick because it *did* sound like something a local reporter would write: It had the ring of truth; as something truthfully reported.)

Preston and Ramona had the last jobs. Ramona was supposed to go out and tearfully say that she'd lost her cat and had thought the coyotes had gotten the poor thing—and then say nothing else, letting Dane and Gloria draw their own conclusions.

But unfortunately, as much as Ramona pretty much *lived* for acting, she really was feeling weak after having fainted. She just wanted to sit. She was sorry, she told Preston, but she couldn't find the reserves to go on out there.

Preston said he understood. He didn't think it'd hurt *that* much if her voice wasn't added to the mix—even though *she'd be the most credible person of all*. (He couldn't help looking right into her eyes when he said that, guilt-tripping her, because after all, she *would* be the most credible, and now she was lost to them). But Ramona either ignored the guilt-tripping, or didn't catch it, because she merely thanked him for understanding.

Well, all right, thought Preston. He still had his job to do.

He slipped out the back of Merle's, ran down the street a good twenty yards, and then, like Skeet, came up the street, and let himself be drawn into the cluster and excitement. At some moment Larry was supposed to 'notice him for the first time,' and you can bet he did it badly, and ask him if he knew anything about all this ape business. And Preston's job was to be the guy who considered the presence of the ape in a matter-of-fact way, telling Larry (but of course, his true audience was Dane and Gloria) that he never let his players walk home alone after evening football practice. They had to go home in pairs. And now he turned to Merle and said that he should *never* have let these two young kids go hiking in our hills. They should have been persuaded to hop over to Taylorville instead—hike the Forestal from *there*.

And now Merle was supposed to put his hands on hips, and look 'chagrined,' as Ramona's stage directions had it, 'while looking off, avoiding Preston's accusing eyes,' but what Merle did, in addition, was cry. Great big guilty tears streamed down his face. He was so caught up in the moment, his character, and the intensity of all this *drama,* that he managed tears!

Preston and everyone else (other than Dane and Gloria, of course) stood amazed, thinking, 'Wow, Merle's *great!*' Larry was jealous. Why couldn't *he* do something like that?

Merle couldn't believe it himself, but *boy* was he proud. Maybe he should try out for one of Ramona's little local shows she put on twice a year!

And wasn't it too bad that Ramona was missing all this! But she sat inside Merle's, eyes closed and fanning herself with her hands.

As Merle swiped at his tears, Gloria rushed to embrace him, and Dane patted his shoulder.

"It's all right, mister!" Gloria said, now crying herself out of sympathy for this poor sinner. "It's all right! No harm was done! We're all right! But now we have to tell the world the truth!"

Chapter Twenty-Three

THINGS TOOK OFF AT A FRIGHTENING SPEED NOW. SKEET published his story, and the online version was read throughout the northwest; and then, as happens on the net, the story went country-wide and worldwide, making its way to places like Brasilia, Brazil, Phnom Penh, Cambodia, Vienna, Austria, and Brooklyn, New York. Per arrangement, the Carnodys let three days pass before they drove to Cascade City and walked into the newsroom of KWCS with Peter's tape. Surprisingly, they encountered no resistance and were only shown courtesy by the bubbly receptionist, a young tape editor who never stopped stroking his beard, and by someone's pale and haunted-looking assistant—who showed them to the station manager's office, which was actually a cubicle.

The Carnodys saw that the man was very busy, but he was polite and asked them to sit down. Mrs. Carnody asked the man if he'd by any chance come across a story in their little newspaper, *The Alpine Voice* about a couple of hikers claiming to see The Alpine Valley Ape.

The manager laughed and said that he had. One of his interns, whose job was to send him links to offbeat stories that might make filler on a slow news day, had suggested he take a look at it. But he had turned it down. It was obvious to him, he said, that the hikers were just a couple of kids who were high on dope and only saw some bear.

Mrs. Carnody, who was quite the best actor in town, nodded, her brow knit in concern, while Mr. Carnody, no slouch himself, said to her, "See, Judy? That's what I thought."

Judy nodded. "Yes," she said, "it's probably just that. I don't know, I guess I just thought...I don't know." She now smiled, a little sadly, but showing relief, too, at the station manager and breathed, "Well, for heaven's sake, I'm a silly goose. I'm sorry to have wasted your time." And she got up—the tape in her hand—actually between two knuckles, so that the station manager couldn't help but see it—and she said, "It was kind of you to see us."

"Very kind," said Mr. Carnody, and turning to his wife he gave a little chuckle and said, "See, Judy?"

As the two were about to step out of his cubicle, the station manager's curiosity got the better of him. (He wasn't a newsman for nothing.) He had seen the tape in her hand and had wondered what might be on it, and he was both interested in, and confused by, the allusive nature of the things the Carnodys had said. Plus, *something* had gotten to these people; something they thought important enough that they'd drive all the way from Alpine Valley to Cascade City.

"Excuse me," the station manager said, "but what are you folks...I mean, I'm not entirely clear as to what it is you're here for. Does it have something to do with the tape in your hands?"

The Carnodys exchanged a look, Mr. Carnody giving his wife a shrug. "Look, Mr. O'Faighlen," Mrs. Carnody began, using the man's name for the first time, "we're not really sure what we've got on this tape. Here, this note—we wrote this note—it kind of explains everything, but we watched it two-dozen times, and it really *does* look like—to *us*—that, well, this wasn't a bear."

"But maybe we watched it *too* much," Mr. Carnody said. "You know? And it *is* just some old bear. But look," he added, looking very serious, and almost—but not quite—glaring at Mr. O'Faighlen, "we're *not* in the business of getting embarrassed and having people call us a couple of old fools—or dope smokers."

"It's just that we had decided," Mrs. Carnody chimed in, as if to forestall her husband from getting angry at this nice man, "to say nothing about what we saw, because what are the odds that what we saw *wasn't* a bear? Astronomical. And, you know, Bill and I *are* getting older..."

"And we're *not* dope smokers," Mr. Carnody said with emphasis.

"He doesn't think we're dope smokers," Mrs. Carnody said to her husband. "But look," she said to Mr. O'Faighlen, "when we read about what those two kids saw—and *where* they saw it, well, our question was, could it only be a coincidence? *Were* they just making this up—or smoking dope? Because, it was not more than a mile from where we saw our...creature."

"Look," said Mr. Carnody, "we've got kids, okay? People have got *kids*. I mean, if a mountain lion comes into town—believe me, you tell people stay indoors. You let everybody know."

By now, poor Mr. O'Faighlen, who had been told several times to 'look,' really did want to look—at that tape. He was *anxious* to look at that tape.

How well the Carnodys had done their job!

"I understand," Mr. O'Faighlen said. "In the end, it might be a public safety issue. Better safe than sorry, right? I get it—maybe it's nothing, but what the heck, why not let's watch the tape?"

Mr. Carnody looked at Mrs. Carnody. He gave her the merest nod yes, and after two long seconds, she extended the tape to Mr. O'Faighlen, who did his best not to snatch it like a dog snatches a treat.

"Here," he said to the Carnodys, "pull up those two chairs. We can watch it on my system here."

He put the tape in. He hit 'Play' on his remote. The three of them watched Peter's tape, the Carnodys seeing things in it that they hadn't seen or appreciated before, especially the timing of things—how natural it looked that he should have jerked the camera exactly when he did; backed up exactly when he did;

decide to run away, exactly when he did!

Mr. O'Faighlen watched the tape six times. Then, with the Carnodys in tow, he walked it down to one of his editing bays and had an editor look at it. The editor watched it twelve times.

"Well," the man said, "I don't know what that thing is, but the tape's real. This isn't faked."

"Faked? We were scared to *death*," Mr. Carnody said.

Mr. O'Faighlen had been reading, and re-reading the note. "Where is this—Big Rock?" he asked them, and then he asked many other questions, like about time of day, and what else they saw that *wasn't* captured on tape—the sounds they heard, for instance, he asked them, did you hear any huge snapping of branches—because that might indicate the creature's strength and size (at which point Mrs. Carnody thought that perhaps *she* had been wrong, and Miss *Ames* had been right, about the issue of the snapping branches, since Mr. O'Faighlen seemed to find them almost *remiss* for not having thought to include in the note what they had *heard*— though Mrs. Carnody found herself a little huffy—inside herself of course—that Mr. O'Faighlen should be expecting them—people like them—not news people—to think about what they *heard*, for heaven's sake).

They answered all of Mr. O'Faighlen's questions and more, after which, Mr. O'Faighlen made several key decisions.

One, he would find Dane and Gloria and send someone to interview them on camera. Two, he'd have someone interview the Carnodys. Three, he'd show this tape. Four, he'd play it safe and broadcast the interviews and the tape on the Friday night 10p.m. broadcast, that being the broadcast where they usually ran short of content and had about a minute or two to fill—and this little story might do that nicely. And five, he'd have his writers slant the story so that it didn't look *in any way* like KWCS was taking seriously what the hikers and the couple from Alpine Valley had seen. No, the station was simply going to present it as a little, *Hey, viewers, can you solve this mystery?* sort of thing. *Some folks in Alpine Valley have seen something interesting. Here's the tape. Tell us what you think.*

And then he, Mr. O'Faighlen, would let it go, and do a follow-up based on viewer response—assuming any kind of viewer response. They might all just have a good chuckle, flip off the TV, and that'd be that.

Chapter Twenty-Four

*B*UT OF COURSE, THAT'S NOT WHAT HAPPENED.

Why would I be telling this story if that's what happened?

And anyway, I already mentioned at the beginning of Chapter Twenty-Three that things "took off at a frightening speed now."

And all that happened went *way* beyond Preston's expectations; way beyond the whole *town's* expectations—and certainly beyond their desires...

This ruse, this prank, this *fun*—and yes, this deception and fraud—went further than anybody anticipated it would, or *could* have anticipated it would. It turned into a beast.

Skeet was the first one to think both, *Oh, boy*, but also *Uh-oh*, because after he published his little write up about Dane and Gloria, he started getting e-mails from some of the places mentioned above (that is, in your past, dear reader), and from other places like Shanghai, China, Papeete, Tahiti, Rota, Spain, and Moscow, Russia. He knew that if this story had aroused a similar interest in people from vastly different cultures, all of whom were vastly far away from where the event had occurred, then a universal, a human, nerve had been struck, and that once the story of the Alpine Valley Ape was more widely disseminated, which is to say hit the airwaves, then it was a good bet that the little story they had concocted would become a lot more than this little town had bargained for. And that's why he had to say both *Oh, boy* and

Uh-oh.

On Friday of the week the Carnodys had met with Mr. O'Faighlen, he followed through and aired the tape—at 10:28 p.m. By 10:31 p.m. the phone lines at KWCS were jammed.

—People were frightened.

—People were fascinated—wanted copies of the tape.

—People scoffed—*It's just a bear!* they said. Or, *It's just an ape escaped from a zoo. You should ask if any zoo has reported a missing ape!*

—People were credulous—said that they themselves had seen the ape (which made everyone in Alpine Valley laugh when they heard that, especially when these people said that that's *exactly* what he looked like).

—People wanted the ape to run for governor—*He couldn't do worse.*

—*So that's where my ex-wife went!*

—*I wondered where my ex-husband had gone...* You can imagine how many people left joke-y remarks like these, especially since it was late at night, and many folk had been drinking a little too much. Didn't matter to Mr. O'Faighlen. The story, as he said, had *popped*, meaning struck a nerve. He couldn't wait to repeat it on the morning broadcast...

By the Friday after that, TV crews from stations throughout the Northwest had descended upon Alpine Valley.

In the ten days after that, these are some of the scenes you would have witnessed if you had lived in Alpine Valley:

—**Saturday night**... Down at Eddie's Bar and Grill, Preston... Boyd and Floyd...Larry and Ramona (sitting together and off by themselves, interestingly...)...and Mr. Pierce and Miss Ames, *also* sitting together (which you probably guessed they'd be doing sooner than later)...all sat at Eddie's big long bar, eyes glued to the TV he had bolted to the wall. They watched a TV reporter from Walla-Walla, reporting from the middle of Main Street.

"It seems," the reporter was saying to his camera, "that

throughout the Northwest, people are talking about a report out of tiny Alpine Valley that the old legend of the Alpine Valley Ape may actually be true…"

—**Sunday night**… Miss Dorothy, Millicent, Gertrude, Peggy Piersall, and Teresa Considine, sat gathered around Miss Dorothy's TV, the volume turned up VERY HIGH, as they watched a CNN news anchor say:

"Hoax or not, it's the story that is quickly becoming the talk of the nation after videotape was broadcast just a little more than two weeks ago of what appears to be an ape-like creature running along a forest path in the little town of Alpine Valley. Here it is…"

And CNN replayed Peter's video. It was the first time Miss Dorothy and the ladies of the sewing circle had seen it. They'd only heard from Teresa's daughter, Shirley, and from Judy Carnody, that it had come out *just great,* and that everybody thought the ladies had done an *outstanding* job on the costume.

The ladies applauded after the video ended and made a fuss over Miss Dorothy at how well her ape head had turned out. She pooh-poohed it all, of course, and only said, Oh, for heaven's sake, and then got up and got the sherry.

—**Monday night**… As Shirley affixed a new oxygen tank to Walter's wheelchair, they watched as the NBC Nightly News began.

"Good evening," the anchor began. "He's an ape-like creature who bounds from trees, and lives in the high mountains of the American Northwest…"

—**Tuesday night**… Ramona and Larry sat on her couch, following a delicious dinner she has made for them, each holding a plate of cake. Larry impatiently flipped through the channels with the remote, looking for more news on the ape—but it was eight o'clock now—all the prime-time shows were on. But as he flipped around, he passed something that made Ramona yell, "Stop! Go back!"

Larry did, finding his way back to Telemundo, a Spanish

television network. What Larry and Ramona saw on the TV was a Telemundo reporter standing near a gaggle of other reporters who were all taking video and snapping photographs of the impression in the mud that Derrick had made.

Larry spoke enough Spanish to translate for Ramona what the reporter was saying, and I speak Spanish fluently, so I can report to you precisely what the reporter said:

"The entire world wants to know, is this where the Alpine Valley Ape slept?"

—**Wednesday night**... Interestingly, not much happened Wednesday night—a few stories, but they only covered old ground.

—**Thursday night**... Boyd and Floyd sat in their cabin and watched themselves on *"Stuart South."* (The whole town was watching them on *Stuart South*.) The brothers had been flown to New York Tuesday, had done the show Wednesday, and were now back home watching themselves on tape. Boyd watched himself holding up a plaster cast of a footprint. Floyd sat next to him. And world-renowned primatologist Dr. Laurence Board sat next to Floyd.

"Dr. Board," Stuart South said, "do you agree with Boyd and Floyd?"

"I do, Stuart," he said, and using a pointer, he tapped several spots on the cast and added, "Note the patterns—here, and here. They are not indicative of any known species in the family Pongidae. On the other hand, note the creases: they bear a striking similarity to those you'd find in your great apes. Complicating things further, note the distinctive curve of the back of the print—here. That's Ursidae for sure."

"So are we looking at something that might be a hybrid?" Stuart South asked.

"I really can't see how," Board replied. "But that's not to say that a heretofore unknown species of animal, which just happens to share physical characteristics of primate and ursine species, could not have left this impression. And as it's thoroughly unlike any bogus Bigfoot print I've been asked to study, I'd say, yes, I agree with them: it seems rather likely that *something* is loose in those woods."

—**Friday night**... Miss Ames served Mr. Pierce a lovely, if simple meal, which Mr. Pierce enjoyed. He had no idea, however, that he was the main course, as far as she was concerned. They both sat on her couch, sipping a little wine, and watching Teddy Revere on the television. He was up on a ladder, and asking his cameraman to move in closer so that he could get a good picture of the claw marks here on the tree. Teddy was saying to his viewers,

"It's clear from these claw marks so high in the tree and so deeply etched in the bark that this creature has strong legs, and very probably strong arms and *brachiates*."

Well, that was just too much for Miss Ames. She could contain herself no longer. There was the sound of breaking glass, a very breathy, "Oh, Stanley," which was almost a cry, more breaking glass, and then poor Mr. Pierce was leapt upon.

—**Friday night** (only about ten minutes later)...Preston leaned against his kitchen counter chowing down some microwave spaghetti as he watched a reporter from the BBC standing on top of a rise that overlooked the valley. The reporter said:

"And is the beast procreating? That's what scientists are wondering now."

—**Saturday night**... Not much happened Saturday night. That is, in terms of media coverage. There was only a re-cap of the stories from earlier in the week.

—**Sunday night**... Peter and Melissa stood in front of the TV, Muffin in Melissa's arms. Peter and Melissa are mesmerized by what they're watching. (Muffin only wants down.)

Annie, her glasses on, with printouts in her hand of apartments for lease in Cascade City, stood behind them. She had been on her way into the kitchen, to ponder new living arrangements, when what appeared on the TV arrested her attention.

60 Minutes. Famed film director Sean Ford was being interviewed.

"I've seen the videotape that surfaced," Ford said. "Everybody wants to know is it real. Here's what I say: Either someone in that tiny little town of Alpine Valley is a cunning and brilliant film director, or we're looking at something, however hard to believe it may be, which is real."

All three LaPeers gave a shocked whoosh of air, Peter most of all.

Larry and Ramona gave a whoosh of air.

Mr. Pierce, and Miss Ames in his lap, gave a whoosh of air.

Chrissy Covington cupped her nose and mouth with her hands and gave a little scream.

Merle gave a whoosh of air.

Edna knitted while watching *Jeopardy*.

Preston gave a fist-pump of happiness. "Way to go, kid!"

Miss Dorothy said, "Oh, my!" and made Winston clap his little hands together as he sat in her lap.

The three scouts who had been mean to Peter looked at each other, shocked.

Melissa gave her brother a little *way-to-go* punch in the arm.

Peter had to sit down. He made his way to a chair and sat, overwhelmed, but looking like no one had ever seen Peter LaPeer look. Joyful. Proud.

Looking at her son, joyous for him, and wiping away a tear, Annie felt something give inside of herself; and you could see something give in her face.

Chapter Twenty-Five

IT'S HARD TO TELL WHETHER SPRING THAT YEAR was the most beautiful it had ever been in Alpine Valley, or whether it was only as beautiful as it generally was there, but that the way people *perceived* of it made it more beautiful than ever. The people of Alpine Valley weren't so much seeing pretty asters, and star anise, and plump trailside blueberries as they were promise, and budding peace—and blooming accomplishment.

On the other hand, I can tell you—this was one beautiful spring. Every day the sky was as beautifully blue as it is in fairy tales, the clouds as fluffy white. The whole length of the river sparkled like something a goddess would, and only a goddess could, pick up and throw around herself, like a boa, and run off with it to the sky; and it ran so clear that even twenty feet from shore, one saw mottled trout holding in the slicks before boulders, patiently waiting for breakfast to come downriver.

You wanted to pick up the wing feathers you might find on the ground, or drifting to the ground, from the birds above, they were so lustrously blue, and black, and white, and red. The squirrels darted about in their glossy furs, showing them off—*Hey, do you see me? How about you, pal? Ain't I something? Hey, you—you see me?* And you knew that if the squirrels in town looked this good, the spring dress of the large creatures in the wood would be no less

136

than voluptuous, which is one of the all-time great words. People should use it more, or have more reason to use it.

What Preston almost couldn't believe; what made him close his eyes and open them again to make sure what he was seeing was real, was how much the town looked like the photos of Willow Creek come to life.

The sidewalks, though still a hazard, were jammed with folk who were too happy at being in Alpine Valley to fret about what lousy sidewalks this place had. Cars circled and circled Main Street's five blocks, looking for parking spots, and no one in those cars minded the too frequent buh-BUMPs and the banging of heads when going over potholes.

While backpackers were generally a familiar sight here during the spring and summer months, you usually only saw them in pairs—a couple of guys; maybe a couple of girls; couples; sometimes a family of four—mom, dad, kids; and of course there were always the hardcore types who passed through on their march to conquer the entire Forestal Range.

But one *never* saw, as now, groups of five and six, and all these mini-expeditionary forces, armed with cameras and audio equipment. Every sixth hiker, according to Preston, had strapped to his backpack a parabola for catching ape sounds, and/or boom mikes with those fuzzy gray oblong windscreens wrapped around the microphones themselves. Making Preston laugh were the people he saw with nets.

But mostly families were here; not families with little kids, but families with young teens—the kinds of teens who were natural-born naturalists and knew everything about dinosaurs, and lizards, and birds, and snakes, and bats, and bears—and who were the ones most avidly following the news of the Alpine Valley Ape. They were the ones pleading with mom and dad to take a trip here—and *now*, Dad, *this weekend*, before it's too *late*, before someone (and not they!) captured the Ape! Please, Dad, please!

In the beginning, it was because of these teens that Alpine

Valley evaded the grim reality it had faced. Their arrival, more aptly, the *cash* they pulled from their pockets, helped the town make good the checks that were bouncing; and literally, kept the lights on here.

Of course, only Annie knew the incredible relief that this was, like gasping for air in a sealed coffin, finding none—but then someone throws back the lid. Still, everyone else knew relief, too. They knew that the town had been dying (if not that it was dead), and that they were living on borrowed time. But now, not only was the town not dying, it showed signs of getting better.

And now, two more weekends in, it was not only showing signs of getting *better*, it showed signs that the town might end up *thriving*...

Because of all the phone calls to the *Alpine Voice*, Skeet had to tape a message prompting his callers, who were mostly parents, to 'Press One,' if they wanted information on the Alpine Valley Ape. Pressing One, they heard Skeet giving them a brief overview about the Ape, the town, and how to get here, and if they wanted more information, including answers to Frequently Asked Questions, he invited them to go to the *Voice's* website, where they would find as much up-to-date information as possible on the Alpine Valley Ape. (Preston loved that clever 'up-to-date' business, as if every day there might be something new to report about the Ape.)

It used to be that the first thing that popped up when you visited the *Voice's* website was a page devoted to Local Valley News. But now, the first thing that did was the FAQ page.

Mostly, Skeet discovered, callers wanted to know about safety. So right away—by question two of twenty-five, Skeet assured them that "while no one at the *Voice* can claim to have discovered proof of the existence of the Alpine Valley Ape," the paper understood from "widespread, if unverified reports," that the Ape was far more afraid of *us* than we should be of him. According to "eight eyewitness reports" (and Preston loved how real the number eight made things sound), "the Ape was timid; and according to one witness, "the only thing that might give you a start was how fast it ran away, if seen."

By the way, and perhaps surprisingly, there was never any particular interest in debating the sex of the Ape. Pretty much everyone was content with calling the Ape 'he.' It's the same with Bigfoot. Think about it. Have you ever heard anyone refer to Bigfoot as she?

In the meantime, if Skeet was more or less the *official* spokesman for the town, Merle had become the *unofficial*, because who had more interaction with visitors than Merle? *Everybody* found his way to Merle's store for everything from snacks, to sunscreen, to soda, to beer, to jerky, to everything else. But mostly they wanted information from Merle. When and where had the Ape last been seen? Had Merle ever seen him? (Once, said Merle, about a quarter of a mile beyond Barney Lake.)

Business had become so good in the store that Merle re-opened the "Café" part of his establishment, which, though he had never officially closed it, had lain dormant since John Chamberlain had closed the mill. He hired Claude to do the cooking, mostly on a wing and a prayer, because Claude had never cooked before. But it turned out the man could not only whip up burgers and omelets and baskets of fried chicken, he could do it for hours on end and quickly. He had, he professed at the time, found his calling. So the Café became a huge success—such chatter and clatter of silverware and moms asking above the din, "He's not actually *rushed* at anybody, has he?" (The Ape; not Claude. No one ever saw Claude. Of course, no one ever saw the Ape, either, but that didn't seem to dampen anyone's enthusiasm.)

Even with Claude taking care of the kitchen, Merle still had to take orders, clear tables, ring up checks, *and* run the store part of his operation. So he needed an assistant. He hired Chrissy Covington to fill in whenever and wherever she saw a need. She'd work as much as possible until school let out for the summer, then full-time after that.

Chrissy's dad said that Merle would probably ask her to take out her studs and tone down the make-up and hair, but it never crossed Merle's mind to ask her to do that. He *did* ask her to stop sneaking free Cokes and ice cream to Derrick whenever he came around; and, both hugely embarrassed that she'd been caught, and feeling her shame acutely (because Merle hadn't made a big deal of it; had even asked her *please* not do it), she paid Merle back every penny she thought she might owe him for the illicit treats, and didn't tell him that she had: she just kept adding to the till.

Not too much farther down Main, Millard made a small fortune thanks to sales of calamine lotion, sunscreen, moleskin, band-aids, sunglasses, Ex-Lax and Gas-X (people were variously affected by the high altitude), iodine, water purification tablets (which Merle also sold), thick socks, hand lotion, antibiotic ointments, athlete's foot ointment, salt tablets, jock itch spray, feminine products, and various and sundry prescriptions Dr. Cabot had to write out, thanks to so many people incurring extra-nasty campfire burns, or taking spills down the mountain, and getting broken arms, ankles, hands, and wrists. Millard (also like Merle) stocked cases of tomato juice. People were *not* behaving with common sense. If you see a skunk, *don't crowd it*—give it wide berth! But twelve times already (twelve!) people had had to take tomato juice baths to get rid of the stink that had gotten on them thanks to an angry skunk.

As for Doc Cabot, he *had* been busier in his life—when the mill was in operation, of course—but *now* was a close second. He rarely got a chance to sneak up to his cabin, he was so busy at his office (which was the whole downstairs of his home). He's the one who treated every one of those extra-nasty campfire burns, spills down a mountain, etc., plus a lot of other things, some of which were rarities, like raccoon bites. As Dr. Cabot could tell you, you had to *really* have been asking for it to get a raccoon to bite you.

Who *were* some of these people?

In the meantime, Walter enjoyed sitting in the sun on the corner of Main and Pine and keeping mental note of all the out-of-state license plates he saw; at least, he enjoyed it until he kept getting bumped by everyone going by and once almost got toppled off the curb and into the street.

Surprisingly—though really *not* surprisingly, and I'll explain why in the next paragraph—for all the people crowding the town, Larry didn't see much of an uptick in crime. Some drunk-and-disorderlies down at Eddie's, quickly handled, because pretty much all Larry had to do was walk into the place and let the sheer fact of his size sober people up fast. There were only two break-ins, both easily solved, a smashed windshield, but nothing taken, and four lost children, all of whom were found within fifteen minutes.

Probably the most important reason there was no real uptick was that there was no way for people to spend the night in Alpine Valley, unless you camped up in the mountains, which plenty of people did. But in the town *itself,* there was no motel, or B&B, or anyone renting rooms. There *had* been a motel, back in the day, but it had closed and looked like something shamed out there on the east end of town.

No, Alpine Valley was, for most of these tourists, a day-hike town. People arrived early in the morning, wandered the town, attacked all the local trails, came back weary, maybe had dinner at Merle's or Eddie's, maybe not, and then even the most interested in the Ape were on the road back to Taylorville—where they *did* have motels—by nine.

And by the way, did all these day-hikers leave disappointed? By no means!

First, most of them visited the spots where the Ape had taken his nap, and had clawed at the tree (Preston and Mr. Pierce imbedded a ladder in front of that tree—and hundreds of folk climbed to the top and had their pictures taken as they pointed to the Ape's claw marks), and they all took their own videos of the *exact spot* where the Ape had been seen. By the way, the Carnodys became *quite* the biggest celebrities in Alpine Valley. If the Carnodys were spotted in town, you'd see no less than two-dozen people rushing up to them and wanting their pictures taken with them. (Mrs. Carnody loved the attention. Mr. Carnody did not.)

And beyond being excited by seeing the three famous spots, many people (that is, kids and young teens—mostly) having the romance (or "proof") of the Ape now rooted in their systems, came back into town from their hikes *quite* sure that the rustle they had heard in the brush, or something they saw out of the corner of their eye, or something odd they smelled, *had* to have been the Ape. And they wanted to go out *again*, the next day, to go farther into the woods. But unless they brought tents and camped, they couldn't. So it was the day visitors who themselves began urging the people of Alpine Valley to build a motel.

And I'll get to the motel presently, but first a little more about what was happening in town:

To raise income for herself and Walter, Shirley had set up a little booth—the kind of temporary-looking thing you'd find at a school fair. She sold Alpine Valley Wildflowers in great big beautiful bunches. (While Walter slept, she got up early in the morning and gathered the flowers from an area just beyond her house.) She also sold t-shirts she'd gotten made in Cascade City. They read either 'Going Ape,' or 'I Saw It!' with '(Ask me what...)' on the back.

In the meantime, in only the third week of our ape madness, a woman named Bettina Billibup, who is not germane to this story, nor a part of it beyond this paragraph and the next three, but whose name I love to both *see* (it's the two capital B's and the double t's and l's I like) and *say* (say it for yourself a couple of times), opened a boutique called Lydia's (named after her departed mother).

Bettina's store is worth mentioning because it was the first business to open in Alpine Valley in fifteen years. Even when the mill was up and running, the town made do with the businesses it had had forever. But somehow Bettina, resident of Taylorville, thought there were now enough people with enough cash here in Alpine Valley to justify moving her store here. She thought they'd come in and buy her clothing (for men and women) hand-crafted jewelry, shoes (women only), and small gifts. And shockingly (as far as I'm concerned) her very first customers were Boyd and Floyd, who were simply walking down the street, eating ice cream cones and observing the hustle-bustle, when they saw on the sidewalk (still not fixed!) Bettina pondering her window display; and they stopped (Floyd first—he initiated it all) to offer her some advice: No, put the purse there—up on the little pedestal where the shoes now are. And move the male mannequin there, and maybe have the female mannequin standing, not seated—and you can put the purse in the crook of her arm, like she's going somewhere.

(Note: I feel I've misrepresented Bettina's importance to a degree, so I want to clear things up before I go on. While Bettina is *not* germane to this story—she remained on the sidelines of it, and was even out of town when all the terrible things took place—she is *quite* germane to the town of Alpine Valley: She ended up marrying Floyd. But their courtship wouldn't happen for another two years after the events of this story, and their marriage wouldn't happen for another year after that. *Lots* of reasons for that, including Boyd's death—and what a mystery *that* was—and remains! But Boyd's mysterious death would take a whole *book* to tell right, and I can't do that here.)

Anyway, Bettina was quite taken with Floyd's advice (the man *did* have his moments—even Boyd had to admit that), and she invited them in to "get a feel for the store."

They walked out in brand-new shirts and pants. Edna walked right past them when they came out of the store, not recognizing them, and when they called her name, she almost (as she said) had a heart attack: How did these strange men know who she was?

Speaking of Edna—and I'm glad I remembered that detail about Edna passing Boyd and Floyd on the sidewalk, because I might not have thought to note this here, where it's logical to do so—she opened up a little booth, like Shirley's, very near the town square. She sold pies. Her sign couldn't have been more straightforward. It read, 'Pies.' They were delicious. They were mince pies, apple pies, key lime pies, pumpkin pies, gooseberry pies, cherry pies, and, of course, rhubarb—which was her biggest seller.

In fact, Edna made so much money off her rhubarb pies that Annie had to wonder if she'd been too hasty in dismissing Edna's idea about how to raise money all the way back in Chapter Two.

What if...Annie thought one day, watching a man and his boy walk away from Edna's booth with *twelve* rhubarb pies...they had all thought of Edna's idea a little longer? Clearly relying on pie sales in *town* would not have done the trick back then, but did Edna *know* that, and was actually thinking about something *large-scale*, like that they send her pies to the cafés in Taylorville and the restaurants in Cascade City...and *beyond*, like throughout the Northwest?

Was *that* where her idea was headed when Annie cut her off? After all, though Edna was strange, she *was* the one who signed the checks on behalf of the town. So she knew what kind of money was going out. She couldn't be *completely* unaware of how much money needed to come in. One day, she'd have to ask Edna this—what did you mean when you said, *We could do pies*?

(And one day, she did; but long after the events of this story took place—'long after,' because Annie was afraid of hearing the answer in the days immediately following the events I'll be relating. Because what if Edna Rasmussen's simple idea to "do pies" had been the ticket—the way out of their troubles? How much could have been avoided! How much tragedy averted!)

And speaking of Annie, she actually sold a house. She sold it to a young family who had come to see the Ape; and though they found the town 'awfully touristy,' they figured that eventually the hoopla would have to die down, and they liked how pretty it was up here. As the father was a writer, and supported his family that way, he wasn't reliant on the health of the job situation in these parts.

And then just like that, Annie sold *another*, this one to an elderly woman whom one would charitably describe as 'eccentric,' and not so charitably as 'bats.' She, too, had come to see the Ape, and *just knew* she'd see him one day. But mostly she was here for reasons she couldn't properly articulate to anyone, most probably even to herself. But she just *felt* that her destiny was to die here (and she did, but many, *many* years later).

Annie had no moral qualms about selling houses to either the writer or to Diana Diana, which was the eccentric woman's name. (She had been born Diana McKown, but had legally changed her name to Diana Diana when she was twenty-one.)

The reason Annie had no moral qualms about these sales was that the writer and his family hadn't chosen to live here because of the Ape, that is, because of something non-existent and fraudulently posited; and Diana Diana, well, Annie couldn't say why she was here, *really*, but the woman was thrilled every day to be living in these parts, and not *once* did anyone ever see her go looking for the Ape—despite what she herself claimed was one of the chief reasons she was here.

Annie did, of course, ask herself what she was going to do, or what she might say, or how she might feel, if someone wanted to buy a house because he really did believe that if he looked hard enough, every day, he might find the Ape. Could Annie bring herself to sell that person a home? Could she hold her tongue and let deceit be the root of the fruit she would enjoy, the fruit being the money she'd make on the sale?

No, Annie decided, she would *not* sell a house to someone who wanted to live here because of the Ape. Because what would her children think of her, she thought, when they got older and understood that their mother had been complicit in, and had taken advantage of, this widespread fraud?

Which prompts the question now, What *was* Annie telling her children about her behavior, about the town's behavior—and how they themselves should behave, should anyone ask them if the ape were real?

Annie's solution came out of her conclusion that she had to perform a delicate balancing act.

These were her kids; and she had the responsibility to raise them up to be moral people. Fine. On the *other* hand, she was a citizen of a town full of people who had been, and still were, leading fragile lives—most of them jobless; most of them broke; most of them close to losing their homes.

They were surviving; but one bad winter, earthquake, or flood—and fire was always a hazard here—and they were done: They lacked the resources to rebuild and regroup; and for many of them—just below their cheerful demeanor—lurked the fear of any kind of serious, meaning *costly*, accident or long-term illness; and if it came, they were done. Homeless and worse.

So Annie didn't want her kids, in telling a reporter or blabby tourist the truth, to be the reason this grand scheme failed; to be the reason this hoax, which was actually *working*, failed, leaving people worse off than before, because hope had raised them up and now *wham*, they were back to their impoverished, fragile lives with no future to look forward to.

Sure, *she* would have been satisfied that her kids had told the truth—and her conscience would be clear—but the lesson might be problematic: Because the LaPeers had served the truth, many others suffered.

So Annie decided that she should tell her kids that if *asked questions* touching upon the reality of the Ape, they were to tell the truth—*No, he didn't exist.* Because doing so was morally good, but also (though Annie didn't share this part with Melissa or Peter), it wasn't going to hurt anything anyway.

Because, in fact, twelve people in town had been assigned the job of being Skeptics. It wouldn't do to have *everyone* in town in lock-step belief that the ape existed. That wouldn't look normal. There had to be *some* people who'd say when asked if the ape were real, "Oh, for heaven's sake, no! The whole town's nuts. They're just seeing bears!" But beyond answering no to questions about whether the ape was real, her kids were *not to volunteer any information.* Answer the question and move on, quickly. Best of all? Don't talk to strangers.

Annie knew that other parents had sat their kids down and launched into a speech about how they weren't lying to *gain,* which was always bad, but lying to protect and save, their thinking coming out of that spectrum of deception wherein a mother bird will feign a broken wing to lure a predator away from her young.

Their argument sounded good on the surface, until, Annie thought, you thought about it a little more and realized that it wasn't the same. The tourists weren't predators. They weren't there to harm anyone here. Quite the opposite, really. It was the *situation* the town found itself in that was bad, that wanted to 'eat them up,' not the tourists, and yet the town was *using* the tourists, using these people to alter their situation. In a way, it was the *townspeople* who were the predators, using their broken wing, their hoax, to lure people in—and then snatch their money.

A few other parents used a different argument with their children, saying that what they were doing was like a reverse of the whole Santa Claus thing, but this time the *kids* could have a wonderful time keeping the truth from the *adults:* So let's not spoil their fun, all right, children?

Annie, however, knew it wasn't like the Santa Clause ruse at all, because no parents ever asked their kids to give them all the money in their piggy banks first, if they wanted to go see Santa.

Nevertheless, Annie kept these thoughts to herself, neither sharing them with her kids, nor with anyone in town, especially as she saw every day beyond the tender hope in their faces how deeply anxious most people were.

Helping Annie steel herself to her decision was the thought that if things kept up like this, they *would* get that road to Taylorville; and that road was a lifeline. Not only could people *here* get to Taylorville with little hassle, but they could do so *every day,*

which meant they could get *jobs* in Taylorville. They could commute! And the hikers, and fishermen, and hunters, who typically
thought that getting here was too hard, would now come explore
what this region had to offer—and they'd be adding their dollars
to the town's coffers.

And look at Shirley, Annie thought, Shirley and Walter. How
much would they benefit; how much would their lives change for
the *good*, if that road could be cut through the woods?

And whenever Annie thought about Shirley and Walter, she
lingered long on the thought—because it justified for her so much
of this *nonsense* (a word, she found, that she was using more and
more, instead of 'fraud' and 'deceit'—and she wondered about *that*,
and then just stopped wondering about it); and she also lingered
long enough on the thought to recall how Walter almost died two
winters ago, almost died on the way to Taylorville, and how Shirley
nearly slid off the iced-over road twice in her panicky attempt to
get her son to the hospital. So a straight, well-groomed road was
key for them—for these two citizens of Alpine Valley. It was key
for the old folk, too.

In sum, Annie thought, thirty minutes to Taylorville would
save this town and the lives of those who lived here, while this current hour-and-a-half of treacherous, near-lethal mountain road,
would *take* them.

But maybe most of all, beyond all these justifying thoughts,
Annie had changed. Something *had* softened in, after all. She would
give herself moral limits, but those limits had stretched. Too much
good was happening here (look at Peter, she thought) for all this to
be *entirely* wrong.

And it was that last thought, about the preponderance of
good, that provided the force behind the *bang* of Annie's gavel, as
she struck the table and declared that the motion carried that the
town *would* divert twenty-five percent of newly derived tax income
into re-building and improving the old "Alpine Valley Motel."

If you go check *The Alpine Voice* photo archives, and look at the file for *Motel, Alpine Valley/Groundbreaking*, that pretty woman you'll see front and center in the picture, holding a shovel and wearing a hardhat, her council members behind her (also in hardhats and holding shovels—except for Edna, who was *told* to bring a shovel for the groundbreaking ceremony, but instead brought that garden spade you'll see in her hand) is Mayor Annie LaPeer.

It's instructive to study her face. That beautiful big smile of hers expresses delight, even pride. But those eyes...there's doubt in them. (I even detect shame.)

But look at Preston's eyes (second row, next to Bulie). There's nothing in them but joy and a real positive energy that clearly expresses, *Let's get it on!* (But of course some people are better than others at managing what shows up in their eyes.) Annie LaPeer was a real *what you see is what you get* kind of person. Preston Mayhugh was a real *what you see is what I want you to get* kind of person.

Of all the council members, only Bulie seemed unhappy about the turn the town's fortune had taken. (Look at him in that photo, standing next to Preston in the second row. Maybe Preston appears joyful to us because next to Bulie, even a small, uncertain smile might look joyous. Bulie looks miserable, like some big bug had crawled up his (and I'm only reporting what Preston said) butt. No one knew why. Bulie only said—quite often—"I liked things the old way!"

What did he mean by that? Was "the old way" during the days he was working at the mill and had twenty-five men under his supervision and was a man of importance in these parts? Or was it after he had retired, but still, his friends were around, and he had money in his pocket? Or was "the old way" in the very recent past, when he was alone, and mostly deaf, forgotten, and having to watch every dime—but it was *okay,* because he wasn't alone in suffering, and that fact offered solace? Was *that* "the old way"? Because what did he see now? Everyone but him gaining in happiness, and more than a few in bank balance.

Sure, the town's gains as a whole would accrue to Bulie, but only in terms of civic improvements and a road that'd make the outside world more accessible. But what did Bulie care about the outside world? Hardly a thing. It couldn't bring back his importance, his purpose, his friends.

In the meantime, in stark contrast to Bulie's unhappiness, was Peter's happiness.

He stepped out into his own now.

Of course, having had none other than Sean Ford call you brilliant and cunning didn't hurt his self-esteem and gave him esteem in the town he had never had before. What the Carnodys were to the tourists, Peter was to the citizens of Alpine Valley.

Really feeling like a filmmaker now, not just a kid with a camera, Peter began documenting all that was going on in Alpine Valley.

At first, he'd only been out shooting the now bustling town simply because he wondered if he could capture 'bustling' through his shooting and editing. That was his only ambition. But in the midst of his filming, on one fine day, in one fine moment—and how I wish he could have remembered that moment!—it came to him that he could do more than just try to capture 'bustling.' He could try to capture 'transformation.'

So he started doing interviews with various people he met in town, and the first person he interviewed was Bulie. It just so happened that Bulie was coming out of Lydia's, and Peter had been filming her display window.

"Excuse me, Mr. Peppersmith," Peter called to him, training his camera on him, as Bulie closed the door behind him. "May I ask you, what do you think about what's happening in town?"

"I liked things the old way!"

"How come?"

"I like things the old way! Now you'll excuse me."

"Nice jacket," Peter said, not that he thought so, and not that he *didn't* think so, it was just something to arrest Bulie's attention a little longer, and also to make the old man feel good: Peter knew intrinsically that the old man had few opportunities to feel good.

"Well, it cost too much!" And off Bulie trudged, and Peter decided to let him be.

He followed his sister a lot. He wasn't sure why, but his sister was always up for being on camera, and he had a half-formed idea of telling his story of transformation through the eyes of a kid (though he realized in later life, it would have been better to have told the tale through Bulie's eyes, so one could see how things *had* been, putting how things were now in better context).

And one day in following his sister, Peter was filming Melissa sitting on a curb licking an ice cream, which she hadn't really wanted—she just wanted to spend a little time with her hero, Chrissy Covington, who scooped up ice cream at Merle's and had no *idea* she was Melissa's hero—and Peter was asking Melissa various questions about the change in this town, and while answering one of them, she suddenly caught sight of their mother coming down Main Street in the back of a canopy-less passenger van. She was standing up in the aisle of it, hand on a seat to support herself, and she was dressed very nicely and pointing things out here, there, and everywhere—that is, pointing out all the progress in the town—to Trevor Westly and The Dudes from the State Capitol, the very ones who had spurned her application for a loan only six weeks ago. But now here they were. And they were nodding and smiling.

"Mom!" Melissa hollered, waving at her.

But Annie didn't hear her, as the van rushed past.

Peter also shot film of Melissa walking Muffin down Main Street, the fur on Muffin's head crested in a pink Mohawk. Peter shot her as she and Muffin stepped off the sidewalk and into the street, just as a car going by too fast nearly ran them down. The driver blasted the horn. Muffin was unfazed—she just looked about and licked her nose—but Melissa turned to the camera and said,

"Did you *see* that?!"

Later that same day, Peter shot film of his mother as she was being interviewed in front of City Hall by an Asian film crew. The Asian reporter stuck her microphone in Annie's face and asked,

"Do you yourself believe in him?"

And Annie replied, "I believe that every place has a bit of magic and mystery to it. Even a tiny place like Alpine Valley."

What Peter didn't film, what he wouldn't have known to film, was Preston out late that same night in an old track suit. Running, running hard down his street, Sequoia. And who should be coming *up* Sequoia but Reverend Flambeau, walking his dog.

Now, that Flambeau was walking up a neighborhood street was no surprise and nothing new. He liked the neighborhood blocks of Alpine Valley, their homey, Norman Rockwell feel, most of the architecture from the Victorian area up through the Forties. That he had a dog was no surprise to anyone, except to you, because I hadn't had an opportunity before now to slip that information in. But he did. That dog traveled with him everywhere, and stayed particularly at his side when they were in Alpine Valley, or so it seemed to Reverend Flambeau. The dog was a mutt and blind in one eye. And here the two of them came, up Sequoia, and Reverend Flambeau smiled and raised a hand in greeting to this running man—but Preston didn't even see him. The man was *right there*, no more than four feet away, and Preston didn't even see him, because though his eyes were open, they were blind to anything present, focused on the past as they were.

Flambeau turned to regard Preston—he thought it odd that the man should not have greeted him back. But Flambeau did not take it amiss. He saw that the man was preoccupied, and perhaps a little more than preoccupied. He was possessed. Oh, not by any demons, per se, but by a thought, and Flambeau had seen enough of the world and the people in it to know that the thought was more than likely a memory, and it made the man run, which is to say, flee.

"Come along, Bandit," he said to his dog, and Bandit did.

And by the time Reverend Flambeau and Bandit were stepping

back up into Flambeau's camper, Preston was a long way from town and taking a forest trail, a small, dark figure racing toward and melting into the dark of the deeper woods.

Chapter Twenty-Six

THROUGH THE WINDOW, THE COUNCIL MEMBERS watched a steamroller make its way up Main Street, as Shirley read from a typewritten report she held in two hands. That odd, muscular, weirdly prehistoric-looking machine was a wondrous beauty in their eyes.

Main Street was getting re-paved.

"Bottom line, Mayor," Shirley concluded, taking off her glasses and flipping back the first two pages of her report, "we're a little more than halfway out of debt."

"If I may jump in," said Millard, "I just talked to the crew foreman on the way here. He said that in seven to eight weeks, the motel should be ready enough so visitors can stay overnight."

"And people from Maine are called Mainers," said Edna.

Annie paused in her note-taking, and Bulie announced/yelled, "What the hell does that have to do with anything?!"

"They're good customers," Edna said. "*They* appreciate good pie—Mainers."

"Unlike Norwegians," Preston said. "No pie sense."

"What?!" asked Bulie.

Preston didn't bother to answer him—it was just a stupid joke, and to repeat it to Bulie would only confuse the poor man. He might wonder all day how anybody would know that Norwegians didn't have a sense for pies; and *why* didn't they? How in the sam hell could it be so hard to have a sense of pie? There it was—apple or whatever—and you ate it or you didn't eat it. What was the big deal? "Speaking of progress," is what Preston said, and he tapped his watch.

"Right," Millard said, checking his own. "Move to adjourn."

Everyone started pushing their chairs back from the table even before Skeet said, "Second."

"Bang and all," said Annie, not even picking up her gavel.

As the other council members filtered out of the council chamber, Annie gathered her notes and files into her briefcase.

Preston had nothing to gather, but watched her, and drummed curled fingers on the top of his chair back, in debate with himself about something. As Annie snapped her briefcase closed and started away, Preston said, "You're losing weight."

"Thank you," Annie said, automatically, as if complimented by someone she didn't know, but who saw her frequently enough to notice, like the checkout person at the store, or the dry cleaner.

"That's not...I mean, you never had weight to lose. So I mean..." Preston was flummoxed. His aim hadn't been to compliment her. It was to have...well, what? Shown concern? "Well, anyway," he said, "have a nice day." He started for the chamber door.

"Look," Annie said, surprising herself and him. He hadn't expected her to say anything to him, and *she* hadn't expected to say anything to him. "I wanted to say something to you."

"Okay," Preston said warily, turning.

"I wanted to thank you for getting Peter..." But what did she want to say? Did she really want to say *For getting Peter involved in all this*? "I guess I just," she resumed—just *what*? "Anyway," she resumed yet again, "he hasn't been this happy in a long time."

"Oh. Okay. Well."

"So. Thanks."

Preston looked at his watch. "Look, I was just going up to Merle's to get a coffee. Can I buy you one?"

"I'll, um, I was half-thinking of stopping there myself.

So I'll...we can go together. How's that?"

"It's a start."

"Okay," said Annie, but then she said, "I mean, no, it's not a *start*, Coach Mayhugh. It's just...I'll just join you."

"All right," he said. "Look. I'm sorry about what I said. That day. At Big Rock."

"I'm sorry I smacked you a *good* one." Annie put a little more emphasis on *good* than she had wanted to. Because, really, she didn't feel as much animosity toward Preston as she once had. Why should she? She had too many things on her mind to even *think* about him, let alone nurse any grudge against him. But what he'd just said, reminding her of that day at Big Rock when she'd found Peter there, *working* with him, when she had made it *clear* that he was *not* to participate in...well, anyway...it brought up both a bad memory and the anger associated with it. Hence, a *good* one.

But feeling embarrassed about the anger that her empha-sized '*good* one' no doubt conveyed to the man, Annie said quickly, "Look. No one wants all this, all that's happening here, more than I do, all right? So thank you for...But I see all this, and I...I don't want my kids to...I want Peter to be a man who's not comfortable with ends justifying means."

"Okay," Preston said, because he wasn't sure what else to say, if anything.

"Okay, look," Annie said, "that little speech there was for me, too, all right? Because, I mean, last night Peter was laughing because he said he'd heard that Mitch Ferguson was offering his services as a trail guide. He knew the best locations for seeing the ape—and he was charging people five-hundred dollars a head. Wow. What breathtaking deceit. On the other hand, Peter was *laughing*. He's gone a couple of years without doing that, and now he's doing it again. And his filming...it's not that he *hadn't* been doing it, but there was no real, what?, *love* in it any longer. *Now* look at him. So I find myself...relieved. Happy. My son's no longer glum. He's no longer depressed, or stressed out all the time. But on the still *other* hand, it bothered me a lot that I detected no sense in him that the people Mitch ripped off might not find it so funny."

Preston was about to say, 'I understand,' but decided not to, even though he did understand and didn't disagree. But he had his own thoughts about people getting ripped off by the likes of Mitch Ferguson, and he didn't think now was the right moment to share these thoughts with Annie. Receptive she wouldn't be—and she might not even understand.

But as for Preston, he just couldn't work up sufficient emotion or moral reservation to worry about any tourists getting conned into parting with their money. Of course Mitch was in the wrong. But it's not like he was selling them a bogus kidney guaranteed to save their life, or a house he *swears* is on good land when it isn't. Further, as far as he had been hearing from everyone, Mitch never *guaranteed* that they'd see the Ape, only that he was giving them the best possibilities of seeing it. So there was *some* regard for decency somewhere in Mitch, right? And how many of those conned tourists would actually *not* have had a good time, traipsing about after the Ape? They might be paying good money for the same thing that other people were getting for free—the excitement that in any single moment, in the *next* moment, just around the bend, you might run into the Ape—but weren't they getting their money's *worth*?

Shoot, Preston thought, parents paid quite a bit to take their kids to Disneyland so that they could have fun in a fantastic world—and c'mon, a good half, probably more, of these cash-paying tourists knew that this was all horse manure about the Ape, but weren't their kids having fun? And weren't *they*? So while he understood Annie's position, and while he couldn't say he disagreed, because she wasn't wrong, he just couldn't bring himself to question his own morality enough to entertain the possibility of not doing what he was doing. He had other things on his mind.

"Anyway," Annie continued, "I wanted to talk to Peter about that, about how he'd feel if someone ripped *him* off—made a fool of him and ripped him off. But how could I say that to him? Because he would have said, 'But, Mom, isn't that what everybody in town is doing? Taking advantage of people?' And the simple, unadorned answer to that question is *yes*. Sure, you probably can justify it. But the point is, you *have* to—which is basically just talking yourself into something. And that's what I've done. I've done what I felt I had to, and that's protect my own; see to their needs and happiness. And it *bothers* me that I can't do it without harming someone else. It's not *great* harm. I get that. But where will it stop. Where will *I* stop? What if the stakes keep getting raised? And what if I have to keep moving that line I will not cross, because now I have no choice but to do it?"

Annie's question was rhetorical, and didn't require an answer from Preston, but it was the first thing she had said that automatically struck a nerve; that got to him, deeply—where his emotions and moral sense *did* lie. She was right about this. It might be five-hundred bucks for a little hike today, but it might be something else and greater—that is, *worse*—tomorrow. Exactly what, Preston couldn't say, but since she had struck a nerve, he knew, instinctively, that it could very definitely be *something*. "I understand that," he found himself saying.

"But I try not to think about that, because *look* at this place, look at what we can see! Look at what we can hope in! This town has a new lease on life. We're going to *make* it—if we can just keep this up long enough...this...*charade*, but then get *out* of it before the cost gets too high. I guess that's what I'm hoping in, that we'll all know when we have to pull the plug on this thing. So, well, look, we've kind of had whatever chat we might have had over coffee, you know? Well, we haven't chatted at all. I've done all the talking and bent your ear. And I'm sorry. But anyway, after all that, what do we talk about over coffee now? The weather? So, thank you and all, but maybe another time."

Annie turned and strode quickly from the council chamber and out through the open door.

Preston wasn't sure what to make of this tsunami of a speech. The woman was conflicted—he got that; and later on, he'd have to sort through some of this to get a better sense of what was going on with her; but right now, pretty much the only thing he could focus on was that she had said 'but maybe another time.' She didn't have to say that, and yet she did. So maybe the door was open with her, if only a little bit? Maybe, if he chose the right moment, he could ask her out? Or maybe she was merely being polite, and 'but maybe another time' was just a stock, throwaway, polite phrase, and she had no intention of letting there be 'another time.'

As Preston gazed at the rectangle of open space through which Annie had disappeared, he suddenly thought, But why do I want to ask this woman out? She's a pain in the butt! Is it because she's pretty? Is that it? But lots of women are pretty; pretty in a million different ways he liked; and let's face it, Preston thought, I'm still that high school varsity player I used to be. Women always flirt with me. I'm almost never rejected. So why am I focused on Annie LaPeer? She's so serious! And bossy!

As for Annie, as she walked down the steps of City Hall, deciding that very *definitely* she was not going to Merle's for a coffee *now*, she pummeled herself for having spewed like that in front of that man. It seemed to her that she was always revealing herself to this guy. She'd done it at Big Rock. She *knew* he saw right into her after she slapped him—it was in his eyes. She *knew* he had pegged her as nothing more than an angry woman, hurt to the core. Damaged goods. Frightened. And *now* look what she'd done! Why had she *said* all that to him? Now he had all this *information* about her and her *feelings*. And he'd use it. Somehow. Some way. Information was power, and she had handed it right over to him. And anyway, she didn't want him *knowing* things about her.

But for *sure,* she had to be less...*reactive* to this guy. He somehow *got* to her. Got her to...act out. She wasn't herself around him. She didn't *hit* people! And yet she'd hit him! And she'd never said so many words like those to any man in her life! Not even to her husband!

She was all the way to her tiny realty office and opening the door before it occurred to her that she'd even walked here.

Chapter Twenty-Seven

MELISSA RODE HER BIKE DOWN THE BUMPETY-BUMP-bump trail along the riverbank. She had on her helmet and a day-pack. Just ahead, she saw Boyd and Floyd by Carson Bridge, which connected the town to this part of the forest, into which Melissa was headed.

The brothers were stringing up their fishing rods.

"Hey, Mel," Floyd said, as she rode up. "Where you going?"

Melissa stopped and straddled her bike. "To read. Miller's Peak."

"The Peak? By yourself?"

"About the only place the tourists haven't discovered."

Boyd chuffed a laugh. "True enough. You got your GPS?"

Melissa patted her daypack over her shoulder. "Yes." She took her seat again and started pedaling around the brothers toward the bridge. "Catch big fish," she said.

"Watch yourself, crossing the bridge," said Boyd. "Planks are getting old. You hear?"

"Yes, sir. I will." And she would. Her mother would have a *fit* if she knew she was going over rickety Carson Bridge. But everyone did! Her mother was always so *worried* about everything.

The river behind her, Melissa started riding up the trail to Miller's Peak. The switchbacks to the peak were long, easy, gentle, for a good mile. That's why the bike: You saved yourself a lot of daylight riding this part of the trail. But after a mile, the switch-backs got shorter and steeper. So when you found yourself standing up from the seat and throwing your body weight left, then right, to get the *right* pedal down, then the *left* pedal down, that's when you decided, 'Enough,' and you leaned your bike against a tree and went the rest of the way on foot.

It really wasn't the best idea in the world for Melissa to go off to Miller's Peak alone, and you may wonder why Boyd and Floyd didn't try to dissuade her, especially since they did voice a little concern about whether she had her GPS, but the truth of the matter is that neither one thought for one second that Melissa was going to make it all the way up to Miller's Peak. A grown man in good shape could get up there and back in the daylight hours, but a twelve-year-old girl? No way. If she got a *quarter* of the way there before she'd have to turn back, that'd be impressive.

As for bears, yes, there were bears in the mountains, moun-tain lions, too, but no one hiking the trails within a couple of miles of town had seen a mountain lion in seven years, and the bears around these parts were pretty used to seeing humans; and not that you *ever* treated a bear in your presence lightly, but just about the time your heart started pumping pretty hard, the bear you encountered went back to eating whatever he was eating, or lumbering along in the direction he'd been lumbering along in. If, however, you came across a mother and her cubs, the best advice to follow in these parts was to make yourself look as big as possible—by taking off your backpack and raising it above your head—and back up and away from the mama, and get out of her area. No one had been attacked by any species of bear in four years, and that attack four years ago was just bad luck: a hiker turned a corner and there was a mama bear and her two cubs coming right at him, only ten feet away. She reared up, the hiker panicked and fell, and she mauled him. Not to death. In fact, the hiker hiked back, but he got airlifted all the way to Cascade City, where a plastic surgeon had to give him a whole new side of his face.

Still and all, despite what a lot of hikers might think of as the tolerably low chance of meeting up with a mountain lion or bear, Annie would never have allowed Melissa to even ride her bike as far as Carson Bridge—let alone cross it—let alone go alone up the trail to Miller's Peak!

In a word, she'd be aghast. But Annie was busy, and Melissa felt no need to inform her mother of her plans beyond truthfully answering her when asked, "What have you got planned for today?" "Do some reading."

Melissa *herself* didn't think she'd get even a quarter way up the trail to Miller's Peak, but she wanted Boyd and Floyd to think that that's what she was going to do. And she liked the image of herself atop Miller's Peak (an image completely made up since she'd never been to the top), taking a careful seat on the least little bit of ledge, leaning her back against the rocky pinnacle, her feet dangling over thousands of feet of air between her and the tops of all those toy trees below, reading. Just her, her story, an eagle going by at her eye level, and looking right into her eyes—and winking.

But that was only an entertaining and fantastical image that kept Melissa occupied for a good minute or two. No, really, her more down-to-earth aim was to find a nice spot off the trail where she knew she'd have quiet and solitude while she read. Because part of her motivation for coming this far from town, to hike this faraway trail, was that she was sick and tired of all the tourists and noise and busyness of the town. For twelve-year-old Melissa the presence of so many people didn't translate into anything, like money for the town—although she understood that the more people who came, the more money the town got, and that was good.

For her, mostly, it was just a bunch of *strangers, crowding* everything all the time, especially crowding what she thought of as *our town's* sidewalks, and *our town's* streets, and going into *our town's* stores, and *our* square, and even stretching themselves out to snooze on what were *our* benches, where she read.

She could have opted for going up the trails whose trailheads were just outside of town, maybe find a nice quiet place up in the local hills. But no, those trails were full of people. It was like a cacophony, a word she'd learned and spelled right on her last spelling test, to hear all those tin water cups that backpackers had dangling from their backpacks and clanking or clanging away against whatever else might be dangling off a loop, or strap. So she wanted to get far, far away; and not that she knew it, but a tiny bit of anger drove her all this way, too. She *would* just keep riding. She couldn't really say why she should be angry, but, as with Bulie, she liked things "the old way."

But, as with Bulie, what did that mean exactly? Life was great when her dad was still around. But then the fighting and yelling she'd hear—and sometimes worse—just...ate her up. And when he was gone, things got better. Weird. Quiet. Serious. But still, better. And anyway, at that point, she still had some friends left, so she could go over to their houses, where things *weren't* weird, quiet, or serious. But then Margaret Riddle left town—her last remaining friend—and things weren't as good.

But she had adjusted. And actually, she was left alone a lot, her mom working so hard all the time, and Peter in his room just generally moping around. But in being left alone, she could do what she wanted; and she did; and she liked that a lot. So for Melissa, "the old way" might have referred to things as they were just before the town got nutso-cuckoo with this Ape thing. Like Peter had gone nutso-cuckoo. Like her *mom* had.

Melissa stopped to take a breather. She took off her day-pack, took out her water, took a long drink. She wiped her mouth and looked around. This was the highest up the mountain she'd ever been. She was sure of it. And she didn't feel particularly tired yet. She looked up at the sun. She still had plenty of daylight yet, and suddenly, she didn't really want to find some spot and start reading. She wanted to keep going; wanted to see how far she could get before she'd have to turn back. And boy, then wouldn't she have something to tell her mother! Oh, wait, she couldn't tell her mother that. She'd flip out. But she could tell Peter, and make him swear to keep it a secret.

She went on. After another half-hour or so, Melissa came up to a plateau in the mountain. It was choked with trees, but the ground was level, and she heard the trickling of a stream ahead, and not too far away from the trail. She wanted to see the stream.

And anyway, she thought, if she headed into those trees, it didn't matter that it was a little darker in there, or that she was off trail. Because all she had to do was turn around and she'd see where it was bright sunshine—and head back for *that*, because that would indicate where the trail would be; and even if she had wandered a little crazily amongst all these trees, still, when she'd head toward sunlight, and emerge from this wood, she'd hit trail— maybe a little farther up it, or a little farther down it—but not so much that it made much difference.

The temperature change as she stepped in among these many trees was instantly noticeable and very welcome. It was cool, refreshing. And it was so quiet here! Melissa stopped and tried to stand as still as a post to see if she could hear her heart beating. She held her breath and listened. Well, she couldn't hear it, but she thought she *almost* could. She walked on toward the stream.

It didn't seem to be getting any closer, and she was getting farther in amongst these trees than maybe she should be getting. She turned around—and there was the bright curtain of sunlight not too far behind her, which meant trail, and so she felt better.

She turned back and suddenly, there was the creek. There was a slight cataract in the earth just here. You had to take a giant, sideways step down, or a jump down, to get to the forest floor at this point. It was like the forest had a lower tier here—and there was the creek not thirty yards past this cataract. And oh it was beautiful!

She made a giant, sideways step down, then turned and hurried to the creek. It ran so clear she could see the bottom perfectly. She counted the different colors in the stones she saw, and saw a pink stone in the middle of the creek and wanted it. She stepped into the water and didn't mind her boots and feet getting wet. They'd dry on the way home, and anyway, she liked the chill of the water. It woke her up.

She plucked the pink stone from the riverbed, and turned and walked out of the water. She saw a nice flat rock, almost like a bench, between a couple of trees and right against the side of an earthen wall—which made another cataract of earth, but this one going *up*, back up to the level she had been on. She thought she'd go sit on the rock-bench, put her stone away, have a little water and snack. Then head back home. What more could she want than this, this place, this moment. This was hers! She'd come back again next Saturday!

She went to the rock-bench and taking off her daypack, sat down, plumping the pack into her lap. There were a couple of apples in there, and a PB&J. She leaned against the cool of the earthen wall—it felt so good—mossy but not *too* mossy; and, in order to absorb a little more of its cool, she pressed her back against the wall a little harder and broke through it and fell backward, down through darkness and so quickly that the light before her winked out. She was too shocked to be scared, and as the evidence from her bumping butt and the backs of her legs testified, she was sliding down a precipitously angled, rough rock hill. It was abrading her legs something awful, and tearing up her shorts—her butt would be next and abraded something fierce.

She hit bottom with a thud she felt all the way through her. Her daypack came next, hitting her in the chin.

Still more shocked than scared, she pushed herself up to sitting position. She looked around.

She could *see*. The darkness of the slide down was replaced here by a twilight kind of light. There was a light source somewhere, and nearby. Oh, she thought, as it registered—from the sun, above this canopy of trees.

She stood. She looked all around her. She understood. This

was just a different part of the forest. A lower part. She was just another tier down. Wow, she thought, this was quite an area for cataracts in the earth, for multiple tiers!

So that was no earthen wall she had leaned against. That was just a flimsy, thick-ish wall of leaf clutter and binding dirt and twigs and spider webs and whatnot that sometimes gathered between trees—as it had between those two trees that bordered the rock bench. It had collected for years; had been substantial for years, like a wall, or moss wouldn't have grown on it. Well, the joke was on her.

Looking up, Melissa thought that she must be about fifty feet below the forest floor she'd been on. That was...neat! And all she had to do was find a way up; which she didn't worry about, because this rock wall that she'd slid down—and it *was* a wall, she saw, not a hill—had lots of foot and hand holds. A one-minute climb would do the trick.

But in the meantime, look at this place! She was in a broad oval formed by high walls of rock. Those two trees she'd sat between up there were like sentries standing guard on top of this wall here. The other walls around here sloped, too, but more steeply than hers. So she was lucky to have tumbled down the wall she'd tumbled down.

Bordering the walls was a lot of brush interspersed with trees. The trees struck her as funny. They looked exactly like the trees up top, except stunted in growth. Like only man-height or a little more. The lack of sunlight, she thought. They couldn't grow tall.

A small leaping creek with pretty white crests flowed straight down the middle of this oval. And though it was like dusk down here, it didn't look gloomy to Melissa. It looked...beautiful. Like peace itself.

She had no fear. Her only thought was, I thought I had found a magical place just up there. But this is even better. *This* was hers!

Melissa brushed herself off and picked up her daypack, and in straightening back up, she noticed how odd the trunks of the two trees directly in front of her looked. There was something almost hairy about them, and as her gaze continued upward toward the tops of these trees, she gasped. These weren't trees at all!

"Derrick! Oh, my god, you scared me!" she said.

Derrick didn't say anything, just stood there holding a branch with berries on it. He looked stunned, and scared himself. "Sorry if I scared *you*," Melissa said, "but isn't this place awesome? How'd you guys know about it?"

She took a seat on a pretty black boulder just to her left. "I didn't know you were filming today. Where's Peter? Peter!" she called.

Derrick dropped the branch and covering his ears, backed away from Melissa. He made a snort.

Melissa laughed. "Oh, stop it." And now she took a closer look at Derrick. "Hey, when you'd guys make another costume? I don't like this one. It's not as realistic." She unzipped her backpack and took out her water bottle. She took a sip and extended it toward Derrick. "Want some?"

Derrick sniffed at the water.

Melissa shook her head. "You've been hanging around Peter too long. All this 'stay in character business.' I know he told everyone that. Like he's all Mrs. DuMonde. She says that. Chrissy told me. Well, it's annoying, Derrick. Sorry, but it is." Melissa rummaged around in her backpack. "Want an apple? I've got gum."

She unwrapped a stick of gum and stuck it in her mouth, then tossed the apple to Derrick, who caught it. Sniffed it. Then popped it into his mouth.

"Whoa..." said Melissa, impressed by that. "Okay, watch *this*." She worked the gum around in her mouth for a few seconds, Derrick watching her, and then blew a big bubble.

Derrick's eyes widened, and then the bubble went pop, and he backed up even farther away from Melissa, making what sounded to her like a bird call. Melissa giggled, getting all the gum off her face and from the few hairs it had stuck to, and she heard a rustling and a faint crunch of pine needles from somewhere behind her, and turning, she was about to greet Peter and whoever else was here—she liked Coach Mayhugh, even though her mom didn't, so she was hoping he was here—and she saw a half-dozen more guys dressed like Derrick approaching, but not saying anything to her, and in fact only glancing at her as they hurried over to Derrick.

They made a protective semi-circle around him, their back to Melissa, as if making one big shield against her.

"Okay, you guys," Melissa said, "you're creeping me out. Peter!" she yelled, at which point all these other guys and Derrick put their hands over their ears, snorting, like they didn't like such loud noise at all.

"Stop it, you guys!" said Melissa. "It's not funny!" And since she'd yelled *funny*, too, Derrick and the others began making a lot of bird calls at the same time, but like the kind you hear when a bird is distressed—like when a mockingbird screams at a crow or hawk when one of those predators gets too close to the nest.

"Stop it!" she screamed, whereupon one of the guys, still holding his ears, bounded over a huge boulder twenty feet away. Not bounded over *to* it. Bounded *over* it. From twenty feet away.

Melissa screamed, and the other creatures bounded away, too, and she turned and ran for her life. She had no direction in mind except *away*, but saw where a rock fall had made a natural series of steps up the sheer side of a wall.

She scrambled up the rock-steps, fear making her more agile than usual, which was good, because she was crying, and it was hard for her to see where to put her hands and feet, because her vision was blurry, and she was afraid to take even a moment to wipe her eyes.

She reached the top of the wall, gasping up air, looked around for the curtain of sunlight, saw it, and raced toward it, every second wondering if one of those creatures was right behind her and going to grab her and kill her.

Chapter Twenty-Eight

*E*ARLIER IN THE DAY, WHILE MELISSA WAS ONLY *considering* whether she should go all the way to Carson Bridge, and how far she should go in fibbing to her mother if she started asking a lot of questions, like, 'Where are you going?,' Shirley, Skeet, and Larry were sitting down for a breakfast meeting at Merle's with the builders of the motel and a man I never met, who was some kind of inspector all the way from Cascade City. Annie was running late, but said to please get started—she'd be there in twenty minutes. And she was.

They were all gathered to resolve certain issues that had cropped up. They were all minor issues, but they *were* several, and were impeding progress. One of the issues was parking.

Everyone at the table knew that Alpine Valley would have to close certain streets to the public, here and there, and at various times, to accommodate the parking needs of all the earth-moving equipment and trucks necessary for building the motel. On the other hand, they all knew that they had to be careful about what and how many streets were closed, and when, and for how long. The town couldn't afford to make their visitors' visits unpleasant. They didn't want them circling forever looking for parking, or parking illegally, which was happening more and more. So, it's a balancing act, Annie reminded everyone. How do we give the construction crews everything they need without impacting upon the town's visitors too noticeably? In other words, how do we balance the needs of the future with those of the present?

Annie knew as she said them that her last words probably made her sound pompous and hi-falutin' to the inspector and these builders...this little mayor (*part*-time mayor!) from Nowheresville, talking this way about one little ol' motel! 'Needs of the future...' For goodness *sake*, what did she think she was building here, a medical center, a *college*? 'Needs of the future...' It was a *motel*! But Annie noted that they were smiling pleasantly at her, with nothing in their eyes to indicate that they were thinking what she was *thinking* they were thinking. Still, these guys had come off really big projects lately, so they had to be laughing at her a *little*.

But you know what, she then thought, who cares? This motel *is* our future. It's important to *us*. It's vital to *us*, if we're to derive the income we need for our straight road...So Annie doubled-down, as they say, thinking, all right, if they want to think I'm pompous, let them think so, and she continued in her grand vein and said, "All you gentlemen *do* understand this, yes?" (Oh my god, thought Annie, that came out far worse than I had wanted it to! There was pompous-sounding, and then...that!)

They nodded or said of course, still smiling pleasantly at her; and what Annie never knew is that neither the inspector nor the builders thought anything of the kind that she was pompous. The inspector actually liked her line and thought he'd use it himself from now on, and of the three builders present, one wasn't actually listening to her as she spoke, but was thinking where was that waiter with the coffee? He wanted a re-fill, and he was getting annoyed; while the second was thinking about getting a couple of those pies he saw at that booth to bring home to his kids; and the third wondered if Annie had a boyfriend, because, boy, he sure would like to ask her out. A little on the skinny side for him, but sure pretty—and he liked her gumption.

(If you're wondering how I know all this, let's just say that over the years, I've learned to be a pretty obsessive researcher and question asker. Like a mosaic, the truth of a story is built bit by beautiful bit.)

And in case you're wondering, the builder never did ask her out. He saw her coming out of Merle's one afternoon, a bag of groceries in her hand, and two kids hurried up to her, and she kissed them both on their heads, and that just turned the builder off. Kids. He was a very nice man, and an excellent builder. But getting involved with a woman with kids? No way, he thought. You gotta be an idiot.

Even though breakfast was only halfway over, and there were still more issues to discuss, Annie decided to leave the meeting. She didn't see why Shirley couldn't handle the rest of things. She was almost a one-woman show with this motel, anyway—and Annie had thought it might be a good idea to spend the day with Melissa.

As Annie had raced out of the house, late for this meeting, she had asked Melissa what she was going to do today, and Melissa didn't have much planned. Just some reading. So today, *now*, was a perfect opportunity to spend some (and she hated to use the phrase, but she did) *quality time* with her daughter.

To put it bluntly, Annie was feeling neglectful. She'd been spending too much time on too many other things, and what made her feel that she *could* was that Melissa was resourceful, and a strong, independent little character. But she still needed her mother, didn't she? And why should she be denied—even punished—because she was an independent little character?

Anyway, this is how Annie felt, so she thanked everyone for their time—just *knew* everything was going to be *wonderful*—and asked Shirley to please carry on in her stead (and she loved it how Shirley just glowed when she said that, making her think, I'd like to put Shirley up for mayor next term...oh, wait...Walter...would she have the time...?) and she walked away from the table, and watching her go, the builder who never did ask her out, told himself, oh, yeah, *definitely* have to ask this woman out.

Annie went home—and was sorely disappointed to find Mel

gone. And who knew where she'd be? Melissa could squirrel herself away with her books anywhere—and she wasn't in the square. Annie had looked for her there as she passed.

"Well, Muffin," Annie said, "I guess it's you and me, kid. Want to go for a...*walk!*"

The magic word. Muffin went happily bonkers.

In the meantime, the breakfast meeting went on. And on. Everyone got stuck on a minor point (and no one ever remembered what it was), and though everyone kept calm, it was vexing. They all ordered lunch, and it was Claude who saved the day, because his food was so delicious, and his home-made peach ice-cream so delicious, that it put everyone in a happy and even generous frame of mind, so that those who were stubbornly sticking to a point gave a little, and that encouraged the others to do the same.

And finally, when the meeting broke up, Shirley, Skeet, and Larry were standing together out in front of Merle's having a little *well, how do you think that all went* meeting, and they heard someone yelling—screaming?—behind them.

It was Melissa, pedaling into Main Street like she was being chased. Whatever she was yelling, it got everyone's attention. The diners at Merle's stood up from their tables to see what was going on, and tourists all around stopped and looked, and Melissa raced past Shirley, Skeet, and Larry without even seeing them.

"He's real!" Melissa screamed to no one, everyone. "They're real! I saw them!"

"Now see," said Larry when she'd passed. "*that's* good. Why can't *I* do that? You almost believe her."

Melissa was off her bike almost before it stopped and raced, half-stumbling, toward the front door, and through. "Mom! Mom!" she cried.

Annie heard the terror in her child's voice and came rushing in from her bedroom. "What's the matter? What's the matter?"

Melissa rushed to her mother and held on to her for dear life, sobbing. "Mom, I saw them! They're real! They're real!"

"What is? Who is?"

"The apes! They're real! There's *lots* of them."

"Mel. Honey. Calm down. What are you talking about? What happened?"

"They're real! And they're not like anybody said. They're afraid of bubble gum!"

"Honey, shh...shh..." Annie said. "You're soaking." She felt Melissa's brow. "You have a fever."

"They go like this," Mel said, and she tried to imitate the bird call sound the apes had made.

Concern—but not yet alarm—spread across Annie's face. "Okay, I need to get you into a cold bath. Come." And Annie seized Melissa's hand and hurried her up the hall toward the bathroom.

"No, Mom, I'm *fine*," Melissa protested, "I've been riding. Let me just *tell* you!"

But Annie wasn't listening. She had a fever to bring down, and if some Advil and a cold bath didn't do it, it'd be right over to Sam's house. Peter had sometimes hallucinated like this when he had a fever. Twice, Annie recalled. He'd seen things not there twice, and both times ended up okay.

After the bath, Melissa sat at the kitchen table with her mother. Her temperature was normal, and Annie felt some relief about that, but her little girl was still saying the most outlandish things. She wasn't speaking feverishly, or as if from out of a hallucination. She was calm. But all this about *falling*...and finding these creatures who did and *didn't* look like apes...and bubble gum...and bird calls...and leaping like no human could...all this had Annie close to tears herself. What was wrong with her little girl? What had happened to her today?

Melissa sat in her bathrobe, her still-wet hair plastered to her head, and she looked fine. She looked as normal as the things out of her mouth were *abnormal*. "So see?" she said—and because Annie was busy with her worry, she hadn't heard what she was supposed to *see*. "You've got to *tell* people, Mom!"

"Uh-huh...uh-huh," Annie said, trying to keep her daughter calm—and herself calm. Oh, dear God, she thought. This is what you get when you neglect your child! I haven't been paying attention, and now she's screaming for it. Sarah was right—about what Melissa's stories were really saying! Why didn't I listen to Sarah?!

"Mom!" Melissa said, ready to explode from frustration.

"Mel. Honey," Annie said, stroking her head. "Listen. Are you angry with me? Is this about your dad?"

"Dad?" said Melissa, confused. How could her mom think that her dad had anything to do with this? And so she said, "This has nothing to do with Dad! I saw the apes! The apes of Alpine Valley!"

Annie could take no more. Tears sprang to her eyes and she lurched forward in her chair and gripped Melissa's hands—hard. "Oh, *honey*..." she cried. "I'm so sorry!"

Melissa jerked her hands free, angry now. "Mom! Please!"

"It's my fault," Annie said through her tears. "I'm sorry. I should have...we never *talked* about it."

Melissa was crying herself now, but her tears were from frustration. "Please. *Please!*"

"We're going to go see Dr. Cabot. We're going to talk. You, me, Peter. Oh, honey, I'm so sorry. So sorry. I handled everything all wrong!" Annie suddenly hugged her daughter, as much to comfort as to be comforted; and as she held on to her mother, it occurred to Melissa that she was *never* going to get her mother to see things by just sitting here and insisting on them. So she changed tactics.

She withdrew from her mother's hug, and sitting back, wiping her tears, she said, "All right. We'll go see him. Sure. Good idea. But look, just come with me to see them. And if they're not there, you can ground me for a year. I promise. *A whole year.*"

"Melissa."

"And no desserts or...anything you *want*! Mom, would I make such a deal if I hadn't really seen them with my own eyes? And they weren't bears! So please don't even say that! Please. One little hike. Not even far. I *promise.*"

Annie looked at her daughter and had no idea what to say. She wanted to take Melissa right now to see Dr. Cabot. But while she loved Sam, he was scary-looking to Melissa—those big glasses and eyes—that face. And it would be so...*intense* for her, right?, to have this man ask her questions that basically were intended to see if she was right in the head. Melissa would get what was going on. *Mom thinks I'm crazy.* Did she want that thought in her daughter's head; or for her daughter to have to entertain it as a possibility that she *was*?

And maybe Melissa is *fine*, Annie thought, but she's twelve, and saw something confusing, or no—something that *traumatized* her. Maybe *that's* it, thought Annie. She saw something she couldn't process...something twelve-year-old girls shouldn't see... maybe some tourist or tourists doing something *awful*...and she made monsters out of it...something like that?...

And, Annie thought, if she herself saw what it was, or could understand better what it might have been, then that'd help. She could tell Sam about it. So, yes, in fact, seeing what Melissa saw was the proper thing to do here. "Okay," Annie said. "One little hike."

"Okay. Good. You'll *see*," Melissa said, and she quickly got up from the chair. She'd pressed her advantage, but worried about pressing her luck, so as she hurried up the hall and away, she said, "But we'd better not go alone. There are lots of them. Get Officer Larry to come."

"Melissa," her mother said, "nobody else needs to know— ."

"Mom!" Melissa stopped, turned, and actually stamped her foot. She hadn't done that in forever. "Get Officer Larry. He needs to bring his gun."

Chapter Twenty-Nine

*W*ELL, ANNIE KNEW LARRY SALISBURY WAS NOT GOING to go off on some wild goose chase and tromp around Miller Mountain. But now Annie was a little scared herself. Something more than pure invention was going on—right? There'd been *something* traumatizing—right? But whatever it was, the bottom line was that Annie was afraid to go up that trail with her daughter alone. What if there were horrible people up there doing horrible things—like a group of Satanists, maybe, conducting some frightening ritual? So, yes, she *did* want a man to come with them. Someone pretty physically reliant, and that meant...oh, hell... thought Annie...

And now here came Preston down the slope toward Carson Bridge. A road ran along and above the river, and Preston had driven here and parked on the shoulder.

Annie and Melissa had ridden bikes here and had arrived a good fifteen to twenty minutes earlier—and that was by plan. Annie's first thought had been to drive here, the drive being no more than twenty minutes. But her second thought, the one she'd gone with, was that maybe a good long bike ride with her daughter was a good thing. They'd have some alone-time together—quality time—and they'd chat, and the lovely space all around them, and the peace of the ride, would give Melissa all kinds of opportunity to change anything about her story that maybe she'd want to change...And if that were the case, then Annie would call Preston and tell him, thanks, but he needn't come: We've got things sorted out...

But Melissa *hadn't* changed her story, and was quite anxious to get going. Where *is* he? She kept asking. And finally, there he was, Coach Mayhugh coming down the slope through waist-high grass, looking at Annie and Melissa standing by the bridge and watching him approach.

"Mel," Preston said to Melissa as he came up to them. "Madam Mayor," he said, turning to Annie, and brushing off his pants, though they really didn't need brushing.

"Mr. Mayhugh," she said, examining something on her forearm that wasn't really there, and brushing it off.

"Ready?" Melissa asked. She shifted her daypack on her shoulder. Almost as if that was their cue to the do same, Annie and Preston shifted theirs, too. Of course, it also gave the two of them something to do, to focus on, rather than just stand there, looking uncomfortable and not at each other.

"Quite a load," Preston said to Melissa, noting how hard it was for her to shift that pack. "Need help?"

"No, thank you," Melissa said. "It's just apples. They like apples." She took a step forward, but then stopped and turned around. "But they *don't* like loud noises. So they'll run and hide if you make loud noises." Melissa turned and continued forward.

Preston and Annie couldn't help sharing a look over this... unusual information; and as they were about to follow Melissa, Annie said, "Thank you for coming."

Preston shrugged. "I haven't hiked here in ages. It was a good opportunity for me. Get off my duff."

"I hope I, we, can count on your...I mean..."

"Discretion?" Preston shrugged. "I went for a little hike today. Just fell in with you. That's all that went on here today." Preston smiled.

"I'm *sorry*," Melissa called from the bridge, "but can we *go*? It's late enough. And you brought a gun, right? Just in case?"

Preston couldn't help but glance at Annie, who glanced at him, and whose face showed...what was that? Appeal? There was pain in the face—a mother's pain—but there was appeal, too. *You see how things are. Please don't judge us.* Well, Preston would do better than simply not judge. He'd help. "Well, no," he called to Melissa. "I didn't bring my gun. But I've got my Chinese fighting stars. I thought that'd be better. I'm more accurate with them."

Melissa studied Preston to see if he were joking.

Preston looked back at her, deadly serious.

"Okay," Melissa said, satisfied, and she turned and continued up the bridge.

Annie exhaled slowly and gave Preston a tentative even close to warm smile.

They followed Melissa across the bridge.

When they were about an hour up the trail, they heard the crack of a rifle in the distance. Annie flinched.

"Probably Rawley Conner out hunting," Preston said. "Not that he hits much."

"It's not deer season," Annie said.

"Rawley doesn't pay much attention to calendars."

It's idiots like Rawley Connor, Annie thought, guys who don't follow the rules, who will make it hard for hunters to come here—not that Annie herself particularly liked hunting, but hunters brought income into the town. But Rawley and his ilk shot at anything and everything all year long. *Bang! Bang! Bang!*

Hey, Annie thought, maybe *that's* what Melissa was reacting to; maybe *that's* what she was—what was the word?—*internalizing*. *She* didn't like the loud noises she had heard—Rawley up here, firing away; or all the noises in town—the jackhammers—the *change* it all means. Maybe *she* was the creature she saw. Oh, my god, Annie thought, maybe my daughter didn't feel *real*, because I've not even been noticing her! Annie's heart began to pump hard.

They went on; and after another hour and a half up the mountain, Annie began to wonder what made her daughter want to climb so high. She had told her that she had wanted to get away from everything—and the way she had said *everything* made Annie feel that *she* was a part of that everything. She and Melissa's dad. And to come so far—out to Carson Bridge!—and then up so high! Yes, that was getting away from everything, all right.

Annie looked at Melissa now, up ahead, her stride quick and purposeful. Annie bet that it was the same stride she had up this trail yesterday. But now Melissa wanted to get *to* something. Yesterday it was all about getting *away*. I didn't drive her up a wall, thought Annie, but worse, right up a mountain!

Annie stopped for a moment to look down into the valley, and around. What were they doing up here? There was nothing to see up here. Was Melissa punishing me?, Annie wondered. Is *that* what this is? Poor Mayhugh—caught up in this...charade.

"Here we are!" cried Melissa. Annie looked up. Melissa stood just above her, Preston now coming up to her. The trail made its switchback just ahead of Annie, and though the switchback, Annie saw, climbed, it didn't do so steeply, and Annie could tell a broad flat area, in fact, a plateau must be behind Melissa, because she lost sight of the mountain face here. It must be recessed, stepped back. This plateau cut into it. Annie hiked to the end of the trail segment and took the turn and headed toward Melissa and Preston.

The plateau was tree choked, she noticed. It ran for at least half a mile. Wow. That was some plateau, Annie thought. The last time she'd hiked Miller Mountain she was a girl—Melissa's age, in fact. But had her dad taken her up this far? Probably not.

Barely waiting for her mother, Melissa went off trail and into the woods. Preston waited for Annie to reach him, and then the two of them followed Melissa.

They heard the stream. They came to the first, small cataract, made the sideways step down, went to the stream and gazed at it for awhile. Then Melissa led them to the rock-bench and stood up on it and pointed down.

Annie and Preston stepped up on to the bench and joined her in looking down.

"So beautiful," said Annie. "It's like looking down into a separate, private forest."

"That's where I saw them," Melissa said. "C'mon."

She led them to the rock slide, told them to be careful, and all three made their way to the bottom.

Upon reaching it, first, Melissa looked up at Preston, just coming down, and said, "You might want to get your fighting stars ready."

"All right," Preston said, and he took off his daypack and unzipped it. He put his hand into it. "I don't want to take them out," he said. "The glint off the steel. We don't want them reacting to it."

Melissa thought this was a good idea. "Look for tracks," she said as her mother came up to her.

The three looked around for tracks, and for several minutes, Annie wondering why she was actually looking for tracks, and not merely pretending to do so. It looked to her like Preston was actually looking for tracks, too. But was he playacting? Maybe not. Didn't someone tell her not too long ago (was it Larry?) that Preston had believed in all those old tales of the Alpine Valley Ape? Yes, it *was* Larry. He had told Annie, "As kids, you could tell that Preston wanted those stories to be true. *I* never did. That old Ape scared the dickens out of me."

Annie looked over at Melissa. She was standing stock still, frowning at the ground.

"Deer tracks," said Melissa. "Nothing but deer tracks. Or mine." She looked over at Preston, questioningly. He nodded confirmation—that's all he was seeing, too.

"But they were *here*!" said Melissa. "The first one right where I'm standing! Okay, let's fan out a bit. Hello?!" she called. "Hello! I've got apples!" She hurriedly took off her daypack, unzipped it, and took out two apples. She held them up, for the creatures to see. "See? Apples!"

Annie and Preston shared a look. It said, *How much should we encourage this?*

Melissa darted worried eyes at them. "There are too many of us," she said. "They're scared." Then, "Apples!" she cried again, and tossed one into the brush bordering the wall, and then rolled one along the ground, hard, so that it rolled almost all the way to the other side of the oval. Even *she* wasn't sure what she thought that might accomplish, except maybe one of the creatures would bound into view and snatch that apple up. It could happen. She'd seen them bound.

Melissa took out three more apples. "Apples! *Apples!*" she cried, holding them over her head. She hurried this way and that, crying "Apples!" and now that way and this, crying "Apples!", and now, seeing her mom and Coach Mayhugh looking at her so strangely, so sadly, she felt tears of frustration welling up in her eyes. "*Apples!*" she cried.

"Mel. Honey," Annie said, seeing her daughter in distress.

"No!" Melissa said. "They're here! Apples!" Then, a sob escaped her. "Please..."

"Mel, honey," Annie said again, hurrying up to her, and giving her a hug.

"Come *on!*" Mel cried, in her mother's embrace, but looking outward, everywhere. "Please. You like these!"

Preston watched mother and daughter and wished like crazy he could be of use; he liked being of use. But what to do?

He wondered what might be going on in Melissa's mind that while she feared whatever it was she had thought she'd seen—or she wouldn't have asked him to bring a gun—she thought, too, that she had the power to placate it—with apples.

Whatever was going on between her ears—it was powerful. She really did look like she'd seen something. But there were no tracks here, other than deer tracks. So. Had she seen deer—maybe a malformed deer? It was spring, so maybe a rutting stag had charged her? It was possible. He and Larry had once made a turn in the forest and had come upon the remarkable and mostly silent scene of an angry stag reared up on its hind legs, snorting and clacking its big teeth, eyes all crazy, and using its hooves to try to cut the hunter before him to ribbons. How easily might a twelve-year-old girl turn that into a monster? He knew from around town that Melissa LaPeer had an active imagination. Maybe it was a *couple* of stags who had frightened her. But maybe that's why she thought she could tame the beasts, because somehow, she still knew they were only stags—*deer*, for god's sake, and so she shouldn't be afraid.

Still, Preston's thinking, his theorizing, sounded neat and tidy; reasonable. And one thing he had come to know. Life wasn't reasonable.

Chapter Thirty

$\mathcal{T}$HE SUN WAS LOWERING BY THE TIME THE THREE OF them got to the part of the trail where they could see the river and Carson bridge in the distance.

"Look," said Preston, "there's some good news." He pointed in a direction between the town and the rest of the valley, where it was flat, like the bottom of a bowl.

At any other time of day, Preston could not have seen what he was seeing from this distance, but now, the lowering sun was at a perfect angle to light up all he saw. It was as if the sun existed only to be a spotlight for that scene.

Where trees had been only a few days before, there was now a sizable clearing. Melissa didn't remember seeing any clearing yesterday on her way up (and certainly she wouldn't have noted it on her panicked way down), but there it was.

The three of them watched a bulldozer backing up in the clearing, and, after making mechanical snorts, charge at a half-uprooted tree stump. The blades of the bulldozer's shovel slipped under the stump, cutting it away from its roots, the shovel part itself banging into the stump and sending it end over end like a wind-blown leaf, like something that had never had mighty presence or anchorage in the earth.

"What are they doing?" Melissa asked her mother.

"The road to Taylorville. The state floated us a loan. Remember my friend Trevor? Trevor Westley?"

"No. Kind of."

"He was here. We got the money. And that, my sweet girl, is the beginning."

"But, it's going to go through the woods."

"Well, it's all woods, honey."

"But, like, *our* woods."

Annie gave her a smile. "It'll still be our woods. Made better with a road."

For a reason Melissa couldn't explain, she couldn't share her mom's enthusiasm. She just said, "Okay."

Chapter Thirty-One

PRESTON HAD OFFERED TO DRIVE THEM HOME. ANNIE had accepted. She and Melissa were exhausted, both physically and emotionally, so a long bike ride home...well, she just couldn't imagine it. So Preston loaded up their bikes in the back of his truck, U-turned off the shoulder, and headed for Annie's house.

It wasn't late—not even seven—by the time they came through Annie's door, but Melissa was sound asleep, Preston carrying her. Annie had tried to rouse her in Preston's truck, but nothing doing.

Annie wondered later if Melissa had known what she was doing and *wanted* Preston to carry her in. Her daughter was smart, but Annie had never thought of her as either shrewd or manipulative. Of course, she might have only been half-aware of what she was doing—or not aware at all, and was just dead-tired. Either way that it was, thought Annie, by pretext or happenstance, Preston's carrying Melissa into the house gave the adults an opportunity to talk; to have a real conversation for the first time.

"Are we home?" Melissa asked, her eyes fluttering open, but they sometimes did that, anyway, so maybe she wasn't being dramatic, thought Annie.

"Yes," Annie said.

Preston put Melissa down.

"Honey, you want to crash? I'd like you to get a bath first."

"No, it's okay. I'm not that dirty. I just want to go to sleep."

Annie didn't have left whatever it was she needed to insist her daughter get a bath. The day had worn her down to a nub.

Melissa disappeared down the hall and went into her room. Turning around from watching her go, Annie noticed a note on the dining room table.

"Your friend Peter," Annie said, reading the note in her hands. "He's out with Derrick Merrick and a bunch of your athletic types."

"Good," said Preston. "I mean...good?"

Annie frowned, putting the note down. This was a good question. "I...Yes. I guess," she said.

"Well. Okay," said Preston, making a move to leave. "This was..." An interesting day, he was about to add. But he changed course and said. "Listen. You feel how you feel about me, I understand. But if I can be of any help here." He shrugged. How could *he* be of help? "It's just that, there's some kind of challenge here. With Mel."

Annie nodded. "I'm going to take her to see Sam Cabot. I mean, I don't think I'm over-reacting. Right? I mean, you were there. You saw."

Preston nodded. "No, it's a good call. *I* would."

Now, while Preston and Annie were having this conversation, Melissa was listening, PJ's in hand. Either the little walk down the hall had roused her sufficiently, or she really *had* manipulated the adults into the house. But either way, she was wide awake now, listening at the door, and *not* hearing the kind of thing she'd been *hoping* to hear in a conversation between her mom and Coach Mayhugh. Whom she *liked*. And whom she was hoping her *mom* would like. Her face grew cloudy. How could her mom not believe her? Her *mom*!

Yes, that she saw the apes was...hard to believe. And yes (it just came to Melissa *right this instant*) she *did* write off-the-wall, hard-to-believe stories, so, okay, her mother might think she was inventing all this. But Dr. Cabot? She *hated* Dr. Cabot! And now

Coach Mayhugh thinks there's something wrong with her, too? Or, wait...does he think she's *lying*? That she's a *liar*? Is that what's going on? I'm either crazy or lying? I know what I saw! I know it!

Or did I dream it? It scared Melissa, this sudden thought. She *didn't*, did she? She really *did* see it, right? I mean, her mom and Coach were *wrong*, right? But...where were the tracks?

"It's just that I didn't think," Annie was saying, "that Mel had taken it so hard. Her dad leaving. I mean, he was such a...jerk. Never paid her any attention."

"Uh-huh," said Preston, wondering what he should say. "But. First of all, she *is* a strong little girl. But stuff she's thinking about? These...worries? Maybe she's turned them into monsters."

Annie glanced up at him. That wasn't half-bad, that thought. She had entertained all sorts of thoughts like that while on the trail. "But what *are* the worries?" she asked. "Because this is incredible stuff she's making up."

Listening at her door, Melissa's face grew red.

"I mean, doesn't she know she's loved? That I love her more than my own life? And that she's...protected. But maybe she feels like she isn't? That I can't protect her? What if that's it—that she doesn't trust me as a mother?" Annie felt herself tearing up at this—but no! None of this in front of Mayhugh! But she had to sniff back her tears.

Melissa heard her do it, and knew what it meant. She'd heard her mother sniff back tears *every* time Dad had hit her and told her she'd better not cry because it would upset the kids, and now Melissa wasn't angry, but wanted to run comfort her mother, and tell her it was all *right*, that I was *fine*, that this had nothing to *do* with her! How could it? The apes were *real*! Then her dad's voice barged into her head loudly, saying, *You can't do a damn thing right, Annie! You're stupid and useless!* And then, insight striking her with all the light and pain of a lightning bolt, Melissa thought, Oh, my god, did Mom go around all the time thinking she *was*?

She crumpled to the floor. Sickened by the thought, hurting

from it, she opened her mouth to call for her mother—then abruptly closed it. She wasn't sure why. But Coach was nice to Mom; and was being nice to her; and *he* didn't think she was stupid. But the hurt, the thought, what her dad did…it was all too much, so she put her hands over her ears and keeping her voice low, said, *La, la, la, la, la, la,* but she wanted to hear her mother's voice—*that* would help—and anyway, what *else* was her mother saying? She hurried back to the door. But she wanted to give her mother a hug and tell her *nothing* was her fault—don't *worry*—because I'm *fine*! But would her mother believe it? No! And then it came to her in a rush: but she *would* believe it, if Melissa could prove to her that she really saw those apes! Then Mom would see that she hadn't done anything wrong!

But what if she *had* dreamed them up? Because, well, there were no tracks. What if she'd been reading and fell asleep and, like Alice in Wonderland, only dreamed her strange encounter?

In the meantime, Preston stood there watching Annie fighting her emotion. Was he supposed to do something here? Put a hand on her shoulder? Too risky. She might recoil. She wouldn't slap him again, would she? No. The vibe wasn't there for that, Preston thought. Why was he always just standing there, when he was with this woman, wondering what to do? And he didn't want to say anything stupid in an effort to be comforting, like, *I'm sure Melissa feels protected.* Because maybe she didn't. How would Preston know?

But he decided he should say *something.* So he said, "You know. Divorce. I've never been married, so how can I say? But it's, it's a lot of bad; all kinds of bad coming at you all at once, from all directions. Hard to know what to feel, or think, or how to behave. With your kids. With others. Yourself. And, I mean, the problem is, you can't *practice* for it. You know? It's a challenge, and yet you can't practice for it. It's one of the hardest things in life to deal with, but you're not prepared. You have no game plan. You aren't sure what to do—what you *can* do—what you *should* do. And people are running all kinds of plays on you, and *trick* plays you've never seen before, and you have no defense for them. And you get run over, and..." Preston trailed off. Enough with the football analogy, he thought. Probably made him sound trite. Cliched.

But Annie looked up at him. There was gratitude—very plainly—in her eyes. "That's...you're right about that. You can't practice. For divorce. And you feel so guilty because you've got kids, and it's something you *want* to do—to get *out*—but what about your kids? Is that good for the kids? So you take it *one* more day, and *one* more day..."

"Until you realize that a mother who's been beaten to a pulp is worse for her kids. So *that'll* help you do the right thing." Preston wondered how he knew this, and wondered if it were even true. It sounded good. But lots of things sounded good.

Annie wondered how Preston might know that her husband used to hit her. Never in front of the kids—she had to give him credit for that, at least. What did people in town know? When they looked at her, what were they seeing? But no, Annie could see that Preston was only saying 'beaten to a pulp' as a metaphor. He didn't know about the hitting. And the pushing down.

But Melissa, still listening, knew about the hitting and the pushing down. But she'd never *said* anything, she hadn't been *brave* enough, and she never knew what to *do!* And her mom had *endured* all that for her and Peter?; had kept trying to keep the family together for *them*, when it hurt, hurt her so much? *Oh, Mommy!* She almost sobbed it out loud, and she *did* cry, and again she wanted to run and hug her, but she wasn't supposed to be listening, so she just ran to her bed, got under the covers and pulled them up over her head, and, as they say in stories, but as she did in truth, she cried herself to sleep.

But back to the adults...

"Yes...yes..." Annie said musingly. "It will—help you do the right thing." He was right. She'd been beaten to a pulp—mentally, emotionally. Dave had made her feel small. Like it didn't matter what she thought, or what she might want.

"Well, look," said Preston, "I guess I'd better— ."

"Would you like a beer or something, before you go? You must be thirsty. I am. Quite thirsty." Annie had no idea why she said that.

"Well. Okay. Sure," said Preston.

"Have a seat," Annie said. "Let's see what we've got."

Chapter Thirty-Two

*T*HIS IS A PARTICULARLY IMPORTANT CHAPTER BECAUSE particularly important things happen in it, and I'm a little fearful that I won't be able to get these things across to you as well as I really must. For one thing, there's my skill as a writer. Can I figure out what to say, and what to leave out, and *how* to say what's important to say, and *when* to say it—so you understand what went on—and why?

I guess you could say I've done enough writing in my life, but nothing like this, nothing so important as this, so I'm not as confident as I otherwise might be about getting you to really *understand* all that occurred on that particular Saturday that is the subject of this chapter.

In addition to worrying about my writing skills, I also worry about my editing skills, that is, my *selecting* skills. More than any other chapter—*including* the still more dramatic ones to come (though after reading *this* chapter, you might wonder, Wow, how much more dramatic can things *get*? Well, just wait. You'll see) — *this* is the chapter for which I have the most interview notes and interview audio.

I have so many old dusty and now browning legal pads, the ink on them fading into oblivion; and so much audio on several of the old media; and so many ancient flash drives filled with so many transcripts from interviews with those people who were a part of the events of that Saturday (or who were at least in town, and could give me second-hand information), that I get lost and overwhelmed.

It's *too* much material. *Too* much to sort through, and piece together, and there are *so* many conflicting stories and disagreements, that, though that's interesting in itself (that there should be so many different ideas as to what *actually happened* on this day), it's impossible for me, after all these years, to come to any single conclusion about the day; or feel confident that I've even got all the facts straight.

I do, however, promise you this: I've done the best I could in piecing together, from so many sources, the most important elements of the day; and I can vouch for the timeline being at least *close* to correct. And while I've had no choice but to here and there speculate on something that may have happened, or *probably* happened, please believe me that the speculation doesn't come out of thin air, but comes out of a solid matrix of reason, my personal knowledge of that person's character, and reference to a person's general pattern of behavior as known to the people of Alpine Valley.

Therefore, in sum, *how* a person might behave in a not altogether verifiable scene will not be uncharacteristic of how he or she *would* have behaved. The word I have in mind is 'essence.' In *essence*, everything in this chapter is true.

My hope is that by the end of this chapter, you will understand that there is only one way this story *should* reasonably end; only one way to *hope* it should reasonably end. And if you hope that, dear reader, then in the end, all will be well. Even if we can't get all our needs met, goals attained, or prayers answered, or can't prevent all manner of wolves and hours from dragging us away, *all will be well*.

Because a boy or girl or man or woman who can *hope* is a person with his substance intact, a person who has something to give to the future, even if it's no larger than the smallest act of kindness, or a smile for a person who could really use one, or an 'I love you,' when it hurts to breathe, let alone speak. Because small acts, like large, are notes in the song of eternity, and all notes, whether the softest, shortest, loudest, longest, are *necessary*, if the song is to be understood as beautiful. If the song is to *be* beautiful.

But anyway, I have decided that the recounting of this day should begin with Miss Dorothy. She is our clock, in truth, and she sews our town together—and that's less a pun than it is a metaphoric truth; and as she's our clock, and as this is a composition of many parts and rhythms as represented by many voices, then let's consider her a metronome—tick...tick...tick... and there she was, coming down Main Street, and Melissa would have been scrambling to get ready for school, except for the fact that it's a Saturday, and anyway, Melissa was up before dawn and already on the most important mission of her life...

Miss Dorothy wore her hat, and had her gloves in one hand, the purse in the crook of her arm, and it was, she thought, a *most* beautiful day; so who could complain that the sidewalks were, ironically, even worse than they were before, since now they were torn up; and in her path there were big piles of jackhammered concrete to sidestep, and places where they hadn't bothered to pile any of it up, so that big chunks lay strewn down big stretches of her path, and even halfway into the street. Progress, thought Miss Dorothy, can wear the face of destruction; and she liked this thought so well that she made a mental note to share it with Millicent and Gertrude later today, not that Gertrude would hear it: the poor dear was deaf as a post now, and Miss Dorothy didn't have the vocal strength any longer to yell. Well, she could write it down. That'd work. So long as Millicent had her glasses.

Now at this point, because orange-and-white-striped construction barriers, one after the other, after the other, angled in on her as she came up the sidewalk, Miss Dorothy was forced to get close, closer, closest to the storefronts, so that even she, of such narrow body, brushed the storefronts as she passed. She wondered what Larry or dear Ramona did when they had to come this way; probably had to forget the sidewalk altogether and walk in the street, which wasn't so great an idea any longer, what with all the *cars* these days. And now in front of her, just at the narrow gap between where Lydia's ended and Eddie's began, was a spot where the concrete had been broken up into four tall jagged slabs. Well now, what was she supposed to do? Those slabs came up to her knees! Miss Dorothy transferred her purse from the crook of her right arm to that of her left, so that she could take hold of the construction barrier, and she lifted her left knee, as high as she could...

Merle, who normally had a sixth sense and a keen eye when it came to Miss Dorothy's progress to his store, was rushing around, beads of sweat covering his face like a strange-looking veil (not that he was unhappy—business was great), because the café was *packed.*

Things had been *insane* since last Monday, when a couple who had paid Mitch Ferguson a thousand bucks to serve as their guide came back from their jaunt in the woods telling anyone and everyone—either in person, or all over the internet—that they had *seen* him!—and had snapped a *photo* of him!

They hadn't seen him, of course. They'd only snapped a picture of a small black bear, halfway up the gentle slope that bordered Barney Lake. But the bear had been standing, rubbing its back against a tree, and he was standing at such an angle that he looked a *little* like the Ape the town had created, and of course Mitch only encouraged these people in their need, and their picture went viral (as they used to say). And now people were standing in line at 5:30 a.m., waiting to get into Merle's Café, which opened at 6:00. The sooner out in the woods the better! So Merle didn't see Miss Dorothy. He didn't sense her.

And she, just across the street, did manage to raise her left knee high enough to get her leg over the slabs, but as she was bringing her right leg over, the toe of her right shoe caught on the tip-top of the tallest slab (leaving a small scrape of black shoe polish), and though she succeeded in getting that right leg over, the catch had made her lose her balance, and she tottered and fell into the dark narrow space between Lydia's and Eddie's.

If Merle had looked across the street; if *anybody* at Merle's had—catching something out of the corner of their eye—and had looked over, all they would have seen was a narrow black chasm between morning bright storefronts. They wouldn't have seen Miss Dorothy in it.

Breakfast went on. Excited chatter about the Ape went on.

In what I think must have been an hour before this, Melissa was making her way down the rock stairs to what she thought of as the secret forest. She had her mother's camera in hand. Her daypack was crammed full of small Fuji apples. Melissa had had difficulty zipping it up.

Reaching the floor of the forest, and keeping those stairs close behind her, she took off her daypack. She unzipped it and calling out "Apples!" began tossing several every which way, and as far as she could.

She waited.

Nothing. So she ventured a little bit farther away from the stairs, then a little bit more, collecting the apples she came across, until she found herself following the contour of the oval and pretty far from the stairs. Her eyes on the ground from time to time, she noted that still she saw no tracks. "Apples!" she called, and then, just to her right, in a gap in the brush, she saw a passageway that led out of this secret forest.

Should she take it? Her heart beat hard. No. She was suddenly afraid. She wanted to go home. But how *could* she? And look, she said to herself, they had run away from *me*. And they liked apples.

Clutching her daypack to her chest, camera still in hand, she went into and through the passageway.

She had walked maybe a quarter of a mile into this new, even secret-er wood—about as peaceful and twilit in appearance as the first, secret wood—when she thought she'd take a breather. She sat on a rock, thought about eating an apple, but didn't, just stared into space, and once again found herself staring at those same kinds of weird hairy tree trunks. She gasped, zipped her eyes upward—and saw two amber eyes blink from out of the darkness of trees.

She wanted to scream, was about to scream, but kept her lips pressed tight. She stood. Slowly, shakily. Slowly, shakily, she took off her pack, unzipped it—slowly—and reached into it for an apple. Withdrawing it, she held it up for the creature to see, then tossed it underhand in his direction.

A great hairy hand darted out of the dark and grabbed it.

"I won't hurt you, if you don't hurt me," Melissa said, or thought she'd said—she couldn't breathe. There was no response from the creature, and of course she really didn't expect there to be one. He probably didn't speak English. Then, she made a heave-ho motion with her pack, like flinging water from a bucket, and apples flew out and bouncing around settled into a big array on the ground between her and the creature. She went to stand behind her rock. Watching, waiting. She saw the amber eyes flick from the apples to her; from her to the apples.

Then the creature emerged from the dark.

The two gazed at each other for several long seconds.

Melissa was pretty sure that this was the same creature she'd seen first, the first time she'd come. There was a filled-in V of silver hair that ran from the top of his head down to the tip of his...would you call that a nose? It wasn't a snout. But it wasn't a nose, either. But anyway, there was that V, and none of the other creatures who had come that first time had had it, that she could remember. Maybe this one was older?

He sniffed at the apples. He took a step toward them.

Ready to run, Melissa picked up her camera from where she'd laid it on the rock. Hands shaking, she raised it to her eye. Now?

Shoot *now*? The sound of the camera shutter wouldn't be all that loud, but it was a strange sound—he wouldn't have heard it before. And worse, what about the flash? What would that do? But she had to get proof!

The creature squatted down and picked up an apple. He popped it into his mouth. He looked up, but not at Melissa, and made his weird bird-call noise, and from directly above him, two more of these creatures dropped to the ground.

Melissa gasped, looking at them, then looked up. It hadn't yet registered with her that, unlike with the forest in the oval, the trees *here* grew normally; grew tall; and that a thick canopy made a ceiling above her. These creatures had somehow descended from the canopy! Had they swung down? Jumped? However they had come, they had done so silently.

Melissa now noticed that these two newly arrived creatures each carried a bunch of branches in his arms. The slightest snap of a branch behind and above her made her turn and look up— and she gasped—as she saw two more creatures—or were they shadows?—racing across the ceiling made of intertwining boughs of trees. One shadow—it became creature as it sped downward— came by vine, the other had jumped. They, too, carried branches.

Vine?, Melissa thought. This wasn't a jungle. But there a vine was, swinging to and fro as the creature let go of it. (A much later, closer look, when the thought again crossed her mind, revealed that the vines these creatures employed had been *made*. These creatures had *skills*. And ingenuity—braiding the stringy material from different barks and plants into supple vines of great tensile strength.)

These four newly arriving apes joined the first in squatting down and eating the apples. The first one—bigger than these other four, and by a lot—made another bird call—a slightly different one, and from the same trees from which he had emerged came yet another creature—this one accompanied by a baby, holding its hand. Melissa knew in an instant that this creature was a female—and that this baby was her child. The female was smaller, slighter, than all of the others. So, the rest were males. She couldn't tell whether the baby was a boy or girl, but she thought of it as a little boy—something about him.

The female and the baby squatted next to the biggest ape. So. These three were together. They were a family. Keeping her eye on Melissa, the female reached out for an apple, sniffed it, then popped it into her mouth. Melissa saw now that these creatures did chew, but maybe only three or four times and quickly, before they swallowed.

What did these creatures resemble?, she wondered. They actually looked a little like the creature the town had come up with—ape-ish. But a little like a bear, too—a black bear. You really *could* think if you saw one of these creatures halfway up a hill near Barney Lake that you were only looking at a black bear. But there was something of the ape in their *faces*, and maybe not right then, but over time, Melissa simply began thinking the word 'ape' when she thought of these creatures. It wasn't accurate, but it was more accurate than 'bear', so that's the word she ended up using—ape.

Both fascinated and frightened, Melissa hadn't realized she had lowered her camera and was simply staring at these creatures as they ate the Fuji apples. She wanted to shoot them. Could she turn off the flash? Did she know how? Would the picture come out? She looked at the back of the camera to see how to disable the flash, and that's when she saw the baby pick up an apple—and he made a sudden leap toward her over the array of apples, landing within a foot of her rock. Melissa gasped. The baby extended the apple to her.

The little ape's mother made a call—it was angry—and was rising to leap for her baby when the big one—the daddy—made a single-note call that made the mother look at him. Something passed between the two, because the mother, though she rose, did not leap after her baby.

The baby took a step closer to Mel, still extending the apple to her. Melissa leaned over the rock, and she took the apple out of his hand. "Thank you," she said. The mother ape made a sound that Melissa thought very clearly meant, "That's enough." The baby didn't leap, but scampered back. On two legs. It dawned on Melissa that these apes got around on *two legs*, not four, like a bear; and she hadn't seen one of them leaning on his knuckles as he got around, the way a gorilla does.

She watched the apes eat a few more apples, and then, leaving only three or four apples behind, they got up as one and turned and walked away, back into the dark of the trees from which the first ape had come.

"Wait!" Melissa said—and it was funny how that one word came out, because when she started saying it, she was saying it very loudly, but within microseconds, she remembered how these apes hated loud noises, so her volume dropped to almost nothing, and the one-syllable word got turned into two: WAY.it.

Then, in as normal a speaking voice as she could muster, she said, "What about my picture? Hello?" It only dawned on her later how dumb that was to ask them about her picture—as if they'd understand, and with apologies, turn around and pose for a nice grinning family photo.

Forgetting her fear (though at this point there wasn't a lot left of it to remember), Melissa took off after the apes, camera in hand.

She entered the deep of the dark and found that, after only a thin margin of dark, created by a triple line of tall trees, everything gave way to a sunlit, thinly wooded expanse. But where were the apes? She couldn't see them anywhere. *Tracks*, she thought, follow their *tracks*! She looked at the ground. But she couldn't see any tracks. She looked left, right, ahead, behind. Nothing. Well, nothing but deer tracks. What was going *on*? Hurrying forward, she saw a tree ahead of her waver. But it wasn't a tree wavering, it was an ape bounding forward. Then another tree did the same; and another. Weird!

She stopped in her own tracks, raised her camera. She waited for the next waver she might see—and she took a picture. She wasn't sure what she'd gotten, but it was something.

Following the wavering apes, she found herself in what was more properly forest again.

How long had she been following them? She looked up and saw the sun through the boughs of tall trees. It was high in the sky, but not near its zenith. It was still before noon.

She had the distinct sense that the apes had been moving west and a bit south, in the direction of Alpine Valley. If, wherever they were going, lay in the southwest, she wouldn't be too many hours from home—and then, of great comfort to her, that distinctive rock she suddenly saw in the distance—which rock grew and grew, as if from the forest floor, as she and the apes neared it—was Big Rock. All she had to do was keep her eyes on it as she worked her way through the woods, and she'd be fine: She knew how to get home from Big Rock.

She was thinking these very thoughts (as she told her mother that night) when she spied the apes coming together in a quick bunch as they stopped behind a natural wall created by four or five fallen trees. They were watching something just over the top of it or through the various gaps.

Melissa thought she was far enough way that the sound of the shutter wouldn't alarm them—and the flash wouldn't go off in all this sunlight. She aimed the camera at them and took a dozen fast shots. She knew they wouldn't be great—it was just their backs—and they were still about thirty yards away. But again, it was something.

Melissa got closer to them, but couldn't see what they were looking at. It was apparent that whatever it was, they didn't like it. They were rapidly trading bird calls back and forth. Melissa identified scrub jay, robin, and seagull (for seagulls were ubiquitous in these parts, come in from the coast). Melissa crept up even more closely, and more closely, and now only about twenty feet from the tree wall, shaded her eyes and squinted through one of its gaps.

She saw an earth mover parked in a clearing—a different clearing from the one she'd seen last week. Melissa thought that the earth mover stood in the clearing like some monstrous, newly resident beast—or that's what she thought the apes might think of it. Somehow, from the way the apes were talking, and from the way the big one, whom she now spontaneously thought of as 'Big Daddy,' was making motions with one hand, Melissa got it that the earth mover stood between them and where they were trying to get to.

Then something strange: Melissa caught sight of something red and white flapping, off to the left of the earth mover. Melissa moved a little closer and to the right, so she could better see this flapping thing off to the left. It was a tablecloth. On a table. A long banquet table. There were four more tables just like it—and four people moving about, setting them. She recognized Edna, a big stack of paper plates in her hands.

Suddenly, the baby ape leapt to the top of this wall made of fallen trees. He made a sound Melissa knew well—the half-bark half-hiss sound of a raccoon. He was calling to the people. But Big Daddy grabbed him, and almost crushing him to his chest with both arms, scolded him in Jay—the perfect language for scolding, because Jays were always scolding—everyone and everything. But then there was not-too-distant sound of an ambulance siren, and Big Daddy let go of Baby and covered his ears. All the apes did.

Now Melissa knew exactly where they were: not more than a mile from town and just below the road to Taylorville at the point where it made a tight curve around Taylor Mountain. Melissa couldn't see the road—too many trees in the way—nor even the briefest flash of ambulance—but the sound of that siren was fading fast, telling her how swiftly that ambulance had to be moving.

Someone from town was in serious trouble, because while the Taylorville ambulance never moved slowly and always used its siren—a good idea on such a twisting road—it would usually go at only a moderate speed when it curved around Taylor

Mountain—for safety sake. But that wasn't happening.

Melissa knew (as she also told her mother that night) just *knew* that it was Miss Dorothy in that ambulance, because Miss Dorothy's face had appeared in her mind's eye the second she heard that siren; and it wasn't like her face had popped in and out. It had *stayed*, and didn't end up disappearing, but faded. So she knew there was trouble.

Their hearing must be amazing and incredibly sensitive, Melisssa thought, because they kept their hands up to their ears many seconds after Melissa had stopped hearing the siren altogether. Big Daddy now chattered like a squirrel, and he and the rest, arced well around the area of the clearing—Melissa took pictures like crazy—and then turned back in the southwest direction they had been going.

They were now almost running, Melissa noted, and slipping through and among trees like quicksilver, and keeping a distance from one another. It occurred to Melissa that you never saw more than one of these apes occupying the same space ahead of you at any one time—and then for only two seconds. (She counted.) They used the shadows of every tree to their advantage.

She had followed them for another five minutes, shooting whenever an opportunity presented itself, before she was treated to a spectacular show.

The apes she most closely trailed were Big Mama and Baby. Baby didn't—couldn't—move as quickly as the others, which Melissa was glad about: she was already running pretty fast, her clothes and hair disordered she knew, but she didn't care. She was, however, getting tired and wondered how much longer she could keep going like this. Then abruptly, Big Mama and Baby stopped. Big Mama sniffed the air.

Melissa couldn't see, and certainly she couldn't smell, what had alarmed Big Mama. Well ahead of them, all of the other apes vanished—simply vanished; and then Big Mama and Baby were gone, too. To say, 'in a flash,' would be wrong, because you can see a flash. Melissa looked up into the trees. The two had to be up there, right, but where?

Amazed, she stood in place for a long time, looking, looking, and wondering what was going on, and wondering what to do; then she thought that maybe Big Mama and Baby had bounded *forward*. So she hurried in the direction the apes had been going, worried that she had lost them; and she was about to call to them, though she knew they weren't going to answer, when up ahead of her, she saw two backpackers coming her way.

In about two minutes, they and Melissa met up. They were an older couple, and they were quite surprised to see a young girl on her own, off trail in the woods. Part of Melissa was thrilled to see them. Witnesses who could back her up! *Adult* witnesses, in case no one would believe a child, and in case her pictures weren't very good, or she was accused of faking them. She would ask them to join her, and they'd see the apes—unless, and here her heart sank—she'd lost them for good now, or the apes would stay hidden, afraid of these new people. But another part of her, a part she felt more than she understood, sensed that it wasn't right to include these people in what was going on. They didn't know the apes as well as Melissa did—not that Melissa knew them, either—but she didn't want these people to scare them. (Interestingly, it didn't occur to her at that moment to worry about whether the apes might scare the people.) Also, who knew what these people would do, say, or want, after encountering the apes. Plus—and this part was hard to admit to herself—she wanted the discovery of the apes to be hers alone. She'd done all the hard work of finding them, and now she was doing all the hard work of getting proof of them—following them and snapping pictures. So she didn't want to share the credit with anyone else. But most of all, for reasons she couldn't put into words at the time, she just didn't think it would be right to say anything to these people.

They asked Melissa if she were lost. Where were her parents?

Melissa answered that she was not lost, she was a local, and knew exactly how to get home. You just head for Big Rock, she told them, pointing at it. The man and the woman visibly relaxed. They had just come from Big Rock, and knew that even off trail, the area was safe...gentle ground...no rivers to cross...no cliffs, caves, or chasms to avoid.

The man smiled and said, "Have you been out looking for the Ape?"

"No," Melissa said, "have you?"

"Of course not," the man said. "What a bunch of hooey. We just come to this part of the Forestal to hike. It's good hiking."

"It's the *best,* isn't it?" Melissa said. "Well, enjoy. I've got to be getting home."

"Wait," the woman said, "tell me, what's the deal with this whole Ape thing?"

"Ah, the whole town's nuts," Melissa said. "Somebody saw a bear doing weird stuff, that's all. But I've seen bears do *plenty* of weird stuff."

"But in that video," the woman said, "that creature looks more like an ape than a bear."

"For god's sake, Delores," the man said. "A couple of yahoos put on an ape suit and got everyone going."

"Dr. Laurence Board doesn't think so. Sean Ford doesn't think so."

"They're probably in on it."

"Oh, for heaven's sake, Kenneth, you think everyone's in on everything all the time."

"Well, I don't know about that."

"Nah," said Melissa. "It's not guys in a suit. I mean, I wouldn't put it past a few people here to try something like that. But they wouldn't have the smarts to pull off something that'd fool big-time people. We're not, like, in Hollywood, where they could do it. Or have people with, like, science degrees that could fake that stuff."

"Well, that'd be true," Kenneth said.

"It's just a bear," said Melissa. "Everyone's gone crazy over some crazy bear. There's no ape here."

They said good-byes, and Delores and Kenneth went on their way, and Melissa continued in the direction she thought she should, every now and again looking over her shoulder to make sure that Delores and Kenneth had indeed gone and weren't for any reason following her. Soon enough, however, she forgot all about them. She had to find those apes! Where had they gone?

She tried to comfort herself with the thought that if she'd lost them, she could probably find them again another day, in the secret forest. They seemed to like it there. And anyway, didn't she have enough pictures? She had *many* pictures, that was true, but she had a funny feeling that they weren't convincing. Most were from pretty far away, or from the back—and maybe she had some pretty good ones of the apes in profile. But—*the money shot*—she'd heard Peter use that phrase a hundred times. *The money shot*. The shot that convinced. Did she have *that*? Maybe. But it bothered her. It *vexed* her. Especially since these days, people could Photoshop almost anything. No, she needed to get close. *Really* close.

And then, as if in answer to a prayer, but even more conveniently, because she hadn't even had to pray for it, she saw Big Mama and Baby loping along about fifty yards ahead of her. When had they descended? Had they *descended*?

She ran after them, closing the gap, and when she'd come within about twenty yards, she slowed her pace, to theirs, and followed.

She guessed that it was about ten minutes later that she saw the apes ahead of Big Mama and Baby bunching up at a rock wall. They looked like people waiting for an elevator. But they were waiting for Mama and Baby to join them.

The apes looked tired to Melissa. Their shoulders sagged. Those apes holding branches had held them high up and pressed tightly to their chests for most of the walk. Now, they held those branches low, about the belly, and not so tightly. All of them panted, and there was a sheen on their fur. They were sweating, Melissa thought, shooting. Whatever was going on, this was a big deal for them; this was a big journey.

Without turning around, because they had heard her or smelled her, the apes at the rock wall parted for Big Mama. When they did, Melissa saw a narrow gap in the wall. Was something hidden in there? Was something hidden in there, and they were waiting for Big Mama to pull it out? Or no, the branches—were they going to stick the branches in there for whatever reason? Or were they waiting for something to come out?

Then shocking Melissa so that she gasped, Big Mama squeezed into the narrow gap, her big body squishing up and disappearing as if some incredible vacuum had sucked her into the mountain. Baby went next, then all of the others, except for Big Daddy, who, Melissa saw, was looking at her. What did he want?, Melissa wondered. What was he trying to say?

Big Daddy extended his arm toward her. He was holding something in that closed fist. He opened his hand. A Fuji apple.

He tossed it to Melissa, who caught it. Then, still looking at her, Big Daddy went through the gap.

Melissa followed.

She could get through, those huge *creatures* could get through, but Melissa doubted that anyone even a couple years older than she could have done it. Maybe Miss Dorothy.

She entered a cave. Sheets and straws of light from gaps in the mountain provided light enough so that Melissa could see. The cave was wide, but the ceiling low.

Squatting, though Baby was kneeling, the apes had formed a half circle around an ape lying on its back on the ground. The ape's breathing was labored. From its size, Melissa gathered that it was a juvenile—not a kid, not an adult. Female. Squatting at the juvenile's side was an ape Melissa hadn't seen before. It was old—withered, fur completely silvered. It was a female.

Melissa took a step closer and saw that the juvenile was

bleeding from her chest, from right where the heart was or might be. Mel gasped. The juvenile caught sight of Melissa and grew agitated, making small, quick snorts. Melissa backed up, toward the entrance. Big Mama put a hand to the juvenile's brow, calming her.

Melissa glanced from the juvenile to the apes in the half-circle. They were all looking at her.

All was quiet except for the raspy breathing of the dying juvenile. Was Melissa supposed to do something?

She got a little closer. She put her camera down and knelt at the feet of the juvenile.

"She's hurt," she said, keeping her voice as low as possible. "She's..." The light dawned. "Oh, my god. She's been shot. Someone...Rawley Connor!...But I don't know what to do."

Suddenly, the dying ape arched her back—and died.

Melissa gasped.

Big Daddy looked at Melissa steadily. The other apes rocked back and forth, making a low, rumbling sound; a drone.

Melissa kneeled there, frightened but transfixed.

The apes now got up one by one and each took one long inhalation of the dead juvenile. Then those with branches lay them over her, covering her. One by one, they passed Melissa and slipped out of the cave. The Old Woman took the longest inhalation of the juvenile, held it in her lungs for a long moment, her eyes closing, then left as the others had.

Melissa found herself alone with Big Daddy, Big Mama, and Baby—and the dead, branch-covered juvenile. Only the juvenile's feet stuck out from underneath the branch covering. For the first time, Melissa noted the soles. They looked so odd, she thought. Right in the middle were pronounced bony ridges. They reminded Mel of something. But what? Big Daddy made a chuff-like sound. Big Mama made it, too, as if she were repeating it. Then the baby did. They inhaled the juvenile. Ah, thought Melissa, she was a part of this family. She studied the juvenile's face. It looked peaceful now, though her fur was all dusty and matted. How long had she lain here, suffering? Had Rawley—probably Rawley—shot her last week? Was that the shot they had heard, she, her mom, and Coach Mayhugh, and she'd been suffering here since then? The area was about right...Baby had passed Melissa and was headed out. Now Big Mama.

Big Daddy came and stood between her and the juvenile. He chuffed at her. She stood—close—he didn't smell, she noticed. Not either bad or good, he just didn't smell. Well, a little, but not a lot more than maybe Muffin might smell, if you got up close to her.

Melissa followed Big Daddy out, her head down, almost as if it were bowed, and maybe it was—the moment had been solemn, after all, and that's when she saw the tracks—the footprints—they were leaving.

Deer tracks.

Melissa's moment of ah-hah was not exclamatory, but gentle; it was an 'of course.'

The soles of these creatures' feet were adaptations. As these creatures had evolved, those who survived were those whose feet grew this way—kind of shortening to deer hooves—big deer hooves, like those of stags or whatever, but hooves nonetheless. And they could squish through narrow gaps because their bodies, though large in appearance, were light, their bones light, not dense. Melissa didn't know all the scientific words to say, or think—she wasn't in Mr. Pierce's grade yet—but she knew that nothing really heavy could walk around on two feet like these. Four, yes. Elk walked around on hooves that didn't seem big enough for something so heavy. But again, their weight was distributed—that was a word that came to her—distributed on four feet, not two.

And the bird calls. And the ability to bound—their leg muscles must be amazing. And the ability to move so swiftly, like the wind. No *wonder* no one ever saw these things, or heard these things—or seldom did. *That's* why there were legends, and had been forever— because there was always somebody at some point—just like her— who ran into them. And how interesting it suddenly was to Melissa that all of the other animals in the woods knew about these apes! And just accepted them as other creatures and had no idea that we would find their existence miraculous. Boy, thought Melissa, wouldn't Mr. Pierce like to know about these guys!

Melissa emerged from the cave, blinking in the sunlight, and her eyes adjusting, she saw Big Daddy and Big Mama loping away, through the trees. Baby loped along at Big Mama's side, playing with something.

Her camera!

"Hey!" she shouted. "Hey!" Big Daddy and Big Mama covered their ears. They bounded away up into the tress, Baby in Big Mama's arms.

"My camera! Give me my camera!" Melissa shouted, racing along the forest floor, eyes on the treetops as much as she dared, because she needed to see in front of her. She ran looking for a long time, never seeing or hearing a thing above her.

Round about this time, and not more than three miles away—but as the crow flies—the Alpine Valley High School Marching Band— all five of them—was blasting out a ragged fanfare, and I wonder if the apes could have heard it, while Mayor Annie LaPeer stepped up to the earth mover those apes and Melissa had seen, a champagne bottle in hand. She looked preoccupied, even unhappy, but as she turned to face the crowd, she slapped on a smile and announced, "Let the road begin!"

The town folk who had gathered—some fifty—cheered. It was lackluster. Annie christened the earth mover. The band played a Sousa March and marched in a circle—it's all they knew how to do—and everyone clapped. Shirley applauded the most enthusi-astically of anybody, tears in her eyes. Walter applauded after his fashion.

Mr. Pierce and Miss Ames stood at the back of the small crowd, arms around each other's waists, each with a hand in the other's back pocket—both in jeans. They didn't cheer or clap. Miss

Ames leaned her head on Mr. Pierce's shoulder.

The crowd drifted off to the long picnic tables. They didn't look eager. It was more like dutiful, as if they were telling themselves, 'Okay, I guess we've go to do this now. Put something on a plate.'

At various points in the picnic, one might have seen Annie, holding a plastic cup of punch, standing in a small circle that included Preston, Millard, and Edna. Annie looked over at one point to see Millicent and Gertrude standing with Sam Cabot. Their faces looked grave as Sam spoke on his cell phone.

Not liking what she was seeing, Annie excused herself from her little group and walked over to these three. "What's going on?" she asked.

Sam looked at Annie, and she knew.

Millicent pulled a handkerchief from her sleeve as she started to cry. Gertrude embraced her.

Annie then embraced the two of them, one at a time. "I'm so sorry."

"I'd like to sit for a moment," Millicent said, and Gertrude escorted her toward the picnic table and sat her down in one of the folding chairs. She sat next to her. They held hands, gazing at the ground; the past; perhaps their future.

Annie wiped her tears and, half in amazement, half in anger, said "But she'd only broken her hip!"

"She arrested on the way," Sam said. "They couldn't revive her."

Annie didn't notice it, but her fists were clenched at her beltline and she was angrily pushing the words out. "She couldn't have fallen *next* year—when we had a *road*?"

No one needed to tell her she was being unreasonable. "This isn't fair!" she said.

Annie had said that so loudly that several people looked over. Seeing her anger, her distress, the pain in her face, they, too, now knew. People bowed their heads, or here and there embraced one another, not a few bursting loudly into tears—like Millard.

Annie made a way to a chair, Sam following her. They sat.

Preston watched Annie and Sam. He inhaled deeply. He shook his head slowly, and then, taking a sip of his punch, saw a kid up on the seat of the earth mover, holding the steering wheel, making big noises, pretending to drive. He couldn't have been any more than three.

The time of his life, Preston thought. Maybe this will be his first big memory. The day they christened the road to Taylorville.

Chapter Thirty-Three

*T*HESE ARE THE THINGS YOU CAN SEE ON THE WALL OF Dr. Sam Cabot's office:

—A picture of Sam Cabot when he was a teenager, stringing up his rod as he stands on the shore of Lake Barney.

—A picture of Sam and his young pretty wife (named Delores—not to be confused with that hiker named Delores). They are waving at the cameraman as they stand on the porch of Sam's fishing cabin. It looks new in the picture—as robust as Sam himself, not weathered, like Sam now.

—A picture of Sam and Delores standing riverside, showing off stringers of trout for the camera.

—A wedding photo. Sam and Delores cutting a two-tiered cake. Several people off to the side are captured in the shot, and darned if that isn't Miss Dorothy, holding a glass of punch in her gloved hands—a veiled little cocktail hat on her head. The picture had to be fifty-some years old, and Miss Dorothy (sad, maybe, but true) didn't look any different then than she did now; that is, than she most recently looked.

—A diploma from Johns Hopkins Medical School.

—Various other diplomas and certificates—all of them with great big red or blue seals and long signatures underneath that look like seismographs for earthquakes you wouldn't want to be anywhere near.

"Tell me a little more about what happened in the cave. The sniffing," Sam said.

He was seated behind his desk in his big, worn-out swivel chair. It was made of a dark wood with a red, faux-leather backing.

Annie, Melissa, and Peter sat before him, each in a big armchair. Their chairs, too, were made of a dark wood, the armrests and the backs done up in green faux-leather.

"It was like, they did that, because they were trying to remember her," Melissa said.

"All right," Sam said.

"They took me there because they wanted me to see her. They wanted me to see what we had done to her."

"'We'?" Sam said.

"Yeah, because I mean, not just Rawley. They're afraid of us. They're afraid of our picnic tables."

Annie shot Sam a worried look. He communicated to her, *Be calm.*

Chapter Thirty-Four

$\mathcal{I}$T WASN'T THAT NIGHT, BUT MAYBE THE NEXT, THAT had you been on Main Street around eight p.m., you would have seen Preston pushing open the door of the AV Bistro for Annie LaPeer, Preston following her out.

The AV Bistro had appeared *like that*. The hardware/sporting goods/forester needs store that had gone out of business a year ago proved the ideal space for what the ambitious restaurateur had in mind for his little restaurant. He'd come here from Vancouver. He was smart, this guy—Martine. He had sniffed out that the town had no money yet, or very little, but it showed every sign of having it soon. So he made the food fancy, but kept the prices low. He'd hook his customers first, build up some goodwill, and *then* raise prices.

He still had no proper permits, or liquor license (though everyone knew if you asked for wine or beer, it would magically appear), and there were still a lot of exposed wires and missing laths here and there. The service was slow, because the waiters he had hired had no restaurant experience—like Miss Ames, who was moonlighting. But she caught on quickly. (Derrick was a busboy here.) Edna was making a little money off Martine, because he bought fifteen pies a week from her. He charged two dollars a slice for blueberry; two for lemon chiffon; two for apple; and three-fifty for rhubarb. "It was just that good," Martine said, and thereafter

215

poor Edna mooned after Martine (twenty years her junior) for the rest of her life.

Preston and Annie strolled up the sidewalk, or, more truthfully, negotiated the sidewalk and all the construction/destruction, and headed, though not really thinking about it, toward the town square.

"That was very nice," Annie said. "Thank you."

"Food's improved around here," said Preston.

"Don't let Merle—or Claude—hear you say that. This place is their competition."

"I mean generally," Preston said. "I know that Eddie's stepped up his game, too."

Annie smiled. It was true. "His hamburgers are no longer as…"

"Burnt to a crisp?" offered Preston.

"Unique," Annie said.

"Ever the town booster," said Preston.

Annie took that in, then glanced at Preston, with something in her face that he could not read.

"Did I say something wrong?" Preston asked.

"No, not at all," said Annie. "But I wonder if we're not paying too high a price for all this…boosting."

"Miss Dorothy."

"We lost sight of her," Annie said. "Literally. And maybe it's that sort of thing that's on Mel's mind. The harm she's talking about."

"I guess the lesson is," said Preston, "eyes on the prize, we've got to remember to watch our step. Or we'll follow Miss Dorothy. Off the path. Into the dark."

Annie gave him a half-smile. "Poetic," she said.

Preston shrugged. "I don't know about poetic, but I know it's true."

Annie nodded, looking pensive. "And we watch our step by…?"

"By keeping an eye on the risks, I guess. Are we at risk of losing our character by all this growth? Are we at risk of not looking out for one another—as very obviously we failed to do with Miss Dorothy? What's next? Who's next? In building that road to Taylorville, are we going to be people who have lost our way?"

Annie looked up at him. She didn't realize there was so much surprise in her face, or she would have masked it. Preston chuckled. "I'm not just a guy with chalk and a whistle."

The two crossed the street and saw John Chamberlain up the street to the right, trying to stick his key into the door of his SUV.

"He's not going to try to drive." It was half-statement, half-question. Annie hurried his way on her clattery heels. "Mr. Chamberlain, you shouldn't be driving!"

"The mayor!" Chamberlain half-shouted, seeing her approach. "You gonna drive me, too? Tell your son he drives like an old lady."

"My son?"

But Chamberlain didn't answer her and once again tried to poke his key into the car door. He saw a hand grab his.

Preston's. "I don't know, Chamberlain," Preston said.

Chamberlain whipsawed his hand free from Preston's and making noises more than words, started swinging wildly at him, left, right, left.

It took Preston no effort to get him into a half-nelson and pushed up against the side of his SUV. He deftly plucked the keys out of Chamberlain's hand and stepped back.

Chamberlain slid down the SUV, passing out.

"Nice date, huh?" Preston asked Annie. He began gathering Chamberlain up from the ground. "Dinner *and* a show."

"What did he mean about Peter?" Annie asked.

Preston got one of Chamberlain's arms around himself and got a good grip around the man's waist. "I don't know," he said. He handed Annie the keys. "Let's stick him in the back."

Annie hurried to the back of the SUV and unlocked it. She opened it up, and Preston maneuvered Chamberlain into the back.

"What do you suppose it's like feeling so...guilty?" she asked.

"No picnic," Preston said. Then he added, "I would imagine."

"I don't know why people have to suffer so much."

Preston had no idea what to say to this, so said nothing.

Annie noticed a change in his demeanor. "Are you all right?" she asked.

"I'm fine. Just...this guy." He shook his head, looking at Chamberlain. "I mean, you knew his son—Kevin?"

"Around."

"He was always my boss at the mill. Summers, you know? I'd come in from Cascade to pick up a little work. I guess if I had any role model in life, it was Kevin. So, you know," and here Preston nodded at Chamberlain, "no love lost here."

"But it was a freak accident. That's the thing. That's what he can't handle."

"Freak. Well," Preston shrugged a shoulder. "I was there that summer. Mr. Greed here was trying to fill way too many orders, as always. But this time he wouldn't even stop production to do the usual maintenance checks. Kevin got in fights with his dad about it. 'Dad, we can't run these machines twenty-four/seven.' Twenty men on the floor when that blade came flying off, and it only took out one guy. Was that freak, or Greek—as in tragedy?"

"Meaning?"

"Chamberlain couldn't escape his character—and that's what did the killing. There was a flaw in the saw, sure—but only because there was a flaw in his character."

Annie nodded, understanding.

"No one," Preston continued, "not one of us—and we all loved Kevin—would go anywhere near that pile of sawdust. But Bulie did. He wasn't on the floor. Someone ran to get him. God bless Bulie. Reached in, blew the dust off. So gently—you wouldn't think Bulie was capable of that sort of thing. And he sat down on the floor, and oh, man, was he crying, and he cradled Kevin's head and rocked it."

Annie had a hard time swallowing the lump in her throat, and her eyes teared up. Neither she nor Preston said anything for several moments. "So that's it for him?" Annie asked, meaning Chamberlain. "There's no escape? What if, what if he went to see Sam Cabot?"

"Yeah, well…Cabot can offer understanding, perhaps even therapy."

"But?"

"He can't offer forgiveness," Preston said. "And that's what he needs."

"You say that like…How do you know?"

"Well. I don't. Guess that was stupid. Look," Preston said, obviously changing the subject, "why don't we just drop these keys off at Larry's office?"

He started away quickly, abruptly. Surprised, Annie watched him for a couple of seconds before she followed.

Chapter Thirty-Five

SAM OPENED THE FRONT DOOR OF HIS HOUSE, AND AS Annie entered, he squinted up at the sky.

"Rains are due," he said. "I feel it more than smell it."

He followed her down the hall to his office.

Sam had pulled two of his armchairs up to his coffee table. He'd laid a nice little coffee service for the two of them. Pastries, too. Annie touched nothing, and he knew she wouldn't. He followed suit.

"So," Annie said, taking her seat, adjusting her realty blazer. "The apes. What's that about?"

"Getting right to it, eh?" Sam said, giving her a warm smile. He sat. "The young ape who died? She died of a wound to the *heart*. Not chest. Do you remember how specific Mel was?"

Annie nodded. "So she's...heartsick? She *does* miss her father?"

"No. Now Peter—that's a different story. But I don't get the feeling he misses his father so much as the *idea* of father, *a* father."

"Okay," Annie said, nodding. "I get that. But the heart thing?"

"Some of this *is*, in fact, about what's going on in town these days. She told me how the apes saw the earth mover and were afraid."

"Too much...change?" Annie said. "No solid...earth under her feet? Is that what it symbolizes for her—the earth *mover*? The world she knows is going...leaving?"

"Very good," Sam said. "Yes. And the apes are solicitous of one another. They have ritual. They work as a large family."

"And we're losing that here. Yes. We're going to have to figure that out."

"Here. Yes," said Sam, shrugging. "But *closer*—in your own family, Annie. She's heartsick for *you*. What's happening to Mom? And maybe it's her fault, because she didn't protect you."

"Protect *me*?"

"From Dave. The walls in your house are thin, Annie."

"Oh, my god..."

Annie looked at her hands in her lap, each hand squeezing the fingers of one, then trading off, over and over. Sam let her sit with her thoughts.

"What she must have suffered," Annie breathed.

"As for Peter," Sam said, "he's far less affected. A simple, strangely profound matter of proximity."

"He couldn't hear anything. His bedroom was—one, two, three...*four* walls away."

"And you'll note that the creatures— ."

"Hated loud noises," Annie concluded, nodding.

Again, Sam let her sit with her thoughts.

"She's not delusional, is she?"

"She's...under a lot of stress."

Annie nodded, looking off, eyes vacant—or was she about to cry? Sam pulled at an earlobe. Had he gone too far? That pause of his—while he had considered whether to use the word 'stress,' or to confirm that 'delusional' was accurate—might have spoken volumes to Annie, might have said to her 'Yes, she's delusional,' as clearly as any utterance might have. He sat forward. "Delusional is not the word," he said. He looked off. "I don't know if it may be of comfort," he added, "but she's not my first patient who claims to have seen these creatures."

Still looking off, Annie raised an eyebrow. "Who?"

Sam smiled. "Well, I can't tell you that. Or even whether it was here, Taylorville, or up in Cascade. But delusion, true delusion, was *not* an issue."

Annie gave a small nervous and ironic laugh. "Small comfort," she said. She now looked at Sam and worked up a small smile. "It would be nice if someone else could see these things."

Sam smiled. "Be careful what you wish for."

After Annie had gone, Sam returned to his office. He sat in an armchair and poured himself a cup of coffee. He looked at his watch. Past eight-thirty. The school kids would all have been delivered by now. He pulled out his cell phone. He dialed.

By the way, if you're not philosophically inclined, you can go ahead and skip the next several pages until you see the paragraph beginning with *"He can't offer forgiveness," he had said.* That part's about Preston and is very interesting, and you won't lose that much of the story if you go directly there. However, some people like to linger a little longer in certain stretches of a path than do others; or they like taking side trails, and maybe in so doing, and maybe not (and they're okay with that, because just taking the gamble is of interest to them), they see a magnificent flower they would never have seen otherwise, or an unusual rock formation that makes them laugh, or a mighty stag bending to drink in a stream—and it will have been worth the digression, worth going off trail. And as *you* might be that sort of person, I'm putting this stretch, this digression, in for *you*; and if you're *not* that sort of person, and like to keep your course, then please do! I'm only letting you know that there is, here, a little fork, and what it leads to has its riches; and as it will always be here for you, however many pages you cover it over with, however you may even close the book and put it on the shelf, you can always come back to it. It will always be here waiting for *you*. You're not obliged to wait for it.

"Thanks for coming up," Sam said. "I thought it might be more private."

"Sure. No problem," Terry Troy said, not winded at all. "Everyone knows I hike, anyway."

"A little stroll down to Barney?"

"Sure."

As the two men headed for the lake, Sam asked Terry the usual inquisitive pleasantries, and Terry answered his questions as he did everything, quickly, impatiently.

Sam didn't take it personally. He got it that for Terry, conversation was like driving down a street that not only had too many stoplights, but stoplights that, no matter *how* fast you tried to go between them, turned red on you, stopping your progress.

Worse yet for Terry, that impatience in conversation extended to everything in life. There was *this* to be done—like this conversation with Dr. Cabot—then the *next* thing to be done, then the thing after *that*, all of which took so much time and worse than that, amounted to nothing. Drive the kids. Park the bus in the lot. Walk to a trail. Hike that trail. Hike back. Get something to eat at Merle's. Eat it. Go get the bus. Drive to the school. Get the kids. Return them to their stops. Repeat the next day. And the next. And the next...

And he had better do it all, or else. Or else *what*? Terry himself didn't know. But it was *out* there, and it would get him—in a moment of idleness; and wasn't it a curse that he'd ended up a school bus driver, having so much time on his hands? But he could never get, well, he couldn't *keep* a second job; not for long. He'd already been fired from his waiter job at the AV. Customers couldn't stand being hurried to place their order; couldn't stand Terry standing there, tapping his pencil against his order pad so that the pencil was a blur.

The only time Terry slowed down was when he was with someone he had affection for. He wanted to mend his pace to theirs, and he could, even past the time he sensed that they had tired of *him*; impatient with *his* company—and he hated feeling their impatience and wanted that feeling out of his system, but that's how much he craved time with them: he was willing to endure that bad feeling in order to be in their presence *just* a little longer.

Sam had sent him many years ago to a colleague he trusted to help him. But the drive...so long. Those roads...so twisty. So Terry had stopped going.

"I know why I'm here," Terry said when the lake came into view. "Melissa LaPeer."

Sam was surprised. But what could he say? He couldn't betray his patient's confidentiality. "I beg your pardon?"

"It's okay, Doc. Don't worry. But I was there on Main Street when she came riding into town like a bat out of hell, screaming about the ape, the ape, and they're real. The rest is two-plus-two. Her mother got worried and took her to see you, and what concerns *you* is that what Melissa said is exactly what *I* always told you. You re-checked your notes, to be sure, but you were right: The similarity is uncanny. So you're wondering what's going on in the minds of two *very* different patients who, independently of one another, and with many years separating the two, end up having near-identical stories about illusory creatures—their look, their bird calls, the fact that they hate our loud noises. Maybe there's a good research paper for you in this. You can publish it in one of those medical journals."

"Terry."

"Okay, you're not so crass as that, Doc, I know that. But still, you're excited about this. A little girl and a nutjob bus driver? Hm. Are there common denominators in their lives and minds? Of course, you have to first assume that the bus driver didn't put the little girl up to it. Unfortunately, that's impossible to verify, because there's no third party watching the two of us—Melissa LaPeer and me. No film or recording. All you'd have is each of us *swearing* that we're not in on something together, hoaxing everyone—and if that's all you've got—each of us *swearing* we're telling the truth—then you've got a gap in knowledge you have no choice but to bridge with *assumption*, assumption about our characters: that no circumstance could lead us to lie—and conspire together; which assumption is only based on faith in your ability to fish out the one right conclusion from two lakes you've observed. And how scientific is *that,* to prop up conclusions by faith in *yourself?*"

"You're not a nutjob, Terry."

"Yeah, well, I know I'm not like others. But still, Doc, why would you assume that whatever makes me different, or whatever might be wrong with me, if anything, would somehow produce in my mind strange-looking *apes*, who hate loud sounds, and make bird calls? How is that logical that because I'm not quite right in the head, that that means the apes don't exist, and that I didn't see them?"

"Good point."

"Of course, *your* question is, why does Terry's *off*-ness restrict itself to those apes? After all, he doesn't also see singing rocks, and clouds made of mixed vegetables, and trombones that deliver the mail. That's what you want to know, especially as Melissa has seen these apes, too, and nothing else peculiar. But I'm here to try to save you a lot of time and energy, Doc; and to keep you from a false road you shouldn't go down: Don't go fishing for psychological answers in my mind or Melissa's, or in whatever case histories you read in your medical journals. Because those apes are *out there*. Not in here." And here Terry knocked on his temple.

"And to anticipate your next question," he continued, "or maybe not your *very* next question, but one not too far down the line, *No*, I couldn't offer an explanation as to why nobody else has seen them, nor why I can't find them anymore. But I *saw* them. And I am confident that Melissa did, too."

The two men came to the edge of the lake and gazed out across its expanse. "Remind me, Terry," Sam said, "where did you see them?"

"About a mile past Slauson's Ridge. It was a three-second look, but they weren't bears. I didn't know it—I didn't figure it out *then*—but two things were working in my favor. I was upwind from them, *plus* there was a rotting deer carcass between me and where the apes were. I almost stepped in the damned thing. But *that's* why they couldn't smell me. The smell of the carcass masked the smell of me. But anyway, I heard two jays squabbling with one another, so just to be funny, I started whistling some crazy stuff back, to mess with their little jay heads, and as I turned a corner, there they were, covering their ears and looking every which way, trying to figure out where that maddening sound was coming from. And when they saw me, it was crazy how they leapt, the one straight up into a tree, the other up onto a rock, and from that rock up into a tree—and they were *gone*. Invisible. Inaudible. No rustling. No movement. And they were such big creatures—so it amazed me, their quickness and agility. I couldn't tell whether they had disappeared from the area, or were holding deathly still until I should pass. Either way it was, I got the hell out of there, I can tell you."

"You didn't tell anybody what you saw?"

"You."

"That day, I mean. Someone. Someone to share this with?"

"Who? Who would that be, Doc?"

"Claude? Isn't he your friend?"

"I didn't know him real well at the time. And anyway, who the hell knows Claude? He's there, and yet not there. He moves among us and is hard to see. And anyway, people weren't going to believe me. Not *me*. They might take the bus job away. So no, I knew I had to keep quiet. I'm not an idiot. Just nuts."

"If they themselves were making such loud noises, why should they be so bothered by *your* loud noise?"

Terry shrugged. "I couldn't tell you. How would I know that? Maybe it's not volume, but something else. Tone? Frequency?" He shrugged again, and now bent down and picked up a stone from the shore of the lake. He gave it a sidearm fling. The stone skimmed the surface of the water six times before sinking. He picked up a second, flinging it, and a third, and a fourth...

Spontaneously, not a word spoken or a gesture made, the men turned and headed east along the shore, toward the slope where the tourists had seen a small bear and had turned it into an ape.

Sam didn't know what to think of what Terry had said. He wanted to call some colleagues; get their take on all this.

Did Terry have difficulty separating fact from fiction? He did not. But among the things Sam had learned about Terry is that no one had told him stories when he was a child; no Grimm, no Hans Christian Anderson, no King Arthur, no folktales, no Sendak, no Hobbits, no Dickens or Twain—*nothing*; and that, Sam always felt, was part of Terry's problem. Children needed stories even more than milk, if they were going to grow strong. Terry never got to defeat pirates, and push wicked witches into ovens, and slay wolves and save the day. He never learned to expect good to triumph over evil; and so he was anxious.

Sam's dad used to tell stories about the Alpine Valley Ape. But his dad's ape had fangs and ten-inch claws. And he hunted people. That's how his stories always went. The creatures were never gentle and noise-hating. On the contrary, they roared. Until they were slain. By the valiant woodsman. So...what was going on inside Terry—and Melissa—that it changed the Ape, so that he *wasn't* aggressive?

His eyes idling on the always-pretty slope—its sunlit boulders here and there, the trees in twos and threes here and there, the wildflowers everywhere between them—Sam mused that there were only three people in this town who had lived here longer than he. Dorothy, Millicent, and Gertrude, and *they* never saw any creature; and *he* had never seen any creature. Not even a sign of anything strange.

"And I'll bet you're now thinking about your own experience," Terry said, as they walked along. "And trying to remember what the old folk used to say about the ape."

"I am," Sam said, turning to him. "You're psychic," he said, chuckling, but inwardly wondering about Terry's perspicacity.

"Not at all," Terry said. "It's just two plus two. You had to wonder if anybody other than me—and now Melissa—had ever said anything about the ape. That is, people other than a nutjob and a pubescent girl; and God knows the things *they* see—angels in grottoes, or voices in dreams, like all those saints. Joan of Arc. What was she? Fourteen? And what's her name at the grotto. Bernadette whoever; and like those boys and girls in Yugoslavia who saw the Virgin Mary? It's never a middle-aged tax accountant from Paramus, New Jersey who sees angels, though he may well see demons. But still, *something* remarkable enough happened to or *for* those young people that at the very *least* it survives alongside skepticism—and it fueled triumph or healing, and continues fueling it. So yeah, Doc, I'll reverse myself and allow that *maybe* the remarkable thing that happened to me was what happened in here." And here, Terry knocked on his temple again.

"Wait," Sam said, "so you think that seeing the apes was healing for you, or a triumph?"

"It gave me something amazing I had never had before. A vision at the very least, and it pleases me. Not least because I survived it. Those apes ran from *me*, but of course I understood that only later—right then, in seeing them, it was too much. I *had* to run. But the lesson that came to me was that it's possible that harm may *not* be around every bend. *Good* might be. Something *miraculous* might be. Hiking as I do, rounding bends, I think it helps reinforce that idea for me. Of course, you'll notice I don't go far. Certainly not to Carson's Bridge. And I'm too afraid to attempt Miller's Peak."

"Terry, in your hiking around, do you think you might see them again?"

"No. But I used to, yes. Now I just hike because it's the best thing I know to do with myself."

"Do you wonder if something like a dream-state or something in the brain—a seizure of sorts—produced those images for you?"

"I do. How can I not? And no, I wasn't high or drunk. You can cross *that* off the list. But I had never had anything like a halluci-nation in this head *before*, and never since. So, yeah, it crosses my mind that something happened in my head. But what's got *permanent* residency is—I *saw* them. I'm not...damaged; not crazy. And I don't think Melissa is, either. Anyway," Terry now said, stopping, "I've got to get going, Doc."

"Okay. I understand," Sam said, and he did to a degree: Terry had done what he could here; helped as he could help; he'd crossed this off his list; and now there was something else he must do "Thank you for your time, Terry. It's very much appreciated." They shook hands and Terry strode quickly up the trail and away.

As Sam stood alone with his thoughts, wondering what it might mean that Terry and Melissa had both ascribed the same behaviors to these apes, a line from Shakespeare's *Hamlet* popped into Sam's head. *There are more things in heaven and on earth than are dreamt of in your philosophy.* Well, that was pretty much what Terry had been telling him, so it was probably no wonder that this quote came to mind. Terry had dislodged it from where it had been planted somewhere up there, and like some pretty sunlit boulder, it had come rolling down to him.

Still, however pretty the line, the thought, the poetry, Sam was a man of science; and though he'd seen some remarkable things in his life, even unexplainable things, there was nothing that he couldn't position in his head as either solved or solvable by use of his reason. And philosophy, science—it could stretch pretty far: down into the deeps of the deepest oceans, and light years into space, and into the nooks and crannies of atoms, and into the nooks and crannies of *those* nooks and crannies. So Sam didn't have a problem with the possibility of amazing, unknown things—somewhere in lands untrodden.

But the lands *here* were *well*-trodden, and there had never been any evidence of these creatures. No fur, no carcass, no track, no scat, no cast-off tooth, or claw—all the usual things one ran across of all the other fauna in this forest. So to insist on creatures out there in the woods, without reference to any evidence beyond someone's personal testimony, was unreasonable.

No, if anything was amazing, it was what was going on in the minds of Terry Troy and Melissa LaPeer. How could it produce those *exact details*? The bird calls...the issue with noise...

Sam now asked himself, other than birds, what else makes bird calls? Well, not *what*, Sam next thought, but *who*. Hunters did. No, not really: They made duck calls—goose calls—and that was about it for around here. A few guys could make grouse calls, and you hardly ever saw a wild turkey in these parts. But Indians made bird calls. The Native Americans who used to live here made all kinds of bird calls—to keep prey and enemies from knowing they were around...And the Indians were now largely displaced—or had disappeared. So. Did Terry and Melissa fear being displaced? Or did they feel that they *were* displaced? Did they feel like they were disappearing? Is the bird call thing an unconscious connecting to—and identification with—the people removed from this land? And the issue with noise...jackhammers in Melissa's case, tearing up the land she knew, the home she knew...kids jabbering on the bus in Terry's case—maybe he didn't like being a bus driver, didn't want to *hear* that this was his fate?

Hm. Sam wasn't too sure about the specifics of that last thought, but he did feel he might be on the right path. And in the meantime, poor Terry: How he must suffer believing what he saw, and yet can't get anyone else to believe.

Well, Sam didn't want that for Mel, that suffering. He'd keep an eye on her...And, yes, she *was* pubescent. Terry was right: young girls's minds were susceptible to the changes in their bodies—so whatever was going on with Melissa might pass simply as a result of natural maturation. He'd seen worse delusions disappear just because someone grew out of them.

On the other hand, Sam thought, as he kicked a rock up the road, and watched it go off trail, he didn't want to live in a world that deprived us of loose ends and what ifs. What kind of world would that be? Everything accounted for, catalogued and labeled? *Confined?* Like some poor animal confined to a cage?

The human mind wants its mysteries and what ifs; wants to wonder what might be around the next corner! In fact, it *needs* to!

Heck, Sam thought, I'd *love* for there to be an Alpine Valley Ape. I'd *love* to stand amazed in the twilight of my life. It's not that I'm bored, but I miss surprises. I miss that feeling of being wrong, of being gobsmacked. Of being filled with wonder. Enlarged by wonder.

He smiled to himself. Of course the ape did not exist, but wouldn't it be great if it did—somewhere out there? And, Sam thought, wasn't it nice to have an 'out there'? A huge swath of unknown? A part of the map not filled in? Yes. And we'd always want that; need that. The Ape was not as important as the great forest. We didn't need the Ape as much as we needed the place where we could imagine he'd be.

It was essential that we always had room to imagine. Where we might find delight, even joy.

In a sense, Sam thought, that's when people might really become delusional—when the forests disappear, when the places where we can go looking for what we need, and can tell our camp-fire stories in, and wonder about sounds, and, yes, see something strange—when we *don't* have that—have that to *go* to, *that's* when we'll restrict it all to our heads, and there'll be no outlet. Nor any communal place of shared experience. So we'll feel confined; become anxious. The apes we need will have no place to be but in our heads. And that's when more and more of us will be living false lives; living in fantasy.

Sam looked at his watch. He had an hour free of duties. He'd get his fishing rod, go fishing; cast about in the lake and, hoping that somewhere in the depths he could not see, something might come and arrest his attention and make his heart race.

"*He can't offer forgiveness,*" he had said. "And that's what he needs."

Preston couldn't get those words out of his head. The evening with Annie LaPeer had gone well. Chamberlain hadn't ruined it, he didn't think. In fact, he might have *added* to it, because didn't it allow Preston to show a little kindness toward that miserable man, that miserable bitter drunk?

But then he had to go ahead and say those words, rub salt into his own wound, but not without first opening it up a little more, let it bleed afresh; and Annie had seen something pass through his face after he'd said those words. She *knew* that word, *forgiveness*, had had impact on him; and she was the type who was a thinker. She'd *know* something was going on with him—that he had some concern about forgiveness. Some need. That he was needy; not whole; not stable—and she'd reject him. Like other girlfriends in the past. Not that Annie was his girlfriend.

He'd never be so lucky.

"Madam Barkeep," Preston said, holding up his empty glass.

The day had gone well, and Preston had received all kinds of pats on the back that nevertheless stung like slaps—in his mind. The pavers had finished paving Main Street. What a fine job they had done, working mostly at night so as not to impede town or tourist. And too much credit had gone to Preston. Any time something good happened in town, Preston got a pat on the back. Because everyone thought of him as the author of all this; and when Gertrude took both his wrists this afternoon outside of Merle's and said, "We're so proud of you, Preston!" that's when he had to break free and get the hell out of town.

And that's why he was here in Taylorville, drinking.

"You're getting those eyes, darlin'," the bartender said, bringing Preston another scotch on the rocks. She placed it down in front of him on a little white napkin. "I'm cutting you off after this. Understand?"

"I do," said Preston. No problem. There were other bars. "Here's to you and your vigilance, Madam Barkeep," Preston said, knowing he sounded like the very caricature of a common drunk playing the role of the mannered duke—it amused him; and not that he thought about it right then, but better she thought of him as a common drunk than as the turd he was, and he picked up his glass to toast her, and it slipped from his hand.

The glass didn't break, but bounced off the bar, and the scotch and ice spilled everywhere, down the bar both ways and water-falling off of it. "Oh, my god," said Preston, and not in the next instant, because in the next instant he was watching his spreading, waterfalling drink, but in the next after that, he had leapt from his bar stool, apologizing like crazy, and grabbing whatever napkins—used or otherwise he found around him to blot up the scotch, and blot it up. He couldn't do it fast enough, and it was a losing battle.

"It's *okay*, darlin'," the bartender said, a bar rag in her hand; and in one fast swipe of it, she made the problem disappear. "But I'm cuttin' you off."

Preston did make his way to another bar, and yes he did get in the car, and yes he did take the road from Taylorville to Alpine Valley.

Who can say whether he would have made it home without harming himself or another person, or worse, because his cousin Larry saved him from a potentially horrible future. He saw Preston not two miles down from Taylorville. He recognized his cousin's truck. He lit him up with his red and blue cop lights and pulled him over.

Leaving Preston's truck on the side of the road, Larry drove him home and sat with him. Preston wasn't a crier. But for two hours, and without moving any one of the large muscles in his body, he sat hunched over the coffee Larry had brewed up for him. Larry had seen this behavior, this posture, this ability?, a couple of times in the past.

Larry knew things about his cousin. Their mothers, God rest both their souls, were as close as sisters could be; and his own mom had cried for days when Nickie had died. Cried for Nickie. Cried for Preston.

Chapter Thirty-Six

THE GRADUATING CLASS OF ALPINE VALLEY HIGH School didn't have to think too hard about who their mascot would be. And neither will you.

Preston of course had already dropped the name 'Bears' and had substituted 'Apes.' But only in his head. He knew it would be another year, at least, before he'd feel comfortable enough to ask for the money a name change would require. He had no doubts that the school board would approve of changing 'Bears' to 'Apes,' but you couldn't do that without taking down the concrete statue of the bear in front of the school—and you'd have to put up a statue of the Ape, right? And the pulling down, the sculpting, and the putting up, would cost money.

You'd also have to remove the growling bear logo from the scoreboard and put up a logo of the Ape, and change the school's stationery so that it would now say in italics under 'Alpine Valley High School,' '*Home of the Alpine Valley Apes.*'

These weren't terrifically costly changes that would need to be made, but still, they would require more money than the town currently had.

Sure, Alpine Valley was pulling itself out of debt, but the town had to keep paying it down, if the state was going to continue giving them financial aid. 'Continued good faith,' Trevor Westley had called it. And whatever didn't go into paying down the debt went into the road and motel. So there was no room for school improvement; and outside of Lydia's and the AV Bistro, there were still no new businesses here generating tax income for the town, nor many new jobs. Not yet. And really, what jobs would there be? This was a mill town—except that it wasn't. All that Alpine Valley could rely on was its new-found tourism. But how long would this tourism bubble last?

So the town would have to be clever about keeping this flow of tourists going; and to that end, it was decided that the time was right for Peter to make a new video. It was time to refresh interest in the Ape. It wasn't waning, but everyone in town knew that, sooner or later, it would.

And summer was coming. If tourism was this good while school was still in session, imagine what it might be like when families from all over the United States would take their summer vacations.

One good summer. Almost the first thing Preston had impressed upon the council in Chapter 8 is the amount of money the town of Willow Creek had made in *one summer*. $2.7 million dollars. If Alpine Valley could make that—even *close* to that—the town was guaranteed getting out of most of its remaining debt; and given the money they had already banked, they could count on at *least* another quarter mile of road being cleared through the wood, plus the possibility that the motel could be completed by mid-August.

One good summer. They needed one good summer of Ape madness...

Here in Alpine Valley, the school year ended May 31st. But the town knew that most kids in the country wouldn't be out of school until the second week of June—and that's when summer would really start for everyone here, financially speaking.

Of course, if you went by temperature, summer had come. Since the middle of May, Alpine Valley had enjoyed temperatures ranging from the low to mid 80s. And today, Graduation

Day at Alpine Valley High, it was a lovely 82.

There were, however, some thunderheads in the distance, and people kept an eye on the sky. This part of the country got wicked summer storms. No one thought that today's festivities would be ruined by any downpour, but the next day or two might see some ugly weather, and that would keep tourists away. They weren't going to take a twisty mountain road to get here in any kind of driving, mudslide-making rain. But that was tomorrow's problem—a problem on the horizon. Today, here and now, things were sunny and bright.

The graduating class—all eleven of them—had an all-are-welcome BBQ in the town square. Per usual, the costs for the BBQ were covered 50-50 by the school and town council. (Actually, the council had voted to slash the funds earlier in the year, but it was one of the first things they put back when a little money started rolling in: The town BBQ for its high school seniors was a big deal here. Keep that future as warmly embraced as possible.)

Annie wasn't sure if she was the only one feeling it, but the BBQ didn't have the same, well, warm embrace it usually had. It seemed...impersonal. On the other hand, how could it not?

Never before had the town a need to put up a sign that read 'Private Event,' because the event *wasn't* private. Everyone in town knew they were welcome. Most everyone didn't show up, of course—only about sixty or seventy people usually did, people connected with the graduating seniors and their families, and people connected with the school, but still, anybody could drop by if he or she wanted to.

But today, quite a few tourists in town had come to the BBQ. You'd think they might get it that this was a locals only, school-specific event—given the homemade banner that read 'Congratulations, Graduates!' and *certainly* given the sight of young people running around in their graduation gowns and mortar boards and taking pictures with their families. But nope—there all these tourists were, probably delighted to be soaking up the local flavor of the town and thinking, well, there's no sign saying, 'Private Event,' and nothing's fenced-off, and since everyone in this town has been so welcoming, why wouldn't they be now? And *certainly* the smell of Claude's BBQ-ing was enticing; so in the end, this is what you got: a lot of people barging in (Annie's words) and getting in line with their shorts and t-shirts and sun visors, along with the well-dressed happy moms and dads and grandparents and graduating seniors, and grabbing a plate and, believe me, *plenty* of hamburgers and hot dogs and cole slaw and chips and everything else.

In fact, by two p.m., the tourists far outnumbered the locals, most of whom, Annie noted, had left a good hour earlier. They felt squeezed out of their own party. Boyd and Floyd, she had noted, were the first to go. They came by to thank her kindly, and when she asked them why they should be leaving so soon, they fibbed so nicely and said, well, they had work to do, which she knew for sure wasn't the case when she saw so many others start to leave not too much after them.

Annie had felt sad about this, of course, but there were other emotions mixed in with the sad. The town had brought this situation upon itself, but on the other hand, next year they'd be serving ribs and chicken again, the way they used to when the mill was running, the humming generator of this town's financial stability, security, and small town warmth. So in a great sense, these unobservant, insensitive, boorish, touristy clods (also Annie's words) were a *good* thing.

She and Melissa had arrived early, with Muffin. They were going to have lunch, then take Muffin as far as Ranger Park for a walk, probably dip their toes in the river since the weather was so wonderfully warm. And she and her daughter would just *be* together. Annie would only shake the hands she absolutely had to shake before they left.

As she watched the smoke from the BBQ drift into the sky and disappear, she wondered for a second time how she absolutely *knew* that Sam had been talking about Terry Troy the other day; that it was Terry who had also claimed to have seen the apes. Maybe it was because Terry was just so weird, Annie thought, and now Melissa was...well, not *weird*, but behaving in a peculiar manner, and the only other person she could think of who behaved in a peculiar manner was Terry. The comparison wasn't accurate, Annie thought, or even logical. Because Terry could be weird for any number of reasons that had nothing to do with seeing any old apes. And also, Melissa wasn't nervous, the way Terry was. But Annie had known Terry since she was a kid, and he used to be *different,* and not nervous at all. Quiet, yes. But not nervous. Not... *agitated.* Then—and everybody talked about it for awhile—something had *happened* to him one day, something that had to be dramatic, because the very next day after that, he was different and stayed different; and overnight, or so it appeared, Melissa became different, too; had come back from her ride up to Slauson's Ridge and now was different. Okay, it was probably a stretch to say that because Melissa had changed dramatically the way Terry had that that meant both had claimed to see apes. Because—yes—there could be a *lot* of different explanations for why Terry had changed. But Annie knew in her *bones* that however reasonable this was to think, it was wrong. She knew, well, *un*reasonably, *intuitively,* that *apes* were what connected Terry and Melissa. And keeping it secret, the way Terry had—because he knew no one would believe him— had turned him more and more—what was the word?—Annie couldn't think of it. But he kept to himself. Mostly. And eventually people didn't like being around him. He became a loner. Alone. And by *god,* Annie suddenly thought, that is *not* going to happen to Melissa! Annie was *not* going to watch people treat her like some oddball and keep away from her, or cross the street to avoid her, the way they did with Terry.

So...what to *do*? Before she'd left Sam's office, he had counseled patience. He'd monitor Melissa...He'd maybe reach out to specialists he knew. But he wanted to go slow. It might do more harm than good to shine a spotlight on Melissa now. She could have seen a peculiar-looking bear; deformed bear...and it behaved strangely. Maybe it had been rabid—a rare thing in bears, but quite possible.

And, Annie now thought, maybe Terry had seen a bear, too, but he's just wired in a way that no one could convince him that he'd made a mistake. Maybe he was just one of those people who just *had* to be right.

Annie looked at the paper napkin in her hands. She had shredded it to bits. She looked around for Sam. But of course he wouldn't be here. These BBQs were never his thing. But where was Mayhugh? Not here either.

So Annie sat there, alone, but receiving a never-ending parade of congratulators passing by. *Look at this town, Annie! Look at all these people, Madame Mayor! Boy, you've really done it!* Shirley and Walter did stop by for a few minutes to chat, but Shirley was all business; which was good, of course—there was business for her to be all business about. According to her, there was a letter she had to get off this afternoon to the landscapers for the motel. They had screwed something up, and if Shirley was going to have that motel up in time to capture at least a *little* of the summer trade, then, by gum, those guys were going to fix their mistake *n-o-w*.

Bulie came by to announce/yell something, but even though he was announcing/yelling, Annie couldn't hear what it was, because just as he had come up to her, the Alpine Valley High School Marching Band, all five members had just started up.

Annie had wanted Peter to come, and he had wanted to—which pleased her—but when it was time to go, he was in the middle of working on his storyboards for the next video. Inspiration had struck, he said. He had gotten the idea he'd been searching for for *weeks*; and he was sorry it had come now, Mom, really sorry, but he had to get it all down before he forgot even a *bit* of it.

Annie understood. She was happy he was so re-engaged in his video-making, and happy about the cachet it had given him in town. She wasn't too certain she liked that so many girls were openly flirting with him now, especially senior girls, several of whom *drove*, and were always wanting to pick him up.

Annie suddenly chuckled, in spite of herself. It was, she thought, a good thing that her son was a little dense about all the attention he was getting. Unless a girl outright said, 'Why don't we get together some time?' Peter had no idea that a girl was trying to get him to notice her. They would just *happen* to run into him almost everywhere and giggle like blithering idiots, Annie thought, or spew all manner of nonsense, lightly pressing down on the toe of his shoe with the sole of theirs when they wanted to make a point, or picking an imaginary bit of lint off his shoulder, or sighing heavily about the fact that they had nothing to do Friday night, whereupon Peter was apt to say something like, Yeah, that's a bummer, but if you have cable, you could watch *Dog Days of Summer*, which starred a young Al Mancini, and was, in Peter's opinion, the best film Stanley Donnelly ever made; and only if the girl—as happened—Megan Meyer—said, 'Oh, I'd *love* that! Why don't we watch it *together!*'—would Peter get it.

Annie was pleased that Peter had had a good time with Megan, and, as far as Annie could see, checking in on them from time to time in Peter's room (she was afraid Megan might get some ideas), Megan had a genuinely good time with him, too. She had also noticed that Peter was losing weight. It was hard to tell whether he did it to look good for girls, or whether he was just so blessedly busy with all kinds of ideas for the next video, that he didn't think about eating all that much. Either way, he began to look once again the way he had always looked, sturdy, but not overweight, a kid who could try out for the football team. But of course, there wasn't an athletic bone in Peter's body.

Annie was also quite pleased, and a little amazed, that the steering committee had given Peter free rein on the next video. Preston was tasked with overseeing the work, but as far as she could see, Preston and Peter hadn't met once. As far as Annie could see, Peter was handling all the responsibilities of the entire production himself—and wanted it that way.

She had worried at first about the pressure on Peter to deliver a second time as much magic as he had the first. But he himself felt no pressure. He was jazzed—his word; and when she learned that the Ape Committee would have final say over the video as to content, believability, and whether it went public or not, she also worried less about the consequences to Peter if he failed. Because only the people on the committee would know it, and she knew them all to be discreet, kind people. They'd tell Peter, Sorry, this wasn't working, and probably have him try again (after all, who else here had his skill?); and this time they'd make sure Preston, or someone, monitored the production. The need for a second effort would all be kept matter-of-factly quiet, the town none the wiser.

On the other hand, Annie would have worried a *lot* about what Peter had decided to do the night after the BBQ—if she had known about it. In fact, she would have forbidden it. So it was a good thing (actually, in the end, it wasn't) that she *didn't* know the scope of Peter's ambition and the lengths he had decided to go to make his next video. But that's the concern of the next chapter. Still, I might add here that *lengths* is the operative word.

Because the new road had pushed deep into the forest. It wasn't yet a road, really, just a very rough, mostly cleared path— the result of the work of earth movers, blasters with TNT, and hard-hatted sawyers felling trees left and right. It looked like a scar on the face of the forest, that is, if you looked at the path from the top of the mountain. It excited everyone to see it, because they felt like pioneers, blazing a new trail, or *blasting* a new trail, as Skeet wrote in the paper, because blasting was one of the first things that had to happen.

A loose succession of towering rocky outcroppings dominated the area and stood between Alpine Valley and Taylorville. These outcroppings were the primary reason no one had ever followed through on building a direct road that might connect the big town to the little. The big town had no interest in making such a connection, and neither did the little town, at least, up til now, with the closure of the mill.

Yes, every now and again throughout the decades a little noise was made about building a direct road, and in the 1950s, there was actually a little start made; but then everything fell apart after a lot of misuse of funds (and outright thievery, some claimed) caused the project to go belly up.

John Chamberlain himself had once come up with a plan to build a new road, and then—as many people claimed—he simply lost enthusiasm for pushing the plan, and meeting all the people he had to meet, and shaking the hands he had to shake. So he let the matter drop. In the end, many claimed, it didn't matter to him whether it took his trucks an entire half-day to get to Taylorville and the highway. After all, it wasn't days or weeks that it took to tote his lumber out, which *would* have made a difference, so why spend time, money, and energy on something that wasn't make or break for him?

As *I* see it, however, the heart of Chamberlain's lack of enthusiasm had to do with the fact that his ancestors had built the existing, winding road to Taylorville in the 1870s, when Alpine Valley wasn't even a town, just a place on the river for a mill and a few big log dormers for sawyers, loggers, and foresters. Chamberlain was *proud* of that patrimony, and proud that the road was named after his great-grandfather on his mother's side. The Sawyer Road—a fortuitous name. If a new road *was* built, who would use the Sawyer road anymore? No one. And, as John Chamberlain had seen in all his years living in the Northwest, a forest overtook an unused, neglected road in no time at all. Roots broke through the asphalt and shrugged off big slabs of it; and seed blown into the exposed earth took root and sent out growth that obscured the slabs, and weather broke the slabs down into smaller and smaller chunks, and finally into a crumble, and eventually trees pushed through where yellow highway markers had been; and then one day—and he knew this because it had happened to him—a hiker thinking he was in the middle of no man's land would come across a chunk of asphalt and wonder how in blazes it got there, not knowing that it had rolled a long way down a mountainside from some long ago forgotten road.

But the new road had mattered to Annie LaPeer. She clearly saw that it was a lifeline for this dying town, in the absence of the mill. She'd get hikers here, and fishermen, and maybe a few hunters, and maybe a business or two; and certainly people *here* could easily get *out,* and get a job in Taylorville to which they could commute—and so they'd survive. She could not have foreseen the phenomenon of this Ape Madness. But it made her dream a blossoming reality.

One good summer...

And already the work crews had blasted a big hole into the first outcropping, and the path makers had cleared the path to and—oh, great victory—*through* an ancient impediment, and now into the heart of the woods.

And as that had happened only a few days back, and was still great fresh news to the town, that's what many of Annie's congratulators were congratulating her for. *We're on our way to better days, aren't we, Madam Mayor?*

Chapter Thirty-Seven

$\mathcal{A}$ FEW HIKERS HAD ALREADY BEEN INTO THE NEWLY cleared, newly disclosed area, and certainly some of the road crew, blasters, and sawyers had, but not extensively. And what they had learned about the area was that a small offshoot of the river curled through it. No one had known that before, and everyone *loved* that discovery. Especially Peter. It served his idea for the new video perfectly.

It wasn't that this area was *that* far from town that it would have worried Annie that Peter was heading here (if she had known he was heading here). But it was a heavily *restricted* area. There was a lot of equipment out there, some of it dangerous; and big holes in the earth; and on top of that, there was the little fact that this newly cleared path pushed into unfamiliar area.

As for Peter, his concern lay in whether the weather would cooperate or not. Like most everyone else, he had one eye on the sky. Storms in the valley could last for days, and he had to get this video made and out in front of the public. Because people all over the country—all over the world!—would be planning their vacations. He didn't want everyone going to the Grand Canyon, or Hawaii, or wherever, because they might be losing interest in his Ape.

His other, smaller, but still significant concern lay in how he and his actors were going to get hold of a vehicle that would get them where they had to go. They not only needed a car, they needed a four-wheel-drive vehicle. That new path was a rough and bumpy, hillocky, dippy bit of business. He certainly couldn't ask anyone's parents to drive them—they'd *never* take a bunch of kids into the restricted area; and the two friends Derrick had who owned four-wheel-drives refused to help him out: they were worried about getting into trouble.

Eventually, the problem was solved. Derrick would simply liberate his Dad's truck for a few hours and hope he didn't notice that it was missing. After all, they'd be shooting at night, and his dad usually didn't go anywhere at night. He didn't usually go anywhere, *period*. Not anymore. Not since he got laid off from the mill and made whatever money he could with his telemarketing job. He was on the phone or computer seventeen hours a day every day.

Normally, Peter would have qualms about helping 'liberate' someone's truck, but, as with not telling his mom what he was doing tonight, he felt he just *had* to do what he was doing. He knew in his heart that this video would be *amazing* and *had* to be made— for the good of the town's future! Also, Derrick had said to him, "Petey-boy, it's easier to ask forgiveness than permission."

So Derrick and Peter had liberated Mr. Merrick's truck, picked up the rest of the Ape ensemble, and headed for new territory.

Arriving, everyone piled out of the truck and walked down to the little curl of river. Peter had heard it ran broad here, about ten feet deep, the current gentle. The information was gratifyingly correct. They stood at the edge of the river, loving the new, surprising fact of it as much as the pretty little body of water itself, their day-packs slung over their shoulders.

A good omen for Peter was how warm the night was. Of course, had this evening been cool, he had a Script B in his pocket. But so far, Script A remained the one he could produce, and it was Script A because he really liked it a lot. A good long look at the sky told him that though there were storm clouds bunched up in the east, they didn't look as if they'd make their way here until very early morning. Still, *chop-chop*, Peter thought, it was better to get things going.

In addition to Peter and Derrick, those now assembled at the edge of the river included Chrissy Covington, Chrissy's BFF, Julie Gleason, Derrick's friend Skipper Reese, Skipper's cousins Maynard and Will Beloit, and Gretchen Barnes, Millard's youngest daughter. (He had four.) They listened carefully to everything Peter was saying.

Inwardly sky-high, but keeping an outward appearance of calm—and *command*, which he knew a director had to have—Peter gave his actors an overview of what he was after here.

"So," he said. "The basic idea is this. Skipper and Chrissy have dashed off to the water. They're going to race each other to the other side and back. The rest of you are here sitting around a fire. You've had enough of swimming. We'll work out later how re-dressed everyone is—like fully, or just shorts and bathing tops, or whatever. Maynard will be taking video of you all having a good time, though of course it'll be *me*—you'll just *say* it was Maynard taking it and— ."

"Wait," said Gretchen. "Why can't it be you?"

"A just-in-case thing. With all the reporters in town, you don't want them wondering if the town's big movie buff might have anything to do with anything. You want me in the background as much as possible."

Gretchen shrugged. "Okay."

"Anyway," Peter continued, now wondering if he had been over-thinking it about having to be in the background—because it sure would help if he didn't have to worry about Maynard's prox-imity to him and Maynard's remembering he had to run with him and say his lines the way Mr. Carnody had, but anyway, he con-tinued, "while Maynard's taking video, you all hear Chrissy scream as she's swimming back to this side."

"Am I ahead of Skipper?" she asked.

"By a lot," Peter answered.

"Wait," said Skipper, "isn't it more realistic that a guy would beat a girl? I mean, I'd be way ahead of Chrissy."

"I don't think so," said Chrissy.

"You want to race?" he asked.

Everyone chuckled, except for Peter. He had stuff to get through here, and anyway, didn't Skipper remember that Chrissy had been on the swim team at the Y in Taylorville? For three straight summers, too, winning every race she entered. Maybe all the piercings and hair had made him forget she was athletic. So he reminded Skipper about Chrissy's aquatic past.

"Oh, yeah," Skipper said.

"And," Peter added, "she's got the trophies to prove she could beat a guy—if any reporter or whoever wants to check things out."

"Okay, okay. I'll gracefully lose."

Everyone chuckled again—their spirits were high. Peter went on.

"So. The scream scares Maynard, and he bobbles the camera. Well, I do. And then when Will says his line, 'What the hell, Chrissy?' really annoyed, that gets Maynard relaxed so he says, 'Yeah, what the hell?', giving a little laugh, and he steadies the camera, and then he's got it pointing at Chrissy hurrying out of the water, and she says, 'Over *there!*' and Will, because you're laughing and saying 'For god's *sake*, Chrissy,' that makes *you*, Maynard, laugh a little, but you swing the camera to see what Chrissy's all excited about—and whoa, there's the Ape along the shore; and then, *really* scared now, Maynard bobbles the camera—but like, a *lot* more this time—and he says, 'Oh my god, oh, my god!' And now Maynard's leaping up— he's scared out of his mind. By the way, Maynard, you don't want to say 'It's the ape!' That's too much."

"I got it," said Maynard, and Peter saw that he really did.

"Meantime," Peter continued, and feeling better, because in talking the scene out to all of them, he saw that not only were they getting it, but it seemed realistic to them, "Skipper's behind Chrissy, and swimming like a madman, trying to catch up, and all of you scream for him to *get out, get out*, and you're all racing out of here, and Maynard is, too, but running kind of sideways, and with his camera just barely catching Derrick disappearing into the woods—I mean, me, of course—just barely catching him. And so we don't *see* Skipper slogging it up through the water, trying to get out and angling in the direction everyone else is taking—we don't *see* that, but we *hear* it, and Maynard is more or less running away with him now—both of them kind of together—and we hear that, too. Mostly what people will *see* at that point is that Maynard is trying to shoot video behind himself as he runs, but he gets nothing. And that's just to show that he was *trying* to, which would be realistic. Okay. That's pretty much it. So, everyone good? Any questions?"

"Wait," said Derrick, "just one thing occurs to me." Derrick looked perplexed, which made Peter nervous. He needed Derrick to be confident, his usual confident self, because this would be a lot for him to pull off tonight, especially since it'd be hard for him to see in the dark.

"Yes?" Peter asked, hoping that his voice didn't betray his nerves.

"What if people look at us and think this was just some teenage goof? Bunch of bored kids with too much time on their hands?"

Peter's stomach sank. He'd never thought about this. And now he felt pressure. Because now, not only did he have to make this video perfect just because it had to be perfect, he had to make it perfect-*plus*, because Derrick was absolutely right: People might look at the video and think, Ah, it's just a bunch of teens goofing on the whole Ape thing.

So now Peter had to overcome a built-in problem. Teenagers! They were all teenagers! And this is what teenagers do! All that time and energy he'd put into his storyboards, into his scenario, and not *once* had this problem occurred to him! Well, too late now, and anyway, they were already behind schedule. Julie had been ten minutes late to the meet-up place, and Maynard had run back home because he'd forgotten a jacket, and *that* took ten minutes. "Well," said Peter, stalling for time—what to say to the troops?— "you're right, of course, they *could* think that, and that crossed my mind, of course, but it didn't bother me all that much because of my cast. I picked you guys *exactly* because you can make this look real. And real is real, no matter what."

Peter knew it wasn't such a great answer back, but Chrissy certainly liked the appeal to her ego, and it looked to Peter that Derrick did, too; and as for the others, they looked so happy to be a part of what was, when you got right down to it, just a teenage goof, that Peter could have said anything, and they'd still be down with the program.

For the next two and a half hours, Peter rehearsed every story element slowly and methodically with his actors. They rehearsed the dialogue and individual line readings. He and Maynard practiced moving as one together, almost as if Maynard were grafted onto Peter, Maynard's chest to Peter's back. The only thing Peter didn't rehearse was, most unfortunately, one of the most important things, and that was Chrissy's and Skipper's parts.

The water was a *lot* colder than Peter had thought it would be. His actors had both gone in up to their waists and had come out shivering. Peter was not some dictator director like Otto Preminger, and he hadn't thought to have them bring robes and warm stuff they could get into, and thermoses of hot tea or whatever. (How much he had to learn!) On the other hand, it had been hot outside, and that had fooled him into thinking he didn't have to worry about the water—so he wasn't *ignorant* exactly, just...fooled. (But again, how much he had to learn! As in, never assume anything!)

All right, then, the complete burden would be on him. But there again, the only real acting part was Chrissy's scream, her one line—'Over *there!*'—and then running like she was scared. How hard could that be for her? He'd seen her in some Agatha Christie play Miss DuMonde had directed at school, and she'd been great.

As for Skipper, he didn't have to say anything while he was in the water, just make sure that he gave Chrissy enough of a lead so that she was where she had to be to scream, with him still swimming like crazy in the background. Then all he had to do was run out of the water for dear life.

He could pull that off, right? How hard was *that*? But Peter wasn't about to say *not hard at all*. Because he had learned from all kinds of biographies of directors that the *second* you said anything like that was the second the weirdest most complicated things happened on a shoot and *not hard at all* turned into three days of shooting.

It was nine p.m. by the time he had everyone rehearsed. They were now all getting cold, but the big campfire they were supposed to build they built, and it warmed them up considerably. And Will, Gretchen, and Julie were actually making s'mores, which was their job in the video, and the food and the warmth of it were warming everyone up inside.

Peter checked the skies. The clouds had moved in. While he'd been busy, they'd been busy. Oh, *please*, he thought, it just *can't* rain. "All right, everybody," said Peter, who waved away the s'more that Julie offered him, "we've got to get it on. Derrick, you ready?"

"As I'll ever be," he said, his confidence back, as Peter saw it, and Derrick put on his head and loped down the river's edge to take his mark.

"Okay," said Peter to the rest of the group, sitting around the fire. "I'm not going to say action or anything. I'm going to sit right here, and Maynard, seriously, like your head should be like *right here* next to mine."

"I get it. I get it."

"Good. Okay, you all know what you're supposed to do and say, and look, you're all *amazingly* natural, I mean just *excellent* at underplaying, so just do what you did in rehearsal, and, like, Chrissy, everything goes off your cue. Just pick your moment to start needling Skipper that you know you're faster, and whatever little, like, sparring happens, happens, and you bolt for the water."

"Got it," Chrissy said.

Peter decided not to say another word and just let things happen, and he was amazed at how well everyone came off, like they *were* just a bunch a kids around a campfire making s'mores and shooting the breeze.

If Peter had any worries it was with himself. He had to resist the temptation to take beautiful video; to frame shots just right and get the sparks flying off into the night. He had to be *Maynard*, just monkeying around, getting his friends. No lovely profiles, no moves...And then, at what Peter himself thought was exactly the right moment, Chrissy began needling Skipper that no *way* was he a faster swimmer. Who was the one with the swimming trophies, thank you very much? And Skipper said, yeah, well against other *girls*. And oh my god what a pig, said Gretchen, which she hadn't said in rehearsal, but what a great idea that was to say it, thought Peter...and everything escalated, and Chrissy was up, and whipping off her sweatshirt and shorts, and was in her swimsuit and running to the water...and then everything went to hell:

In giving chase, Skipper tripped over his own feet and landed hard on his knee, but gamely, he got up, and hobbled on after her; and though Peter *almost* yelled cut—because who was going to believe that a guy who was hobbling was still going to try to swim?—he didn't, because, well, maybe Skipper would be smart enough to ad lib something. And Chrissy would *certainly* be smart enough to realize she had to ad lib, and so Peter kept shooting her, keeping an eye on what Skipper might contribute, and Chrissy reached the other side of the river, touching the raised bank, and, god bless her, there wasn't even a hitch or a look, she just *got* it that something had happened, but no one had told her cut, so she was going to keep doing what she was supposed to be doing—what a pro!—he was suddenly in love with Chrissy Covington—and she was swimming back when it appeared to Peter that she had launched herself upward out of the water almost vertically, and she was screaming, *perfectly*—but *way* too early, and this time he really *did* have to yell cut because that too-early scream would throw off the timing of everything else, and what was the deal with that leap of hers?, but he *didn't* yell cut, or he might have, he never could remember, because there was *another* scream, and it startled him, and he wasn't sure whether it came from Chrissy, but there was a black shape next to her that also seemed to be leaping vertically up out of the water. And what *was* that? But Chrissy shoved it away— and it cried out in fear and pain, and it was Baby Ape—and Chrissy lit out for shore.

Though Peter saw all this happening, it wasn't registering with him what was going on. He was confused. Not scared. He had had no experience with Baby Ape before, and all that was penetrating was that maybe Chrissy had collided with a bit of log in the river; unless maybe that was a beaver swimming by.

Then Skipper was screaming lines like, "Run! Run!" And "Chrissy, swim!" And the lines were delivered unbelievably well, but he was *way* off script now, altering the story completely, and he didn't understand why Skipper was hobbling away for all he was worth, nor why Maynard, was running away, too. He was supposed to stick to Peter like glue! And where were Will, Julie, and Gretchen going? It was just a bit of log, or a beaver—and it was already gone!

But though he was confused and angry with everyone, Peter had learned enough from reading biographies of the masters that a lot of times it was good to keep the camera rolling. You could always yell cut and make things stop; but what if what was happening was even better than what had been planned? Of course, now *Derrick* would have to be the one to get it that it was time to ad lib.

But Derrick, way up the shore, was jumping up and down and yelling, though of course no one could hear him through that ape head. "What are you all doing?" he hollered. "You're doing it all wrong!"

He couldn't see because of where he was—and Peter couldn't

see because he was focused on looking at things through his camera—that all of the following had or was taking place:

It would appear that in shoving Baby Ape, Chrissy had knocked the wind out of it, and it sank under water.

As Chrissy broke Olympic records trying to swim for shore, Skipper and those around the fire saw Big Mama and Big Daddy swimming the way a bear swims, and heading toward where they'd seen Baby go under. It would appear that all three had been swimming down the river—a little family swim of an evening—and who knows whether they had detected Chrissy or not, probably they had, but Baby hadn't heard—or had ignored their call—and had banged right into her.

Then, scaring the kids, there was suddenly a cacophony of animal noises, and three more apes appeared in the river—so maybe this was a communal swim of an evening; and as these new apes raced toward Big Mama and Big Daddy, Big Daddy pulled a coughing, choking Baby into his arms. Big Mama made a sniff at Baby, possibly to see if he was all right, and then turned, and turned all her attention on Chrissy, who was still swimming for shore. Big Mama disappeared under water, but it was quite obvious she was coming after Chrissy.

At this point, or right around this point, Peter had had enough of this confusion, and in frustration and anger, he lowered his camera and called to Chrissy, "Never *mind*, Chrissy! You don't have to swim so hard! We have to start all over!"

It was clear to Peter that she couldn't hear him—she was swimming so hard—so he stepped closer toward the water and cupped his hands to the sides of his mouth to yell—and that's when a dripping Chrissy started scrambling on all fours, and now upright, as she found ground under her feet and began struggling out of the river, crying, Big Mama surfacing behind her and now lunging for her ankle, but missing, as Chrissy ran onto shore. "Peter, run!" Chrissy screamed.

But Peter didn't. He was trying to remember what you were

supposed to do when you saw a bear—and run wasn't one of those things. And then he saw four more bears swimming his way, and "Chrissy, you're not supposed to run!" he hissed.

At this point, the lunging Big Mama picked herself up from the mud of the riverside and was about to take off after Chrissy, but Big Daddy vocalized something that was clearly meant to convey, "Don't! Stop!" Big Mama turned, vocalized nothing, but clearly communicated something to Big Daddy with her eyes, then turned around and bounded after Chrissy.

Derrick, still in costume, and not having seen Big Mama at all, ran up to Peter and said, "What the hell is going on?!" And then he, too, saw what he thought were bears, emerging from the water, but angling away from him and Peter. They were clearly after Chrissy, and maybe the other kids, too. One of the bears, however, couldn't help but pause for a second when he got a look at Derrick. He looked confused; but then he ran on after the others.

In the meantime, with Peter and Derrick frozen in terror and trying to figure out what to do—and not yet wondering why these bears were running on their hind legs, Chrissy was running for her life. She had entered the woods, her goal being to get to the truck, and hoping like mad that Derrick hadn't locked it.

Big Mama was behind her, but closing in.

The truck wasn't far away now, dark in the night, but giving her glints of hope from off the chrome of the door handles and the glass of the windshield; and reaching it, she saw dark figures inside—Skipper, Maynard, Will, Julie—and Gretchen, who opened the door for her on the side facing her—the driver's side—and then slid over in the seat so that Chrissy could get in, and Chrissy did.

Big Mama leapt on to the hood of the car and started screaming at Chrissy, who covered her ears while curling up in the front seat into as little a ball as possible. Big Mama started pounding at the windshield and succeeded in making it crack into a spider web pattern.

Big Daddy then bounded to within ten feet of the car, and,

handing Baby Ape off to one of his pals, began remonstrating with Big Mama to stop and consider what she was doing—or so that's what the kids thought he was doing. But Big Mama wouldn't get down from the car. Big Daddy, it appeared, was not only scared for her, but scared of the car. It was definitely scaring the other apes. They kept a safe distance from it.

Then the windshield broke through. Big Mama hadn't struck it again, but all the vibrations she was causing by slapping the hood of the truck in frustration at what Big Daddy was telling her had to have been the reason it broke. The sound of breaking glass scared Big Mama, and she put her hands over her ears, and the glass falling all over Chrissy freaked her out, but not as much as it freaked out Gretchen, who screaming, opened the passenger door and got the hell out of the truck, running away like a mad woman.

Their ears covered and making vocalizations of complaint, the apes stomped their feet on the ground, and Baby made what sounded like crying sounds. Then, either confusing Gretchen with Chrissy, or not caring, Big Mama took off after Gretchen.

Who knows what Gretchen's fate might have been, had she not seen the earth mover they had passed in coming here? And as she recalled in narrating these events to me, that earth mover had been on her mind when she had leapt out of the truck. She had thought they were all goners when that windshield collapsed, leaving no shield between them and the apes, and her only hope was to take refuge in the cab of the earth mover—not more than thirty yards away.

Reaching it, she climbed up into the cab and shut the door. She thought about hiding—dropping below the seat so she couldn't be seen, but there was no room for that she saw, and that's when she saw that there was no place for a key, just a black button to push. She pushed it. The earth mover started right up. She whipped her head around to see how close Big Mama was, and the answer was surprisingly close, except that the start of the earth mover's engine had terrified her, and she stood not fifteen yards off, covering her ears.

Gretchen had no idea how to drive this thing, but she could drive a stick shift and realized that a lot of these knobs and levers had to do with earth-moving, not driving. Her hands flew from one lever to the next, pulling and pushing, trying to determine what did what, and her foot found the gas and clutch, and because the machine was still warming up, it only bucked forward once, as if it were balky, when she gave it the gas. But Gretchen geared it up again and gave it more gas, and though sluggish, it moved forward.

She bounced it up onto the cleared path proper and, giving it as much gas as she could, got it to go as fast as it could—which, after several seconds, proved surprisingly fast.

But Big Mama was surprisingly fast, too. Her target was getting away from her, and though scared by that monstrous machine, she uncovered her ears and bounded after it.

At this point, Gretchen saw a few lights of the town wink into view—the outskirts of Alpine Valley. But she didn't have time to feel even a scintilla of relief, because *thump* Big Mama had leapt on to the earth mover.

Gretchen screamed and saw Big Mama reflected in the rear view mirror. She was covering her ears, but now uncovering them and advancing on her. Gretchen screamed again, and Big Mama covered her ears again. This was her weapon, Gretchen realized, or her defense. But when Big Mama uncovered her ears the third time and Gretchen screamed a fourth, Big Mama ignored it and advanced on the cab.

Gretchen screamed yet again, this time more out of mortal fear than out of any hope that it would stop Big Mama, and it didn't stop Big Mama.

But her scream did awaken Rawley Conner, who sat up fast in his bed. Had he really heard someone scream—a woman? And there it was *again*. Yes, a woman was screaming, a woman afraid for her life. Rawley ran into his front room, tore open the door of his gun cabinet, and pulled out a rifle.

As the earth mover rumbled into Sequoia Street, Big Mama

made repeated smashes at the glass of the cab. It finally broke through. She began slapping Gretchen's head. Not grabbing it, not grabbing Gretchen, not biting her, just slapping her head.

Gretchen of course was terrified and knew only that this creature was attacking her, and so she screamed for the umpteenth time, finding a decibel level she didn't know she was capable of.

Lights had already begun flicking on, because Rawley wasn't the only one who had heard Gretchen's scream, and as the earth mover kept moving down Sequoia, toward Main, Gretchen screaming, more lights flicked on, and as the earth mover rumbled onto Main, Big Mama gave Gretchen one last slap on the head and leapt off the earth mover, whereupon Rawley shot her through the heart, and, quite surprised, trying to cover her ears, trying to keep her balance and failing, Big Mama fell on her back onto the street. She made a big gasp for air; then a smaller one; and died.

Looking through the scope of his rifle, Rawley thought he'd shot a bear—a crazy-looking bear, and now he saw another bear—on its hind legs—rush up to the one he'd killed and gather it up into his arms. Rawley looked up from his scope to look out through the open window. What the...?

And then he had a moment of sheer, vertigo-inducing panic. What if he'd just shot that kid who was playing the ape? What if this was another of those videos? And then Rawley blacked out from his panic and collapsed to the floor.

On Main Street, Big Daddy cradled Big Mama in his arms and then lifting his head to the sky, made a great, horrible pure animal cry. And as if he'd provoked it, or as if it had only been waiting for the beast to cry, a thunderclap sounded overhead and shook the valley.

The rain fell as if all at once. Big Daddy bounded away, Big Mama in his arms, and he disappeared into the darkness.

Gretchen, still up in the cab of the earth mover, sobbed.

The residents of Sequoia Street, who had been looking through their windows at the entire bizarre and tragic scene, now came out of their houses and into the rain. Preston was among their number. They walked toward Main, toward Chrissy, toward the great pool of blood spreading across their newly paved pride and joy.

No one noticed the rain. They stood in the sun of revelation.

The legend of the Ape was *true*.

The Ape was *real*.

Apes...were *real*.

Chapter Thirty-Eight

ONLY THE CLOCK COULD TELL YOU WHAT TIME IT WAS.

Dawn.

Otherwise, it looked like the blackest of black nights.

The clouds had gathered and dominating the sky blocked the light. Only here and there, the result of friction, did lightning penetrate the funereal atmosphere and reveal the presence, the solidity, of reliable objects—signposts—by which anyone out could find his way down the street or along a path, to where he should be.

There was Miss Dorothy's house.

The town square.

Good old Eddie's.

I know where I am.

City Hall...

Annie was on the phone, pacing in a circle around the oval table in council chambers. She looked bedraggled, like she'd been up through the night, which she had been. She wore a good old-fashioned yellow slicker over the jeans and sweatshirt she'd thrown on.

Peter and Melissa sat at the table, watching their mother. They were similarly dressed, similarly bedraggled, Peter in particular. In fact, Peter looked hollowed out; but for good reason: What did he know anymore?

Creatures he could only have imagined, creatures that only had existence trapped in celluloid, had raced past him and looked

him in the eye in so doing. And what did they see but a boy transfixed by fear. He couldn't have helped Chrissy or anyone. He
couldn't have helped himself.

Only when everything was quiet—deathly still—did he and
Derrick take frightened, most tentative steps, through the trees
toward the truck. Neither had been more relieved in his life to see
it still there, the dark figures of their friends inside—and they,
seeing the two boys, yelled, "We're in here! Run!" They did, doors
opening for them, and they dove in, though Derrick, forgetting
that he still had the ape head on, bonked it pretty good in trying
to get himself through the too narrow space Maynard had made
for him: Maynard wasn't about to open his door any more than he
thought he absolutely had to. "Derrick!" Maynard hissed, as if it
had been Derrick's fault. Derrick got himself up from the ground
and tried again, this time Maynard getting it that he had to give
him more head space.

Even though it was Derrick's dad's truck, Chrissy drove home,
because she was already in the front seat and nobody wanted to
spend any time switching spots, especially given how it might
involve Derrick, so bulky in his costume, getting out of the truck
to get back in, to take the driver's seat. "Give me the keys, Derrick!"
Chrissy yelled—she didn't have to yell; it was just the fear talking.

"They're on the floor. Don't you see them?"

There was a strange, awkward, silent moment after that key
bit of information was related. *They were on the floor? They'd been
there the whole time?*

"*I* didn't have them," Derrick said. "This thing doesn't have
any pockets."

"You don't have pants on?" Will asked.

"Gym shorts."

Chrissy took deep, nostril-flarings breaths. She was having
difficulty with this. She could have gotten out of there before the
ape had attacked them; before Gretchen had run off in panic. The
others were thinking this, too, but also thinking, *My god, if we'd*

left, we would have left Peter and Derrick behind...

It was Julie who expressed for the group everything they were thinking when she gave one long relieved, but self-revealing *whoooo* of exhalation.

No one said a thing about the missing windshield—not even Derrick, who might not have even noticed it: his mind was still occupied with his fright and the wonder at what he had so lately seen—as Chrissy drove them home.

They were almost at Sequoia before it dawned on Derrick to ask, "Wait. Where's Gretchen?"

"We don't know! Shut up!" cried Chrissy.

"She just ran," Julie said.

"Where?" Derrick asked

"We don't know!" repeated Chrissy. "Shut up!"

And he did, and Chrissy bumped the truck off the dirt road that led from Sequoia Street into the sequoias and onto the pavement of Alpine Valley. It got even more quiet in the truck thanks to the smooth surface of the asphalt street.

In the light of the first streetlight, Skipper noticed the waxen look of Peter's face, the vacancy of his eyes.

"Are you okay, man?" Skipper asked him, because he certainly didn't look okay.

And that was the same thing Melissa now asked him, "Are you okay, Peter?"

And he didn't—couldn't—answer her any more than he could have answered Skipper six hours ago.

"I've been on all night with everybody," Annie said to someone on the phone. "I can't get them *here*. We need to work this *through*."

Melissa now got it that her mother was talking to Coach Mayhugh. She just kind of had a tone of voice that was different when she spoke with him.

"*Guns*?" Annie cried. "What do you mean, 'guns'? Where's Larry? Where's your cousin?"

I won't take you through the whole nervous conversation,

Annie's pacing around the table picking up speed. But I will tell you what she heard from Preston, who had also been on the phone with fellow council members, trying to get them to calm down and come down to City Hall.

But they weren't having any of that. They were frightened. They hadn't seen, as Preston and his few neighbors had, what had gone on. They had only *heard*, and so their minds went to even more wild and dark places, where things turned into things too horrible not to imagine. And wild talk had picked up through the night, so that now people were arming themselves and were forming a posse—not that that was the word they used, but that was pretty much what it was.

And Larry Salisbury, Officer of the Law in these parts, was on a date with Ramona DuMonde in Taylorville. He wanted to celebrate her completion of another successful school year. They weren't due back until tomorrow—well, *today*, at this point—and meantime, he wasn't answering his cell.

Then through all the rain pounding on the windows for admittance, Annie heard car horns honking, and voices—raised voices. She looked through the assaulted window and saw splotches and smears of headlights, as a large number of townsfolk pulled up in front of City Hall. Dark, wavery figures got out of cars.

"Stay here," Annie said to her children.

When she emerged into the dark and rain, Annie saw a large number of people gathered at the foot of the steps. She couldn't identify individuals right away because of the hoods and umbrellas and bulky foul weather gear. But she knew the vehicles—the trucks and Jeeps and cars. She knew that her council members were amongst those present, except for Shirley—because she'd be home with Walter. She wouldn't bring him out in the rain. And Bulie, she knew, hadn't heard his phone ring. She had tried four times and given up. She was hoping to see Boyd and Floyd in this crowd, since they were slow, methodical, step-by-step types who'd resist any action based on emotion. But only in now looking for them did she realize that she had never thought to call them (and as it turned out, no one had).

"We have to eradicate them!" Millard said above the rain, even before Annie was halfway down the steps of City Hall to stand before them.

"Let's go inside!" Annie said to everyone, making a sweeping gesture up the steps, thinking that if they couldn't hear her in the back, they'd see what she was after. But no one moved; and Annie couldn't understand why no one wanted to get in out of the rain. Just then, she saw Preston's truck pulling up. She felt enormous relief. He had told her he was on the way, but he'd had a few more calls to make. He was trying to convince the two hotel managers and five motel managers in Taylorville to please see if Larry Salisbury was registered there—big guy?...big woman with him...?...please, it's an emergency...but no—there was no Salisbury registered there or anywhere. (Only later would anyone learn—and it would be Annie who had—that they had checked into a Bed and Breakfast—one of four in town. It had never occurred to Preston to look up "B&B's in Taylorville.")

Preston dashed from the truck and against the rain into and through the crowd. He wanted to stand by Annie's side, but thought she might find that presumptuous (while meantime Annie was hoping he'd stand by her side), so he dashed to the front of the crowd, anyway, and turned toward them, Annie a step above him. He had arrived just in time to hear Mr. Pierce say, "No! These creatures are a wonder! They just saw Chrissy as a threat to the baby. That's all!"

"That 'baby' attacked my daughter!" Millard said. Millard was mixed up, as most of the town was. In all the telephoning through the night, one neighbor to the next, and so on, the facts had gotten mixed. The Baby Ape had merely banged into Chrissy in the river—not *attacked* her. It was Big Mama who had attacked (as it were) Gretchen, Millard's daughter, as she tried to escape her in the earth mover.

"Wait! Hang on!" Preston said, growing confused himself. He had caught sight of Chrissy in the crowd. "Chrissy, can you describe what happened to you?"

"It attacked *me*!" Chrissy cried, trying, in her way, and out of her own perspective of events, to shed some light, but in effect only making things worse, because in correcting Millard that the attack was on *her*, not Gretchen, she managed to create confusion in Millard's mind, and Millard was a man who was not at all comfortable with confusion. He liked things black and white; on or off; and if he couldn't get that certainty, he grew angry.

But then a man cleared things up for him, but not really, by shouting, "It was *two* apes! One who attacked Chrissy, and one who attacked Gretchen!"

"That's right!" shouted Chrissy, who was the de facto spokeswoman for Gretchen, who was at home with her mother, warm and safe, but only in a bodily sense.

"Look, this is stupid!" another man cried. It was Rawley Conner, who had recovered and now, oh so relieved that he hadn't killed anybody, and angry that he had been made to think he had, wanted to make those apes pay. "We're getting wet!"

"He's right!" Annie cried, "so let's— ."

"So let's get it on and go *get* 'em!" Rawley said, which is not at all where Annie was going with this. "Who's with me?"

Several men in the crowd cried, "I am! We are!"

"Wait! *Wait*!" Preston cried out in the rain. "Let's dial this back! First, let's please just consider what we've seen. We've got a lot to...to...process here. Rawley!" he hollered to Rawley, who was toward the back of the crowd, "We can't go off half-cocked here!"

"Let's put it to a vote!" Millard cried.

"Second!" Skeet cried.

"All in favor of eradicating this danger say, 'Aye!'"

Everyone but Preston, Mr. Pierce and Miss Ames said 'Aye!' Annie said nothing, because she was so busy trying to figure out how to stop this locomotive of emotion, while she herself was trying to apply the brakes to the outrage gathering in her throat and about to burst through her teeth. How dare they vote like this! This was a council issue! A governmental issue! And there was no Law here at the moment, other than what she and the council could provide.

"The 'ayes' have it!" said Millard.

"No!" Melissa said—and Annie jumped—she hadn't seen her daughter join her at her side. "This isn't right! You can't hurt them! They're gentle!"

"Honey, please," Annie said. "Go back inside."

And then there was Peter, on her other side, saying to the crowd, "They ignored Derrick and me. And that one ape was little—like a *baby*."

Someone in the crowd started shouting—something, I don't know what—but he was clearly shouting Peter down. Whereupon Preston said, "Quiet! Let him speak! He was there!"

Peter darted eyes at Preston, grateful, but also a little afraid that all eyes were now on him; and that he had the floor and must speak. On the other hand, he was, well, he *was* the one who'd put this town on the map, wasn't he? Not to be egotistical about this, but without his video, where would all these people, who kissed his ass every day now, be without him? On the still other hand, he was the scared little boy who stood motionless and did *nothing* as that creature took off after Chrissy Covington. So he took a deep breath, his jaw quivering, and his voice cracked, but out came, "Look, I don't think he attacked Chrissy. It was, like, they just banged into each other in the river. It was an accident. And Julie told Skipper that Gretchen told her the ape just *slapped* her."

He wanted to say other words, more words, to make things clearer to these people—it wasn't quite coming out right, it was like a badly edited sequence in a movie—*there*, but not as persuasive as it could be, but someone else, a woman, maybe Edna, was scoffing, "Julie told Skipper told whosey-pusey..."

"The mother just got mad," Mel was saying. "I know it! I've

seen it! But I mean, not *really*. Not—it's not like you all are! She never shot anybody!"

"Honey, calm down," Annie said, and at that moment, she got pushed in the back by a gust of wind. It had been storming, but wind hadn't been much of a presence. But now it suddenly was.

"Just let them be, and they'll let us be! I promise!" Melissa said.

"Let's go!" Rawley yelled from the back, and he turned and all the men around him turned to and went to their trucks.

"No!" screamed Melissa, and she ran off, skirting the crowd, and dashed away. But where was she going?

"Melissa!" Annie cried. "Melissa, come back here!"

"Wait! Just stop! Everybody!" Preston yelled, angrily, like no one had ever seen him, and it occurred to Preston that, man, he should have thought to bring his whistle. "This is...outrageous! It's stupid! You don't even know where they are! This is..."

"We know where they are! Where the kids were!"

And then everyone heard a Jeep screeching as it tried to gain traction in the rain, and they looked—and it was Melissa, in Annie's Jeep, fishtailing wildly.

"Melissa!" Annie screamed, the wind snatching her words away.

The Jeep got traction and Melissa drove off.

"She doesn't know how to drive!" Annie screamed, to Preston.

But by all evidence, Melissa did, because that's what she was doing down Main Street, and at a very high rate of speed.

Even with everything going on as it was, Peter couldn't help being impressed by his sister—and jealous of her. He would have been afraid to drive like that—so fast, and in the rain.

Chapter Thirty-Nine

I'VE NEVER GOTTEN A FULL PICTURE AS TO EVERYTHING that happened next. But I know this:

Rawley and the men who had left with him, all of whom were armed with rifles, made a quick, quite bumpy way to the curl of river, where Peter and company had attempted to make their video. Not seeing the apes there, as they thought they would, they played army rangers fanning out in twos into the blowing woods all around for about two hundred yards deep, keeping in touch by walkie-talkie, huge flashlights lighting their various ways.

But they found nothing.

Preston and Annie had pulled into the area about five minutes behind them. In her panic and confusion over Melissa, Annie thought that maybe Melissa had gone home—in tears?...out of anger...? But she didn't find her there. So the next logical conclusion was that she had gone to the spot in the river where Peter—and the creatures—had been. Where Rawley and everyone else had gone. And they had guns. And her little girl was in that area—probably tromping about in the dark and rain yelling, "Apples!" into the wind.

Annie shook. From fear. Not cold. Preston wanted to comfort her, but there was no time.

They got out of the truck, and I really don't know what they said, and to whom, though at one point Preston lost his cool and sent Rawley to the ground with a punch, and then lost all kinds of time apologizing to him like a mad man and helping him up, when Annie was really wishing he'd kill him. But at that point, the men playing army came filtering back through the wildly waving trees, at which point Annie screamed. Everyone jerked from fear, and fingers went to triggers, and eyes darted around, but the scream was only the thunder of a frightening bolt of insight that shot through Annie's mind: She knew where Melissa had gone! Carson Bridge! She'd go look for these creatures in the spot she had found them— and she *had* found them! She had been *right!*

"I know where she is!" she said to Preston, clutching his arm, and then, regretting it immediately, because others heard her, she said, "She's going to where she saw them—where they *live!*"

No one is quite clear what happened immediately after she said that. But the next thing everyone can agree on is that a long, cross-purposed caravan of cars and trucks was making a way through the storm to Carson Bridge.

In the meantime, Melissa had roared up to Carson's Bridge in Annie's Jeep. As Preston had the day he joined her and Annie on the hike, she parked on the shoulder of the road and made a way down the slope toward the river. Unlike Preston, she slipped and she slid in the wet grass most of the way down, leaving a telltale slick chute down the slope.

The river was high and wild. White-capped waves collapsed over the bridge, and the bridge was undulating in an S pattern.

Melissa picked herself up. She had nothing with her. No daypack. No apples. No means of communication. She hadn't stopped to think. She had no idea what she was doing beyond trying to warn these creatures of danger.

Rawley pulled up in his truck, parking next to Annie's Jeep. Though Preston had been in the lead of the caravan, Rawley, in an effort to be first, had accidentally (or so he would claim) forced Preston off the road—and into some mud. Though Preston had four-wheel-drive, it still took him precious panicked minutes to get the truck moving forward again.

When Melissa heard all the trucks pulling up, she threw a wild glance up the hill, seeing Rawley, and two other men, coming down the slope with their guns, and slipping but not falling. She screamed something, but the wind snatched it away and carried it off.

At that moment, an uprooted tree raced down the river and slammed into Carson Bridge, making the wood of it shudder and the joints groan. A part of the river now used the tree as a kind of ladder to get up and over the bridge, and the bridge stopped making the S pattern it had been making and started to belly, looking more C-shaped than anything else.

Melissa ran away from the men with the guns, ran toward the bridge, toward the forest, toward the apes.

"No! No!" Rawley and the other men called to her.

But she raced onto the bridge, and holding onto the railing—hand over hand—as she got buffeted by wind and water, she made as fast a way across as she could, and then she fell through rotten planks.

Even in the wind, the men heard her scream and saw the river whisk her away.

She disappeared.

Men newly arriving screamed and ran down the slope, but in the direction Melissa was going. They ran but felt in their bones the futility of it.

Several whipped out walkie-talkies and screamed into them, and as Mel's head reappeared above the water, Preston and Annie pulled up. But seeing Melissa, while Annie screamed a blood-curdling scream, Preston turned the wheel, hit the gas, and went down the road in Melissa's direction.

She slammed into a collection of flotsam that had gathered mid-river and was withstanding the assault of raging water. Choking, she grabbed for something, anything, and got hold of the end of a slick wet branch from a chunk of tree.

There was no slope to deal with where Preston turned off the road, angling his truck toward the river. But the ground he drove over was hillocky, and he and Annie got tossed around in the cab. As he got to within twenty yards of the raging water, the ground flattened out, but turned muddy.

Annie leapt out of the truck before Preston had completely stopped. The mud wasn't deep, only rising to halfway up the shoe part of Annie's rain boots, but still, it made it very difficult for her to run, but run she did.

"Mel!" she screamed to her daughter, who could not hear her, could not see her. The water leapt higher in this part of the river and, already fast, was even faster, freed from the impediment of the bridge. The tree that had slammed into the bridge now came hurtling down the river as Annie ran stumblingly to and now into the river. "Mel!"

But Preston, running after her, and yelling for her to stop, which she didn't or wouldn't hear, now caught her from behind at the waist and started dragging her back out of the water.

"No! No!" she cried, hitting him, kicking him, "Let me go!"

Melissa lost her grip on the slick end of the branch, and as her head went underwater, a frantic hand found a trailing vine and gripped it. She tilted her face up, but it was barely above the surface of the water, and she coughed and choked, every time the water slid over it.

"Let me go!"

"Annie!"

"Please, God, my little girl!"

"Preston! Preston!" And out of nowhere, or so it seemed, came Boyd and Floyd. Someone—they never remembered who—but a man—had thought to call them, and they had come, as they were now, running.

"Take hold of her!" Preston yelled to the brothers, who took transfer of the wildly struggling Annie. Floyd was still famous among the older residents of the town for fighting with a mountain lion and living to tell the tale, which the scars on his neck and right arm still very loudly did—and he would later say that he had an easier time of it with the mountain lion than he did with Annie that day.

A thunderclap directly overhead knocked the wind out of the brothers and they fell to the ground, Annie going down with them.

Preston ran back to his truck. He grabbed a rope out of the back of the utility box. He made a cross-secure of rope between his thighs and around his shoulders.

Seeing him, Boyd yelled in the wind, "Don't be crazy!" But Preston, the big remaining coil in his hands was running toward the water, and then out of nowhere, Mr. Pierce was at his side, but now in front of him, running backward, and trying to hold him back.

"This is suicide!" he said. "You can't!"

But Preston shouldered his way past Mr. Pierce, and seeing Bulie (who wouldn't have known to come had Miss Ames not gone to his house and thrown a rock through his window—which finally had done the trick of waking him up), he handed him all the rest of the rope and raced to the water, as Bulie let the rope pay out. Preston ran upriver, in the opposite direction from where Mel was, and then, checking over his shoulder to see if he'd gone far enough to get to and catch the current that had taken Mel, he stopped, and before launching himself into the raging water, he looked up at the sky and said, "Okay. It's really okay."

He flung himself into the water and with powerful strokes got himself into and caught up in the current that carried him in a parabola up toward the opposite bank, and then in Mel's direction.

There was another clap of thunder and a bolt of lightning, which hit a tree on the other side of the river.

Sobbing, the brothers holding her, Annie watched Preston—only a little head bobbing along at this point—racing toward Mel, or at least in Mel's direction. Her grief, the brothers noted, was working in their favor, because it re-directed her energy into heart-breaking, heaving sobs, and so they had a better hold of her, though still she struggled to be free.

Not too far from where Annie stood, Bulie was digging his heels into the mud, but was at one moment either sinking into it, or in the next, getting yanked forward, and falling to knees and elbows. Seeing this, Merle and Claude, newly arrived (again, thanks to Miss Ames—but no rocks for them, only loud pounding and then a lot of screaming at them for turning off their phones at night—a peculiar habit in both men), grabbed the rope behind Bulie and joined the tug of war with the river, or it was like they were fishermen, and they had Leviathan on the end of their line, who was trying to pull them in, while they tried to pull him out.

Now Boyd came up, leaving his brother alone to contend with Annie, and there was Stan, and Derrick, and Peter. Peter had run to Derrick's house after Melissa had driven off in Annie's truck, and even in the midst of Derrick's dad screaming at his son for taking his truck without permission (his dad, in his anger, missing the big picture of all that had gone on that night), Peter had run right up to the two and ignoring Mr. Merrick, said, "Derrick, let's go!" Derrick wasn't sure to where or why, but Peter's face and demeanor scared him, and anyway, he wanted to get the hell away from his dad, who stood nonplussed as the two boys ran off—and took his truck again!

It must have been at this moment, all those men playing tug of war with the river, that John Chamberlain, taking a swig from his bottle, drove by. He had nowhere to go, nowhere to be, and only because of a life-long habit of early rising in order to get to the mill, was he up so early, but without aim or purpose, except to drive, to keep moving, to keep drinking, and he hit the brakes, seeing the strange early morning game of tug of war at river's edge. And all these cars...What were these people doing?

And what Chamberlain saw was these men losing the tug of war and either slipping and falling in the mud or getting dragged knee-deep through it, as if together they made one long plow tooth. They repeatedly lost their grips, too, their hands mud-slicked. It was the lack of proper anchorage in the ground, he saw, and the lack of a good grip, that beset them more than the pull of wild current and whatever that was they were trying to haul in.

"The truck!" Bulie yelled into the wind, but those just behind him heard and understood his meaning. Muscles taut and ready to burst from effort, the men dug deep and backed up toward Preston's truck, the game now whether they'd sink to their waists and immobility first or make their goal of reaching the truck; while meantime, Preston appeared and disappeared in the white water, though he was closing in on Mel, or at least closing in on the big collection of flotsam, mid-river.

Mr. Pierce was nearly parallel to the ground, pulling, by the time the men reached the truck and Bulie could start tying the rope around the bumper—though Boyd, who could not see what Bulie was doing, because of his position among the men holding the rope, but who nevertheless understood the goal, began shouting, into the wind, so fruitlessly, "No! It won't work!"

Which Chamberlain understood from his vantage point on the road. He said, "No, that's stupid. Don't do that."

Bulie no doubt knew it was stupid, too, and Mr. Pierce *certainly* would have known that it was—that the physics of the thing would not allow it—but he was so concentrated on the physical effort of vying with the force of the river, that he was only half-aware of what Bulie was doing or even, exactly, what the goal was. He knew it had something to do with the truck, and that was it.

Of course, if you're anxiety-ridden and feel close to hopeless, you might grab for anything, too, anything that looks like hope; and Bulie had snatched at the solution of using the truck to help them against the river. The truck would do the work of all these men, and now they could race down toward the river and toward the *beginning* part of the rope and help guide Preston's descent downriver.

The men were now spaced out more than they had been, needing to be so, to help guide the lifeline and keep slack out of it as Preston hurtled toward Mel. Peter was the last in line, or first, depending on how you looked at it, but anyway, the one nearest the truck.

Between leaping white-capped crests of water, Preston could see Mel, her uptilted face still just above the water, though under it more frequently now.

Peter couldn't see his sister from where he was, but he could definitely hear the steadily building shriek of metal as the bumper got pulled from the car. Above that sound and in the wind, he heard someone calling to him, or yelling at him, he didn't know, and he looked hard right, almost behind him, and beheld John Chamberlain running his way, and repeatedly poking at all the air in front of him as he ran, as if trying to poke holes in it, but he was pointing at the bumper at about the level of Peter's knees.

Peter understood now, and it confirmed what he had half-understood only seconds before—this bumper was going to come flying off—and knock him down, maybe kill him, and even worse, that'd mean the end of his sister's chances; and Coach Mayhugh might be a goner, too; so Peter pulled on the rope now for all he was worth to keep as much tension off the bumper as possible.

Preston, now less than twenty feet from Mel, called to her. "Mel! Mel!"

She heard him, but could not respond, she was gurgling in the water, choking.

By the truck, there was a terrible, pterodactyl-like shriek as the bumper tore off and flew at Peter's head. Instinctively, stupidly, both, Peter turned to see his fate coming at him and saw Chamberlain leaping on him and driving him to the ground, the bumper streaking just over them and go like flying evil after the other men, who instinctively dropped the rope and dove out of the way, none of them actually seeing the bumper, but, having heard the shriek and noting the change of the tension in the rope in their hands, and perhaps hearing in the wind, a tell-tale, frightening whoosh of air, knew that death was on its way just overhead.

Annie, in the meantime, kept calling and calling to her child, to whom this terrible man holding her wouldn't let her run. But even she had heard and responded to the pterodactyl shriek of the bumper flying and had instinctively turned—and saw John Chamberlain leap on Peter as the bumper flew over their heads. Normally, a witness, just catching sight of something like that, wouldn't be able to put all that had happened in sequence or perspective, so that there could be understanding. But this was a mother, and that was her child, and he was about to die, and someone saved him. A mother whose child is in mortal danger puts things together very quickly. And it was John Chamberlain who had saved him, and Annie did not wonder what he was doing there, because what he had done was save her boy.

The river threw Preston against the collected bunch of flotsam and he made a grab-where-he-could way to Mel, and then he grabbed her, at the waist, lifting her up from the water as much as he possibly could. She coughed; she gasped for air.

But in that small moment of victory, which others on the riverbank observed, Mr. Pierce's attention was elsewhere—on the rope the men had dropped. It was current-whipped away from them and sliding fast in a great arc toward the water, into which it was about to go. He pushed himself up from the mud and raced after it. "The rope!" he cried to the others, and he dove headlong to try and grab it—and missed, landing in the mud.

At about that moment, the flotsam island imploded, and Preston and Mel were sped downriver toward a cataract. The Roebuck's Cataract, everyone called it, and no one knew why (even Miss Dorothy hadn't), and though it wasn't more than twenty feet high, there was an array of boulders below it, death below it.

Annie shrieked, and because Floyd, jolted, sickened, by seeing Preston and Mel being swept to their deaths, had let go, she ran away from him and downriver after her daughter.

Everyone else on the riverbank ran, too, and if anyone involved in the ill-fated rescue attempt could have paused to look around, they would have noticed that most of the town had gathered along the river or along the road that bordered it, and those on the road were running, too. Who knows why? To what end? You just run.

Preston had a death-grip on Mel, trying to determine how he might keep her alive when they went over the cataract. If he could go backwards over the falls and keep her head and body pressed to his chest, he would absorb most of the impact on the rocks below, and she might have a fighting chance to get purchase on one of the rocks and hold on. It was a pipe dream.

The two were within thirty yards of the cataract when those closest to Preston's and Mel's position heard a jay, which Mr. Pierce could not account for, since jays would not be out in a storm, and then Big Daddy emerged from the line of trees on the shore opposite. The Old Woman Ape darted out after him, and obviously agitated by, and frightened of, the humans she saw on the side opposite, she made huge slaps on the muddy ground in protest. But only with one hand. She was holding Baby Ape in her silvered arm, and Baby Ape was struggling to get away from her to be with his father. Now several other apes emerged from the trees and made a hue and cry, slapping the muddy bank. No!

Big Daddy dove into the river and disappeared.

Closing in on the cataract just ahead, Preston and Mel got swept sideways into a whirlpool, and the force of the water ripped Mel from Preston's embrace and flung Preston like so much ejecta downriver ahead of her.

He said no prayer, and didn't cry or call out, but kept his eyes on the sky and was quite resigned, when suddenly he was being lifted up out of the water and pushed toward the sky. Big Daddy had come up underneath him, and now he flung Preston as if he were a rag doll toward the bank of the river the apes were on. Preston didn't land quite on the bank, but enough in the rocky shallows that he could get to all fours and hold fast against the swiftness of the river now piling up around his body as it passed. He had no idea what had just happened to him.

Big Daddy swam after Mel, angling toward her against the current, trying to get himself between her and the cataract. The river kept buffeting his side and tossing him a bit downstream... force of nature versus force of nature, the cataract now only fifteen feet away.

The townspeople had stopped running, had stopped moving, and transfixed couldn't move. Their mouths were open, the women with both palms to their cheeks, the men with their hands bunched into impotent fists at their sides, looking grim, expecting the worst.

Old Woman and a couple of the other apes began to make what sounded to Mr. Pierce like a keening sound, as if all were lost as far as they were concerned.

With only ten feet separating Mel—and at this point, Big Daddy—from death, Big Daddy made a vocalization, a call, to Mel. Though dazed, Mel heard it and shifted her eyes toward it. She saw Big Daddy. He extended an arm, battling the river with only one now, stroking furiously to keep himself from being swept over the falls. Mel extended her arm as far as she could, and with a last effort, Big Daddy grabbed it and in pulling her to himself, the river took him, took them, toward the falls, only three feet away; and Big Daddy, with all he had, with all one free arm could give him, stroked with panicked animal fury against the current. For the longest time it looked like the best he could do was hold his position.

"Come on..." Mr. Pierce found himself saying.

"Come on..." Boyd and Floyd said.

"Come on!" Bulie announced/yelled.

Annie couldn't speak.

"Do it...*do* it..." Peter said, tears streaming down his face.

And the town was crying, "Go! Go!"

And Big Daddy, slowly, but not surely, gained ground, or

water in this case, and gaining in confidence, he gained in power and angling toward the riverbank, he now found ground under his feet and, Mel in his arms, emerged from the river.

Safely on the bank, Big Daddy turned around and faced the townspeople across the divide of the raging river. His body enlarged and contracted with his great breaths.

They watched him, and watched the other apes bounding down the riverbank toward him. Big Daddy put Mel down into a sitting position. She stared toward the riverbank, and only by happenstance in her mother's direction, because she was too dazed to have done that on purpose, or to have even thought to seek her out in the crowd.

But Annie thought her daughter was looking right at her, and she dropped to her knees and cried out to her, "Mel! Oh, my Mel!"

The townspeople regarded the apes; the apes regarded the townspeople, the noise of the river between them, the noise of the wind all about; and then the apes, on some cue no one heard or saw, began filtering away through the trees that bordered the river, disappearing, Big Daddy among the first, Old Woman, Baby in her arms, the last, leaving Mel to keep her gaze on the townspeople.

Chapter Forty

*B*ANG! BANG! BANG!

Seated on the stage of the auditorium, Annie rapped her gavel for order.

Night showed in the rectangles of windows above everyone's heads.

Half the crowd was sitting, half standing. A lot of people kept close to the big urns of coffee set up on a table pushed up against one wall. Most everyone had gone home and cleaned up; slept some, eaten something. But they were all still storm-weary and looked the worse for wear. Most didn't really need the Styrofoam cups of coffee they were holding, but they wanted them; to hold on to something, I think; or the warmth and familiarity of it, anyway.

"Quiet, please, people," Annie said. She didn't have much energy for a lot of volume, but she had her gavel. "Millard, you have the floor."

The council members sat on the stage, shoulder to shoulder at two rectangular tables pushed together. Only Edna looked perfectly put together, her beehive perfect, which was remarkable and, it must be said, spoke well for her, because she, like everyone else, and longer than most, had glopped about in the mud and rain for hours today, and since dawn. Shirley, who hadn't been out because of Walter, looked the most bedraggled of all, but perhaps that's because she had turned all her energy against herself and had spent all day getting beaten to a pulp by her fear and anxiety, while hoping for news of anything, from anyone out there.

Preston sat subdued, his face and hands scratched up from the rocks onto which Big Daddy had flung him in trying to save his life. He sat still, and almost...rueful. Regretful, one might say, if one studied his eyes, which I did.

"Yes, thank you, Madam Mayor," said Millard. "Okay, look, folks," he said to the assembled, "we witnessed a great tear-jerking moment. It was a terrific thing that creature did, for whatever reason. But let's not forget, they're wild creatures, and *unpredictable*. We're not safe if we allow them to wander freely. Or need I bring up my daughter and Chrissy Covington as examples of what can happen?"

"And," said Skeet—and he continued over Annie's objection that he was "out of order"—"not only are they a threat to us, but if one tourist gets mauled or killed, you can kiss those dollars good-bye. And then what?"

For some strange reason, or it wasn't strange at all, but came from a very tired mind, Annie wondered if Edna was going to answer that question by suggesting, 'We could do pies.' (But she didn't.)

I noted John Chamberlain, alone in the balcony. He had his feet up on the railing, and though he looked uninterested, a disinterested party, swigging from a flask, he couldn't have been: He was here in the high school auditorium, after all. I'm pretty sure I saw him laugh sardonically.

"*Unpredictable*, Millard?" Annie said, ignoring Skeet's interruption, and addressing Millard's point. "Their behavior is *unpredictable*? Is that true? Why not go on evidence? What have we seen? What made them mad would have made us mad. What moved them is the same thing that moved us. I don't think they're any more unpredictable than we are. And, okay, they're wild creatures, but they're evidently capable of compassion and bravery. Are they not?"

"I guess," Millard began, "but— ."

"We have to respond in kind," Annie said, interrupting him and knowing she shouldn't have. She was the mayor and allowed floor liberties, but interruption showed worry; a worry about control over things, and it made others think that interruption was acceptable, and in short order, you had a mess, followed by a lot of *bang, bang, bang*. "If we can't behave as they did, we're less than they are. I propose we do two things. Stop the road, because it's obviously pushing into their home— ."

"No! We can't do that!" shouted no less than two-dozen people from various parts of the auditorium.

"And *two*," Annie pressed on, "I agree with what Stan Pierce said earlier. We've got to re-think our growth plans here, or we'll crowd them too much and expose them. And look—that's exactly what's happened already, right? And then we build this, and then that, and more people come..." Annie shook her head. "And the second they're exposed, the whole world will come here—and you know that will be the end of them. Then us, too. Consider that. That's the end of Alpine Valley as anybody ever knew it."

Annie saw Shirley waving her hand from the front row of the auditorium. When Annie had first taken the stage, she had noted Shirley seated there and wondered why she wasn't taking the stage with the rest of the council. But then she saw the oxygen tank and the tubes in Walter's nose. This was one of Walter's bad days. Shirley never left her son's side on one of his bad days.

"Councilwoman Considine," Annie said, "you have the floor."

Shirley stood and half-addressing the council members, and half-addressing the assembled, said, "Ladies and gentlemen, for me, there's only one way to look at this problem. What brings us the road to Taylorville the fastest way possible? Answer: tourist dollars. And what will bring the tourists the fastest way possible? The road. Madam Mayor, it's to our credit to be as good to these creatures as we can be. It's also to our credit to do the utmost for our children. We need—*need*, Annie, Madam Mayor—those tourist dollars for another year at least, if we're going to get asphalt all the way up to Taylorville."

Millicent, sitting next to Shirley, spoke up and said, "She's right, Annie, dear. Mayor, dear."

"What's the shortfall?" Preston asked. Annie was surprised to hear his voice—he'd been so quiet.

"Seven point two million dollars," Annie replied.

The auditorium was quiet—well, as quiet as a buzzy auditorium full of agitated people can be—as they thought this number through; this very large number through, most concluding that Shirley was being more than optimistic to think that the town could raise revenue like that in one year.

"So what's on your mind there, Preston," Skeet asked. "You haven't said much."

Preston nodded slowly, to show agreement, but mostly to buy himself enough time to put some words together; words he wasn't sure he wanted to say. "I think," he began, "I think we need the tourists. Stan," he now said to Mr. Pierce, seated in the second row, "you said we know too little about these creatures to say anything definitive about them." When Stan nodded in affirmation, Preston said to him, "So maybe they'll read the writing on the wall and move?"

Before Stan could answer, Annie said, "And maybe they won't. Look at all of us here. This town was doomed, and yet none of *us* wanted to leave his home."

"Well, then," Millard piped up, "I'm sorry, but it's them or us. Survival of the fittest."

"Pretty stark, Millard," Preston said. "But Annie—Madam Mayor—Shirley's right. I mean, that creature saved my life, too. But we'd be—I'm sorry—irresponsible to put the concerns of their young *above* the concerns of our children—and our future."

"Soooo," Skeet said, really dragging the word out, and as if for the umpteenth time, though it was only for the second time in this meeting that he said, "we round them up and fence them off at Miller's Peak. Nice secure barbed wire. No one will go there. It'll be like a little nature preserve for them."

"Skeet," Annie said, "once again—we know nothing about them—their needs, their habits. In trying to preserve them, we might destroy them. In the meantime, we have no clue as to their number, and even *how* one might round them up."

"'*Might* destroy them'" said Skeet, ignoring the second part of Annie's remarks. "Come on, it's a pretty fair gamble. I move for a voice vote."

"Second," Millard said.

"All in favor of a round-up, 'Aye,'" said Skeet, who was quite out of line, since only Annie could pose the vote.

"*Aye!*" most of the town roared, and so loudly you could almost *see* the word—like it was a thick forest sprung up. There were a few who didn't say aye, including Mr. Pierce and Miss Ames—and Preston, who thought *something* had to be done with these apes, but that rounding them up couldn't possibly be the solution.

And in the relative quiet after, the town waiting to see what happened next, and the council waiting for Annie to bang her gavel and certify the vote, Annie said, "Well. I cannot certify."

"Annie, you have to," Skeet said.

"Madam Mayor," said Millard, "this is...this is...You *have* to!"

"Not if I'm not mayor," Annie said. "I'm sorry, I'm going to have to resign. And move...forthwith." It was only in the moment *after* saying the word 'move' that she realized she didn't mean it in the governmental way of 'move,' as in 'I move that we adjourn,' or whatever she was actually going to say, but never did.

There were more than several gasps and 'Oh, no's' from people in the auditorium, who may or may not have understood what Annie meant by *move*, but certainly understood that this most excellent mayor was resigning. But Preston understood her very well, and he closed his eyes, which was an interesting reaction to something he didn't want to hear.

Up in the balcony, John Chamberlain took his feet off the

railing and sat forward. He held the railing in one hand, his bottle in the other.

"I'm sorry," Annie said, "but if I can't help these creatures, I at least don't have to be party to harming them. And that's how I see this playing out. Barbed wire? Look, that creature saved my child. Which is to say he saved my life. And. I mean. I understand what you're saying. This town is everything to me. But it would no longer be the same kind of place if we do that—what you propose, Skeet. We'd lose...ourselves. Our best selves—*they'd* be in a kind of prison. And we'd be so busy keeping them there. When, really, they want out."

Chamberlain put down his bottle. He gripped the railing with both hands.

"So, anyway," Annie continued, "someone else will have to certify. Edna, as comptroller, that's you."

"The ayes have it," Edna said promptly and crisply.

"And now," Annie said, "invoking Rule Ten-Forty-Seven, I, Annie LaPeer, do hereby resign from the office of Mayor of Alpine Valley effective— ."

"Wait!" John Chamberlain roared from the balcony.

There were quite a few gasps from the crowd, this surprising outburst scaring a number of people, most all of whom didn't know anybody was up in the balcony. As one, the crowd turned to look up to see who was interrupting things—and then there were more gasps when people saw, behind the railing, that it was John Chamberlain.

"I have an idea!" Chamberlain said.

And it was a most remarkable one.

Chapter Forty-One

*L*ITTLE CARRIE SEVY ('LITTLE' BECAUSE OF HER SIZE, not age) banged her cymbals together so hard that I couldn't help but wonder if the Apes out there somewhere heard her and were covering their ears. Then she and the other four members of the Alpine High School Marching Band did something they had never done before. They marched in a line, and it was almost straight; and they marched in that almost straight line almost straight down Main Street.

And when they reached the end of it, and because they had enjoyed themselves so much, they turned right around and marched up the other way, and then repeated the process a half-dozen more times before Little Carrie got tired of banging the cymbals, and Porky Blair started complaining that the bass drum strap around his neck was really beginning to chafe his skin, so they stopped and went to Merle's for ice cream.

But they had to stand in line, because Merle's was packed, so Tiffany Westley (Trevor Westley's cousin), decided it would be very nice for everyone if she played the trumpet for them while they waited. She only knew two tunes by heart, and they were short, and the line was long, so she played them through several times, and the people in line started getting *out* of line and going over to the AV Bistro, where they had pie; and though Little Carrie saw that people were getting annoyed, so maybe Tiffany should stop, Porky saw that the line was now moving along more quickly, so told Little Carrie to shut up and encouraged Tiffany to keep playing.

If you weren't standing right there with that horn in your ear, it really did add to the festive atmosphere all along Main Street, across which hung a huge professionally made banner that read, *First Annual Ape Days Festival!* The banner came courtesy of John Chamberlain who had it made in Cascade City. He had also paid for advertising in all kinds of newspapers and on all kinds of websites. He really wanted a *lot* of tourists to come for Ape Days.

Claude sweated happily over three large BBQs, cooking ribs and chicken along with hamburgers and hot dogs, and Terry Troy assisted him—an actual smile on Terry's face, for vindication is a wonderful feeling. Doc Cabot had come to his house the next day after that night of death and discovery on Main Street and had apologized to him. Terry had accepted Doc's apology, but he also told him that he certainly understood how Doc could have doubted him. "You didn't know me well enough to justify taking a leap of faith, Doc," he had said. "And with no evidence to support what I saw, why would you conclude that what I said was true?" They had talked at length, and easily, Terry showing no signs that he had somewhere else to be.

People wouldn't know it for a little while—though they began to get inklings of it at this very festival—but Terry was becoming less antsy; less peculiar. You could have a brief chat if not an out-right conversation with Terry without either one of you trying to tear yourself away from it as quickly as possible. He had lunch with Claude a couple of times a week. Edna, of all people, reported that she found Terry "excellent company lately." But as I've told you, Terry died not too many months later than this very day, alone, a picnic for two in his basket, but at least looking calm, and in fact, looking like he'd wait forever for whoever he was waiting for. Maybe he really did think that someone, anyone, might join him now, if only for a moment—and he'd be prepared to offer them something, anything—a sandwich? some fruit? some cheese? a cookie? Maybe his enthusiasm and expectation outran the town's ability to catch up with the changed—or renewed—Terry Troy. I do not think he was waiting for Claude, as some people speculated. I have my own ideas about Terry Troy and the little mystery of Ranger Park, but that's another story, dear reader, and a quieter one, if no less dramatic in its way.

Speaking of Edna, for the first time in the history of Alpine Valley, Edna's beehive wasn't perfect. It tilted on her head, and reminded more than a few people of the leaning tower of Pisa. But Edna was happy. It was one o'clock, and she had already made three-hundred dollars selling rhubarb pie.

"We sure do love this pie," a woman said to Edna as she and her husband stood in front of Edna's booth, forking it up.

"You must be from Maine," Edna said.

"Why yes," said the woman, quite surprised, "how did you know?"

Shirley and Walter were having a blast handing out free t-shirts to every tourist who walked by. The t-shirts read, *I've Gone Ape for Alpine Valley*. John Chamberlain had commissioned Shirley to come up with that slogan, design the shirt, and see to production of it.

While all this was going on, Preston, Peter, and Derrick stood together in a fringe of woods just outside of town, watching the happy hustle and bustle. Peter had his camera. Derrick was in the ape costume, ape head in his hands.

"Now's as good a time as any, I guess," Preston said. "You dialed in for this, Peter?"

"The money shot is for sure, Coach."

"Whatever that means," said Preston, "and the acting—you think you can pull it off?"

"I rented a lot of Al Mancini movies. I'll just do Al."

"Uh-*huh*," said Preston. He wasn't too sure Al Mancini was quite what was needed for what they had in mind. He thought Tom

Henries might have been a better—but never mind, it was too late. "All right, then," he said, "go get her done, son."

Peter hurried toward town. He was dressed like a tourist, wearing one of Shirley's t-shirts, a pair of sunglasses, and a sun visor advertising some other tourist spot the lucky lad had been to in his life, a camera in hand.

When Peter entered Main Street, Preston turned to Derrick and said, "Okay, you ready? Game face on?"

Derrick nodded and put the ape head on. He clapped his big paws together a half-dozen times, psyching himself up.

In the meantime, Larry was practicing his lines in Ramona's living room. Ramona stood in front of him, listening—the proud encouraging teacher.

"'Uh-oh!' recited Larry. "'Uh-oh! Oh, *no!*' How was that?" he asked Ramona.

She clapped her hands together in joy. "Oh!" she said, that was so, *so* close to adequate I could just kiss you!" And she did, and Larry beamed.

Not too far away, Peter had the camera rolling on a couple he'd stopped on Main Street. Not yet doing Al Mancini—that would be for later, at the critical moment—he told them he was Dwight from Albuquerque and he was making a video about the ape for a summer school science project.

"So," he said to them from behind the camera, "tell me. Do you think the ape is real?"

"Of course the ape is real," the couple said, pretty close to simultaneously, and then overlapping each other they said, "I've seen the video. Couldn't fake that. No way."

In the fringe of woods, Preston said to Derrick, "Okay, kid, go for the gold." He gave Derrick the ol' football slap on the butt, and Derrick took off running.

His camera rolling, Peter, still playing Dwight, conducted another man-on-the-street interview with another happy couple.

"Well, we're from Milwaukee, Wisconsin," they said to the

camera; and the man said, "I don't personally believe there's an Alpine Valley Ape, but you know— ."

As the man was speaking, you heard in the background (and later, you heard it on the camera's audio) several people up the street yelling things like, "A bear! A bear! Look out! It's not a bear!"

"—it's still a lot of fun!" the man concluded, while his wife, turning around said, "What's that noise?"

Keeping the camera on the couple, Peter watched through the lens as they watched the commotion, and then he adjusted his position and zoomed in on Derrick as he charged into town.

And Derrick growled and made feints at tourists—and boy did they run. A few, however, thought this was all in fun—a part of Ape Days—and they laughed.

But Peter had anticipated that some would, which is why he had Chrissy strategically placed inside of Lydia's and dressed like any other tourist. Peter had asked John Chamberlain for the money to buy the kind of squibs the movies used for making blood burst from an actor, and he had wired one on Chrissy.

Peter was a little worried about asking Chrissy to take the kind of fall she would need to take, but Chrissy was not only game for it, she asked him if she could make it worse. "I mean, then we'd get *real* blood!" she said. Peter said no, the squib would be enough; but already a little in love with Chrissy Covington, he was now smitten and really sorry that she was so into Derrick the way she was, but they were both seniors, and seventeen, so what chance did he have, anyway?

So here came Chrissy out of Lydia's, sunglasses on, a Lydia's shopping bag in the crook of her arm—quite oblivious to all the fleeing and screams of alarm—and here came Derrick, charging in her direction and now, seeing her in his path, 'slashing' her across the chest, whereupon Floyd, inside Lydia's looking out, pressed the remote for the squib, and blood appeared all over Chrissy front. She fell, tumbling so realistically that Peter's instinct was to run help her up, before reason reminded him that Chrissy, who had rehearsed all night on the mats in the gym, was only acting like mad out there. So he kept shooting.

The tourists near her ran away in panic, one woman screaming in such horror that Chrissy later said she didn't think anything else in life would *ever* give her such pleasure. (Boy, was she wrong. Talk about a charmed life. But, like Terry Troy's, that's a different story.)

Derrick now turned, and he, too, was doing a great job. He really did look like a confused, angry ape, as fearful about being here as the tourists were fearful of him, and only doing what a creature like him did when panicked—lash out. As Derrick now headed back up Main Street, Larry 'just happened' to be turning on to it, making short pop-bursts of his siren, to let people know he was coming, his red and blue lights twirling.

He got out of his car and, seeing Derrick heading his way, tourists crowding behind him, he said, "Uh-oh! Uh-oh! Oh, no! Look out, it's the Alpine Valley Ape! Run!"

And then, Larry seized his moment, the moment that convinced Ramona she would marry this man; the moment no one had thought of; and might well have rejected as way too risky— even inviting a lawsuit; but Larry, like a good actor, was caught up in the scene and character, and he pushed a young mother and her child into the back of his squad car and slammed the door on them. Who would take such liberties with people he didn't know; *risk* taking such liberties, if this was only a goof? Now, even those who had still been thinking that this was just a stunt for Ape Days, ran.

Preston, who had slipped into town unseen, not that that mattered really, was also watching events unfold through Merle's window. His eyes went from Peter, shooting, to Derrick, acting. "*Now*, fellahs," he said, more to himself than to Ramona.

Peter, who had also, that moment, felt that the moment was right, got into position, and by tilting the camera up twice fast, cued Derrick that the moment of truth had come.

Seeing his cue, Derrick made a last rush at a few more tourists, and then fell and took a dramatic tumble, while discreetly pushing up on the ape head with his hands, so that now, the head flying off and bouncing up Main Street, it appeared to be doing so as a consequence of the tumbling.

As Derrick lay groaning in the street, holding his elbow (a nice touch, thought Peter), Peter rushed up, his camera on Derrick and rolling.

"No! Please!" said Derrick, trying to cover his face so that it wouldn't be seen on camera, "It was just a joke! Don't tell my mother!"

Still filming, Peter unleashed his inner Mancini and said, "Are you the ape, my friend? Did you just *hoax* all this? Was this just a *hoax*? Oh, *boy*!"

Inside Merle's, Ramona bit her lip. "Clearly his future is *behind* the camera," she said.

Even the blood-stained Chrissy bit her lip—a gesture she probably got from Ramona.

"I wasn't alone!" Derrick said. "There were others!" Very dramatically, but still believably, he pointed at Preston, who 'just happened' to be standing nearby, in front of Merle's. "*He's* the one said do it! He cooked everything up!"

Peter turned the camera on Preston, who now, seeing the camera on him, turned his face away, and then, as if having given it quick consideration, thought he had better get out of there. He took off running. Peter kept the camera on him for a bit, catching Preston's figure every now and again as he ran, the tourists something of a wall between him and the camera.

"And she's in on it, too!" Derrick said, pointing an accusing finger at Chrissy. All heads turned Chrissy's way. Chrissy looked defiant, standing there under the glare of public scrutiny, but she was also staring daggers into Derrick and doing an amazing job of it, and then she broke down and half-collapsed, half-sat in the street, tearing off her bloody blouse to reveal the remains of the squib pack attached to a t-shirt. "Damn it, Hugo!" she said—the name she had thought perfect for Derrick's character—"why did you *say* anything!"

Derrick now thrashed around on the ground, completely out of his gourd from anger at his exposure. "Everyone's in on it!" he said toweringly. "Him, and him, and her! The cop!"

Peter got footage of Floyd and Merle and Ramona, and Larry, who was now apologizing to the mother and her daughter as he escorted them out of his car.

"This is...this is...you all made this *up*?" a man in the crowd said.

Another said, "The whole thing?"

As no one said anything, but only hung their heads in shame, or looked away, not wanting to say a word, the crowd had its answer.

A silence followed, and then a boy in the crowd was heard to say, "You mean the ape's not real?"

His slightly older brother said, "They just made it up, dodo-head."

Quiet again; but only for a moment; and perhaps it was that word, 'dodo-head' that did it, because a man standing next to the boys laughed. Then the man standing in front of him laughed, too. A woman elsewhere in the crowd didn't want to laugh—you could tell—because she was mad, but a laugh escaped her mouth nevertheless.

But not everybody thought it was funny. As one man laughed, his little boy burst into tears and said, "He's not real!" The man slipped his arm around his kid's waist and hugged him to his side, though still laughing himself.

A woman standing next to Floyd threw the t-shirt she'd bought from Shirley at his feet. "You people!" she said and stormed off. Her ten-year-old daughter punched Floyd in the arm as she followed her mother.

"Ow..." said Floyd, rubbing his arm.

In the meantime, a few tourists had rushed Derrick, wanting

video of him and to have their pictures taken with him. Derrick knew to drop the act at this point, and laughing and joking with them, he happily consented to put the ape head back on and make all kinds of menacing poses and silly feints—whatever the tourists wanted.

Chrissy was thrilled to put her bloody blouse back on and pose for her own share of pictures.

The others, less amused, were getting into their cars and slamming doors in very point-making ways. They sped out of town, and Larry thought about going after them and giving them citations, but then decided that might not be a good idea.

At some point, amidst all this, Preston caught Peter's eye and gave him a big thumbs up, while Peter, still filming (as Dwight) gave it back (discreetly)—while going through the crowd and every now and again channeling his inner Mancini by saying things like, "Hoax? These people thought they could pull off a *hoax*? Oh, *boy!*"

No one was listening to him, though, which Ramona, and Peter himself, thought was to the town's benefit, when they watched playback of the video later that day.

By five that evening, when most of the tourists had gone, Peter and Derrick walked together to Alpine Valley's one and only mailbox. Using the rounded top of the mailbox as his writing surface, Peter addressed a padded envelope. Derrick, newly showered and dressed in jeans and a tee, watched proudly. Finished writing, Peter took the copy of his latest, greatest, video and popped it into the envelope. He sealed it as Derrick opened the mouth of the mailbox for him. Then Peter dropped into it the proof that Alpine Valley had made this whole thing up, proof addressed to *Mr. Connor O'Faighlen, Station Manager, KWCS-TV, Cascade City.*

Chapter Forty-Two

*T*HE JAWS OF THE BOLT CUTTER CLENCHED, AND THE shackle of the padlock snapped in two.

John Chamberlain laid the cutters to the side of the door and picked up the now useless padlock from the ground.

He didn't know what to do with it. Toss it away?

He put it in his pocket.

He pushed open the door, and it creaked, rust flying away like dust from the hinges, and Chamberlain coughed.

He looked into the dark down the one shaft of light that came through the open door.

Silenced saws in his path, and the ambient light filtering deeply into the expanse of dark revealed more silenced saws. It took Chamberlain three tries with the side of his work boot to get the doorstopper down. It, too, had rusted shut in place; then it coughed rust, yielded to Chamberlain's work boot, and came down, holding back the door, and, as I like to say (so will), holding back the weight of the past, as Chamberlain passed into the mill for the first time in years.

He saw a hardhat on a worktable. He picked it up. Blew the dust off it.

I couldn't learn whether it was that day or not, but it was certainly within that week, that Boyd, Floyd, Stanley Pierce, Miss Ames, and Bulie, working together, built, painted, and, on what they all remembered as a *most* beautiful day, put up a huge sign on an open space near where Main Street turned into the road that led to Taylorville—the old, original road that led to Taylorville. The new one under construction was abandoned.

As the sign rose up from the ground, you saw the words come out of shadow and into light, and they read, "Future Home of the Miss Dorothy Dodd Acute Care Clinic." Underneath those words you saw, in italics, *Made Possible by the Generosity of John Chamberlain.*

Shirley and Walter applauded when the sign stood upright and proud in the sun, Shirley also wiping a tear from her eye.

Here and there in town, the few men and women who had once worked in the mill and hadn't left to seek greener pastures, opened their closets and took out their coveralls, work boots, and hardhats. They shook out wrinkles, clopped the dust from soles.

Claude was the first person John Chamberlain called and asked to come back to work. He'd be the new Bulie; and since you can't become a Bulie overnight, Chamberlain asked Bulie to come back on a consultancy basis, so Claude could learn how to manage scores of men. "I'll do it!" Bulie announced, the first time a smile had been on that man's face in this entire story.

As for Dr. Cabot, occasionally shaking his head, and quite frequently smiling, he marveled at what he thought of as the many miracles of little Alpine Valley—the discovery of the Apes, the validation of the legends, and of Terry Troy, and the redemption of poor old John Chamberlain, and how it led to a rebirth of the entire town.

He was too wise not to appreciate that the teacher had the chance to once again become the pupil; to have the rare and wondrous chance, so late in life, to look at everything anew, and from the perspective of a man who knew, as he never had before, how the world at large, and the earth, and life, defied one's very reasonable ideas about it, and had as much capacity to surprise as we had capacity to be surprised. It's not that he became an even better healer than he was, nor that he stopped making diagnoses of delusion, it's just that he felt joy to live in a world outside of his head, a world where he couldn't be absolutely sure of too many things. He lived in a world once again of, *What's around the bend? What's out there—in the dark?* And he, who had been certain that he'd never see his beloved wife Delores again, now wasn't so sure he should be so certain about things he could not see, nor might experience. *There are more things in heaven and on earth than are dreamt of in your philosophy.*

I think it was also in that same week that John Chamberlain opened the mill, that Preston went to school to do a little end-of-term work, and while he didn't do much while there, he did do two small things, small things which stuck in his memory as joyous— though to anyone else who hadn't walked a mile in his shoes, they might seem mundane, forgettable, not worth mentioning.

He got a ladder, a wash bucket full of sudsy water, a good brush, and he hooked up the hose, and he gave the bear in front of the high school a good bath. Before doing that, he had taken out of his filing cabinet a folder that contained several mock-ups he'd made of the Alpine Valley Ape for the athletic teams' logo. He tossed the entire folder into the trash.

After giving the bear a good bath, Preston remembered feeling fairly good about things, so he got in his truck and drove to Main Street and Merle's.

You didn't need a reservation to get into the café anymore, but that didn't seem to bother Merle one bit. He was a *little* bothered that Claude would be leaving him in a week, to go back to the mill. But Claude was a miller, happiest as a miller (knowledge about himself that he had recovered) and Merle understood that and was happy for him. But no way was Merle going to run the whole show by himself any more. So whom would he get to replace Claude? The answer was Derrick Merrick's dad. The man actually cried when Merle called him up to say that he had the job. And he took it seriously, and he did it well, some saying that Claude had been the better cook; some saying that Mr. Merrick was.

Preston sat at one of the outdoor tables of the café. Chrissy took his order—coffee and a tuna salad sandwich—and Preston opened up a copy of The Alpine Valley Voice that carried as front page news, *Local Woman Wins Tri-County Pie Baking Contest*, and there was a photo of Edna holding out toward the camera a nice big piece of...Boston Cream pie. Will wonders never cease...

As he turned the page, Preston caught sight of Annie LaPeer over the top of the newspaper heading up Main on the opposite side of the street. He watched her for a moment or two.

He put down the newspaper and got up. He made a way through the tables toward the grocery store part of Merle's establishment. There were a couple of white plastic buckets outside the store's door filled with bunches of Alpine Valley Wildflowers. Preston's gaze went from one bunch to the next, to the next. Which was the prettiest?

Since her t-shirt enterprise had folded, Shirley relied solely on her flower picking as a little extra source of income. It didn't bring much—Merle and Martine at the AV Bistro were her only steady buyers—but it brought *something*, and she could come close to making ends meet, as she had since the mill had closed, and would, until it reopened in what everyone estimated would be one to two months. Since so many former residents had left town, Shirley would be about the only one left who had a real grasp of how things went in the accounts receivable department, so John Chamberlain asked if she'd come back as its supervisor. She wouldn't. That'd call for too many hours and occasional weekend work, and Walter was her priority, but thank you anyway, and might I come back in my old position? Of course, said Chamberlain, secretly hoping that somehow he'd figure out a way to change Shirley's mind.

Preston selected what to him looked liked the best of the bunches and went inside the store to pay for it. Merle wasn't anywhere near the register, but was toward the back, stocking a shelf with canned goods. He called to Merle, asking the price on the flowers. Oh, just take 'em, Merle called back. You can come in and buy a can of yams sometimes—which Preston thought was a strangely specific thing to say, until he realized that Merle had probably picked that to say because he was at that moment stacking cans of yams.

He left the store and, crossing the street, headed after Annie with the flowers. He had no idea what he wanted to say to her, but something about how glad he was that she wasn't leaving town, after all, and had decided to stay on as mayor. But now he stopped, as he saw Annie head up the steps to Sam Cabot's door and knock. He saw Sam open the door and welcome her in.

Preston looked at his watch. It was ten after noon. Annie had probably made a noon appointment to talk to Sam, and was running late. But now what would Preston do?

He'd wait. Forgetting he had ordered a sandwich and coffee at Merle's, he walked to the town square, just steps away from where he now stood. Heading toward the benches near the war memorial, he saw Reverend Flambeau on a bench, feeding the pigeons. As Preston started angling away from Flambeau, Flambeau saw him and gave him a smile. Preston gave him his usual quick nod and hand up in greeting and continued toward a bench several away from Flambeau. But then he stopped. You could count one. You could count two. You could count three. Then Preston turned and walked back toward Flambeau.

Reaching him, he asked if he might join him, and Flambeau scooched over on the bench. Preston sat, holding his flowers for Annie. The two men began to chat.

I never did learn what my mother and Sam talked about that day, or during any of her appointments that she kept for over a year. She kept that private. I suspect of course that a lot of it had to do with coming to terms; coming to terms with divorce, and re-building self-esteem and dealing with her ridiculous guilt.

What I *do* know is that it worked, and Mom, rather quickly became a woman I hadn't really met before, but someone, I don't know, *lighter* might be the word. *Funny.* And certainly she learned to trust.

And in case you're wondering, yes, she did marry Preston Mayhugh, who himself seemed, I don't know, happier, and very seldom preoccupied. He lived in the moment now, and more often than not, seemed to enjoy it. For all the years of the rest of his life, he was my most loving stepdad, though *dad* is far more like it. (Except for one brief weird and awkward phone call from my biological father on my twenty-first birthday, I would never hear from that man again.)

My brother became a filmmaker, as he pretty much couldn't avoid becoming, and, among many other films he made—some famous—he ended up making a documentary film about our stepdad. The film won several of the big film awards and was about the year Preston took the Alpine Valley Bears Football Team all the way to the state championship. They lost, but that a tiny school got as far as it did was victory in itself.

As for me, well, I've written this account for you, but have done so from the vantage point of forty years later. There are, as you might imagine, so many more things to tell you, and also, as you might imagine, things I *cannot* tell you.

Alpine Valley does exist, as do (or in many cases now, *did*) the very real people who inhabit or inhabited it. But of course I've had to change people's names, and of course *Alpine Valley is* not our town's real name. Further, you've certainly gathered that I've always been vague about where this town exists. In fact, I wonder if I'm not unwise in letting you know that we're in "the Northwest," as I've mentioned several times.

On the other hand, it's quite possible that I've only said "the Northwest," in order to throw you off.

But if that's what I've done, I hope you'll forgive me, because I have friends to protect. I've named them Ben and Andrea and Seth and Bill, and they are the great-great grandchildren of Baby Ape. They themselves have children, and they are not in any preserve, but roam the forest through which we once tried to cut a road.

No one in this town says a thing about them or will. We don't even talk about them among ourselves. Their existence is a secret passed down generation to generation.

As for those rare occasions when a hiker, fisherman, or hunter claims that he saw something strange in the woods, we're all very good at letting him know in a very kind, gentle way that the poor dear might have had a little too much sun, and perhaps he should go to Gretchen Barnes' pharmacy and see if there isn't something she could recommend.

And if I write this story at all—risk exposing my friends in any way at all—it is because the world all around them is changing, and closing in on them, and I worry for the future of their children.

Please, let those dark woods that are dark woods be; the forests that should be forests be; the wilderness—let it forever be.

It is for the good of all.

And here, now, is how I want to end this story, with the happiest moment of *my* life.

I think it was, coincidentally (or not) the day my future stepdad waited for Mom while chatting with Reverend Flambeau in the square. I was up in the Carson Bridge area. I was standing among trees and looking out at a crew of men in a clearing. They were loading up an earth mover onto the bed of a huge transport flatbed. Several other men were going around the area and pulling surveyor pins up from the earth. They were done. There'd be no more earth moving, no more clearing. They were clearing out.

That day when John Chamberlain stood up in the auditorium and said he had an idea, it was that he'd re-open the mill—if the town agreed to leave the apes alone; which also meant, he said, that we had to stop cutting road into their habitat.

Though people were still worried about the apes, not accepting Chamberlain's offer was out of the question. This was a mill town, and everyone in this auditorium, to a man or woman, would have his job back. So the ayes had it, unanimously.

It was not, as I learned years later as he lay dying, that John Chamberlain cared about the apes. He cared about Peter. Who had stopped to try and help him one night. And my mother. Who had stopped to try and help him one night. And Preston Mayhugh—who had stopped to try to help him, too, and who, he had put together, would never want my mom to leave this town. It was basically for them that John Chamberlain had stood up and said, "Wait!" He knew what a broken heart was like, he said, and he saw that our hearts were breaking, or would. "I didn't want your family to suffer one, too." And he patted my hand, and held my hand, and later that night, he died.

But back to the happiest moment of my life...

Every day for three weeks, I'd been coming up to the Carson Bridge area, now only reachable by going another two miles upriver to Kindall Point and working back. I wanted to find Big Daddy so I could thank him for saving my life.

Of course, I didn't know how I might do that, but I knew he liked apples, so every day, like today, I brought a daypack stuffed full of them. But in three weeks, I hadn't seen him—not in any of the several spots I thought he might be.

I had begun to worry, and even believe, that he and his family had gone. To where, who could say, but I guessed that maybe he thought it was too dangerous for his kind here. As I watched the giant transport chug off with the earth mover chained to its flatbed, I thought, well, I guess I'd better go, too, and that's when I heard a jay behind me. I turned to look at it, to see what it might be on about—and there was Big Daddy. He, too, had been watching the men at work.

I wanted to communicate so *much* to him, to thank him, but to tell him first that what we were seeing was *good; good* news. *They* were going. *He* didn't have to go. *Please* don't go! But how could I possibly get any of this across to him?

I opened my mouth to speak—to say what?—but just then, he tossed something to me. I couldn't tell what it was until I'd caught it. It was an apple. A Fuji. And it didn't look any worse for wear. He had saved it.

He then said something to me. One little word, and it sounded very much like the call of an owl. *Hoo.* Then he turned and, looking over his shoulder, gazing at me, started away.

I didn't hesitate. I ran after him, into the woods.

In Gratitude

THANK YOU FIRST TO MY MOTHER, LISA CREHAN. I'LL say it simply: No her, no book. No kidding.

I'd also like to thank—and therefore I will—Brook and Joe Larios, Founders of PlainClarity Communications, and their associates, Natalie Smithers and Lourdes Frame. Their insightful critiques and close reading of the manuscript in its final stages, as well as their spot-on ideas for the design of the book's cover, proved, taken as a whole, the sine qua non to the novel's completion. I'd also like to thank—and I'd like to see anyone try and stop me from doing so—Grace Peirce of Great Life Press—whose beautiful design of the printed book makes the total experience of it so pleasurable.

And where would I be without Olivia Nossiff, my brilliant sixteen-year-old YA reader? Well, I won't hazard a guess, but I certainly wouldn't be all the way here at the acknowledgements page, acknowledging her.

To all my many friends and colleagues who read various chapters and offered their own insights and encouragement throughout the journey here—*thank you*. Without you, I wouldn't have an entire novel under my belt. Well, it's not actually under my belt. How odd would that be? (It's under my shirt.)

I also want to thank my psychologist, Philip Pierce, Ph.D. He does nothing less than free my mind from the many shackles that constrain me from all sorts of things, like achievement and comfort with happiness. Who knew that blue skies were to be enjoyed and not feared? I mean, I know that's a radical idea, but it's one I'm learning to embrace. Perhaps soon you'll find me with a beard, a megaphone, and a bunch of pamphlets explaining how that the sky is not, in fact, falling.

About the Author

*P*AUL CREHAN ALMOST GOT AN ACADEMY AWARD-winning director shot, ruined a famous comedian's car, cost a well-known production company a fortune when he hired a schizophrenic alcoholic, and ruined another director's chances for selling a movie by making the stupidest but most consequential clerical error in all of TV history.

On the other hand, he got a former SS officer to admit on national television that of course the Nazis killed millions of Jews; lured a fugitive out of hiding when the FBI couldn't; and helped a gang member turn his life around.

Adored by his dog, unknown to millions, friend to President* and King** alike, Paul Crehan is a television writer and producer who loves writing novels.

His first, *The Secret of Alpine Valley*, is the result of a lot of research he conducted while working on TV's "Unsolved Mysteries" and "Proof Positive."

That's pretty much it. He hates zucchini. That may be worth mentioning.

* *Burt Baxter, President of the local Mountaintops Club in Keokuk, Iowa*

** *Joe King, Paul's dry cleaner*